VIII

VIII

H. M. Castor

SIMON & SCHUSTER BFYR

New York London Toronto Sydney New Delhi

SIMON & SCHUSTER BFYR

Library of Congress Cataloging-in-Publication Data
Castor, H. M. (Harriet Mary), 1970-
VIII / H.M. Castor. — 1st U.S. ed.
p. cm.
Summary: Hal, a young man of extraordinary talents, skill on the battlefield, sharp
intelligence, and virtue, believes he is destined for greatness but, haunted by his
family's violent past, he embarks on a journey that leads to absolute power and brings
him face to face with his demons as he grows to become Henry VIII.
ISBN 978-1-4424-7418-5 (hardcover) — ISBN 978-1-4424-7420-8 (eBook)
1. Henry VIII, King of England, 1491–1547—Juvenile fiction. [1. Henry VIII, King
of England, 1491–1547—Fiction. 2. Kings, queens, rulers, etc.—Fiction. 3. Great
Britain—History—Henry VII, 1485–1509 4. Great Britain—History—Henry
VIII, 1509–1547—Fiction.] I. Title. II. Title: Eight.
PZ7.C26874167Vii 2013
[Fic]—dc23
2012021550

For Richard

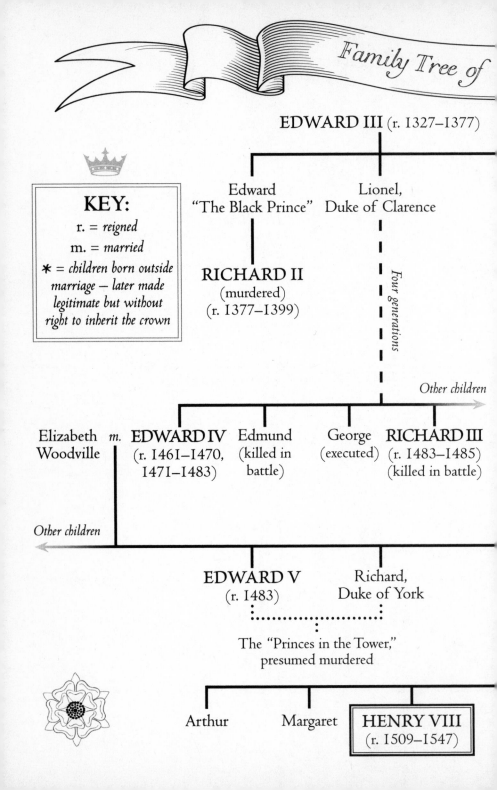

Family Tree of

EDWARD III (r. 1327–1377)

KEY:
r. = *reigned*
m. = *married*
✱ = *children born outside marriage — later made legitimate but without right to inherit the crown*

Edward "The Black Prince"

Lionel, Duke of Clarence

RICHARD II (murdered) (r. 1377–1399)

Four generations

Other children →

Elizabeth Woodville *m.* **EDWARD IV** (r. 1461–1470, 1471–1483)

Edmund (killed in battle)

George (executed)

RICHARD III (r. 1483–1485) (killed in battle)

← *Other children*

EDWARD V (r. 1483)

Richard, Duke of York

The "Princes in the Tower," presumed murdered

Arthur

Margaret

HENRY VIII (r. 1509–1547)

Henry VIII

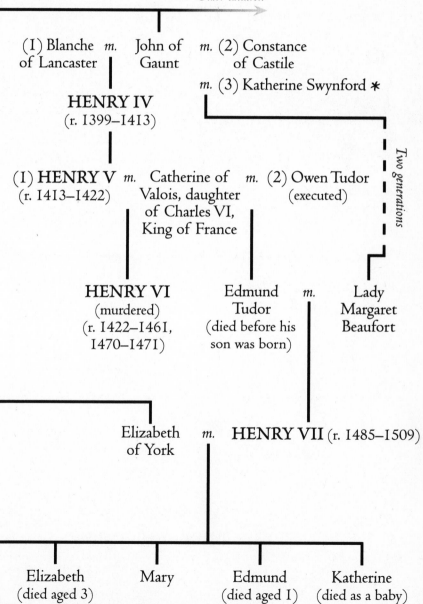

Other children

(1) Blanche *m.* John of *m.* (2) Constance
of Lancaster   Gaunt   of Castile

m. (3) Katherine Swynford ✱

HENRY IV
(r. 1399–1413)

(1) **HENRY V** *m.* Catherine of *m.* (2) Owen Tudor
(r. 1413–1422)   Valois, daughter   (executed)
of Charles VI,
King of France

Two generations

HENRY VI   Edmund *m.* Lady
(murdered)   Tudor   Margaret
(r. 1422–1461,   (died before his   Beaufort
1470–1471)   son was born)

Elizabeth *m.* **HENRY VII** (r. 1485–1509)
of York

Elizabeth   Mary   Edmund   Katherine
(died aged 3)   (died aged 1)   (died as a baby)

The mind is its own place, and in itself

Can make a Heav'n of Hell, a Hell of Heav'n.

John Milton, *Paradise Lost*

PART ONE

To the Dark Tower

I'm still half asleep when I feel strong hands grabbing me.

I try to kick, but it seems like I'm twisted up in the bed-clothes, and the next minute I've been swung up into the air, and whoever's carrying me is walking fast, and I'm going *bump bump bump* against his chest.

He smells of beer and horses and sweat. And my cheek is rammed against cold metal—a breastplate—so I know he's a soldier.

He must be one of the rebels. Only I didn't think the rebels *were* soldiers. I thought they were a mob of stinking peasants from Cornwall, with butcher's knives and farm tools for weapons.

"Let go of me! Let—"

The man changes his grip; a glove clamps across my mouth. It reeks. "Whoa! Don't struggle, sir. You're quite safe."

The words are a trick, of course; I know I am about to die. The rebels have come for me because I am the king's son, and they want to kill me and my brother and my father. So that someone else can be king.

"Hnnff dnnf yff!"

"Your mother's orders, sir."

"Lhhfffh!"

"No, I'm not a liar, sir, and you need to stop kicking. Little *shit!* Pardon my French, sir, but your teeth aren't half sharp."

In the struggle, the blanket I'm wrapped in has been pushed back from my head. The soldier's holding me across his body, facing outward now, one of his arms clamped round my hips, the other under my shoulders, with the hand curled up over my mouth, pressing harder than before. My feet are free to kick, but they're making contact with nothing but hangings or—painfully—walls and doors and pillars.

At least, in breaks from the struggling, I can see where we're going. I'm at the Coldharbor—my grandmother's London house—and the soldier is carrying me down the front staircase, the grand one. It's dark in the house, but the big window we pass glows softly blue—it must be nearly dawn. When we get to the bottom of the stairs, I see orange torchlight spilling out the door to the great hall, winking off and on as dark figures move hurriedly through, blocking and unblocking the light. Are they servants or more soldiers? And where's my grandmother—and my mother? Have they been captured too?

"Nearly there," says the soldier as he turns down the passageway toward the back of the house. "We'll be outside in a moment, sir; it's really important that you're quiet."

So I breathe in through my nose, filling my lungs as deeply as the panic will let me, and then—as the soldier steps out through a door into the cold air of the courtyard—I yell as loud as I can into the muffling hand.

"Hllfff! Hllfff! Suuwu hllfff!"

Even I know that the sound is pathetically thin, lost in the wide damp space. And—oh, mercy—out here, soldiers are everywhere.

They won't take me—they won't; I twist and thrash for all I'm worth.

"Hey, don't kick the horse, sir. It's not fair on the poor beast."

For a flash I think I'm going to be slung on my stomach across a saddle, the way Compton says prisoners or dead bodies get carried, but the soldier swings my legs up and I land on my bottom—hard, but the right way up.

I hear the soldier say, "Sorry, ma'am. He was asleep when I picked him up. Got himself a bit agitated." He puffs out a breath. "Strong for a little 'un, isn't he?"

And an arm grips me around my middle, pulling me back against a body, warm and solid, and a voice in my ear says, "Calm yourself, Hal. It's me. We're in a hurry, that's all."

My mother.

I want to snuggle into her and cry with relief. I don't understand what's happening, my heart's still banging, my lungs and stomach still heaving, but if I can cling to her, I can cope.

As my mother tugs quickly at my blanket, draping it over my head like a hood and wrapping it firmly round my body, I sit, dazed for a moment, staring at the horses that fill the courtyard. They stamp and snort and toss their heads, harnesses jingling. Each one of them has a soldier in the saddle.

Then I say, in a thin, croaky voice that doesn't sound like my own, "What's happening, Mama? Are we running away?"

"No, sweetheart. Just moving to a safer place. Hold on. Here." She pats the front of the saddle. I grip it and look back, trying to squint up at her. But my head turns and the blanket stays where it is, so I can see only with one eye, and nothing more than the edge of her face.

She's hooded too, in a black cloak. I catch sight of the tip of her nose, and part of her cheek. In this weird light—not dawn yet, but not proper night either—her skin looks blue.

As I turn back, she reaches around me to adjust the reins and says, "Let's go, Captain. Steady pace."

Hooves clatter on the cobbles as the mounted soldiers form a guard around us. Then we set off, filing out through the courtyard gate and turning right, up the lane, away from the river. Though it's summer, dank mist creeps into the streets from the water behind us; the air tastes wet.

The lane is narrow and dark, squeezed between black walls. The soldiers riding at the front are carrying flaming torches; when we turn right again into a wider street, they fan out to surround us.

There's something exciting about being out at this time, but I know that no one moves in the night for a *nice* reason. And it's the second time we've had to move in just a few days.

First we came from Eltham, outside London, to my grandmother's house here, because it's inside the protection of the City walls. Now we're moving again. Last time we went in daylight. Now it's barely dawn. And there hasn't even been time to get me dressed.

My feet are bare and cold: I reach the left one backward, tucking it under my mother's skirts; the right curves toward the warm flesh of the horse, trying to hug it.

Over my head I hear my mother say sharply, "No faster

than this. We'll attract too much attention. I don't want to spread panic."

A man's voice—one of the guards—replies, but I don't catch the words.

She says, "I was told the rebels' plan was to march at dawn. They won't come in sight of the City for a couple of hours, surely?"

The man twitches his hands on the reins, and his horse moves closer to ours. "It only takes one, ma'am, to've ridden ahead. Any doorway, any alley entrance could hide a man with—"

"I understand."

She's cut him off deliberately. I see him glance at me, then he drops his horse back again.

He must be the captain of the guard; a moment later I hear the same voice bark an order, and every horse quickens its pace.

Through chattering teeth I manage to say, "W-will we be killed, Mama?"

"No, of course not." She sounds faintly impatient. "Where we're going, we'll be very safe."

But, as the man said, it only takes one.

Pushing the blanket back from my face, I keep a lookout— through gaps between the soldiers on either side of us—for doorways and alley entrances. Anywhere where the mist collects and thickens—anywhere a man could hide. As we pass a monstrous lump of a building, the mist thickens in what looks to me like a human shape, crouching at the corner of the wall. My heart's in my throat. Do I yell to my mother? Scream to the guard? But then the shape rolls and thins and vanishes into the black air. Just mist—no assassin. I can breathe again.

A gap in the buildings yawns suddenly on our right: the entrance to the docks. The river looks oily black and vast— and then it disappears as buildings again block the view. Rats scatter from a rubbish heap as we pass it. Shops and town houses, now, are showing chinks of light between the shutters of their overhanging upper stories; servants are lighting fires in their masters' bedrooms, as Compton does for me. But shabby people are already in the streets. I catch glimpses of them—filthy, like the rats, slipping in slimy gutters to stand flat against the house walls as we pass. They frighten me, with their blank stares and pinched faces.

A bell begins to clang. It doesn't stop. Dogs, chained in unseen yards, bark and yelp. Now there's another bell, some- where farther off. And a man's voice, thin in the cold air: "Every man to arms!"

Running feet, somewhere behind us. Another voice, closer: "To arms, to arms! Man the walls!"

My mother mutters something I don't catch. She uses her crop and our horse lurches forward. The guards around us match her pace.

I don't see him at first—the man who runs in from our left, straight in among the riders as if he's crossing clear ground. But when I turn my head, a face looms; he's close enough for me to see his bloodshot eyes and his grabbing hand with its grimy, broken nails. He reaches for me, saying something urgent, bellowing.

My mother's horse tosses its head in alarm and tries to veer away; I cling to the saddle, hunched low, desperate not to slide. At the same moment the nearest soldier lashes out with the butt of his spear.

The man's down. Down and half-trampled and we're past him, already half a dozen buildings on.

"Who was that?" I squeak.

"Drunken beggar, sir," says the captain. "That's all."

But I feel so frightened I want to be sick.

The guards ride in closer formation around us after that. Reaching the top of this long street at last, we turn left past some old stone ruins. The sky is streaked with orangey pink now; against it, on our right, I see gray walls, layers of them, rising one behind another and, beyond, the turrets of a vast whitewashed fortress. And I know where we are. This is London's ancient stronghold: the Tower.

Ahead of us the street runs uphill and widens into a huge grassy space. We turn to the right, crossing the lower reaches of the slope, and then my mother says, "Here. Thank God."

We come to a gateway made of brick, its edges all sharp and new. We stop. The captain of the guard speaks to the gatekeepers. Then the horses move again, and we pass through, across a small space, to the next gate. It's older, this one: an arch made of huge lumps of worn stone, sealed by an ancient wooden door.

"See how thick the walls are, Hal?" my mother says, as

the door is dragged open for us. Her voice sounds lighter, almost cheerful.

I look.

"Count the drawbridges. Count the gates. No one can harm us here."

I count them. At gate number three a drawbridge stands lowered, but so do two portcullises. The warders raise only one portcullis at a time, and we have to wait in the space between, while with loud grating noises the cranks are turned—to shut the portcullis behind us and then open the one ahead.

Gate number four. It looks like a big black mouth as we approach—and I think of being swallowed by a monster. Again there's a drawbridge, again a lowered portcullis, screening a great nail-studded door. We wait in front of it, and I see through its chinks the orange light of the warders' torches getting brighter as they approach on the other side. Chains rattle and massive bolts screech and scrape as they're drawn back—and scrape again as they're shot home behind us.

No one can harm us here, my mother said. I believe her. How can this place ever be captured? My mother doesn't say anything now, but somehow I know she is getting happier with each gate we pass through.

At the fifth, as we wait again for a portcullis to be raised, I hear a hoarse croaking of birds and look up. Large black shapes wheel against the lightening sky.

And then suddenly the skin on the back of my neck prickles. It's like an animal instinct: I feel that I'm being watched. Not by my mother, not by the guards—by someone else.

Above the pointed center of the gateway's arch there's a window. Before I've properly looked at it, as my gaze slides down from the birds to the building, I think I glimpse something: the smudge of a pale face moving—a white oval against the lattice. By the time I'm looking at the window directly, it's gone.

The portcullis is up and the horses begin to move, their clopping footsteps echoing as we pass under the gateway's vaulted roof. I feel stiff from gripping the saddle so hard, and I'm shuddering with whole-body shivers now, which makes it hard to keep my balance.

It's not just the cold that's making me shiver. A scary thought has come into my head: What if the danger isn't outside after all? What if there is something inside, waiting for me to arrive? And the bolts screeching home behind me are shutting me *in with it?*

2

"For the love of God, have someone dress the boy, Elizabeth. He looks like a peasant."

I don't like to be called a peasant, even by my own grand-mother. And anyway it's not true. What peasant wears a sable-lined blanket with embroidered velvet slippers? (Even if the slippers *are* much too large—a groom just found them for me.) I scowl down at my fist. I'm trying to pick a bit of dried food out of my garnet ring.

"Don't fidget," my mother whispers, rubbing my hair.

We're deep in the heart of the Tower: We've come through so many gates it feels like the center of a maze. I'm surprised: I thought it might feel like a prison, but the hall we're stand-ing in isn't grim and bare—it's very like the hall at Eltham Palace, which is the place I call home. A fire is blazing in the huge hearth, and friendly faded ladies and knights ripple at me gently from the painted hangings on the walls. I have pushed all thoughts of eerie faces from my mind. I would like something to drink. The only thing making me feel uncom-fortable is the fact that my grandmother is here. She must have set off from the Coldharbor too: How she got here first, though, I have no idea.

Servants are rushing about, carrying candles, piles of linen, trestle tables, and benches. My grandmother stands in the middle of all this commotion, her yellowish face edged by a white wimple, her bony hands resting on her plain black gown. She dresses like a nun, but you do not forget for a moment she is the mother of the king. She has a manner you could graze yourself on.

I know, too, that I must not show my grandmother how much she scares me. She's like my father: She will kick a dog if it whimpers; if you show fear, she'll look at you like you're a piece of maggoty meat. Tudors aren't afraid. It's my mother's family that are weak and tearful and full of foolish feeling. I've heard my grandmother say that my mother's parents married for love. She says it like she's picking up a dirty, stinking rag. I think it means: No wonder your mother is so soft, no wonder she hugs you and kisses you and treats you like a baby.

My mother gathers me in now against her skirts. She says, "Have you heard any news, ma'am? Are the rebels at the City gates? At the bridge? Are they south of the river or north?"

"They are not at the gates," says my grandmother. "The report that they were so close to London has turned out to be a false alarm. We have been informed that they are still thirty miles away." A passing page boy is holding down the top of a huge pile of napkins with his chin. In one smooth movement she stops him, whisks the top cloth off the pile, yanks his arms out in front of him, and cuffs him across the head. I wince, as if she's hit me, too.

As the boy rushes past, his eyes brimming, she adds, "Lord Daubeney is encamped with a force on Hounslow Heath to hold the rebels back from the City."

"How many men in Daubeney's force?"

"Eight thousand."

I feel my mother's hand tighten on my shoulder. She says, "The last estimate I heard, the rebels had nearly twice that number."

"Our scouts have been reporting desertions. And, in any case, the king will bring his force to join Daubeney." My grandmother says this as if my father only has to turn up to be sure of winning any battle. Is it true? I could well believe it. My father is a fearless warrior.

"The earls of Oxford and Suffolk have mustered good numbers too," my grandmother says. "Daubeney simply needs to hold out until they arrive."

"And . . . there's been no report of—" My mother hesitates. "No report from the Kent coast?"

"Of a landing?" My grandmother smiles thinly. "Nothing yet. But if the rebels have a plan to take London by storming the bridge, *that person* will most likely sail up the Thames and assault the City from the water, don't you think?"

I know who my grandmother means when she says *"that person."* It's a man who wants to push my father off the throne and be king instead. Sometimes people call him "the Pretender." He's been talked about for as long as I can remember: how he moves from country to country, from court to court of the kings who are my father's enemies, getting money from them and trying to build an army so he can invade England. I imagine him like an ogre, striding across kingdoms with a few giant steps—*stomp, stomp, stomp.* He's had coins minted threatening my father, with a quote from the

Bible stamped on them: *Thou art weighed in the balances, and art found wanting.*

Now, after years of waiting, they say this man—the Pretender—is coming for real. The rebel army closing in on London isn't his—it's a band of Cornishmen, rebelling against taxes. But this is the Pretender's chance: While the country's in chaos, he's going to invade. I glance fearfully at the hall's great oak door, as if he might knock it down right now and come crashing in to kill us all.

My mother mutters, "God preserve the king."

"Oh, he will," says my grandmother. "I have faith in that." She hands the crumpled napkin to a passing maid. "Arthur is not being moved?"

"He has a garrison protecting him at Ludlow. It's best he stays where he is."

My grandmother grunts, which I think means she agrees.

"And the girls will be safe enough at Eltham," adds my mother.

My grandmother doesn't even bother to reply.

Arthur is my older brother and, being the heir to the throne, has his own household at Ludlow. He is also my grandmother's favorite. I don't think, in fact, that she knows what younger brothers like me are for, let alone sisters—of any age. She had only one son herself: my father. She gave birth to him when she was thirteen years old, and people say that he ripped her insides so badly she could never have another child.

"Mass will be said in the White Tower at eight," my

15

grandmother is saying. "Your chambers should be ready soon." She is about to leave, heading for the door behind us at the far end of the hall. But, as she comes close to pass by us, she stops. "By the way, Elizabeth, it occurs to me that I haven't asked you . . ."

"What?"

"Who you are hoping will win, my dear."

I feel my mother stiffen. She whispers, "Not in front of my son, ma'am. Please."

There's a tiny moment of silence. Then my grandmother sweeps past, flicking a bony finger painfully hard against the side of my head as she does so, and says, "Stand on your own, boy." I jerk to attention, leaving go of my mother's skirts.

When she's gone, I let out a breath. My mother does too; we catch each other doing it and grin. Then my mother puts her hands on my shoulders and bends to look me full in the face.

"May—" I begin, but she cuts me off.

"God favors your father," she says. "You know that, don't you, Hal? There is nothing to fear."

"I know," I say. "May I have a drink now, please?"

When my drink has been fetched and my mother and I are in her chamber, I say, "Why did Grandmama ask who you want to win, like that?"

My mother's been busy with two of her gentlewomen, unpacking some clothes from a newly arrived trunk. Now she looks at me sharply. For a moment she seems to hesitate, then she comes over and takes my hand. She says, "You've heard of the man they call the Pretender?"

I nod.

"Well, he claims he is my brother: Richard, Duke of York."

"But I'm Duke of York!"

"Exactly—so you are. It's the title given to the king's second son. When I was a child, my father was king, so the younger of my two brothers was made Duke of York. And your father is king now, so you—as his second son—are Duke of York too."

"You mean there are two of us with the same title?"

"No, sweetheart. My brothers died years ago. This man, the Pretender, is telling lies. He isn't my brother, and he has no right to any title."

I'm sitting on a wooden chest. She sinks down next to me and sighs, putting my hand back in my lap and patting it. "But your grandmother . . . is worried I might not believe that. She thinks I'm hoping my brother is still alive. She thinks I'm hoping the Pretender really *is* him. And that I might want him to come with an army and take the crown and be king. It's all completely ridiculous."

We're both quiet for a moment. I drain my cup. I say, "Why doesn't Grandmama like you?"

"Oh!" My mother stands up suddenly. She takes my cup and puts it on a nearby table. "She *does*, she just . . ."There's a pause. More quietly she says, "For complicated reasons." She looks at me. She can see I'm still expectant; bending to hook my hair behind my ear, she whispers, "Because I have more royal blood running in my veins than either she or your father do. She can't stand that."

I stare at her for a moment, my eyes wide.

I don't think that's the reason, though. I think it's that my mother laughs and makes people happy. When I was younger, I thought she might be an angel. She's certainly the most beautiful person I've ever met. I wish she could live all the time at Eltham, with my sisters and me. Every day we could shoot together, and go riding—I'd love that. Instead she has to live at court with my grandmother who doesn't like her, and my father who is so serious and scary—it can't be much fun.

Our family seems divided: My mother and I are on one side, my father and grandmother and my older brother Arthur are on the other. I can't think why, but that's how it's always been. We even look different: I'm like my mother's family—all solid and rosy cheeked, with red-gold hair— while my brother is like my father: dark haired, and wiry like a whippet.

My mother is standing near me now, giving instructions to her women. I reach out and slip my hand into hers. When I tug it, she looks down at me, and I say, "Don't worry, Mama. When I am a man, I will look after you."

For a moment I think she's going to laugh. But then she puts her face level with mine and her expression is very serious. "I can see him, you know, Hal—the man you will be one day. I can see him looking out through your eyes." She hugs me tightly. "May God keep you safe, sweetheart."

Later, when I've been shown to my own bedchamber, I catch sight of myself in the looking glass. I am big for my age and usually I think I look quite grown up. But today my reflection seems young, and rather scared. I twitch my face— pull it into a confident shape. Then I try to fix in my mind how this feels from the inside. So I can make sure I don't look scared again.

3

My father is never scared, I'm certain of that. Somewhere out there, right now, he's marching at the head of his army. His sinewy body is encased in magnificent armor. His broadsword is ready to swing into men's flesh, to visit God's anger on those who dare rebel against him. I kneel up on the window seat and try to imagine it.

It's not much of a view I'm looking at, though—I can't even see out of the Tower. The window of my bedchamber looks inward, onto a courtyard. Even early on a June morning, it's not cheering. In the shadows, the walls weep damp green streaks. I breathe on the window and start to draw a dragon with my finger.

Behind me something's rustling, like a hedgehog in a pile of leaves. It's my servant, Compton, who's kneeling on the rush-strewn floor, rummaging in a trunk. He's already helped me to dress, in an outfit of my own colors as Duke of York: mulberry-red and blue. So: fine white shirt, red doublet and hose, and a short, loose blue velvet jacket on top, embroidered with gold. Now his task is to search for the matching hat: blue velvet, with a pearl and ruby brooch and a red feather. I can't go to Mass without my hat.

"I don't think . . . no . . ." He's carefully lifting the last few layers at the bottom of the trunk. "I'm sorry, sir, I must have packed your hat case in one of the other boxes. I'll have to go down to the hall and see if they're in yet."

I'm drawing the flames coming out of the dragon's mouth. I say, "How long do you think we'll have to stay here?"

Compton stands and brushes stray rush stems off his legs. "A few days? A week or two? Until the rebels can be persuaded to disperse or else there's a pitched battle. It can't be long, either way."

"And what if that man comes with an army?"

"Which man?"

"The Pretender."

Compton shakes his head. Being fourteen, he is a man of the world and always seems to be up with the latest news. "He won't dare land here, sir—not unless the rebels defeat your father's army. And they won't manage that. So. You don't need to worry about him."

Compton makes for the door now, but an idea occurs to him and he turns back, with a new look of helpfulness on his face. "Would you like to put a stake on it, sir? Not, obviously, on the outcome. God knows"—he crosses himself—"we are certain of that. Just on the number of days we'll stay here?"

My belt and purse are lying on the table beside me. I open the purse and count the contents carefully. "Sixpence says five days or more?"

Compton sucks in his lips.

"I don't have much with me!" I tilt the purse toward him as proof.

"Beggars can't be choosers. Five days exactly, though." He

catches the coin I throw to him, tosses it into the air, bounces it off his elbow, and, catching it again, secretes it somewhere inside his doublet.

As he closes the door behind him, I turn to the window again and rub off the dragon with my sleeve. Down in the courtyard a covered cart is coming in through the Inner Ward gate, and servants are running from the hall doors opposite, ready to unload it.

I watch them and think of Compton's confidence. I pick through his words carefully, like counting out coins. I often do this with things grown-ups say.

He won't dare land here, sir—not unless the rebels defeat your father's army. And they won't manage that. So. You don't need to worry about him.

Compton's certainty is like a blanket, comforting and warm, but a tiny part of me still wonders: How does he know? I've heard some of the servants say that God is angry because people are bad, and so he is sending more wars to punish everyone, and that this man—the Pretender—will start up the civil wars again, the ones that raged for years and years before I was born and that my father put a stop to.

But Mistress Denton, who is in charge of our household at Eltham, slaps anyone she hears talking like that, so maybe it's not true. Or maybe it *is* true, but it's wicked to talk about it. Mistress Denton's always on a sharp lookout for wickedness.

There's a tap on the door.

"Excuse me, sir. May we put this in here?"

Two servants shuffle in, carrying another trunk between them.

I say, "Did you see Compton on the way up?"

"No, sir. Shall I fetch him, sir?"

I shake my head.

If he's not on his way up yet I can look for Raggy, my old scrap of cradle blanket. I hope it's been packed. I'm always afraid Mistress Denton will throw it away. She threatens to all the time; she says I'm too old to be attached to something so babyish. But I need Raggy, especially at a time like this.

I'd like to find my book of stories about King Arthur and the Knights of the Round Table, too. I've just got up to a really exciting passage about Sir Galahad, and I want to know what happens next.

So, when the servants have shut the door behind them, I climb down from the window seat and grab the bunch of keys Compton's left on a shelf by the door. One by one, I try the keys in the lock of the trunk they've just brought in. The fourth fits. Turning it, I lift the lid.

The trunk is full to the brim. First layer: large bags of dried rose petals to perfume clothes; I discard them on the floor. Next: my red and black cloak and two doublets. Then I fling out three pairs of hose. Raggy, to my joy, is lying just beneath, on top of something hard that's covered in black velvet. It's not a book box, this hard thing; it's large, curved unevenly and—running along the center—there is something ridged like a spine.

I prod it. For a moment, staring stupidly, I can't think. There is something horrible about how solid this thing is—I sense that, even before I register the curl of straw-colored hair at the collar, even before I see that it is a person: a boy, bigger than me, folded over, face down, inside the trunk, with his forehead to his knees. There is no movement in his back, no breathing, and a terrible thick feeling to the flesh beneath the clothes, like a lump of cold meat.

Scrambling up, I lurch back across the room until I bang into one of the bedposts. I've got Raggy rammed against my mouth; I can taste vomit. I swallow, breathing hard. My heart's hammering, but in the room there's silence. Nothing moves.

What should I do? Wait till Compton comes and finds me, quivering here like a hunted hare?

I make myself walk to the trunk, though I keep my focus to one side of it; I can't bear to look at it directly. Slowly, slowly, my fingers reach down to the black velvet. Summoning all my courage, I watch them as they touch it. And freeze, confused. Then I spread my fingers and grab. The velvet crumples in my hand. It is one of my doublets—it is empty.

I am scrabbling now, clutching fistfuls of cloth and flinging them out of the trunk. Nothing, nothing, nothing— except the clothes and, beneath them, the bare wooden floor of the box. The body is not there.

"What on earth are you doing?"

Compton is standing in the open doorway, staring at me. He's holding a hat case in one hand and one of my best daggers and a sword belt in the other.

I sit back on my heels, panting, and wipe a hand across my mouth. Clothes are strewn everywhere. I say, "I don't know."

4

"If you see something that isn't really there . . . ," I say slowly, "does it mean something's wrong with you? In the head?" I can't bring myself to say the word "mad."

My mother looks down at me, her eyes hidden in shadow. The room is dark, the fire damped for the night, one lonely candle casting a pool of yellow light across my pillows. I'm lying under the covers, Raggy hidden out of sight. My mother's shadow stretches itself across the floor and runs straight up the wall, like spilled ink running the wrong way.

She's standing near the end of the bed. For a long moment she doesn't move or speak, then she comes closer, frowning a little, and perches on the edge of the quilt. She says, "If you see what kind of thing, Hal?"

I say, "Oh, anything." I turn my head away, reach one hand up to the nearest bedpost, and trace over its pattern. "You know, like in stories."

On the quilt under my other hand there's a book. My mother gently slips it from my grasp and opens it to look at the title page. "Well . . . in this story Galahad sees a vision of the Holy Grail before he really finds it, doesn't he? Have you got to that bit? And stories of saints' lives often mention visions too."

"And no one thought they were mad for seeing things? The saints, I mean?"

My mother smiles. "No, of course not. God was speaking to them. They were blessed. Though the message he gave was not always easy to hear, I suppose." She closes the book carefully, fastens its silver clasps, and moves into the shadows to stow it in a box on a shelf. She says, "Sweetheart. Why all the questions about seeing things?"

"No reason. I was just wondering."

I haven't spoken to anyone about what happened this morning. Not even Compton. I told him the clothes were everywhere because I'd gotten frustrated looking for my book. At Mass I prayed about it, though. Begged God not to let this be the first sign of some awful brain disease.

My mother moves round the bed, tugging shut the curtain at the far side and the one at the foot. Some of the lining, she notices, is moth-eaten. As she tuts over it, I think: *If my vision of that body—that dead boy—in the trunk was God's way of speaking to me, what could he possibly have been saying?*

That this is my future: The rebels will defeat my father and make someone else king, and I will be murdered and put in a trunk?

I sit bolt upright as my mother pulls the last curtain half-shut. I blurt, "Does this place scare you?"

Her pale eyes widen. "No. Why should it?" Gently, she lays me down again. "It's old. A bit musty. It could do with redecorating, couldn't it? But it's a safe place, not a scary place. Now, go to sleep, Hal."

"Don't leave me."

"Hal, don't be silly."

"Is Compton here?"

"Of course. He's waiting outside—I'll call him in. Now, settle down."

Some hours later I open my eyes, very suddenly, to blackness. I feel I've been woken by something, but I don't know what.

I squirm toward the edge of the bed and pull back the curtain. I can just about make out the window, by a sliver of dim moonlight where its curtains are not quite shut. But the window is in the wrong place.

For a moment, I panic: I have no idea where I am, or what kind of room the darkness hides. Then memory slides back in, like a cloth across a table: I'm not at home in Eltham Palace—I'm in the Tower.

And one thing, at least, is the same as always: Compton is asleep, on his pallet, somewhere beyond the end of my bed. I can hear his steady breathing.

The sliver of moonlight winks, then disappears; wind whistles through gaps in the casement. Then a noise comes, outside in the passage. A door unlatching, opening. Soft footsteps—and urgent whispers.

I sit up, holding my breath. Very slowly, I peel back the bedclothes and swing my feet to the floor. Across the other side of the room, beneath the door, there's a faint, flickering line of orange light from the passageway. Sliding my feet forward instead of lifting them, I head toward it, feeling for obstacles as I go. The rushes are prickly against my bare ankles. Suddenly a great gust of wind lashes the window. I stop, tense; but, though Compton stirs, he doesn't wake.

Reaching the door, my fingers search carefully for the handle. I apply the gentlest pressure possible and open it a crack, just wide enough for one eye. It gives me a view of the passageway, looking in the direction of my mother's bedchamber, which lies next to mine. Her chamber door is open, light spilling from the room, and a dark figure in a nightgown and shawl stands on the threshold, its back to me. This person—a woman—is looking along the passage. Beyond her, I see why: My mother is walking down it, holding a candle—a flickering spot of light in the darkness. As she walks, her free hand trails slowly against the wall. She is dressed for bed; her hair hangs loose down her back. Two of her servants are shuffling along with her, sideways like crabs, looking anxiously at her face, their arms half-open toward her as if hoping to shoo her back.

Something is wrong, but when my mother speaks, it's in a perfectly normal tone of voice. She says, "Keep turning left, isn't that what they say? Always turn left, and eventually you come to the place."

Near to me, at my mother's chamber door, a second, younger woman emerges to stand beside the first. "What's wrong with Her Grace?" she whispers. She sounds as if she's only just woken.

The first woman hisses, "Sleepwalking."

"What's she done?"

"Done?"

"People sleepwalk when they've got a guilty secret, don't they? My cousin told me that."

"Then your cousin's a fool," the first woman snaps. "Her Grace, poor lady, is looking for her brothers."

Now my mother has stopped walking and laid the side of her head against the wall. She says, "Don't you hear it?"

One of the ladies with her says, very gently, "Hear what, ma'am?"

"A tapping. No, no—more like a scratching. Listen—there it comes again. They're here. I must be quick."

"What does she mean?" says the second woman at the door. "Are her brothers hiding?"

Her neighbor tuts. "I forget how young you are." Then she whispers something in the younger woman's ear.

"Oh, Christ have mercy upon their souls!" The woman crosses herself. "And them only little children, too!" She clutches her companion's arm. "Do you think their spirits are unquiet here? Oh, it makes me afraid to walk the passageways on my own!"

"Pull yourself together, girl. If the spirits of all the people killed in this place were up and walking, we wouldn't be able to squeeze down the passageways for the crush."

"Well, *that* doesn't make me feel better!"

"Shh. Keep your voice down. I'm going to follow. Madge has to persuade the queen to turn back before she reaches the guards. It would be shameful for her to be seen like this."

As the older woman starts down the passageway, and the younger turns to go back into the bedchamber, I dart sideways into the darkness of my room.

I wait until the sound of soft-slippered footsteps has faded to silence, then I push my door gently shut again and feel my way back to bed.

The rest of that long night I lie awake, my eyes open in the darkness.

6

I have a tiny painting, on parchment, which I often carry rolled up in a pouch on my belt. It shows the three nails used to fix Jesus to the cross. Each nail is shown driven through a chopped-off part of the Savior's body. So, one of the nails is driven through a bleeding right hand, another through a bleeding left hand, while the third goes right through two feet, laid one on top of the other and also dripping with blood. A crown of thorns lies like a garland around the whole grisly arrangement, and in the middle there is a bleeding heart.

Beside the picture it's written, in ink as red as the painted blood, that the pope has promised that if you carry this picture with you and say five Lord's Prayers, five Hail Marys, and one creed every day, then your enemies will not defeat you, neither will you die suddenly; you cannot be killed with a sword, or a knife, or with poison, and you will be defended from all evil spirits, on land or on water.

This morning, despite feeling sick with tiredness and so distracted that Compton almost despairs of getting me toileted and dressed, I am still very careful to tuck the picture into my belt. As I stand, tugged and jostled while my points are tied—to fix my sleeves to my doublet and hold up my hose—bits of the conversations I heard yesterday repeat, over and over, in my head. I feel confused every time I try to piece them together: My mother said her brothers were dead; my grandmother thinks she might not believe it—which is strange; and then the lady at the bedroom door said my mother was looking for her brothers. And: *If the spirits of all the people killed in this place were up and walking, we wouldn't be able to squeeze down the passageways for the crush.*

I don't know what to think, but I have a feeling of dread, as if something evil is approaching through the shadows, though I don't yet know its form.

When I'm dressed and have eaten (after much nagging from Compton) a little bread and cold meat, I go out into the orchard that lies to one side of the royal apartments. Here, two targets have been set up at opposite ends of the grassy space. Both are made from packed straw, covered with a white cloth. In the middle of the cloth is the mark you're supposed to aim for: a black painted circle.

As I approach, my mother is standing at the far end of the orchard, shooting her longbow. I watch her loose a shot smoothly. From where I am, I can't see which part of the target she's hit, but it's probably the black circle—she's an expert archer. She starts walking toward me, to change ends.

It's a beautiful morning, and the sunlight makes a halo around my mother's figure as she walks. Her quiver swings from a leather belt at her hip. The hems of her skirts are darkened with damp from the grass. Birds sing, perched on the rooftops and the twisted boughs of the old fruit trees. From the south, beyond the curtain wall and moat, I can hear the calls of the watermen on the river; there's no sign of yesterday's fear of a rebel attack. Only the clanking of the Royal Mint at the other side of the Tower breaks the peace. It's a metallic drumbeat that sounds like an army of demons on the march.

A waiting woman tugs the arrows out of the target; my mother takes them and slots them into her quiver. Then she walks across to me and kisses me on the forehead.

She says, "You look tired. Didn't you sleep well?"

I shrug. "All right."

"Poor thing." Her fair hair—loose last night—is plaited up on top of her head, as usual. Today it's covered with a linen cap and a velvet bonnet over that; no veil to get in the way of shooting. She looks neat and entirely in control. But beneath her eyes there are heavy shadows.

"You look tired too, Mama."

"Do I? You're a caring boy. I slept like a log."

She says it lightly enough, as if she believes it. If you sleepwalk, do you know about it in the morning? I suppose not. Not if your servants don't tell you.

I follow my mother as she makes her way back to shoot again. "Has there been a battle yet?" I say.

She takes up her stance, replying over her shoulder, "Lord Daubeney's sent your father's best spearmen forward to attack the rebels. There's been some fighting at Gill Down."

"Is Father fighting?"

My mother's movements are unhurried, smooth. She pulls an arrow from her quiver, nocks it, draws, and shoots. All in three seconds, or four.

Then she says, "Not yet, I think. He's testing the rebels. To see if they will hold their ground."

"And will they?"

She shoots again, aiming and releasing two arrows in quick succession, then lowers her bow and turns to look at me.

"We must wait for more news, sweetheart. I've told you all I know." She hands her bow to her lady-servant. "Now, let me see you shoot."

Behind me, Compton is waiting with my longbow and a selection of blunt-tipped practice arrows. I take the bow, tuck three arrows into my belt, and walk forward to take up my stance.

My mother shoots to hit the mark, but I'm still learning to keep a length. This means aiming the arrow correctly over different distances so that it will reach the target and not fall short. You can't learn to hit a mark until you know how to keep a length.

Today, here, it's a tricky task: the sight line lies between the trees of the orchard, which aren't spaced regularly, and the distance is difficult to judge.

"Don't forget to check the wind."

"Oh yes." I pull up some grass and toss it into the air. It drifts gently sideways as it falls; the wind's coming from the south, off the river. But it's not strong.

I take the first arrow. With my arms held low, I rest it on the knuckle of my bow hand, and position the nock—the groove at the feather-end of the shaft—against the string.

Then, as I lift the bow into position, I draw the string back—right back until the thumb of my drawing hand skims my ear.

This is where you need the strength. The more powerful the bow, the harder it is to draw. My father's bows have a drawing weight of over a hundred pounds.

I hold—no longer than the count of three—and loose the arrow, trying to open my fingers cleanly and quickly, without jerking. If you don't get your fingers smartly out of the way of the string, you know about it; it's a mistake you don't make twice.

"You held that one a fraction too long," says my mother, shading her eyes to see where my arrow has hit: I've made it to the straw target, but low down, and over to the left. "And, look—as you loose the arrow, think of squeezing your shoulder blades together a little and pressing forward with your bow arm." She lifts her arms to demonstrate.

"I was. That's exactly what I was thinking."

My mother narrows her eyes at me and smiles. I take another arrow from my quiver; nock, draw, hold, and loose again. This one scrapes a tree and scuds into the grass well short of the target. I growl in frustration.

"Mama . . . ," I say, as I pull out my third arrow.

"Mm?"

"How did your brothers die?"

I'm looking down at my bow, but I can sense that she's suddenly very still. She says quietly, "Why do you want to know?"

"I mean, was it some disease or . . ." I hesitate, wondering if I'm brave enough to say what I'm thinking. "Or was it a knife, or a gun, or what? An arrow?"

"Who have you been speaking to, Hal?"

"No one." I raise my bow, hold only a moment, and release. It's a better shot. "But were they murdered? And did it happen here, at the Tower?"

My mother doesn't answer. I'm still not looking at her. I add, "You said this was a safe place." Then I set off, walking toward the other end of the orchard to retrieve my arrows.

After a moment I hear a swishing; she catches up with me and walks alongside. Her skirts are dragging against the long grass—she grabs a handful of them and puts her other arm round my shoulders. "Hal. Yes, they were murdered. Yes, it happened here. But it was before you were born, sweetheart. During the old wars. It was . . . it was a different world back then. I don't think you can imagine just how different."

We've reached the target. My mother's three arrows are all in the black circle; my two are more spread out, one way above it, the other low. I've already picked up the one that fell in the grass. Now, pulling the other two out of the packed straw, I say, "So, was it a knife, then?"

She lets out a quick breath. "Can you stop asking about it?"

"I just want to know." I watch as my mother tugs out her arrows and puts them back into her quiver. Two patches of pink are showing high up on her pale cheeks. I say, "If you don't tell me I'll ask the servants."

The waiting woman has followed us at a distance; as she

steps forward to hand over my mother's bow, I see her dart a look at me.

My mother, weighing the bow in her hand says, almost in a whisper, "No one knows for sure. No bodies were ever found." Then, briskly, she takes up her stance and shoots again. The arrow hits the target, but way off the mark.

My brain is fizzing. I'm thinking of ropes slung over walls, of daring escapes. "Does that mean . . . maybe they weren't killed at all? Maybe they got away?"

"I don't think so."

"But it's possible?"

"It's possible." She says it reluctantly.

"So . . . if the Pretender says he's your brother and calls himself Duke of York—"

My mother releases another arrow. "You're the true Duke of York."

"Yes, but you told me that one of your brothers *was* Duke of York. So—*that* brother could have escaped. And the Pretender could really be him, all grown up . . ."

She looks at me, fresh arrow in hand. "I don't believe it."

"But he *could* be."

She takes aim and shoots. From here it looks as if she's hit the very center of the mark, but as she turns to me her expression is grim. She comes to stand close and says in an urgent whisper, "Listen to me, Hal. Don't let anyone hear you talking like this. It's dangerous—do you understand? Your father is king—the true king. There've been imposters before, and your father's enemies are always behind them, using them to stir up trouble. The last one was a baker's son, who'd been trained specially for *years* to pretend he was a cousin of mine. When your father caught him, he set him to work in the kitchens. This man now, who calls himself York—he belongs in the kitchens too. He's not my brother."

Her eyes look fierce, almost frightened. I think: *How do you know for sure?* But I don't dare say it.

7

Compton disappears around the corner and my smile fades. It's exhausting, hiding how scared I am, but how can I explain? What would I say?

I saw a body in a trunk and then it disappeared. Oh, and I've found out my uncles were murdered here when they were boys. Probably. Although they might have escaped. So—is one of them abroad now, waiting to invade? Or is his body hidden somewhere in this building? And if he is buried here, was it his ghost that I saw—was it his corpse, in the trunk?

Only two hours have gone by since dinner. I can't concentrate on reading, and I've had to stop playing cards with Compton because I'm losing too much money. If my grandmother catches me scuffing about, she'll hiss something about idle hands and give me a chunk of Latin to learn by heart. So I've sent Compton to ask if I'm allowed to visit the Tower's collection of animals: the menagerie. It's somewhere near the outer gates, and I think it has lions and leopards, kept in wooden cages. Compton says there used to be an elephant, too, but it died.

I hope he'll be quick. I'm nervous on my own. It's sunny outside, but the rooms and passageways of the Tower are cold. I think maybe they don't ever get warm. The shadows seem to collect in odd places, too, black as deep wells, and there is a worrying kind of pull when I walk near them, as if they could suck me in. When I'm alone, like now, I move from one room to the next, not with a princely stride but with a scuttle.

Despite my fears, though, I'm exploring—padding up and down staircases and along dim passageways, trying every door that I pass. Most are locked. What am I looking for? In my head there's a silly idea that this is an enchanted castle, and that something horrible is behind one of these doors, waiting for me to find it. I don't know whether it's more frightening to search for the horrible thing, or to hide in my room, imagining it.

It's odd, but I feel right now there are two *me*s. One me is being grown-up and sensible and opening doors to prove to myself there's nothing there. The other me has a horrid fascination: *That* me is opening doors *hoping* to see something frightening. Which is crazy.

Still, while my imagination is filled with wispy-haired skeletons, bloodstained floors, and grisly murder weapons, in reality, behind the few doors that I can open I'm finding nothing but old trestle tables, broken stools, and iron bedsteads.

The only dead thing I've found so far is a mouse, lying on its side with its little scratchy paws bent up and its front teeth showing. When I saw it, I knew straightaway it was dead, so when it started moving—shifting a little, this way and that— I wanted to scream. But soon I saw the reason: Its stomach was full of maggots, crawling in and out through a hole in the skin. The maggots were making it move. I poked it with a bit of old kindling from the fireplace, then left it alone.

Now, passing the entrance to a staircase, I find I'm almost at the end of a passageway. I'm not exactly sure where I am, but I think it's somewhere north of where I started, somewhere close to the White Tower. Pushing open the last door before the passageway's dead end, I look into a small chamber, where one narrow window lets in a slice of watery light.

I wrinkle my nose because the room smells musty. In the far wall there's another door—shut. Near it, some pieces of furniture are huddled together as if they've been shoved out of the way: a round table covered with worn black velvet, a bench, three stools, and two folding chairs made of painted wood. The only other thing in the room is a rickety-looking portable altar near the window, with a place to kneel—complete with fraying cushion—and a picture hanging on the wall above it.

The picture looks familiar—I want to have a closer look. I come fully into the room, closing the door softly behind me, and approach the altar. Yes, it's a painting of the three nails used to fix Jesus to the cross, very like the one I'm carrying.

I pull my picture out of my belt-pocket to compare. Looking at it, it occurs to me that perhaps I should say a couple more Hail Marys; I always worry that I may have lost count and said four rather than five (in which case the protection against murder and evil spirits won't work, will it?).

So I kneel on the cushion—which puffs out a cloud of dust—and begin in a whisper, not daring to shatter the silence of the empty room: *"Ave Maria, gratia plena, Dominus tecum. . . ."*

Hail Mary, full of grace, the Lord is with thee. . . .

And stop. I've heard someone speak.

For one mad moment I think it's the Virgin Mary replying. But then I hear another murmur—muffled, but close by—and footsteps. They're coming from my left—from beyond the door in the far wall. I'm frozen, not breathing—listening.

Then the handle begins to move. I don't even consider racing back to the other door, the one I came through—there's no time for that. Instead I dive for the corner beside the altar, crouching low, so that the width of the altar shields me.

Instantly, though, I can see this is not enough. I'm hidden from the door, but someone only has to move into the center of the room, and I will be in plain view.

The door begins to open. My mother's voice says, "This is the best place—no one comes in here."

My back's resting on a piece of wainscot with a pattern of small holes in it. I realize it's one of the doors of a press—a cupboard set into the wall. Quickly, still crouching, I open it a little. The cupboard is quite deep, lined with shelves in the upper part. The space below them is empty and, though not high, it is wide: plenty big enough for several people to hide in, let alone just me.

This is the moment of decision: Do I hide? Or do I stand up and admit I'm here, take the telling-off for roaming around without Compton, and go back to my room?

I don't stand up. I edge into the cupboard. Perhaps because I'm scared. Perhaps because, if my mother has secrets, I want to hear them. And later I wonder if there was something else at work too: maybe the three nails. Maybe God.

They're entering the room now: my mother and whoever she's talking to. Slowly, carefully, my ragged breathing sounding loud in my ears, I pull the cupboard door shut, hoping they're still not far enough into the room to see it move.

I brace myself for being found out—for an exclamation— but it doesn't come. Instead my mother says, "We don't have long. I must be quick."

"Yes, ma'am," says a man's voice.

Through the pattern of holes in the cupboard door I can see only a slice of the room straight ahead of me; there's a wall to my left, and, to my right, my view is blocked by the side of the altar. For a moment I catch sight of the edge of a brown robe—a monk's robe—and I know, from the voice, that the man who's spoken is Father Christopher, my mother's confessor.

My mother says, "Well—did you go into the City? What are the people saying? Are there prophecies circulating?"

"Yes, I'm afraid so, ma'am. As always at a time of crisis, the people distract themselves with any bill or rhyme or ditty they see pinned up on a tavern door, when they should be praying, or listening to their priest—"

"I know your feelings, Father, but did you collect any? The prophecies, I mean?"

"There is a notary of my acquaintance who has been

collecting prophecies as a hobby these past few years. I asked him for his latest findings. He gave me this."

"You didn't say it was for me?"

"Of course not."

I hear paper crackling as if my mother is opening a package.

Father Christopher says, "There are a few manuscripts, I think, and a few cheap printed folios. My acquaintance pointed out though, ma'am, that many prophecies circulate in a town by word of mouth only."

There's silence for a moment. Then distractedly, as if she's reading at the same time, my mother says, "There's no one outside that other door, is there?"

The plain figure of Father Christopher comes fully into view as he crosses to the door I entered by, opens it, checks the passageway, and shuts it again carefully. He turns to face my mother and shakes his head.

My mother says, "Do you really think there's nothing of value in any of these?"

"There *can* be. . . ." I see Father Christopher frown as if he doesn't want to admit it. "In certain cases. Many of the prophecies that Saint Bridget made are recorded, for example. A truly holy and blessed lady . . . But every one of those papers in your hand is untraceable, ma'am. I would want to meet the author, ask how the message came to him, gauge his devoutness, the purity of his soul . . . He *may* have an angel at his shoulder, whispering in his ear. But it may equally well be a devil crouching there."

My legs are getting stiff; I shift carefully.

"'The Turk will come this year to Rome . . .'" my mother reads aloud. "'A great king will rise in the north who will destroy the power of all Frenchmen.' Well, that would be convenient." She makes a nervous little sound, like a swallowed laugh. "Gosh, I'm shaking. How silly. There's probably nothing to the point in here at all."

Another silence. I watch as Father Christopher lifts one hand, smoothing the fringe of gray hair around his shaved head.

Then suddenly my mother says, "You understand this is a last resort for me, don't you, Father? I would consult a respected person, if I could. I would consult our court astrologer. But you know how the king's mother watches me. It would be just what she has been waiting for: to catch me asking Dr. Parron to cast my brother's horoscope! Can you imagine? She already suspects me."

"Of what, ma'am?"

"I wish someone would ask her that: Of what, precisely?" My mother's tone is scornful. "Of wanting my brother to be alive? Of *course* I want him to be alive! What loving sister wouldn't? But that doesn't mean I want him to invade with an army and slaughter my husband and my sons and make himself king. She does not allow any separation of those things. To hope my brother is alive is, in her eyes, to be a traitor."

I swallow a gasp. I am hot and cold at once. My mother sounds like a stranger—not capable and sure and comforting as she usually is, but frightened and angry. And now I know she has lied to me. She is *not* certain her brother is dead. The Pretender *could* be him, after all. And if he invades and my father is pushed off the throne, it's just as I feared: He will kill us. Kill me.

Father Christopher's voice interrupts my thoughts: "The king is devoted to you."

"He is devoted to his mother more. He listens to her. And she drips poison in his ear. . . ." My mother groans. "She hates me. She always has. We were on different sides in the old wars. She only made a deal for her son to marry me because it made political sense. She hates that my claim to the crown is stronger than his, and she hates that he loves me too."

Softly Father Christopher says, "So, this Pretender—you think it really is him: your brother?"

"You sound like her!" my mother snaps. "Forgive me, Father. No, I don't 'think it really is him.' I *don't know*—that's the whole point. How can I possibly know? That's why I asked what the prophecies are saying. . . . I want to find out. Or at least to be given a clue.

"Is that so very bad, Father? Can you say you wouldn't do the same? Imagine it: Your brother, a little boy, is dragged away by soldiers in front of your own eyes, and you are told he has been murdered. You weep and wail, but of course nothing will bring him back.

"And then, fourteen years later, someone in a distant land declares he is your brother, escaped and grown to manhood. Wouldn't you want to know if it's true?"

"Yes, ma'am, I would."

There's a silence. And it's in that silence that I hear breathing beside me. Someone else is with me in my hiding place.

I freeze. I daren't turn my head, but I must. And when I do, every instinct in me wants to cry out; I shove my knuckles against my mouth.

The holes in each cupboard door, together with a thin strip in the center where the two leaves haven't quite shut properly, let in enough light to make out a figure slumped against the wall at the other side of the space. It's turned away from me, kneeling or crouching, I can't see which; but the hunched back, the curl of pale hair at the collar, are horribly familiar.

That body in the trunk, in my chamber, yesterday—it's here with me again.

Out in the room my mother says, "I feel as if I am being ripped in two, Father. I fear this rebellion. I fear an invasion. I grew up in the civil wars; I've seen enough horror."

It's a horror that I'm seeing right now: unlike yesterday, the body isn't deathly still—it's moving. I think of the maggots, wriggling in and out through the hole in the mouse's skin.

"But still," my mother goes on, "there is a part of me that cannot stop hoping that my brother is alive—that he is *not*, after all, a little rotted corpse somewhere in this place."

No maggots this time. This body—this boy, this thing— is breathing, making little shuddering movements, the chest heaving in and out. Whimpering sounds are coming from it too, soft and horrid like a terrified animal. Like a rabbit caught in a trap. It turns my stomach. If it *were* a rabbit I'd want to snap its neck.

My mother says, "I can't stop hoping that he is alive and . . . and perhaps that he *is* this Pretender. But if he is, I pray God he will lay down his arms, let us all live in peace."

"Amen to that," says Father Christopher.

Amen from me, too. Let me live in peace. Let this spirit, this nightmarish vision—whatever it is—stop appearing to me. Please, God, take it away.

I hear a shuffle of papers. My mother says, "Listen to this one: 'And there shall be signs in the sun, and in the moon, and in the stars: and upon the earth, distress of nations; the soil drenched with more blood than rain. The word of God shall be transformed into a serpent, and good interpreted as evil. But when these things begin to come to pass, look up and lift up your heads: because your redemption is at hand.'"

Trapped in my terror, barely breathing, I listen to the words. They seem eerily beautiful.

"'The one who has been prophesied will come, full of power, full of good devotion and good love. Oh blessed ruler, I find that you are the one so welcome that many acts will smooth your way. You will extend your wings in every place; your glory will live down the ages . . .'" My mother sighs. "That sounds wonderful, doesn't it? It makes me shiver."

The boy is still whimpering. I reach out my hand toward him. He has to be real—he looks so real, he sounds so real . . .

Father Christopher says, "It is wonderful, ma'am, but

entirely unspecific. No names or dates, you'll notice, nothing to tie it to a particular country, even."

My hand is shaking. I watch my fingertips edging forward through the air, as warily as if the boy might at any moment turn and bite them off.

"Oh lord," my mother says.

"What is it?"

"You want specifics? Then here—listen to this one. 'York will be king.'"

But just as my fingers reach him, he is no longer there. The darkness somehow seeps into the space he occupies and rubs him out.

Father Christopher says, "What else does it say?"

"'He will begin as a lamb and end as a lion.'" My mother sounds shaken. "That's it."

I feel forward as far as I can. My fingers meet nothing but empty shadows.

"The Pretender calls himself Duke of York, doesn't he?"

"Yes," my mother says quietly, "he does. So . . . if 'York will be king' is correct, it means he will invade and seize the crown . . . and, no doubt, 'the soil will be drenched with more blood than rain.'"

I hear rapid footsteps. Looking out through the holes in the cupboard door, I see that my mother has crossed to Father Christopher and is clutching his hand. She says, "I must warn my husband!"

"How? Without revealing that you have been reading these?" Father Christopher indicates the papers.

"I don't know. I could say I have had a bad dream—a premonition . . . Oh, God . . ." She covers her face, the papers scrunched in her fist.

"Calm yourself, ma'am. Do any of the other prophecies make any mention of York?"

"No—no. I've looked at them all."

"Then it's just one. One scrap of grubby paper. The king, your husband, has many enemies. Any one of them could have written this with no more divine revelation than a clerk has, copying out an account book. It could simply be political agitation—the Pretender's supporters could have sent it into London to try to persuade people to join them. Nothing mystical in that. No need to say anything—no need to endanger yourself."

My mother takes a shaky breath. "You're right. Of course." She folds the scrunched papers and hands them back to Father Christopher. "I shouldn't have asked to see them, should I? What a fool I am." Her voice is clipped. "Be sure to burn them all, won't you? Straightaway. Filthy things."

"Yes, ma'am." Father Christopher bows. "I'll go and do it now."

I'm vaguely aware of them leaving the room—Father Christopher through the door by which I entered, my mother through the other one. For several minutes I'm completely motionless—stunned, very scared, and wondering if I'm about to be sick. But there's something else too: something small that's tugging at my attention like an annoying page boy tugging my sleeve. At first I ignore it—my heart is racing and

I can't move and I need to move: I need to get out of here.

Tug, tug. *What?*

A picture comes to me: my mother in the orchard. Her strong fingers snap straight; an arrow flies; she says, "You're the true Duke of York."

I take in a slow, shaky breath. I sense that something delicious is unfolding in my mind even before I know what it is.

What did my mother say, just before the boy—the thing, the vision—disappeared?

York will be king.

And now, in my head, I can hear her reading from that other paper:

The one who has been prophesied will come . . . Oh blessed ruler . . . you are the one so welcome that many acts will smooth your way. . . . Your glory will live down the ages . . .

I feel a warmth spreading from the center of my chest, tingling through my limbs. It's as if an invisible sun has come out from behind a cloud and is shining down upon me.

Pushing forward against the cupboard doors, I stumble out into the room and fall to my knees. I lay my forehead on the bare dusty boards of the floor.

Nothing has ever been clearer to me or more obvious. *York will be king* and *your glory will live down the ages*—those two prophecies are talking about the same person. I know it in every inch of my being. And it's not the man waiting abroad, this Pretender.

It's me.

8

I have only one thought now: I must speak to my mother.

It's the end of the day when my chance comes. After evensong and supper I go looking for her and find her alone in a chamber near her bedroom. The soft light of the summer evening shows through the half-drawn curtains, but the thick stone walls keep out any warmth, and the only other light in the room comes from a fire, blazing in the hearth.

My mother doesn't hear me enter; she's facing away from the door, sitting in a high-backed chair. The bonnet she wore in the orchard this morning has been replaced by a gable hood and veil—from behind I see the long black cloth crushed against the chairback where she's resting her head.

I approach hesitantly, fidgeting with my belt buckle, my dagger hilt, scrunching my toes inside my shoes. The fire hisses and cracks. The figures carved on the ornate fireplace, lit from below, seem to grin demonically. My mother doesn't move—I wonder if she is asleep.

Moving round the chair to stand before her, I see that her eyes are open, but she stirs and looks confused for a moment, as if I've woken her from a dream. "Mama!" I blurt. I probably look crazy—bright-eyed and barely able to stand still. "You don't have to worry, I've realized what they meant!"

"What, sweetheart?" With an obvious effort, she is smiling at me, trying to look interested.

"Those prophecies from the City." The smile is gone: My mother is instantly alert, aghast. I hurry on. "I was hiding in the room. I know I shouldn't have been—I'm sorry—I just happened to be there. Anyway, 'York will be king'—it's not him, the one they call the Pretender. It's *me*. Mama—aren't I Duke of York too? Aren't I the proper one? It's *me* who will be king!"

The blow reaches me before I know what is happening. Her left hand, ringed and surprisingly heavy, slams across my face with the force of a leather strap. I find myself twisted round, looking suddenly at the floor.

There is a moment of silence.

One of the tiny claws holding the stone of her ring has caught the skin below my right eye. My fingers drift up to it, absently—I look at my hand and see blood.

The next moment she has bundled me to her. I am pressed, too hard, into her bodice, my cheek rammed against the jeweled border of her neckline, so that the stones make painful pits in my skin.

She is weeping—huge shuddering sobs. I think: *I have made her weep.* And she is rocking me. "Hush, hush," she says at last, when her breathing has steadied. "Hush . . . hush." But I am making no noise.

At last she puts me at arm's length, her hands on my shoulders. Her face is blotched, her eyes puffy. "You must never say such a thing again, Hal," she says, shaking me slightly. "Understand?"

I am the one crying now. I nod, gulping.

"Those prophecies were complete nonsense. The ravings of charlatans, agitators, enemies of the crown. They've been burned. Your father is king and—God willing—your brother will one day succeed him. Listen carefully." I can't bear the way she's looking at me: It's ferocious, piercing—like nothing I've seen before. "*Never* mention those prophecies to anyone. Lives depend on it. My life. Maybe yours, too. This is a time of danger: Rebels are approaching London; your father is leading an army to meet them; foreign rulers are trying to stir up trouble . . . Ridiculous prophecies are always circulated when there is unrest like this. Do you understand?"

I nod energetically and press my knuckles against my eyes. I can't speak.

"If ever you *do* mention the prophecies—to anyone—I will deny all knowledge of them. I will say you have made them up. And you will be flogged for it. Understand?"

I nod a second time.

"Don't spy on me ever again, will you? Will you?" She peels my hands from my eyes—makes me meet her gaze.

I shake my head miserably. My cheek is throbbing now where she hit me. I want to run away.

"Oh God, look at you. I'm sorry, sweetheart. I'm sorry." She searches in her purse for her handkerchief, wets it on her tongue, and wipes the blood from my cheek. "There. Better now. Aren't we?" And she smiles at me valiantly. It is so vulnerable, that smile. It makes my heart lurch inside my rib cage, like I've missed a tread on the stairs.

So I mumble, "Yes," and do my best to smile back.

The jewels round my mother's neck wink in the firelight as she takes a deep breath and opens her eyes wide. "Oh! Aren't we silly sometimes?" She is brushing herself down now, finding a clean corner of handkerchief to blot her eyes. I know what she is thinking—that if my grandmother sees her, she must not look as if she has been crying.

That night in bed I hide under the covers, clutching Raggy tightly. I feel that the world has jumbled itself up: shattered into pieces and reformed, like a broken jug that's been mended. And though on the surface it looks as it always did, I know that underneath everything has changed.

Sometimes—I have learned—appearances are no more than masks. And that knowledge terrifies me as much as anything I have seen here at the Tower.

9

The following day—the day after my mother hits me for announcing my glorious future—five hundred of my father's best spearmen, commanded by Lord Daubeney, meet the rebel army at Gill Down and drive them into retreat. The rebels regroup and make camp by Deptford Bridge, near the River Ravensbourne. Three days later, my father's army attacks at dawn, taking the rebels by surprise.

By two o'clock that afternoon, my father is entering the City of London on a magnificent war horse, a livid scar showing fresh on his cheek and one of the rebel leaders lying, shackled, over the saddle of a horse led behind him. Unlike the thousands of dead even now being dragged from the field, this man has been saved for a slower and more public end.

A battle is a test of God's favor—I know that. A battle proves who is the rightful king. So, now, God has shown his favor, not to the rebels, or the Pretender—whoever he might really be—but to my father.

That same afternoon, as my father parades through the City streets in triumph, I suddenly turn hot and shivery. My joints ache and my legs feel like jelly, and the women servants put me to bed. I stay in bed for days and days—I have no idea how long. And when my mother leaves the Tower to join my father for the thanksgiving at Westminster, I have to stay behind. I'm in a cocoon of sickness. If my mother comes to say good-bye, I'm too ill to know.

During those feverish days in the Tower I have an odd dream.

In the dream, I am lying in the dark, underneath something—it is like lying under the covers in bed. Except that I am cold. I don't mind. It's restful. Perhaps I am asleep. And then it occurs to me: I'm not sleeping; I am dead. Covered by a layer of earth. Of course! How silly that I didn't notice it before.

And I am just thinking: *So this is what it is like and it's quite all right really; why do people worry about dying so much?—I must tell my mother when I see her*—when a black dot appears in the darkness. Or rather, a black dot that has light all around it.

And the dot rises up and gets bigger as I watch it, until it's as big as a sun, and the light from it is beaming down like strange sunlight on a clear day.

And at first I think there's just the dot, and something about the dot is moving, but then I see that the moving thing is a little boy, coming down the beams toward me, walking on the light as if it is a road. He gets nearer and nearer.

As the boy draws close to me, I see that he is very pale, with a halo of straw-colored hair; he looks like the Christ child in an old painting, except that his eyes are so deep-set they're completely hidden in shadow. It looks as if he has strange dark hollows instead of eyes. And the golden hair and the shadow-eyes make a contrast of light and dark like the brilliant black sun, and I am chilled and I shiver.

The boy stretches out his hands to me—pudgy hands,

the hands of a toddler—but when I put my own hands in his, the grip is strong, like a grown-up's.

And the moment he touches me, being dead isn't restful anymore. I'm drenched in terror, and I grip the boy desperately, as if he can keep me safe.

All at once, too, we're no longer in darkness. I see that we're in a field on the edge of a gorge. The spot where I've been lying is right by the drop. Somewhere far below I can hear rushing water.

The boy pulls me to my feet. He's smaller than I am, and dressed in a coarse gown like a poor man's child, but there's something fierce and powerful about him.

At that moment I hear a terrible noise from the gorge. I turn to see a huge serpent hauling itself up over the cliff edge. Its legs are short and muscular, and from its back vast wings unfold, with skin stretched across them like a bat's. Its eyes are red, its nostrils wide; with a terrible swinging motion of its head it seems to be searching for something, roaring in pain and rage. The smell from its open jaws is rank—of rotting flesh. Step by relentless step it comes, dark water sliding off its scales.

The boy tugs me sharply, pulling me away. He breaks into a run and I stumble after. Up ahead, a horse appears. The boy must somehow have grown taller, because it's a large horse and he mounts it with no problem and hauls me up in front of him into the saddle, just as the serpent's teeth snap the air where I stood. However close I am to the boy, still I can't see his eyes.

His arms reach round me as he holds the reins and spurs

the horse into a gallop. I grip the front of the saddle; against my back I think I can feel the sliding metal of a mail-coat, as if the boy is wearing armor under his peasant's gown.

Away we speed through open country, across scrubby moorland, fields, and ditches, so fast that we lose the serpent; there is no sign of it following. Soon the great dark mass of a forest looms before us. As the horse slows to a trot, we dip under a canopy of low branches, immersing ourselves in the cool, moss-green light. Far above us, brighter light shines in a dappled, broken pattern—beneath, I hear the horse's hooves crushing soft bracken underfoot.

The cool of the forest, the dark green shadows, the welcoming, delicious safety—how I would love to lose myself in here.

I wake with such happiness. Somehow, days have passed. The fever is lifting.

PART TWO

Acts Will Smooth Your Way

10

Four years later

"Tell the boy to move, Elizabeth. He's blocking the view."

My mother's fingers press my shoulder. She's behind me but she must be leaning forward; her voice is right in my ear. "Hal. Sweetheart. Your father wants you to move along."

I get up. On the sand-strewn floor of the vast hall in front of us, youths clad in various quantities of half-armor and leather padding are grunting and sweating, slicing and chopping at each other with blunt-edged swords.

"Go and sit over there. Next to Meg."

I edge along, holding the sword that's slung on my belt upright, so it doesn't poke anyone, and excusing myself as people are forced to stand up to let me pass.

"Relegated to sitting with the girls," says my elder sister Meg when I arrive. She speaks sideways out of her mouth; her jewel-encrusted hood is heavy, and I'm not worth the effort of a direct look. "What have you done?" She is sitting poised, straight backed, speckled with rubies and pearls the size of bilberries. Beyond her my little sister Mary, who is five, is sitting similarly ramrod straight, confined by a tight-laced bodice and the beady-eyed supervision of her nurse.

"Done?" I whisper back. "Only worn a hat with a feather

when sitting in front of the Spanish ambassador." I settle into my seat. "I wish Father would tell me himself. To get out of the way."

Meg gives a tight smile. "He hasn't said one word to me since I arrived."

We are in Westminster Hall. It makes me think of a cathedral: It's a huge cavern of cool, echoing stone. The windows—arched, churchy ones—are set high in the walls. When I look up, there's an entire world of sunbeams and dust motes up there, swirling about. Beyond that—way, way up—the roof is an amazing construction: wooden, ribbed like the hull of an upside-down ship, and decorated with carved angels.

Above us, then: the angels. Below, on the hall floor: the fighters, working like devils. One of them is my elder brother Arthur. We, meanwhile, are suspended in between, sitting on a raised and canopied platform along with half the court and a party of Spanish envoys.

The envoys have come to London to negotiate a treaty between England and Spain. To seal the deal my father wants a marriage: The groom will be my brother Arthur, his bride a Spanish princess. It's a prize my father has been trying to secure for years, I know: The Spanish royal dynasty is ancient and powerful. By comparison we Tudors are puny newcomers; we need to convince the king and queen of Spain that their precious princess will be in safe hands. Arthur's fighting display is intended to prove, physically at least, that we are built to last.

Which would be fine if he were any good with a sword.

"Block! *Block!*" I mutter now, my eyes on the fighting. My shoulder twitches because I want to join in.

It's Charles Brandon that Arthur's grappling with, a youth my father shows much favor to, since Brandon's father was his standard-bearer and died in the battle that made my father king.

Brandon is seventeen and big and beefy; it's like watching a tree in combat. Arthur, two years younger, is slight. If he trained hard enough he would be all sinew and gristle, like Father. As it is, he prefers to spend time bent over his desk, his soft white hands pressing open the pages of books. And it shows.

"A gap! Urgh, why didn't he attack?"

"Shh! Try to sit still," hisses Meg.

She's on my left; to my right, a little farther away, there's a Spaniard—one of the more junior members of the embassy. I lean forward to see past him, pretending to watch the fighters at the other end of the hall, but really I'm looking along the row of spectators to catch my father's reaction. Arthur is his favorite; usually Arthur can do no wrong. But surely Father's noticed that Arthur's a complete donkey when it comes to fighting with a broadsword?

Sitting at the center of the platform, next to the Spanish ambassador De Puebla, my father has his public face on: It is warm; it smiles; it laughs. But the eyes—I think the eyes always give him away. They are small and sharp, very bright. Not warm at all. Watchful. I can see he is observing everything—everything on the hall floor, everything up here on the platform—and even as he laughs he is not missing a thing.

He must be ashamed, I think. Secretly, he must wish Arthur could give better proof that we are a family of strong warriors, fit to dominate our people and crush all challenges to our power.

I sit back again and find my Spanish neighbor looking at me. I smile politely. It occurs to me that I probably ought to be making conversation.

"Do you have a handgun?"

The Spaniard looks mildly startled. "No, my lord. Only this." He pats the hilt of the sword at his hip.

"I mean at home."

The envoy shakes his head.

"I'd like to fire one. Someday."

I turn to watch the fighting again. There are *oohs* and *aahs* and ripples of polite applause; down in the hall, thuds and scuffles and violent exhalations. The fighters step in, step out again to dodge, lock together, pause as a mortal strike (placed but not, of course, driven home) is acknowledged, disengage.

"I think you would like to be down there with your brother, hm?" says the envoy.

"He should have used true guardant just then."

"I'm sorry. My English isn't good enough to understand this word."

"True guardant. It's a defense position. Like this." I raise my right arm in front of my face, hand angled down to show the direction the sword's blade follows. "Then if your opponent tries an overhead blow you only have to straighten your arm to block it. He doesn't anticipate that move very well. In a battle someone could come in and split his head straight down the middle."

"Yes, I see."

"That's the trouble with practice like this. Brandon's not going to do that. . . ."

"Not split his head down the middle, no."

"So he can carry on making the same mistake, not learning—oh, nice hit."

I can sense that the Spaniard is studying *me* now, rather than the fighting. He says, "I should like to see you fight, my lord."

I glance at him to see if he's joking, but he seems to be in earnest. I look back to the fight again and say, "I'm good. Broadsword, backsword, sword and buckler. I'm going to start with two blades soon. I do longbow shooting, too. Hit the mark pretty much every time. I'm better than all my friends."

On my other side, Meg clears her throat pointedly.

The envoy says, "You must be very accomplished, my lord."

"And I've just started with the quarterstaff."

"So young? That's impressive."

The Spaniard turns to speak to his neighbor on the other side.

"Hal, stop showing off," Meg says in a low tone.

I whisper into the side of the jeweled hood, about where I imagine her ear must be: "I'm not. I just think it would help if they knew there was someone in this family who knows how to handle a weapon. Don't you?"

But before she can reply, the Spaniard leans across to me again. "With your leave, my lord, my colleague here will ask your father's permission for you to fight a bout for us."

"What, now? I'd be delighted."

I hear a groan from Meg; I ignore it, watching instead as a servant relays the request to my father. He reacts with surprise. I can see him shrugging, spreading his hands, indicating that there is no need. But beside him Ambassador De Puebla is delighted with the proposal and presses his fingers on my father's sleeve, and I see my father give in with good grace. *Of course. Of course you must see my beloved younger son too. What a marvelous idea.*

A herald approaches and bends to me gracefully. "At the request of our honored guests, His Grace the King invites you to fight a bout, my lord. Is there harness for you?"

"Compton will find it." I'm on my feet so fast I've almost collided with the herald, and now I set off, picking my way through the crowd, brushing past velvet skirts and slashed sleeves, trying not to tread on silk slippers or furred hems or trip over exquisitely expensive scabbards. I can feel my cheeks burning—I'm eager, excited, terrified.

And I'm thinking: *This is my chance. Father is a soldier; if I can impress him with my fighting, he will notice me. Really notice me. I will count for something.*

I climb down the steps of the spectators' stand. My stomach is tight, and my heart seems to be beating twice as hard as usual. There's a pavilion at one end of the hall for arming and disarming, and I make my way toward it, keeping close to the wall, feeling sure everyone must be staring. Inside the pavilion it's dark, lit by candles. Shadows stretch and loom over the fantastic creatures of the cloth wall, which ripples softly when someone walks by.

Soon Compton arrives with my armor. My breastplate glows green and gold in the flame-light. He helps me into it and tugs tight the soft leather straps. "You're shaking."

I snort. "Cold. There's a draft, can't you feel it?"

He hands me my helmet and gloves, and I bat aside the cloth to get back out into the hall.

11

It has to be a joke. I'm standing in front of the viewing gallery, having just been helped into my helmet, and when I push the visor up, I see Brandon walking toward me, for all the world as if it's him I'm supposed to fight.

I'm tall for my age and broad framed, but still—surely this is ridiculous? I glance up to the canopied platform. My mother is looking anxious. My father is looking away.

"Can this be right?" I ask the herald who's to act as referee. "Are you certain it isn't supposed to be someone else?" I turn my head, scanning the hall. There are several smaller boys fighting nearby. I catch sight of Arthur, taking off his helmet. He looks amused.

"His Grace the King's orders, sir," murmurs the herald, dipping his head.

I swallow. Brandon's even bigger than I thought, now I'm close up to him.

Compton's team of page boys has been efficient in fetching my equipment; he hands me my broadsword, and I weigh it carefully, feeling for the right grip. Its point and edge are blunted, but still it's a serious weapon—long, tapered, and beautifully balanced. The air whistles and sings if you slice it fast.

Down the center of the hall runs a wooden barrier, like a fence, which prevents collisions in a joust. The herald positions Brandon and me on the near side of it, closest to the viewing platform.

Brandon's visor is raised—I can see a section of face. It grins. "Be gentle with me, sir," he says.

"Not a chance." I slap my visor down.

Then the herald lifts his baton and says loudly, "On guard, gentlemen! Seven strokes each, by order of His Grace the King."

And so we start. We skirt around each other, keeping a good distance.

It's all about who moves first. In attacking you seize the initiative but leave yourself vulnerable. If you wait for your opponent to move, you need lightning-quick reactions to avoid or block the blow *and* counterattack, preferably all in the same movement.

Brandon has adopted the inside guard stance now, his sword-arm held across his body, the blade pointing upward at an angle. I mirror him. We're both shifting, one foot in front, one behind, knees softly bent, as light on our feet as we can be in our half-armor, ready to move, fast and hard.

He attacks first. The blow swings in toward my head; I move my sword to block it, and the blades clank together. I don't feel much force in Brandon's arm, and he makes no attempt to slip my block and land another blow; instead he disengages and moves back, on guard again.

And I realize: He's going gently with me—just playing at it, putting a little boy through his paces. The thought makes me feel sick.

I go for him now, and yell as I do it, loud enough to

be heard up on the platform. Everyone laughs when I miss. Brandon's reach is longer than mine; he only has to lift his sword-arm, and my strike, making contact with nothing but air, swings me off-balance and sends me stumbling side-first against the barrier.

But I'm angry. Back on guard for an instant only, I attack again, aiming high—at Brandon's neck. As he wards off the blow, I slip my blade down to cut his thigh, but he blocks me again, and in the same move lands a thrust to my body, jabbing hard against my breastplate.

Before the herald's even declared the hit, we've sprung apart again. I'm breathing hard.

Damn. A point lost. But at least the laughter's died. And I see Brandon shake himself and take up his stance again with purpose, as if he's suddenly taking this seriously.

Fighting bareheaded, your opponent's eyes are what you watch, not his hands or his blade. You get an instinct for the moment of decision; you sense the move a split second before it starts. I love it—that feeling of being locked in together . . . daring each other . . . and then exploding into action. You don't feel the bruises until later.

But with helmets, and no view of your opponent's face, it's much harder. Occasionally I glimpse dark eyes glistening behind the grille of Brandon's visor, but I can't read them at all.

And now he's coming at me in earnest, aiming for my head; there's a clash of metal as I block and shift to the side. We disengage and then I'm in again, my arm across my face, sword high, as if I'll strike his right ear. But it's a trick: As

Brandon blocks, I turn my wrist, swinging the blade back over my head, and land a blow to the other side of his helmet.

He staggers; the spectators cheer and clap. But by the time the herald has declared the point, Brandon's recovered and we're grappling again. After two bungled engagements he grabs the wrist of my sword-arm and yanks it back, twisting outward, off-balancing me. The next instant his blade comes down heavily from above.

My head feels like it's ringing inside my helmet like the clapper in a bell. I'm dizzy; against the blackness of my visor, thin strips of the scene before me fuzz and swoop sickeningly. I stagger back so far I could be accused of running away.

Bang. I collide with something behind me: It's the contraption they use for jousting practice—a wooden horse mounted on a wheeled trolley, which has been parked at one end of the barriers. Playing for time, I hitch myself up to sit on it, sending it trundling a short way backward under the impetus of my landing. The crowd laughs.

My view of the hall stops swooping, but I'm enjoying the moment, so I don't get down. I jump my feet under me, stand up on the horse's back, and leap from there onto the barrier. Sticking my arms out like a tightrope walker, I run along it until I'm past Brandon, then wobble and drop down some way behind him. I find myself not far from Arthur, who is leaning against the barrier farther along, helmet under his arm, blotting his face with a gold-fringed cloth.

In an instant I've snagged the cloth with the tip of my sword and whisked it from his fingers. With a sharp flick, I send it flying through the air. It seems to hang suspended for a moment like an airborne pancake, and then lands—more by luck than judgment—on Brandon's helmet, covering his visor.

The crowd whoops and cheers. Brandon, for whom the world has suddenly gone surprisingly dark, turns about in confusion. Meanwhile I bound over and thwack the hardest blow I can to his shoulder-guard, bursting one of its buckles and causing its owner to kneel heavily in the sand.

I can hear muffled swearing from inside Brandon's helmet. The noise from the platform is marvelous. I glance up, looking for my father, but before I can spot him the herald distracts me: Maintaining a professionally straight face, he signals that the fight is over.

Brandon is now sitting in the sand with his legs out in front of him. He wrenches off his helmet; his brown hair is flattened and sweaty. He casts a squinting glance up at me and grins. "My God, you're good, sir," he says, rubbing his hair. "Remind me not to fight you when you're older, won't you?"

By the time I've disarmed and emerged from the pavilion again, I'm starting to feel my bruises. I find the hall's been cleared of the foot-combat boys, and an archery target's been moved into place at one end of the barriers, ready for the next display. Servants are laying out bows and arrows on a long table covered with a cloth, embroidered with my father's crest in gold and red and blue.

Arthur is selecting his bow—drawing one, putting it down, trying another. He's changed his armor for an outfit of expensive black velvet; above it his face looks pale. Brandon's hovering near him, clearly expecting to shoot too, but as I make my way toward the viewing platform a herald waylays me to say that the Spanish would like Arthur to compete against me.

I nod my agreement, my face calm, hiding my excitement. As I change direction, walking with Compton toward the table, I hiss, "I'm impressing the Spanish! I'm actually *helping*. Is he looking? Is Father looking at me? Is he smiling?"

"I can't see, sir," says Compton. "Shall I send for one of your own bows?"

"No, I'll be fine."

Right now I feel I could draw any of those bows lying on the table, even the heaviest.

The mark to shoot from is placed on the hall floor directly in front of my father's position on the platform. Arthur takes up his stance first, nocks his arrow, draws, holds, then shoots. The arrow flies smoothly and embeds itself at the edge of the bull's-eye.

I'm fizzing with energy as I walk up to the mark. The bow I've selected seems to have almost exactly the same drawing weight as my own, but I'm beginning to wonder whether I'll be able to relax enough to shoot fair.

As I take up my stance, I try to breathe deeply. I try to forget where I am, block out the hall, the distractions around me, the colors, the faces, the shuffles and coughs and muted conversations.

I uncurl my fingers. My arrow, straight and deadly, thuds into the bull's-eye, just off center.

We each shoot twice more, Arthur and I. Then, out of

the corner of my eye, I see someone approaching. It's a herald, the man who refereed my bout with Brandon. "Would
you like to try to hit this, my lord?" he says to me. He is
holding out a glove—a leather gauntlet, its cuff embroidered with gold. "It is a challenge, if you will accept it, from
Ambassador De Puebla."

My eyes flick to the viewing platform. I see the ambassador, his neatly trimmed black beard turned toward my
father as he speaks. My father's head is inclined a little, his
gaze dropped—listening, concentrating. Neither of them is
watching me. But talking about me? Perhaps.

I look at the glove, still offered on the herald's palm. An
expensive item. Does the Spanish ambassador really want it
ruined—or does he think I don't stand a chance of hitting it?
I've played this game many times with Compton—usually with
an old cap or two, out in the woods by Eltham. It's easier than
shooting birds—but then I can do that, too.

I say, "I accept."

The herald pads away in his soft-soled shoes, carrying
the glove carefully, as if it's a basin of water that might spill.
I step up to the mark, nock an arrow, and, as the herald stops
and turns, I half draw it in readiness.

Up on the platform, conversations pause—heads turn.
The herald shows me the glove, then throws it high into
the air.

A glove flies differently from a cap, of course. The
weight's distributed differently—the heavy cuff with its trimming makes it spin differently in the air.

It's the work of a moment—a half moment. The full draw, the movement of the bow as you train it on the object's line of flight, the release.

Yet in that half moment, my concentration falters. My eyes slip from the spinning glove to a face beyond it—a face I have the weird feeling of recognizing. The hair is straw colored and the eyes so deep set as to be in shadow. Behind the face, wings are spread wide.

It's a carved angel, gazing down at me from one of the hammer beams of the roof. It holds a shield: the fleurs-de-lis of France quartered with the lions of England. I see it all in an instant—the hair, the wings, the shield—but even as the arrow is loosed I know that that instant was crucial; I can't have shot true.

The glove lands in the sand, but I've already turned away. It occurs to me, as I go back to my place at the side of the shooting area, cursing myself silently, that the applause is particularly generous considering I've missed. Compton grins at me when I reach him, so broadly that it gives me a flicker of uncertainty; I look back. The herald has retrieved the glove and is holding it up high, turning round so that all can see. My arrow has pierced the leather through the palm. I stare at it in disbelief.

Then I glance again at the roof, looking for the face. It has no golden hair, no color at all—it's just plain carved wood. I don't recognize it now. Who did I think it was before? I don't remember. I shake my head, as if I've come in from a rain shower, just as Arthur starts forward and signals that he would like to try this game too. A glove is hurriedly found for him, donated by another Spaniard; the herald throws for a second time.

On the viewing platform, a hundred faces tip upward as Arthur's arrow flies toward the mighty oak ribs of the roof. Arrow and glove pass elegantly, like the jets of a fountain. They land in the dust, ten feet apart.

There is a short silence.

Then the spectators break into applause. I see that Ambassador De Puebla has risen to his feet as he claps—the rest of his party is following suit. After a moment they turn and begin to move away from their seats—they're coming down.

As they approach across the sandy floor, Arthur's suddenly at my side. He hooks an arm round my neck and ruffles my hair. As if he's fond of me.

My father leads the party, limping slightly as always. He has a permanent stiffness in his left leg—scar tissue from an old wound: His battlefield credentials are on display at every step. As they reach us, De Puebla is saying, "... but remarkably skillful for his age. He is a talented child. Congratulations, Your Grace."

My father smiles. "You are generous in your praise, Ambassador. I am proud of the boy. He has a fine spirit. He works hard." A bony hand reaches out and grips my shoulder.

"Added to which," De Puebla turns to me, "you have all the natural talents God could bestow, my lord prince. You are built like a warrior already. Nearly as tall as your brother when there are, what, five years between you? Impressive. Very impressive." He bows to Arthur. "And, my lord, a most excellent display of your skills too. We will be happy to make a report back to the king and queen of Spain, full of the highest possible praise."

Arthur and I bow, and express our humble thanks.

My father turns to his guests, opening his arms to herd them away. "Come, gentlemen, it is time to take some refreshments in more comfortable surroundings."

I watch them go.

I am proud of the boy.

I look around me, blinking. I glance up to the angel on the roof again—but there are rows of them, one on each hammer beam, and I can't remember which one it was I thought I recognized. The viewing platform is emptying. Arthur has melted away. A hand gently takes my elbow. It's Compton. He guides me out of the hall and into the warren of passageways leading to the royal apartments. I can't stop talking.

"Did my father see the strike before the last—with Brandon? Not the last one—I had open season on that, it doesn't count—but the one before. I truly found a gap, such a small one; I was *so* fast!" I stop walking abruptly and slap my gloves against Compton's chest. "Tell me he saw that one."

"He saw it."

"Really?"

Compton shrugs. "I don't know. I expect so, sir. I was watching you, not the king."

We walk again. "Brandon's good. He landed some amazing blows. I really should've seen that one at the side coming. And the way he twisted my arm, Christ—I want to practice that. I'll get him to show me sometime. Do you think he'd practice with me if I asked? Regularly, I mean? I suppose he'd have to come down to Eltham, and maybe that'd be a problem."

We've reached my bedchamber now. Entering, I sling my gloves on a table and see that I have a visitor. "Oh." I stop, staring at him. "Hello."

It's Arthur: I don't remember that he has ever voluntarily sought my company before.

He is standing, accompanied by several of his gentlemen-servants, beside the window. He says slowly, "I wanted to congratulate you on your excellent performance back there." He pauses, looks at my servants. "Compton. Boys. You may leave us."

The pages who have entered the room behind me bow and scamper away. Compton hesitates, looks at me. I nod to him to go.

Then I give a shrug and bend down to scratch my calf. "I just practice a lot. You can't be best at everything. Don't let it get to you."

As I straighten, I see Arthur signal to his men. Two of them move to stand on either side of me; they take my arms.

"What's this?"

He doesn't answer me. Struggling, I quickly discover, only makes the men tighten their grip. Arthur says, "No, no. This isn't the time for showing off."

He's pulling at the fingers of his gloves, one by one, unhurried. He slips the gloves off, places them one on top of the other and hands them to a servant. Then he curls the long white fingers of his right hand into a fist. And punches me hard in the stomach.

It knocks the wind out of me and leaves me gasping, stooped forward as far as the strong hands on my arms allow. I cough and can't do anything about a drip of saliva that stretches down to the floor.

"What was that for?" I croak. "What've I done?"

No answer—just another blow. This time the knuckles make contact with my left ear and temple. There's a ringing in my head.

Arthur says, "It's not about fighting skills, you see. It's about power. And power is, among other things, having someone to hold you still while I hit you."

By the time I can look up, Arthur has taken possession of his gloves again and is examining them, removing minuscule traces of fluff, dust, dirt. "Or having someone to hit you for me." He nods to someone unseen to my right, who slams a knee, hard as a cudgel, into my kidneys.

Nothing on my face, of course. Nothing where a bruise might be visible.

Hanging limply, wondering if I'm about to vomit, I'm aware of a small pleasure: He is five years older than me, and he daren't take me on alone.

I manage to say, "You'll pay for this. I'll tell Father."

"Oh, Father already knows." The voice has come from behind me, from the doorway.

I can't turn, but I don't need to. Automatically I start trembling, like my dog Angwen when she's wet. Arthur's eyes glitter, triumphant.

I hear uneven footsteps approaching, and then my father swings into view, leaning on the slender stick he sometimes uses in private. He's agile with the extra limb, like a spider.

He says to me, "Your brother thought you needed to be taught a lesson—and I agreed with him."

I grit my teeth, fighting the shakes, and glare at Arthur. "What lesson?"

My father's stick whips up under my chin, lifting it uncomfortably high. "You have no control. No discipline. You have been *indulged* for too long."

He points the stick at Arthur. "You may go."

The stick swoops back to jab me in the chest. "Not you."

12

Arthur's men release me and follow their master out, shutting the door behind them. My father and I are alone. Despite my best efforts, I am still trembling. I feel sick at the thought of more blows.

He begins a little tour of the room, poking with his stick at the bed-hangings, a footstool, twitching aside the curtain covering a mirror. I flinch every time he swipes the stick through the air. He catches me cringing, and I can see his disgust. I could so easily cry; my throat is tight, my eyes prickling. I mustn't. It will only make him worse. More angry, more disgusted—he will beat me across the room and back. It's happened before. And I know that a beating hurts ten times more than sword practice with the strongest opponent—though it's a mystery to me why.

My father stops, facing me again, both hands on his stick. His hair is graying, and he's thin under his plush velvet gown. If someone saw him on the battlefield, they might think they could take him out, no problem: That little collection of twigs? I'll snap him over my knee. They wouldn't realize each twig is as strong as steel.

He smiles now, but not pleasantly. "That was some display," he says, jerking his head. "Out there."

"Tha—" I squeak. I clear my throat. I mustn't sound like a mouse. "Thank you, sir."

"Quite a swordsman already, aren't you? A crack shot, too. Better than Arthur, would you say?"

I hesitate—decide. "Yes, sir."

"And so charming. The Spaniards warmed to you, didn't they?" He nods. "Yes. But you know that. You know what you are about."

"I am honored to have merited their approval," I say.

My father's eyes widen in extravagant surprise. "Did you think they *admired* you? They were laughing! Not *with* you—*at* you. Your childish swagger! It *was* quite funny, even I had to admit that. They said to me: Contain that one. We can see he's a problem already."

Perhaps I'm shaking my head, though I'm barely aware of it, because he goes on, "Oh yes, I'm afraid it's true. You *are*, you see. A problem already. Don't blubber. A boy crying is a sight that makes me gag."

But I can't stop. My father moves quickly, and the stick lands with a thwack across my bottom. I hit the floor, on hands and knees.

"You pathetic little insect. Get up! *Get up!*"

As I scramble to my feet, my father is slipping off his long gown, keeping hold of his stick. He barks, "Take off that doublet. Take it off! I won't have expensive cloth ruined."

I undo the laces with quivering fingers. I'm still crying. My father grabs the garment from me and slings it onto a chair.

"It is all a great game to you, isn't it?" he shouts, hitting me across the back.

"No, sir!"

His arm whips round my neck, doubling me over, my head gripped against the side of his body, my back and bottom and legs in front of him. "Remember this!" he roars, hitting me rhythmically now. "It is the way to learn! It is how I was taught and I have *never* . . . for*got*ten . . ."

"Stop! For the love of God!" someone shouts.

My father suddenly lets go of me; I collapse onto the floor, unable to break my fall. From under my arm—lifted in front of my face in case of more blows—I see my mother fly into the room and my father catch her by the wrist as she heads toward me. She swings round to face him, her skirts swirling.

"No, don't go to him!" my father growls, breathing heavily from his exertions. "This is *your* doing, Elizabeth! The boy has been spoiled. He needs to learn his place."

"Not like this!"

"If he learns now it may save his life."

"But he doesn't understand!"

"Doesn't he?" My father releases her, grabs a wooden stool from near the wall and bangs it down in the center of the room. "Then let me explain. In simpleton's terms." He sits, and points at the floor in front of him. "Stand here, boy. Stop crying unless you want another beating."

I get up, painfully, and stand where he indicates. Behind him my mother's face looks wild with agitation and concern, but she holds herself very still, her hands clasped in front of her, the knuckles white.

My father stares at me, his small black eyes gleaming. He

says, "You are my second son. What's a king's second son for?"

"I don't know, sir," I say, thoroughly miserable.

He hits me, open handed, across the face. "What's a second son for?" he repeats.

I swallow, blinking hard. I say, "So that if the first son dies there will still be an heir, sir."

"That's right. You are a spare. A backup. In case our beloved firstborn son dies. From which calamity God in his infinite wisdom has been merciful enough to spare us." Both my parents cross themselves. My father goes on, "And when the firstborn son marries and has sons of his own to continue his line—guess what? That second son is not needed anymore."

He leans forward, gripping his knees. "Now. The Spanish envoys are here because Arthur is about to . . . ?"

"Get married, sir."

"Very good. And, God willing, the birth of Arthur's sons will follow soon after. So. What does this mean for you, I wonder? The backup, who is not needed anymore? Hm?"

"I don't know," I whisper, afraid of being hit again.

My father leans in and whispers back, as if confiding a secret: "It means you must be very, very careful."

He straightens, spreading his hands. "So. You have a choice. First option: generally make a loud noise, draw attention to yourself. Like you did in the hall just now. Prove yourself a man—eh? Eh? You want approval! You want to be noticed! You want to be *loved*." The way he says it, it sounds like the word means something shameful.

"Well, what do you think that leads to?" Springing up, my father stumps to a table under the window where my chess set is laid out. He takes a knight—a St. George on horseback—and slaps it down in the middle of the board. "Here you are: the Duke of York. Powerful landowner, brilliant military commander, charming, popular—with a large following of loyal retainers. Sounds good?"

He's staring at me beadily. I have to respond. I nod, feeling sick.

"Oh dear, oh *dear*. Not good at all. What if some half-wits get it into their heads that you might make a better king than Arthur, hm? It sounds to me like *civil war*."

"I am loyal to Arthur, sir."

My father pretends to consider. He says, "Does he really believe that? I think he might have you killed, just to be on the safe side." With a flick of his finger he knocks over the knight. It rolls in a semicircle and lies still.

"But, how astonished you look! 'He wouldn't kill me, I'm his little brother!'" my father sing-songs in a baby voice. Then he starts toward me again across the room. "Don't believe that *sentiment* will save you, boy. Sentimentality is the ruin of a king. I have stripped myself of feeling; I have flayed it like a skin from my back. And I am teaching Arthur to do the same."

A pause. I suppose he is standing looking at me, though I don't know, since I'm staring at the floor now. "Option two, then," he says in a lighter tone. "You can fade quietly away. Join the Church. Why not go to Rome, throw some money around, try to get made a cardinal? That might even *help* Arthur."

My father comes forward and bends, twisting his neck to look up into my face. "What? What?" he taunts. "Are you thinking you have no wish to be a priest?"

"No, sir."

"Yes-sir-no-sir. Understand this: I am not interested in your preferences."

He moves away. I hear a rustle of skirts as my mother moves too. She is helping him on with his gown. "God has ordained a destiny for each of us," he says. "My destiny has been to bring stability to this blood-soaked, war-ravaged land. Arthur's destiny is to be the first great king of the golden age of peace. And your destiny"—the tip of his stick suddenly prods my chin up again so that I meet his gaze—"is to keep out of his way."

13

"Don't harden your heart against your father."

"He hates me."

"No," says my mother. Several hours have passed since my father's visit. I am lying facedown on my bed, and my mother is sitting beside me, skillfully applying a poultice of comfrey leaves and crushed parsley to my bruises and weals. "You just frightened him today, that's all."

"*Frightened* him?" I turn my head to squint at her. Gently, she presses my shoulders flat again. I stare out sideways across the bedcovers at the tapestry on the wall, where a blindfolded Lady Fortune rides through the sky, scattering roses to her left and stones to her right.

My mother says, "You win hearts, sweetheart. You are so gifted. . . ."

"They laughed at me."

She murmurs, "It wasn't like that." Then she says, "Do you know, in all the years I've been married to your father there isn't a night he's spent with me when he hasn't been plagued by bad dreams? He dreams of battles. He has seen things, Hal—horrors—that will haunt him all his life."

She has finished with the poultice; carefully she tugs my shirt down over my back and begins to collect up her bowls and stray stalks and leaves. "He is trying to look after you, in his way—to keep you safe. He doesn't want you to see what he has seen. And he finds it hard to trust . . . anyone. He spent so many years on the run, you know, before he became king. Afraid of spies. Afraid of men sent to befriend him and betray him. Even as king there's hardly been a year of his reign when he hasn't had to combat uprisings in the shires, and plots against his life here at court. Sometimes I think he doesn't even trust me. Not really. Not in his secret heart."

I raise myself gingerly on one elbow and watch my mother as she crosses to the table. A large basin of water has been put there; she rinses her hands. "He's terrified that after he's gone, his achievements will be torn to shreds," she goes on. "Above all he wants security for the succession. For Arthur and Arthur's sons."

"But how can he be afraid when he's so brave?"

My mother smiles. "A brave man still feels fear, my love," she says. "Everyone does. Unless they are stupid—or lying to themselves." She picks up a linen towel to dry her hands. "It's just that a brave man knows how to turn his fear into energy—for battle. And that's a skill worth learning, don't you think?"

Later, when she is long gone, and the view from my window is turning blue and gray in the twilight, I slip out. Compton and my other attendants are busy preparing for my supper and the night ahead. Only a page boy sees me go; I pass a coin to him—a penny for his silence.

My rooms are on the side of the palace farthest from the river—the side that looks out, instead, onto Westminster

Abbey and its precincts. Prickly with pinnacles, the impressive bulk of the abbey is a dark shape now, with just a flicker of color, here and there, where candlelight illuminates stained glass.

Standing in its shadow, inside the palace wall, is an orchard, where the grass is left to grow long. I walk there now, getting wet, turning my face to the darkening sky and feeling the rain on my skin and my open eyes, stinging like pinpricks.

I will have to go back soon—they'll be looking for me. Compton will be agitated, afraid for my safety and his own position.

But it is a luxury to have no one here to see me cry. My back is stiff and aching—hurting more now than it did straight after the beating. I stretch out on my front in the sodden grass.

I think: *It is a lie that I am unimportant. I feel it in my gut. I feel it in the ground and the sky and the rain. A long time ago I heard a prophecy—and I have not forgotten it.*

My hands close into fists and I cling to the grass angrily, as if the ground would like to throw me off.

14

"Three shillings says she has a wart."

"Where?" says Compton. Behind me Charles Brandon laughs.

My horse is jittery. I let it walk forward a little way, and then I turn it again, saying, "I thought we were sticking to facial disfigurements."

Beneath the leaden skies of a November morning we are waiting on horseback in St. George's Fields, an open space on the south bank of the Thames, not far from London Bridge. We're preparing—along with numerous bishops, an archbishop, and a crowd of earls and lords—to line up as a welcoming party for Princess Catherine of Aragon, Arthur's Spanish bride.

It's been drizzling for the last ten minutes. The surface of my cloak is covered with a fine mist of droplets, my legs are beginning to feel distinctly damp, and my nose is so cold I've lost all sense of whether it's still there or not. The only thing cheering me is the possibility that Princess Catherine will be ugly.

"How about smallpox scars?" suggests Francis Bryan, beside me. Bryan is one of the well-born boys I spend my lessons and my leisure time with—his father is a trusted servant of the king.

"Harry Guildford's put money on that already," says Compton.

"All right, a moustache. Two shillings. And no quibbling, Compton: Any dark hair visible on the upper lip and you pay out."

"I thought she was fair-haired," says Thomas Boleyn.

Of the friends and attendants who serve me, some are boys like me, and others are older: grown-up young men who advance their careers by working in my service. Boleyn, an ambitious knight's son, aged twenty-four, is in this last group. Francis Bryan is my own age. Harry Guildford, whose father is a royal councillor, is a couple of years older. Compton, who is nineteen, and Brandon, seventeen, are somewhere in between. But age does not decide seniority: I am the master here, and I am ten.

"Fair-haired?" Bryan echoes Boleyn's words. "And Spanish? Is that possible?"

"If she's really awful," cuts in Brandon, "is Arthur allowed to refuse to marry her?"

"No," I say, grinning. And that's why, of course, my hopes are running so high. Since this marriage, as my father's explained so clearly to me, turns me into a nobody—the backup son who's not needed anymore—I want it to make Arthur suffer too. As much as possible. And I think a hideous bride would be an excellent start.

Now a scout brings news that the Spanish party is close by, approaching over the open land that lies between here and Lambeth. We form an order. Being, of course, the senior duke present, I position myself at the front.

Coming into view, a strange sight: a collection of oddly dressed figures, making toward us not on horses, but on mules. In the center there's a girl, her face hidden by the broad brim of her hat. She's sitting very upright on a saddle no less foreign looking than the rest of her outfit: It has a cross brace that lies like a stepladder on the mule's back. She is perched on top, swaying as the beast walks.

The Spanish party halts, leaving a stretch of damp, marshy grass standing empty between us. It's my job to make the first communication.

I walk my horse forward, somewhat squelchily.

Dear God, please let her be ugly. . . .

The girl—Princess Catherine—looks up. Beneath the hat her face is softly rounded, with a pink and white complexion and a pretty dimpled chin. Her long auburn hair is loose, and blowing sideways in the wind.

Damn.

I have prepared a greeting in Spanish—I've learned it by rote. I declaim it, thinking, *All right, then, pretty but ill natured . . .*

Hearing the Spanish, Catherine breaks into a delighted, grateful smile. She nods encouragingly when I stumble over the unfamiliar pronunciation.

All right—pretty, sweet tempered, but slow witted . . . please, slow witted—

And when I have finished, she replies, thanking me elegantly, in fluent French.

Smelly?

It's my last hope.

An unlikely one, though, going by the clean, shining hair and the beautifully kept clothes, with ruffles of spotless white linen just visible at her neck and wrists.

I give in. I'm disappointed. Even so, I can't stop watching her, as my father's heralds organize us, dovetailing the two companies—Spanish and English—into a single long procession. It's as if I think she's a mirage, and any moment now she's going to transform into something else—or disappear altogether.

Catherine and I head the procession, riding together. The drizzle, thankfully, has stopped. Our task now is to make a formal entry into the City of London, so that Catherine can receive its welcome. First we have to cross the river.

We approach London Bridge, where the rotting heads of executed criminals are splayed at crazy angles on pikes above the entrance gate.

Catherine's hat must be shielding her from the view; she says, "How beautiful your country is! I am so happy to be in England."

"Thank you, ma'am," I say, "and England is overjoyed to welcome you."

The bridge crouches across the river on twenty stone piers, a crush of fine houses and shops on its back. When we're halfway over, we stop to see a pageant, which is to say a little show—part of the City's welcome. The stage is a specially built wooden tower, where City ladies dressed as St. Catherine and St. Ursula stand, attended by heavenly maidens, who all seem a bit shivery. The saints make speeches—long ones—in verse, and entirely in English.

Glancing to my left, I see Catherine's delicate brows drawn together.

I say in French, "Can you follow the sense of it?"

Nodding and smiling for the benefit of the performers, Catherine replies in a low voice, "Nothing after the 'welcoming, aiding, and assisting' bit. I'm afraid my English isn't good enough."

"Saint Catherine's saying that Christ is your first husband, and Arthur your second. You need to love them both, but in that order."

Catherine whispers her thanks to me, then calls out a loud "Amen!" and smiles and thanks the performers, raising her hand to acknowledge cheers from the crowds lining the street on both sides.

They're cheering me, too, chanting my name: the common people, packed body to body behind the line of guards on each side. The smell of them, even in the cold November air, is like animals being herded to market.

We press on, over the bridge. In front of us, the City sprawls: a mass of roofs and smoking chimney stacks, bustling shopping streets, grand houses with their gardens stretching down to the river, landing stages, busy wharves, and a forest of church spires pointing to the sky. I think, with a sudden surge of pride, that no city in Spain could possibly be so glorious.

In Gracechurch Street we stop again, the procession

bunched up behind us—the horses stamping and farting. This street is packed even more tightly with people than the bridge. Faces, faces, everywhere you turn—squeezing out of overhanging upper-floor windows, gazing down from rooftops, eyes wide at the sight of costly fabrics, gleaming jewels, and royalty in the flesh.

Here, another pageant. This one's mounted on a mock castle, complete with turrets and covered in my father's emblems: golden crowns and portcullises, dragons, greyhounds, and red and white roses. Two knights marked POLICY and NOBILITY look out from upper doorways. Beside them there's a bishop labeled VIRTUE, at whom someone in the crowd seems to be aiming small missiles that look like bits of bread.

As the speeches begin, there's a loud crack to our right, and a piece of guttering gives way under a man's weight. For one delicious moment he's dangling in midair, apparently in danger of peeling the entire length of pipe from the wall—but then, after a struggle, his friends bundle him in through a window, to a loud cheer from the crowd.

Catherine and I applaud—and are cheered for that, too. This is marvelous enough; what then must it feel like, I wonder, to be cheered by the people as their *king*?

And then we're off again, the procession jingling, winking in the watery sun, as it snakes slowly along the packed streets.

In Cheapside—an impressive street of goldsmiths' shops—we're faced with God the Father, plus warbling angels and a variety of wise men and prophets.

"You need to understand," I say, "they've dressed up the person playing God to look like my father."

"It's a fair likeness," says Catherine. "Why so many more guards here?"

I look about. Yeomen of the Guard, plus huge numbers of liveried servants, are ranged in every window, on every rooftop, and are standing several deep in the street around us. This amount of security can only mean one thing.

"Ah," I say. "I think God himself is watching."

Catherine follows my gaze. There's a merchant's house to our right; behind one of its diamond-paned windows I think I've glimpsed a face. My father no doubt planned this as a secret visit, but Catherine bows her head in that direction anyway. I do the same.

She looks back to the pageant. Another man dressed as a bishop is already several verses into his speech. "Any help you can give me with this one?"

I listen. "Um . . . To save us all from our sins, God made a marriage between the divine and the human by sending Christ to live among us . . . He's saying the king of heaven is like an earthly king who prepares a wedding for his son. No prizes for guessing *which* earthly king."

"So—your father is God and your brother is Christ. Who, then, are you?" She looks at me, eyes twinkling. "The Holy Ghost?"

I smile, though not especially happily. "I am no one in particular."

"Oh, I can't believe that," says Catherine. "And the people clearly don't think so. Listen to them."

The chanting has begun again. Some people are calling my name, some hers, some shouting out "God save the king!" and flinging their caps into the air, causing occasional struggles in the crush when the wrong people catch them.

As we move on, I say, "No, it's true. I'm just a fill-in, for when my brother isn't here. You'll meet him in a minute—when we get to Saint Paul's."

"What's he like?"

"Oh . . ." I'm suddenly at a loss. "Very accomplished. You'll find he's, um, taller—well, not taller than me, actually. Older, though—yes. And more, er . . ."

Catherine smiles. "I'm teasing you. We've met already. He and your father came and inspected me on my way up from Plymouth."

"Ah, I see." To check for warts, I want to say. But don't.

We ride into St. Paul's churchyard. The bells are ringing, and the booming sound echoes across the open space of the yard, rebounding off the buildings. Near the west front of the cathedral is the Bishop's Palace, and before that a crowd of courtiers stands waiting. Catherine leans toward me to speak—it's hard to hear anything over the bells. "The king wanted to reassure himself that I wasn't ugly, I think."

"Yes," I say automatically. "I mean, *no*."

She laughs. "In my country, you know, a bride never shows herself to the groom or his family before the wedding day. But your father insisted. He said he would storm into my bedchamber if necessary."

"Honestly?"

As the procession halts, she smiles, biting her lip, and nods. "He suspected, I'm sure, that I had something to hide."

Wooden blocks of steps are brought so that we can dismount. I'm first to the ground. Catherine takes my outstretched hand as she steps down from her mule.

"*He* might have been suspicious," I say, "but *I* was hopeful. That you would be ugly."

Her eyes widen. "I could take offense at that! Why did you think so? Because all Spaniards *must* be ugly? I've been told the English think badly of foreigners."

I escort her toward the palace. Walking side by side, I realize how small she is; she's six years older than me, but still we're eye to eye. I say, "No. It's just that it would give me some small happiness if my elder brother didn't have *all* the best things. There, now you know how ungenerous I am."

Catherine laughs again. "I'll be glad to have you as my brother when I'm married! I had sisters at home—and I used to have a brother too. We always talked to one another—*really* talked—and laughed and joked and argued. You're the first English person I've had a proper conversation with. Everyone else has been really polite, but so . . . formal. Some people in Spain say the English are cold, and I was starting to believe it."

We're almost at the entrance to the Bishop's Palace. The

courtiers stand aside as we approach—to reveal my brother, waiting for us in a blue silk doublet and a matching cloak, slung across one shoulder and fastened with a huge diamond.

"Most beloved Princess Catherine, you are heartily welcome," he says. He bows and offers her his hand, taking no notice of me whatsoever. About that, I couldn't care less. But I think: *There's cold for you, my lady, right there in the blue cloak.*

Two days later, in the ancient cathedral of St. Paul's, dressed in matching shimmering white satin, my brother and Princess Catherine of Aragon are married.

The celebrations last a week.

On the fourth day, after the dinner boards have been cleared away—along with creations the cooks have labored over for hours, only for them to be picked at, half eaten, and left—we head outside to the tiltyard.

I am dressed in cloth of gold, and feeling uncomfortable, as if my clothes don't fit—except they do; or as if I have an itch—except I don't. Not on the outside, anyway. Maybe in my head.

The tiltyard—a vast open arena outside Westminster Hall—is chilly and damp. I draw my outer gown tightly about me as I make my way, with the rest of the royal party, to the canopied grandstand. The remainder of the court and the City dignitaries sit in separate uncovered stands, while the lower orders are crammed behind barriers at the far end of the yard. Torches flare; it's only one o'clock, but it seems barely light.

I'm directed, with my friends, to the edge of the royal enclosure. It suits me fine. In the center, next to my parents, the bride and groom sit stiffly side by side, Arthur managing to look smug and awkward at the same time. He doesn't seem to be having much success in thinking of things to say to his wife.

Then trumpets sound, the great doors of Westminster Hall open, and out into the cold air trundles a mountain on wheels. It's pulled by a red dragon. On top of the mountain sits a (real) maiden with a (not-so-real) unicorn, lying with its head in her lap.

The mountain performs a tour of the arena, circling the wooden barrier that runs down the middle, to cheering that drowns out the efforts of the trumpeters. At last, it comes to a halt in front of our royal stand. Then a door in one craggy side opens, and out rides a knight on a black horse, his saddlecloth decorated with castle-shaped pieces of solid gold.

"How do they *do* that?" Beside me, Harry Guildford's eyes have narrowed as he stares at the pageant-car. "How do they make the mountain? How do they stop the horse from going crazy and trying to smash its way out? And what on earth's inside that dragon?"

"Count the legs," says Francis Bryan on my other side. "It's four men. And I bet there's swearing in there fit to shock a ferryman."

Never mind the dragon, my attention's on the knight, who is busy bowing to my father. It's the first tournament I've seen in ages, and I'm gawking at the armor—in this case a perfectly fitted suit that's gilded all over and topped with a plume of ostrich feathers sprouting from the helmet.

"What will Brandon's pageant-car look like?" I ask the

boys around me. Today Charles Brandon will ride in his first public tournament.

"Can't remember," says Bryan. "What's he being? A hermit in a hill? A pig in a poke?"

Compton leans toward me. "He's in a tent made to look like a chapel, sir, accompanied by a wise man and two lions."

And just as he says this, the chapel (on wheels) emerges into view through the doors of the hall. We cheer ourselves hoarse. Brandon—whom lots of the court ladies seem to find very charming, God alone knows why—emerges from the chapel with his helmet under his arm, grinning like a maniac. As he rides past the courtiers' stand, a lady's handkerchief is thrown and flutters down onto the sandy floor.

Brandon sends a page to collect it. When it's handed up to him in his saddle, he makes a great show of kissing it and then tucks it into the band of silk that decorates the top of his helmet. The crowd whoops and whistles.

More arrivals follow: a knight dressed as a Turk; another in a tent covered with roses; and an unidentified Spaniard, without coat of arms or emblems, whom the heralds haven't, it seems, been expecting. It must be a member of Catherine's escort party; out of deference to her the heralds accept him as a competitor, and he's paraded round the tiltyard like everyone else.

More trumpet blasts. More cheering. And then, at last, the jousting starts.

The knights are divided into two teams: the challengers and the defenders. Their task is to take turns to ride at one another, almost head-on, separated only by the wooden barrier. Each knight carries a long wooden spear—a lance—with which he aims to hit his opponent. One point is earned for a hit to the body, two points for a hit to the head, four points if your lance shatters when it strikes.

I've forgotten just how exciting jousting is. Two minutes in, and I'm on the edge of my seat. The riders thunder toward each other at breakneck speed. There can be no dodging, no failure of courage, though on any run if something goes wrong one of them might die.

And as I watch I'm thinking: *I could do this.* I want to be down in that yard right now. What must it be like? Like sword combat—only *more* terrifying, *more* thrilling? I try to imagine my opponent's lance speeding toward me, its metal tip aimed at my head; the sense of terror and excitement only just under control; the joyful sharp simplicity of the world when everything disappears except *this* and *now*.

On Brandon's first run his opponent—the anonymous Spaniard—thwacks his lance into Brandon's breastplate. The lance slides and shudders. Brandon is knocked backward half out of his saddle, and we all yell in alarm—but he clings on and manages to grab the reins again. And when he reaches the far end of the yard, he turns his horse straightaway, eager for the next run.

He sets off, his supporters starting a rising roll of cheers that crescendos until the moment of impact. This time the Spaniard aims high. The lance hits Brandon's helmet; his head jolts back sickeningly fast. The next moment he's falling, head over heels over the back of the horse, pulling and twisting the reins as he goes, and I'm on my feet, clutching Bryan in alarm. The horse rears then tumbles, its round belly rolling in the sand, hooves flailing. By sheer luck, Brandon has fallen free of his mount.

A team of grooms rushes forward to help both Brandon and the horse, while a couple of spectators vault the barriers and run to collect gold trinkets that have fallen off Brandon's tabard and the horse's trappers. The horse has been cut on the nose by its armor and is bleeding, but it scrambles up and is led away.

Miraculously, Brandon himself seems unhurt. He pulls off his helmet. He's flushed, his sweaty hair is sticking up at angles, and he looks delighted as a puppy, as if he's just had a gentle gallop round the park on a sunny afternoon. After bowing to my father, he takes the lady's handkerchief from his helmet with a flourish and mops his brow, to cheers from the crowd. It looks as if he would happily do it all again.

Meanwhile the anonymous Spaniard is parading his horse round the arena, to loud appreciation from the Spanish party and some of the more sporting Londoners. He holds his lance aloft in triumph. His helmet is still on, his face concealed.

As I sit down, I feel suddenly so jealous of them both—of Brandon and the Spaniard—that it is like a physical pain.

And then something begins to stir in the back of my mind. A thought—a memory from old storybooks I've read. An adored hero . . . a mysterious stranger . . . The tales of

King Arthur and his court are full of knights fighting anonymously, their identities hidden behind their visors.

An anonymous knight is a *nobody*, of sorts—a heroic nobody. And a nobody is what my father wants me to be.

As the next two competitors come forward, my eyes are on the tiltyard, but my mind is lost in a waking dream.

I see myself arriving at the court of a new King Arthur: my brother. Dressed in coal-black armor, without crest or emblems to identify me, I refuse to give my name or show my face. Instead I challenge the bravest knights of the court to a joust. They accept.

The tournament is long and arduous. Many lances are shattered, many riders unseated, but I triumph over all, my skill and courage amazing both king and court. The crowds shout for me, and King Arthur's queen—the lovely Catherine—bids me wear her glove on my helmet, as a mark of her favor.

When the tournament is over, the king begs me to stay for a banquet, where he promises I will be treated as his most honored guest. I thank him graciously but decline the offer, then turn my horse and ride away into the dusk. The whole court stands at the windows of the palace to watch me go, until I am lost in the shadows of—

"What about you, Hal?" says Bryan next to me.

"What?" I blink at him.

"Armor—I was talking about the armor. I said I'd have the blood-red—look, that suit there. Given the choice."

"I'd take the gold," says Guildford.

"Black," I say. "Definitely the black."

At the end of the tournament I go looking for Brandon. Compton directs me to a chamber near the Lesser Hall.

Walking in, I find it filled with several of the more junior jousters, some being dressed or washed, others sprawled out, resting, examining injuries, or flicking cloths at their page boys to get them to hurry with their tasks.

As awareness of my presence ripples through the room, there's a scramble to get up and bow. But I signal that it's Brandon I want to speak to—there's no need for everyone to stand to attention. He comes over, and I say, "Teach me to joust."

He grins. "You're rather young for it, Hal."

"Did I ask for your *opinion*?" I'm not the king's son for nothing: I know how to use a commanding tone.

A look of surprise flits across Brandon's face. The next moment he's a picture of perfect respect. "No, sir." He bows to me formally. "I'll do my best, sir."

Anonymous knight—winner of tournaments—mysterious warrior, face hidden behind my black visor. This way I can be the nobody my father wants *and* the hero of my dreams. For the next few months it's my secret plan for survival.

16

"Get him!"

The water arcs through the air and descends in a splatter, with glorious accuracy, on the head of Harry Guildford.

Francis Bryan plunges the nozzle of the bellows into the bucket again, pumping the handles furiously.

Guildford is sitting, blindfolded, on the wooden horse mounted on a wheeled trolley that we've been using for jousting training. Compton and Brandon, who have hold of the ropes attached to the front of the trolley, have been pulling him as fast as they can round the hall, while Bryan and I try to drench him with water missiles.

Bryan has taken the bellows from the fireplace. I am making do with cups and jugs from the kitchens.

Guildford's got a lance in his right hand with which he is trying to take his revenge—a huge great long thing, one of the training lances with replaceable end sections. It is—as I know from experience now—heavy, and hard to balance even when you can see what you're doing. Since he can't, the lance is making extravagantly wild sweeps and several times almost topples him off his mount all by itself.

Now Brandon, who's dropped his rope, empties a full bucket of water over Guildford's head from behind and dodges out of the way as Guildford sends the lance swooping about in reply. Guildford's gulping and roaring, purple in the face, with his wet shirt stuck to his back like a milk skin. The rest of us are shrieking with laughter.

The next moment Guildford thwacks Bryan an almighty blow on his bottom.

"He can see! He can see!" yells Bryan.

"WHAT IN GOD'S NAME IS GOING ON HERE?"

The voice is a roar. We stop and turn as one, all except Guildford, who—startled into a final loss of balance—slides sedately off the horse and lands in a heap on the floor.

The chamberlain of the household here at Eltham Palace, a white-haired man with a long furred gown and a fine sense of his own importance, is standing in the doorway at the far end of the hall, eyes wide and cheeks puffing as he surveys the room.

"Look at the floor! Mother of God, look at the *hangings!* What on earth has possessed you, gentlemen?"

We are wet, panting, hiccupping. I double up to get my breath back, my hands on my knees. Looking between my legs I can see Bryan, behind me, calculating the trajectory needed to aim the bellows at the chamberlain.

"Get up, boy!"

Brandon has seen fit to join Guildford on the floor; he is flat on his back, presenting the soles of his very wet shoes to the old man.

"Do I have to point out that you are not supposed to bring that wooden horse into the house?" says the chamberlain, his voice quieter now but quivering with rage. "In fact,

I would like to know whether Master Simpson has given you permission to use it at all. Well?"

Not as such, is the answer, though no one offers it.

The chamberlain flaps his arms. "Away with you—all of you! Go up to your chambers! Do not think you will get away with this! There will be consequences! And you are not exempt, my lord prince! Your father will hear about this!"

We file past the chamberlain, attempting to look contrite, as he calls household servants to fetch mops and cloths. As soon as we make it to the stairs, we're laughing again, running and jostling up the steps and scuffling along the passageway to my rooms.

Bryan stops off for his lute, Compton instructs a page boy to run and find dry shirts, and Brandon sends for jugs of ale, which he persuades his favorite serving girl to bring up the back stairs without alerting the chamberlain. Then we pile into my bedchamber.

Bryan sweeps aside a scatter of chessmen and lies full length on one of the window seats.

Brandon sits down on the other window seat, springs up, shoves aside a comb and a tennis racket, and sits down again. "Hal, does no one ever tidy up here? Your gentlemen are neglecting their duties."

"On account of how he keeps us jousting and fighting all day," says Guildford from inside his shirt, which a page is helping him to strip off.

It turns into a pleasant enough evening. Bryan, from his horizontal position, sings us a song with lute accompaniment.

I discuss armor with the newly shirted Guildford, whose father and older brother are in charge of the Royal Armory. I fancy designing my own jousting armor, but I can't see my father agreeing to pay for it. Brandon and Compton, meanwhile, play a ridiculously competitive game of shuffleboard.

Later, I grab the lute from Bryan and start on a madrigal that I love, and the boys join in with the other voice parts, with varying degrees of success.

At the end Brandon clears his throat. "I usually don't sing except to impress girls."

"Know some deaf ones then, do you?" says Bryan. Brandon picks up a puck and throws it at him.

Deftly dodging it, Bryan gets up and pulls a card table toward him. "Hal, come and lose some money to me, would you? I could do with a new pair of boots."

"Oh, aim a little higher. What about a horse?" says Brandon. "Or a house? Come to think of it, count me in. I could do with both."

"I haven't lost to you, Charles, in a month," I say, putting down the lute and walking over, "and I don't intend to start now."

"Only because you ply me with drink while we're playing," Brandon says, pulling a mournful face.

I grin and hitch the stool under me.

"Primero?" says Bryan, hands poised with the pack, ready to deal.

I nod.

"For serious money?"

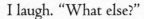

I laugh. "What else?"

Two hours later I've won a fair amount of cash, and Brandon has downed a large quantity of ale. On account of having lost a forfeit, he is currently kneeling on the bed pretending to be my Spanish sister Catherine, who for the past three months has been presiding over her married household at Ludlow, along with my brother. Bryan is taking the role of Arthur, which is all the funnier because he is so much smaller than Brandon.

My bed is a sight to behold: It has a crimson cloth-of-gold canopy and striped curtains made of purple and yellow silk. Brandon has grabbed the curtains in a fistful under his chin and has poked his head between them; it looks like a puppet show. Now he's squawking (in an attempt at a Spanish accent), "Oh, Arthur! Be gentle with me!"

Bryan can mimic Arthur's drawl perfectly. "Be patient, sweetheart, while I fetch my books. I'm sure there is a diagram of the female body somewhere. . . ."

Guildford and I are laughing uproariously. Compton seems to have disappeared.

Brandon's body is entirely hidden by the bed-curtains. As Bryan approaches, riffling through a copy of some book he's grabbed from my cupboard, the blade of Brandon's dagger appears, poking out between the curtains some way below his face.

Bryan looks up from the book, and gasps. "But, my love, I thought you were a woman!"

"Did your book not tell you, sir? This is what women's

parts are like." Brandon bats his eyelashes. "Where can I put it, sir? Do we not fit together?"

Guildford falls off his chair and carries on laughing on the floor.

"Hal . . ."

"What?"

It's Compton, evidently returning from a conversation in the outer chamber. He says, "Master Denys is here to see you."

"Oh, God." Hugh Denys is one of my father's most trusted servants. "Let him come in." I look round at my companions. "Behave yourselves, boys—try to look respectable." Bryan salutes, ironically, and Brandon hauls himself off the bed, sheathing his dagger. I'm wondering what message my father could possibly have sent. . . . And Lord knows what the chamberlain will have reported already to Denys downstairs. As the door opens, I turn and say, "Please tell the king we'll pay for the damage to the hall floor, won't we . . ."

I trail off. Hugh Denys has entered, still in his mud-spattered riding boots and cloak; he's clearly ridden hard. As he straightens from his bow, his gaze flicks round the disordered room, then back to me. He looks exhausted. "No, my lord prince. It's not about any"—his eyes shut for a moment—"floor. It's news from Ludlow."

Ludlow. I attempt to think. What could possibly be the news from there?

"Ah," I say suddenly, spreading my arms in a grand gesture, "Princess Catherine is with child, is that it? Already? Hang out the bunting, my redundancy is complete."

Denys frowns, puzzled. "No, sir. It's your brother, sir. I'm afraid . . ." He hesitates, turning his hat in his hands. "I don't know whether word reached here of his fever, but, well . . . it pains me more than I can express to bring you this news, sir. Prince Arthur is dead."

I stare at him. Denys has an oddly crooked nose—I've never noticed it before. Was he born like that, I wonder, or did he have an accident in his youth? And it really is quite strange because I thought he said, just now, that my brother is dead.

Suddenly the room tilts, and the ground swings up to where the wall should be. Something hits me hard on the side of the face.

The next minute—or later, I'm not sure—I hear voices nearby.

"Steady—"

"Lift him—"

"Mind your shoes—he's going to be sick."

"There, sir . . ."

"He's shivering—get a blanket."

"It's the shock of it—the grief."

But even as they ease me into a chair, fold a blanket around me, and place a basin in my lap—a basin into which I stare, dazed and stupid, as if an explanation will appear there . . . even now I know it's not grief.

It's not grief at all.

17

I'm sitting at the window, reading from the book of Psalms, translating from the Latin as I go. The April sunlight streams in on me, and the gilded, painted borders of the page dance; I run my finger along under the words to stop them jiggling.

The Lord is on my side; I will not fear: What can man do unto me?

At my feet, my dog Angwen twitches and whines; she is asleep, basking in the warm light, and seems to be dreaming of chasing rabbits.

The Lord taketh my part with them that help me: Therefore shall I look in triumph upon them that hate me.

My finger pauses; I am awed by how the words seem written just for me.

This is the Lord's doing; it is marvelous in our eyes.

Three days have passed since I heard the news of Arthur's death. I've hardly slept.

I will be king.

This phrase repeats in my head, over and over. It gives me a thrill that is half like fear, that squeezes my guts and sets my heart racing.

I will be king.

When I'm alone I say it, experimentally, out loud. While sharpening a pen . . . drawing a bow . . . buckling a dog's collar. As if the object will respond.

I hold my hand up to the light and see the flesh between my fingers glow orange red, and I think: When I am king, when I am anointed with the holy oil at my coronation, this flesh will become sanctified. Every inch of me will be infused with the Holy Spirit—how will that *feel?*

Meanwhile, I can't seem to summon up any pity for Arthur. I try to picture him in his last hours, weak with fever, but the image won't come. Lying awake at night, I am afraid he will haunt me, his thin white shape rising from the foot of the bed, pointing a ghostly finger, accusing me of callousness. But he doesn't appear. And in the morning what surprises me is how *right* it seems that he is gone and that I, now, am standing in his place.

But then, haven't I known for years?

York will be king.

And how did the other prophecy go?

Oh blessed ruler . . . you are the one so welcome that many acts will smooth your way. . . .

I wrote them down, those prophecies, the same day I heard them in the Tower—or rather, I scribbled the bits I could remember—and kept the paper tucked carefully in the back of a book. The stories of King Arthur—I think that was the one.

Getting up now, I leave the Psalms lying open on the table and cross to the cupboard where I keep my books. Angwen, who has woken up, scrambles to follow me and stands beating her tail enthusiastically against my leg as I look along the shelves.

I'm still looking when there's a knock at the door and Compton appears.

"My lord, Her Grace the Queen has arrived from Greenwich."

It's unexpected, and there's no time to prepare—before I've even pushed the leaves of the cupboard door shut my mother is sweeping into the room and Compton has hold of Angwen's collar; he bows himself and the dog out, to leave us alone.

The door clicks shut. My mother and I look at each other. And I realize it hasn't occurred to me until this moment to wonder how she feels.

No need to wonder—it's all too obvious. She looks like a paper doll in a downpour. She's not crying; she's entirely controlled—standing there, taking off her gloves—but her skin is so pale it's almost translucent, and her eyes look huge, damp, and red-rimmed, the shadows beneath them mauve and blue.

What was I expecting, *congratulations*?

I approach my mother and kneel, as I always do after a time apart; she raises me and hugs me. The hug feels too tight; she holds me a fraction too long.

Then she puts me away from her and studies my face. "Compton tells me you're not sleeping, my love."

I nod, feeling agitated; I can't think what to say.

"I know you were never close, you and . . . Arthur." She says his name so softly it is almost a whisper. "How could you be, living apart all this time? But, knowing that, I wasn't sure how much it would affect you . . . now . . ."

She strokes my hair. "Forgive me, sweetheart, I can see the pain in your face. It does you credit—you have a loving heart. But remember, Hal, we must not grieve too much. We may incur God's wrath if we do not submit ourselves humbly to his will." Her eyes are swimming. She blinks, and two fat droplets spill down her cheeks. "And that is what it is, you know—God's will—that Arthur should be taken—from us—so young . . ."

She crumples me against her because she's crying properly now, making no noise, just shuddering and shuddering. I cling to her, my arms round her waist, urgently wanting her to stop. But then I realize something awful. Something obvious, too—it's as if a flash of lightning has shown me a thing hidden in the corner of the room, something that's been there *all along*—how stupid have I been not to notice it before?

The awful, obvious thing is this: It's no accident that Arthur has died; it is not by chance that the prophecy is coming true. That is not, after all, how prophecies work. God has killed my brother *for me*. And I have done this to my mother. It is my fault.

"I'm sorry, I'm sorry," my mother says, taking my hands from round her waist and turning away. She produces a handkerchief from a small bag at her belt and presses it firmly to each eye in turn. In the sunlight from the window, the wisps of hair escaping from her hood look golden and fragile.

I stand utterly still. I have an awful hollow, winded feeling in my stomach—as if I have done something terrible, and it is too late to undo it.

"Ah, good boy." My mother moves to the table by the window and rests her fingers on the page of Psalms. She takes a deep, steadying breath, and lets it out gingerly. She says, "I have been finding comfort in scripture too."

I can't reply. My eyes follow her as she walks about the room, minutely adjusting the position of objects, straightening them, lining them up—a box of hawks' hoods, a pen-and-ink holder, a writing slate.

Without looking at me she says, "Your father doesn't want to make changes to your household immediately. You will, of course, become Prince of Wales instead of Duke of York—but exactly when, I don't know. He may well assign you another tutor. And at some point he will bring you to court to live with us, but not just yet."

In the silence she looks up—I'm expected to say something. I swallow hard. "I will do whatever he wishes."

She smiles, her face full of sympathy, then walks back to the window, where she gazes out at the sunny gardens, tapping her fingers on the sill. "He cried, you know," she says. "Your father. I have never seen him cry before. And he came to me to do it." There's a note of defiance in her voice. She's thinking of my grandmother, I suppose—that the king didn't go to *her*. I try to picture my father weeping with anyone. I can't.

My mother says, "Don't expect too much of him, will you? Not at first. He—he had high hopes for Arthur. He saw so much of himself in him. And all that meticulous planning, all those years of training . . ." She breaks off, gives a little shake of her head. "But we must deal with reality—it is fruitless to dwell on what might have been."

Then she turns and stretches out her hands toward me. "We are so fortunate, so blessed to have another son."

"I will be good," I say fervently. "I will be *so* good, Mama, I will work hard, I will please God, I will—"

"It's all right, my love," she says. "I know you will." And she half turns to the window again and says in a light tone—matter-of-fact, "Anyway, as I said to your father—we are both young. God willing, we can have more children."

She doesn't mean children, she means sons. To secure the succession.

"But you don't need more." I move toward her. *See me,* I think. *See me. Standing, solid, before you. Here I am, Mother. Turn back and see me properly.*

It's as if she's heard me, because she does turn back. She reaches out, black sleeve trailing, a long finger uncurling, and smoothes a lock of hair away from my brow. "Ah, but sweetheart," she says quietly, "which of us knows the date of our death?"

My mother spends the whole day here at Eltham, listening to my sisters read, attending chapel with the three of us, and then inspecting my schoolwork and Mary's sewing while Meg plays us a few somber tunes on the virginals. Before nightfall, she rides the five miles back to Greenwich, and I am left trembling with some dark feeling that I can't understand.

After supper I return to my room in search of that book I was looking for earlier—the King Arthur stories. At first, scanning the shelves, I fear it's at Greenwich or Richmond—I have book collections in all three places—but at last I see it, tucked at the end of the lowest shelf. I hook a finger behind the top of the spine and pull it out. The cover is blue velvet, embroidered with gold and silver flowers and fastened with silver clasps—inside, the pages are handwritten in black and red ink, the illustrations individually painted.

In the very act of turning to the back of the book I imagine finding nothing—the paper vanished—and my heart starts thudding. But then I see it: a single sheet, folded several times.

I take the paper, smooth it out, and, moving closer to the candlelight, I frown over the words, which are written very small (as if, I suppose, that would keep them more private) in my best childish handwriting:

The one who has been prophesied will come, full of power, full of good devotion and good love. Oh blessed ruler, I find that you are the one so welcome that many acts will smooth your way. You will extend your wings in every place; your glory will live down the ages.

And, beneath this, I've written the other prophecy:

York will be king.

So, you weigh it in the scales, don't you: a good thing against a bad, to see if the good thing is worth the trouble. And this is what must be weighed against my brother's death and my mother's grief: my glory.

It *will* be worth it. I will show her. She will see me become the greatest king of England that has ever lived.

18

I can't wait to see my father. As the days pass, I expect the summons with growing impatience, while a mixture of triumph and guilt fills me with an uncomfortable, fretful energy. I'm hardly able to bear sitting at my studies, even though I'm determined to work harder than ever. I can't sit down at all without my fingers tapping, my knees shaking. It's much easier to keep moving, from the moment I wake up until it's time for bed again. Hunting, hawking, sword or jousting practice, playing tennis or music, even card and dice games with my friends: I must be occupied, occupied, occupied.

And all the time, my anticipation grows. Always, my father's behavior toward me has been defined by my position in the family. He has never seen me as a person—he has seen my function: the backup son, the spare . . . the spare that could become a rival to Arthur.

Now the barrier to him loving me has been swept aside. *I* am the precious one—I am his heir. All my talents, all the reasons why I was a threat to Arthur will now become advantages—traits to be cherished and praised.

When the summons finally arrives, it is late April, almost a month since Arthur's death, and my father is at Richmond. With Compton and Guildford, I ride from Eltham to Greenwich, and from there take a boat upriver.

It is a fresh spring day, and as we approach the Palace of Richmond, the light gleams softly off the pale stone of its many towers, each topped with a dome and a lantern and a glinting golden weather vane.

My heart lifts. I have it all planned out in my head—how it will happen. My father will smile at me and put his hands on my shoulders. He will speak gently to me and perhaps even apologize. It will be like a Biblical scene—like the tapestry that hangs in the Great Hall at Eltham, illustrating the parable of the prodigal son: The penitent young man kneels before his father; the father (in a modern gown of vivid blue and gold) bends to embrace him tenderly. Except that today, here at Richmond, it will be the father who is begging forgiveness.

When we enter the palace, gentlemen-servants tell me the king is in his private rooms. I must pass through the grand public chambers to reach him: chamber after chamber opening in sequence, like a puzzle toy made of boxes within boxes. These rooms become smaller and more intimate as they go; the people allowed through each door become fewer and fewer.

Finally, as yet another pair of guards steps aside, a door is opened for me into a bedchamber where the walls are hung with cloth of gold, and the bed is emblazoned with my father's emblems: portcullises and roses, dragons and greyhounds.

The first thing I see on entering is my dead brother's face: A portrait is fixed between the hangings on the wall opposite. My eyes slide quickly away, and I look about for my father.

For a moment I can't see him. Then I spy a chair facing the window at the far side of the room; above its back a section of black velvet cap is visible.

"Approach, my lord," says Hugh Denys, nodding me on.

A length of vivid blue velvet drapes over the side of my father's chair; as I walk round to face him I realize that this velvet is a robe, laid across his lap. He's stroking it absently, as if it were an animal: a robe of blue velvet, lined with white damask—a robe of a knight of the Garter.

I kneel.

"Rise," he says. His voice is flat.

Speaking, even focusing on me, seems to be an effort. "All my advisers—Fox, Warham, the others . . ." He waves one hand vaguely in what I suppose must be the direction of his Council Chamber. "All of them seem to think this meeting is necessary. I'm not sure I understand why. Your position has changed—but you know that. There is a great deal of hard work ahead of you—but I assume you have enough wit to realize that too. Beyond that, there is nothing to say. Unless you have any questions?"

This, I had not expected. I rack my brains. "Am I to go to Ludlow, sir?"

There is a brief moment of silence. Then suddenly my father's chin juts forward and the eyes fix on me, alive and accusing. "Do not imagine you will take his place," he snaps. "You will *never* take his place."

He sinks back against the chair again, looking down at the robe on his lap. I realize, with a twisting feeling in my gut, that it must be my brother's. "I may send you to Ludlow; I don't know," he says. "I may make you Prince of Wales—I must, at some point, I suppose. But . . ." He lets out a breath. "Arthur and I understood one another. I have never understood you. Right from your earliest years you seem to have had an innate capacity to . . . irritate me. I don't suppose you can help it."

He looks up at me. "I will oversee the changes necessary in your education. It goes without saying that you will be expected to put your all into your work. If I receive reports from your tutors that you are shirking in any way, the punishment will be severe. Is that understood?"

"Yes, sir."

"That is all. Off you go."

I hesitate, momentarily confused. Can it really be over so soon?

A flick of his fingers: "Go!"

Feeling numb, I bow and exit the chamber. Compton and Guildford are waiting for me in the anteroom outside. I keep walking, on into the Presence Chamber; they fall into step beside me.

"You all right, sir?" says Compton.

"Yes. Yes, I'm fine."

Beyond the Presence Chamber lies the Great Watching Chamber, where guards with sharply polished halberds stand in lines along the walls. There we meet the king's mother, coming the other way.

There is nothing to distinguish my grandmother in

mourning from my grandmother at the height of happiness. She is dressed entirely in black, except for the white wimple around her head and throat, and her face seems to be carved from wood—grim and gnarled. As I greet her, she surveys me with something that looks very like loathing. With my solid build and my red-gold hair she sees me, I know, as entirely of my mother's family; and now for her it must seem, I suppose, as if the other side has triumphed—the louche ones, the ill-disciplined wastrels.

One bony hand stretches toward me and fingers the stuff of my doublet at the shoulder, as if feeling *my* quality. "Well, well," she says, "and what can we make of you, boy?" She does not sound hopeful.

"I am willing to learn, ma'am."

No reply. She sweeps past me, flicking the train of her black dress out of the way as though to brush against me would pollute it. Behind me, boots and weapons clatter as the guards at the door to the Presence Chamber stand to attention to let her through. Then the door shuts behind her with a thick boom.

We walk down the grand spiral staircase, and then, taking a shortcut to the water gate, we head past some of the service rooms for the royal lodgings: the king's wardrobe and his private kitchen. From the latter I hear a raised voice—someone is being scolded—and as we pass a serving hatch, I turn my head. I catch a glimpse of a scene, partly obscured by Guildford beside me and framed by the oblong opening in the wall. We walk on so fast that I don't register what I saw until we are halfway down the passageway. I hesitate, wanting to go back and look again, but I can think of no good explanation to give my companions. I walk on, the image lingering in my mind, though it was ordinary enough.

It was a boy my age, doubled over in pain. I couldn't see his eyes. But his hair was the color of straw.

19

When we reach the water gate, we find the bargemen aren't ready; they hadn't expected me to set off home so soon. Neither had I. Although it's still sunny, a hovering cloud is providing a short, sharp shower, so while Compton stays to chivy the bargemen, I take shelter in the palace with Guildford. I am troubled by the glimpse of the boy: It's as if I recognize him, as if I know him from somewhere. He seems significant. But how can he be?

I want to avoid the royal lodgings, so I head across the moat to the gardens, where a newly built gallery provides some cover. At ground level, the gallery is an open arcade. Above that there's a long enclosed room, attached to the palace at one end and the nearby friary church at the other, and lit by a series of huge mullioned windows on both sides. Wanting to be alone, I leave Guildford propping up one of the open arches and climb the stairs to the first floor by myself.

I open the gallery door, hear music coming from inside, and hasten to shut it again. But I've been seen, and a voice calls out in French, "Don't run away."

The music has stopped. I put my head round the door.

Princess Catherine, my brother's widow, is sitting at a table beneath one of the windows, her fingers poised over a virginals' keyboard. Beyond her the gallery stretches on into the distance, sparsely furnished—a corridor of light. Catherine smiles, drops her hands in her lap, and tips her head to one side. "Won't you talk to me? I don't see many people these days."

My heart sinks—I am not in the mood for conversation. Catherine's duenna—her governess—a fearsome-looking Spanish lady, has risen from her chair some distance away and is glaring at me. I don't know whether she is more offended by my presence or the suggestion that I might not stay.

Feeling trapped, and annoyed, I bow to each of them. The duenna sits down again and begins to stab at some embroidery with her needle.

I say to Catherine, "I'm sorry, ma'am—don't let me disturb you. I didn't realize you were here."

"You wouldn't. Not many people do. Realize I'm at Richmond, I mean—I don't sit in this particular place the whole time, obviously." She lifts her chin to the window. "But I do like the view. It makes a change from my bedchamber, and I don't seem to be needed anywhere else."

I smile, reluctantly.

The sunlight from the window gives Catherine's face a pretty glow. She is dressed in deepest black—dress, sleeves, hood, veil, all—and if the thought of *why* did not give me a sick jolt of guilt I could have said it suited her. As it is, my eyes stray to the only patch of color: a tiny book resting against her skirts, the silk rope it hangs from lying slack, since she is sitting down. The book is enameled and jeweled—and full of dirges for the dead, I imagine.

Another knotting of my guts. Must I feel responsible for her grief too? I say, "I am sorry for your loss."

"Thank you. Your brother was kind to me." She looks at me thoughtfully. "I'm sorry for your loss too."

I bow, but say nothing. There's a silence. The faint sound of rain drifts in through the windows.

"It's quite a change for you, isn't it?" says Catherine. "For both of us."

Another silence. She smiles, still watching me. "You're not 'no one in particular' anymore."

I want to answer. I want to say something witty or at least interesting. But I can't. I walk to the nearest window and stare out at the dripping hedges and herb bushes. I say, "I'm going back to Eltham in a moment. I'm just waiting while they prepare my barge."

Catherine plays a little, breaks off. "I've been addressed as Princess of Wales since I was three—did you know that?" she says. "I spent all my childhood expecting I would come here and marry your brother. I thought it was my destiny to be queen of England."

I think back to that day in Westminster Hall. The Spaniards never let on to my father that the deal was done and had been done for years; there was so much hesitation; we were made to feel there was so much to prove.

Catherine is saying, "But none of us knows our true destiny, do we? We make plans . . . and God's plans for us turn out to be quite different."

I think: *That may be how it is for everyone else. But I know I am to be a great king.* I say, "You must be disappointed."

"I'm sad for Arthur. Though I shouldn't be, should I, because he's past his pain and with God. But I'm not sad for myself. I'll go home now. When I left Spain I thought I would never see my parents again."

In my mind, I am still in Westminster Hall. I remember shooting an arrow and being distracted by a carved angel on the ceiling that looked for a moment like . . . like that boy in the kitchens just now. Am I going mad? Why do ordinary things I see suddenly remind me of someone—though I can't think *who*? Perhaps it's someone I once knew and have forgotten. Perhaps someone from a dream.

"Can you sight-read?" Catherine asks.

"What?"

She taps a sheet of music propped in front of her.

"Oh. Of course."

The instrument she's sitting at is a double virginals, with two keyboards side by side. She slides along the bench to make room for me. I hesitate, then come to sit next to her. I'm terrified at the thought that there may be some dangerous part of my mind that I cannot trust: something that produces visions, that recognizes things I do not know. Now I concentrate ferociously on the notes written on the paper, trying to block out everything else.

"You play well," says Catherine when the duet is finished.

"I'm not a baby."

"I know that! I'm not patronizing you. You do play well, compared to anyone."

"I write, too. Melodies."

"Play me something of yours, then." She gets up and moves away, leaving me in charge of the instrument.

I play. And play. Relentlessly. I play every melody I've ever written for my music master and some, too, that aren't mine. Then I stop, and put my head down on the edge of the instrument's wooden casing.

Somewhere outside a dog barks. The duenna asks a question in rapid Spanish and Catherine replies.

And I think: *There was a dream . . . years ago. . . . A boy came toward me on beams of light. He rescued me from a serpent. . . .*

Catherine says in French, "It can't be easy. For you now. I mean, I don't imagine this is an easy time."

Without lifting my head, I say, "Do you want to go back to Spain?" My voice is muffled; I'm speaking into the keyboard.

"Of course. I miss my mother very much."

"Will it be soon?"

"The timing is up to the king, your father. I am an English subject now."

I look up—someone has knocked at the door. It's Compton, telling me my barge is ready to take me downriver. We will pick up horses at Greenwich and from there ride the rest of the way to Eltham.

I kiss Catherine's hand when I take my leave. I don't suppose I'll see her again.

20

"He saw it—with his own eyes. The bodies of the French lying in piles higher than a man. The English soldiers climbed on top of them to carry on fighting!" I'm delighted, almost laughing—thrilled at the astonishing, against-the-odds victory won by a small band of Englishmen almost a hundred years ago.

At the other side of the room my mother, who has been at best only half listening, says, "God bestows victory upon whom he chooses."

Pray to be chosen, then. God's favor certainly rested with Henry V of England that day he won the battle at Agincourt. This book, which I'm translating from Latin into English (an exercise set by my tutor), was written by a man who was there. He says Henry had six thousand men against an army of sixty thousand French. But, he says, it was impossible for misfortune to befall Henry, because Henry's faith in God was so sublime.

My mother says, "Hal, you don't have to study so long."

"I know." I sit back, one knee shaking, and hold my pen to the light to see if the nib needs recutting. I think: *I, too, must have a faith so sublime that no misfortune can befall me.*

My mother is sitting with an apothecary's book open on the table in front of her, turning the large, crisp pages carefully, running a finger down them. I wonder what she's looking for. Something to do with her pregnancy, I suppose.

Without lifting her head, she says, "Why don't you take the dogs out—go and hunt a hare in the woods?"

"Yes, I already did, before breakfast."

"You are so diligent, sweetheart. I only worry that you push yourself too hard."

Not hard enough. I want to be *sublime* not just in faith, but in everything. Though, sitting with my mother now, there's one imperfection I can't seem to correct: irritation at her pregnant state. I'm uncomfortable just being in the same room as her these days. I don't like to see the loosened lacing on her dress. I don't like to catch sight of her hand softly rubbing her swollen belly. I shall be a glorious king, like Henry V—no backup heir is needed. So why must she complicate matters by bringing a new brother into my world?

I shake myself, push a hand back through my hair, bend over the next paragraph of Latin. "Those lands Henry the Fifth conquered," I say, "they're rightfully ours. Why hasn't Father taken them back? And the crown of France, too—since Edward the Third's time it should have belonged to the king of England. Why hasn't Father pressed his claim?"

"You need peace at home before you can think of conquest," my mother says, still turning pages. "Though your father did lead an army to France the year you were born. He got good money out of that, I remember—the French paid a lot to secure a truce. But it's taken all his effort, all his resources, to establish himself as king here, and to make sure there is a secure realm to hand on to you." She looks up. "I've been meaning to ask—what do you think of Catherine?"

"What do you mean 'think of her'?" I write a couple more words, chewing my lip. "I *don't* think of her. Isn't she back in Spain now?"

"Well, no, actually," my mother says, her eyes on her book. "Your father doesn't want to have to pay back the dowry—he and the Spanish are wrangling about it. I've been thinking perhaps there's no need to pay it back. The alliance would still be useful."

My knee stops shaking.

"Though—" She frowns into the middle distance, one finger marking her place. "I suppose marrying your brother's widow is not . . ."

"Allowed?" I suggest, staring at her. "In the eyes of the Church she's my sister. No one's allowed to marry his sister, surely?"

My mother smiles. "Not *ideal*, I was going to say. But there'd be no problem as long as the pope granted you a dispensation—which I expect he would. Do you like her?" She raises her eyebrows in mild inquiry. It's as if we're discussing a bolt of cloth I might buy. Or a horse. "We could contract it now, hold the marriage ceremony—but it needn't become binding until you turn fourteen."

Quite what the expression on my face is, I can't imagine. I'm reeling. Do I like Catherine? Me? *Like her?* As my *wife?*

My mother waggles her long fingers at me. "No hurry, sweetheart," she says. "Have a think about it." She closes her book and, hauling herself up, moves closer to the fire. One of her ladies—who has been sitting sewing in the shadows all this time—comes over to help her settle and then leaves the room on an errand.

My mother places the toes of her slippers neatly together on the edge of a footstool and rests her head back against the chair, her eyes on me. She says, "I regret that you and Arthur didn't know each other better. I would like to do things differently this time." One hand is resting on the curve of her belly.

"I will bring him up alongside you, this baby. In the same household. I hope the two of you will be close. It is important to have love in a family. Even a family such as ours. *I* think so, anyway."

I look down at my work again, turning back the pages, murmuring some sort of agreement. But I don't know what my father's view will be of raising loving brothers. After all, by his reckoning, this child she's carrying could become a dangerous rival; I might have to kill him one day, just as I was told Arthur might have to kill me. Certain phrases catch my eye as I scan the text: A knight who rebels against Henry V is called "this son of darkness . . . this raven of treachery."

My mother's woman returns with a small dish and a napkin and, bobbing a curtsy, places them within my mother's reach. I know what is inside. For the whole week she's been here at Eltham, my mother has suffered a craving for—of all things—eggs.

Today's is hard-boiled. I watch as she peels off the shell,

picking at it with her fingernails, dropping the pieces into the dish at her side.

I think of ravens' nests—black-feathered chicks hatching.

"Where will the baby be born?" I ask.

"At the Tower."

I yelp. "Why *there?*"

"Your father chose the place. It has a symbolic strength. The ancient fortress."

"But . . ." They say that a woman's thoughts and dreams affect the nature of the child growing in her belly. I saw my mother sleepwalk, once, at the Tower.

"But what?" She looks at me blankly. Is she pretending to have forgotten that her brothers were murdered there—or instructing me to forget?

The glossy white egg is peeled now: smooth and perfectly rounded, like a miniature version of her belly. She flicks off the last traces of shell.

"Nothing," I say. "I can't imagine it's very comfortable there, that's all."

"On the contrary—wonderful preparations are being made. I've visited already to check on progress. I'm to have a bed embroidered with clouds and red and white roses. Everything will be just as I want it."

As she lifts the egg and bites clean into it with her sharp teeth, I suppress a shudder. The Tower, I think, is a place where a woman might give birth to—what? Something monstrous. A serpent. A son of darkness.

21

January, Greenwich: The light across the wide expanse of water is bright and cold as we emerge from the palace gateway and make our way toward the river. Barges bob and tug gently on their mooring ropes; water slaps against the landing stairs. A cutting wind whips veils out sideways and ruffles the gray surface of the Thames.

At the head of the procession, my mother stops and turns. Courtiers hang back, while family members fan out around her to say their good-byes, one by one.

This elaborate occasion—a procession through the palace and now this formal farewell at the waterside—marks my mother's departure for the Tower. There, the chambers specially prepared for her lying-in are ready to receive her. She will be alone with her attendants—the rooms are a secluded and exclusively female domain. And once my mother enters them, she will not emerge again until the child is born: It could be weeks from now.

My grandmother, dressed for once not in black but in cloth of gold, grasps my mother's elbows and presents each papery cheek to receive my mother's kiss. Then my mother turns to Meg and me and kisses us, too.

She smiles cheerfully. I smile back, wearing a perfect

shell. But inside I am nursing a sullen fury, which sits in my stomach like a stone. I think: *My mother believes she knows me, but she doesn't. She has no idea what it's like to be in here, looking out through my eyes.*

On the jetty, my father is waiting; he will accompany her as far as the entrance to her chambers, though even he is not allowed inside. Behind him, musicians on the escort barges saw thinly at their instruments, battling the wind. A huge red wooden dragon at the prow of the royal barge dips as my father steps stiffly down into the hull. He turns back to offer my mother his hand, to steady her as she steps aboard, and then leads her to her seat under the royal canopy.

Somewhere beneath my mother's gown, Meg told me, is a holy relic: a girdle that belonged to the Virgin Mary and has miraculous powers for relieving the travails of childbirth. And somewhere beneath that girdle, lying smug in his place of safety: the child.

I don't want to see the boat leave. I turn away and find my grandmother watching me oddly. Walking past, I snarl at her, just a sound in my throat, like a dog.

22

Our shoes squeak on the floor as we circle each other, breathing hard.

Guildford lunges and grabs my shirtfront. I seize his hand, twist, and ram his elbow joint the wrong way.

"Jesus!" shrieks Guildford.

"Head butt him, Guildford—go on!" yells Simpson, my sword master.

"Am I allowed to?" Guildford pants, his eyes watering at the pain.

"Yes!" shouts Simpson.

"No!" I yell at the same time.

Guildford does it anyway. But I dodge and send him sprawling onto the floor. He rolls to his feet, wiping his mouth and laughing. Guildford's tough. Blows bounce off him like hailstones off a roof.

He goes for me again, a fist aiming at my face.

"Wait!" Simpson steps forward. He's a bald, red-cheeked man with calves that bulge like the fat legs of a fine table. He fought in my father's army at Bosworth and at Deptford Bridge. He knows all the elegant moves—and all the rough and mean ones too.

"Now look, sir," he says to me. "When he's approached you side-on like this, just step in behind him—pass your arm in front—and heave him backward over your leg."

I try it. Guildford hits the painted plaster floor with an almighty thump.

"Yes! And now he's down, stamp on his knee!"

"Hey, sir!" Guildford protests.

I put my foot on Guildford, and bounce a little of my weight on it, taunting. He grabs my leg, tries to sweep me off balance . . .

"Aargh!"

I hop, flounder, and fall heavily on top of him. We disentangle ourselves, laughing again, and when I get up I find Compton's standing by the rack that holds the quarterstaffs, waiting to speak to me.

"Sir. A messenger's come from the Tower." He's holding a paper—I suppose it'll be my mother's official announcement. The wording's the same every time—the clerks write it out beforehand: *It has pleased Almighty God, in his infinite mercy and grace, to send unto us good speed in the deliverance and bringing forth of* . . .

I say, "Is he born, then?"

"*She* is born, sir. See, here—it says the queen has been delivered of a princess."

A princess—a girl! I grab the paper. This is wonderful news. Girls count for nothing—useful for a marriage alliance, that's all. This little scrap of flesh will be no threat to me.

I hook my arm round Guildford's neck—show him the paper. "We must celebrate!" I say. "Simpson, come and have a cup of wine with us—"

Compton puts his hand on my shirtsleeve. "But I need to tell you: Your mother is unwell."

"Seriously?"

He dips his head toward me and says in a low voice, "Don't worry unduly. I'm told it's happened before, other times she's given birth. I just thought you should know."

I release Guildford and say to Compton, "I want to see her."

"You know the rules, Hal. They won't let you in."

He's right. I'm silent for a moment. "What can I do, then?"

"Beat Guildford to a pulp? It passes the time." Compton grins, hoping to cheer me. When he sees it won't work, he adds soberly, "I don't know, sir. Wait. Pray?"

23

I do pray—for hours. Here at Greenwich, where I've been since my mother left for the Tower (my father, for once, has not immediately sent me back to Eltham), there is a church adjacent to the palace, belonging to a community of Franciscan friars.

I daren't go to the palace chapel for fear of meeting my father, so I spend the evening in the friary church, my old picture of the three nails of the Crucifixion clutched in my hand.

I am God's chosen. *The one who has been prophesied will come, full of power, full of good devotion . . .*

Surely, then, I only have to pray—to demonstrate my *good devotion*, my faith as sublime as the conqueror Henry V's—and it will follow that no misfortune can befall me.

The church is as cold as a vault. The candle flames flicker and bow to the swirling drafts. When it is time for evening prayers, a single bell starts to toll, and around me the black-robed friars glide in, silent as specters. No one speaks to me; no one questions my presence. When the service is done, they disperse again through drifting clouds of incense, their hoods raised against the cold.

In bed that night I dream of the black-hooded figures, but now they are mourners at a funeral, following a coffin across snowy ground. I wake in a panic.

"Get up."

Compton stirs on his pallet as I dig at his blanketed bulk with my foot. He tries to pull the covers higher.

I crouch down and shake him. "Get up. I must go to the Tower."

I've only lit one candle; it throws our shadows, hugely magnified, onto the arras-covered wall. I look like a hunched monster grasping my sleeping victim. My victim swears blearily and rolls out of bed.

Ten minutes later we're both dressed. Compton is pulling on his boots while I buckle my sword-belt.

He says, "They won't let you in."

"That's the third time you've said that."

"Because you're taking no notice. And it's true."

"Look." I catch his wrist. "One day I will be king, and when I am king it may count for something that you have served me now. Or it may not."

Compton understands. He stops arguing and hurries to the door. But, with his hand on the latch, he turns back.

"You must have a guard."

"I can't. At this time of night? The captain will want it agreed with my father. All hell will break loose."

Compton passes a hand over his face—imagining, no doubt, a whole range of possible calamities. "We'll get into trouble, going without one."

"We'll get into trouble anyway. Just get me a boat, will you? Stop wasting time."

He closes the door carefully behind him. He has a few

delicate negotiations ahead—to get me out of the palace past the guards, and then into a boat with some plausible excuse for going to the Tower. But I will leave that to his ingenuity—what is he for, after all?

I snuff the candle and grope my way to the window, where I pull back the curtain and look out into the night.

The moon is high and almost full. Its light skitters across the surface of the Thames. Beneath the window flaming torches mark the landing stairs and the gatehouse, where guards remain on duty through the night. Across the dark water, marshy fields and woods on the far bank are invisible against the distant higher ground—a mass of black against midnight blue.

Compton comes back, holding a candle. His face, lit from below, looks ghoulish.

"We can go."

"What did you tell them?"

"That my Lord Prince is still awake and has ordered some clothes to be brought from the Great Wardrobe at Baynard's Castle for the morning. You're a servant, coming to assist me." He sets the candleholder on a stool and throws open the lid of a trunk. "You'd better borrow one of my cloaks—they're plainer than yours." He pulls a gray woolen cloak from the trunk and slings it to me. "I suppose we'll have to come back with something that passes for a chest of clothes."

"But we're not going to Baynard's Castle."

"I'll break that to the boatmen once we're on the water. It's the guards that are the bigger problem. Come on."

Compton has done his work well; the guards inside the palace let us through without question. We emerge into a courtyard half bathed in milky light and turn left to the gatehouse, where another guard unlocks the small wicket door within the big gate. We step through.

We're not far from the water's edge—a dank wind flaps at us like wet washing. Underfoot, the flagstones of the path to the landing stairs are black and glassy.

Ahead, a mountainous boatman waits for us, his young apprentice at his side, both standing in a gently rocking skiff. They've been roused from their rough beds by the look of them.

It's not the type of vessel I'd expected; the barges I usually travel in have a covered section at one end to provide shelter. "No luxuries for servants," mutters Compton, nudging me on.

I step aboard, the hood of my cloak well down over my face, and sit with my back to the boatmen. Even wrapped up like this, I can't quite believe that I pass for a servant.

We cast off. Out on the open water, it is cold. Cold—after the first few bracing minutes—beyond imagining, the chill reaching inside your clothes like a freezing pickpocket, reaching inside your flesh, frisking your bones.

As we slide through the darkness, the boatmen steer us along one side of the river, as close to the bank as is safe. The strongest pull of the tide is in the central section of water, and it's running against us. I face away from our direction of travel; by the lantern's light I watch the water: rushing, rushing the other way, as if fleeing the very place we're heading for.

My mind is filled with indistinct pictures of a sickroom, shadowy figures stooping over my mother. I want to go faster. It takes strong men to row us against the tide at any decent speed, and our boatmen are strong—no doubt Compton has given them enough of my money for it to be worth their while making the effort, too. But I wish I could row with them, to speed us on, to get warm, and to stop myself from thinking.

Near Limehouse, as we pass the massive hulks of ships at anchor, Compton tells the boatmen about our change of destination and indicates that there will be further payment.

"Secret visitor for one of the prisoners, is it?" the older man says. I turn to look at him and catch an unpleasant wink. "Don't worry, gentlemen, I won't ask questions. Safer for me not to know, eh?"

We pass lighters, barges, and cranes moored at wharves and jetties, but no other travelers awake like us and moving on the water.

Until, that is, glancing over my shoulder to try to make out what is ahead in the blackness, I see a boat approaching from the other direction, farther over toward the center of the river. It is a skiff like ours, traveling smoothly with the tide, its lamp illuminating three figures: two boatmen and a single passenger—a hunched figure in a gray hooded cloak like mine, the face obscured in shadow.

Without reason, I am gripped by a sudden terror of this figure. My eyes are pinned to it, as if it is something monstrous—my mother's corpse, already stiff, propped up in a sitting position and shrouded by a cloak, being rowed to the underworld on the river of death.

Since the two boats are moving in opposite directions, there is a tiny instant when we come precisely level, some thirty feet apart, and I see the figure side-on, just a profile view of a hunched cloak and hood, sitting exactly as I am sitting, facing the same way as me, wearing a cloak like mine, the only difference being that it has not turned its head.

But as the two boats pull away from each other, the figure *does* turn, shocking me as badly as if a corpse moved. The figure looks at me as if it's felt my gaze, and the hood falls halfway from its head as it does so. In the swaying lamplight I see a youth, his hair the color of straw, his eyes so deep-set they're just two bone-edged shapes of black shadow.

I want to cry out. Deep in those shadows I sense rather than see a glittering gaze trained directly on me—I sense that this boy, this *thing*, knows who I am and why I am there and is not surprised: He's been expecting me.

I put out a hand and steady myself on the edge of the boat. It is the boy that I have seen before. The boy in the kitchen. The face of the angel on the roof. And perhaps . . . It is as if in my mind there is a locked room, a door I do not open. Behind it I have hidden the image of a boy that I am terrified to recall: at first as congealed and unmoving as cold meat, then hunched and whimpering—those apparitions that I saw in the Tower, years ago. I only ever saw him from the back, but wasn't his hair this color—didn't he look like this too?

Mother of God, what is it? A ghost? A restless spirit that has some business with me? Or some incubus, some devil that is not out in the world at all, but *in here*, in my mind, projecting visions onto the world I see—onto a carving on a hall roof, an anonymous kitchen boy, a stranger in a boat . . .

In my churning mind only one thought about this boy rises clearly to the surface, horrifying enough and inexplicable: *I know him.*

Or rather, something in me knows him. Some instinct, something unreachable and dark that stirs far below the surface of my thoughts.

The eerie boat, moving faster than us with the help of the tide, has been swallowed by the night. We are almost at the Tower. The boatmen maneuver us across the river, across the dragging current, and the jagged battlements of the ancient fortress loom at my back. In my mind I see mouths, the mouths of beasts: portcullises with rows of spikes like teeth. My own teeth ache with the cold, and I realize my mouth's ajar; I'm panting, my heart's pounding, sweat prickles under my arms.

And now a sudden wild feeling floods through me, as if I have been trapped, or am about to be. All at once the Tower seems like a living thing: monstrous, malignant. I have lost all thought of reaching my mother, deep inside it. I feel alone and vulnerable, as if I am something's prey and about to be swallowed.

We are coming past the entrance that leads to the Traitors' Gate, coming to the wharf steps near the Byward Tower.

"Turn back."

"What?" Compton stares at me from his place at the stern.

"I said, turn back!"

"But we're here, sir. Look—"

I am amazed they cannot feel it, if not for themselves then rising off me: this animal fear.

Is my mother asking for me, somewhere deep in there? She could be asking for me right now.

I clutch my head. "Pay them double, triple, I don't care— just *get me away from here.*"

The older boatman mutters an oath; Compton tells him sharply he'll not be paid at all if he complains—but he's already turning the skiff, his oar working in the water, the other angled up.

Then the men begin to row in earnest and we pick up good speed, running with the tide.

I look beyond them, searching for the boat that passed us. Might we catch it? I am terrified to, but eager as well: I want to know if what I saw was real. But however much I strain my eyes, I can make out nothing but thick soupy blackness, punctuated here and there by flaming torches marking wharves and water stairs or the jetties of grand private houses.

Guided by one feeble lantern, we are tiny specks, skimming over the depths of this great river. I think of the hundreds of drowned there must be below us, swaying upright like reeds. And above us, in the infinite blackness, how many other dead, speeding as phantoms through the air, brushing their vaporous fingers over our faces with the wind? Even the boatmen look sinister; even Compton, in my fear, looks unknown and unknowable—a grotesque stranger in the night.

24

Morning—a gray, grinding morning in February. The world is solid, leaden, and unmysterious. I am in the tiltyard.

Last night we made it back into the palace thanks to Compton's imaginative storytelling. He reported to the guards that I—his assistant, bundled in my cloak, leaning against him—had been taken ill and that we'd had to turn back before reaching the Great Wardrobe. In the safety of my chamber I slept only fitfully for the rest of the night. This morning, having woken feeling drained and sick, I have chosen the most difficult physical task I can think of. I am hoping it will drown out my thoughts.

There is much to be learned from tilting at a stone wall. Slamming a lance into a solid, unmoving object, at speed, is the hardest training there is.

The wall's corner is the part to aim for. The force of the impact travels along the lance (whether it breaks or not) and delivers a hefty blow to your right arm and shoulder. Meanwhile you have to stay in the saddle as the horse is brought round in an arc by the blow, and keep your touch light on the reins with your left hand.

Considerable strength is needed—in your thighs to stay with the horse, in your torso and shoulder and arm to control the lance and take the impact.

In competition all this is done, of course, while wearing eighty pounds of plate armor. Oh, and against a live, moving opponent instead of a wall, with the risk of someone else's lance slamming into your head at the same time.

I've been practicing all morning, using one corner of the wall that borders the tiltyard. Lone, meticulous training builds trust between horse and rider, and I have been training up several mounts, learning with each one how best to keep in rhythm—how to keep my backside stuck to the saddle no matter what the animal does.

It's a bitter day. Even inside my gloves, my hands feel raw.

I jump down from my horse and sit on the sandy ground, tugging on one stirrup and the reins. I am teaching the horse not to drag me if I fall off.

A shape blocks out the meager sunlight.

"Sir?"

It's Compton. I carry on with what I'm doing. He waits.

"Sir?"

And waits.

"Will you stop, sir, for one second?" he says at last, exasperated.

"No." I get up and walk past him.

My hand hovers over the lances laid out in a rack; I can't quite decide. Then I pick one.

Compton says, "Bishop Fox is waiting to speak with you." He's come to stand beside me. "There's some news."

I turn to him for the first time. He looks stricken, agitated.

The wind is blowing the fur on the collar of his gown flat, showing the pale roots of the hairs.

Somehow I know what the news is without being told: My mother is dead. I say, "When did it happen?"

Compton looks at me searchingly. Then he says, "In the night. I'm really sorry, Hal."

High above us, the flags crack and slap in the wind; somewhere a bird takes off, screeching. I search my mind for something to say, but all I find is a great emptiness, like an expanse of gray sea.

Beyond Compton, a tall figure stands waiting: Richard Fox, the bishop of Winchester. I can see his long, lined face from here, his black cap pulled well down over his ears. He's one of the men closest to my father—one of the gang who shared his exile in France during the old wars. Well-rewarded for his loyalty, Fox is now a high-ranking minister.

"Send him away."

"I can't, sir," says Compton. "The king ordered him to come."

So I approach, and suffer the telling with perfect calm. My mother is dead, and the baby, too.

I ask, "Where is my father?"

"His Grace the King has retreated to his chamber," says Fox. "He cannot receive anyone. He is deep in sorrow."

I thank Fox, wish him good day, and turn to the nearest groom: "Tack up the black mare."

By the end of the day I've trained with five different horses. It is slow, hard work. But I am getting better.

25

February drags on, as Februarys do, and the weather gets worse. Damper, less decidedly wintry, and all the drearier for it. I return to Eltham and continue my studies. I don't see my father. By day I try to fill every waking moment with work, with sport, with gambling for distractingly high stakes—anything. By night my dreams float toward me on black rivers, full of visions of my mother, white-faced and unreachable.

And then an idea comes, and fixes like a tick to my mind, resisting removal, growing fatter and fatter until I must do something about it.

I persuade my tutor to arrange a visit to Westminster, arguing that it would help my studies to have access to my father's impressive library there. The real purpose of the visit, however, lies elsewhere. Just a short scull downriver from the palace there is a set of landing stairs at what, for a private house, is an impressive waterside gate. This gate belongs to Durham House, the London residence of the bishops of Durham—a grand house, currently used as lodgings for the Dowager Princess of Wales: in other words, for Princess Catherine.

I instruct Compton to find some pretext for getting me into a boat during a break from lessons. He does it. I don't even bother to ask what story he's made up.

And so, after three hours spent sweating over Latin and Greek texts, Compton and I and a couple of guards are on the river. Swans accompany us as we glide along, passing Lambeth Palace on the far bank and approaching, on the near bank as the river starts to curve west, the first back gates of a whole row of great houses, whose faces give on to the Strand, and whose gardens reach right down to the river.

The third of these is Durham House. We disembark at the landing stairs, and Compton speaks to the guard at the gate, who stands aside smartly to let me pass.

I've heard that Catherine has retained a whole Spanish household about her, and I'm cowed at the idea of a roomful of women like her duenna, their critical black eyes fixed on me as I try to talk. So I send Compton to present himself at the house, and to ask whether Catherine might come into the garden to meet me. In the meantime, I loiter in a squally corner among the spiky bare branches of fruit trees. I lean on a wall, pushing the gravel about irritably with my foot.

I'm there for some time. It occurs to me that, in this weather, she may prefer to say she is indisposed.

But at last a side gate opens and Catherine emerges, attended by her duenna, with Compton following. I push myself off the wall, and she sees me and threads her way toward me on the pathways. She's wearing black still, but after so long with my mind filled by pale mournful figures what strikes me is how robust, how capable she looks, with her healthy blooming cheeks and the stripe of glossy apricot hair showing beneath her hood.

When we've wished each other good morning, Catherine says, "My sorrow at the news of the queen's death could not have been deeper. She was a lady of such wisdom and generosity. She was always kind to me." Her eyes are bright with sympathy.

I manage to grunt some thanks, ducking my head (sympathy right now is unendurable), and try to steer her away from her duenna.

Catherine sees the target of my glances. She says, "You can speak freely. Doña Elvira understands no French."

"All right, then." I can't do this elegantly; I'm too ragged to be capable of it. I know how I'm going to seem to her: twitchy, confrontational, demanding. I say, "Don't go back to Spain. Stay here and marry me."

She stares. "But you're . . ."

"What? What am I?"

"Where do I start? Too young."

"To get married? Or too young for you?" I don't wait for a reply. "We can contract the marriage now—it just won't be binding until I turn fourteen. And you're only six years older than me—that's not much. . . . She said we should."

"Who did?"

"My mother. Oh, and don't worry about the fact that we're related. The pope will give us a dispensation, apparently."

There's a silence, in which I'm vaguely aware of Compton trying to engage the duenna in conversation some distance away. Catherine's not answering. She looks pained—and sorry for me.

She touches me lightly on the arm. "Let's walk."

As we crunch along the gravel, the clouds begin to clear. Patches of sunlight make the yellow flowers on shrubs of witch hazel and winter sweet glow gold. The air is crisp; shouts from the river carry to us on a thin breeze.

Catherine talks about the gardens in Spain and the castles—the Moorish palace at Granada, the fortresses of Aragon and Castile. She still hasn't said whether she'll marry me. But why wouldn't she want to? She told me she'd grown up expecting to be queen of England.

We pause by a fountain, where water cascades down two tiers of fantastical carved beasts into a sunken square pond at our feet. The beasts of each tier support a great dish on their shoulders, gripping it with claws that protrude from batlike wings. Jets of water gush from their mouths, the pipes hidden between fangs.

In the sunlight each stone face is covered with a bright sheen of water; at the point of each beastly chin, stray droplets collect, cling, and fall. I watch them. And without planning to, I find myself saying, "I heard a prophecy once. It said I would be king."

Beside me Catherine says, "Where did you hear it? When?"

"Oh, years ago. Long before Arthur died."

"That gives me the shivers."

I shrug; that's just how it is. I say, "But I didn't have Arthur poisoned or anything—to make it come true—if that's what you're thinking."

"No. Of course not."

"The prophecy said I'll be . . . not just any old king. God has chosen me for greatness. My glory will live down the ages."

"Oh!" She's smiling. "That's nice!"

"Yes, go on—have a good laugh," I say savagely. I turn, swipe at a bush, and come away with a handful of leaves. "You think I'm useless, just like my father does."

"No, I don't. Sorry, Hal. Look, I'm not laughing. I believe you."

"Doesn't matter if you do or not. It's true."

There's a silence. I open my hand, and the leaves scatter in the wind.

Catherine says quietly, "I really am sorry about your mother, you know."

Another silence.

I say, "I want to . . . *grieve*." I bare my teeth, pushing the word out as if it has a foul taste. "But I can't. Because it's my fault she's dead."

"That's crazy. Don't say it."

"It *is*. Arthur died because God chose me to be king. And Arthur's death was the reason my mother had another child. So she died because of me."

"Even if that's true, it's not your *fault*. You didn't ask to be chosen."

I stare at the ground. "God tests his chosen ones—he finds out if they are worthy by sending them trials. It's all over the Bible: Job, Abraham, Joseph—"

"And Christ."

"Exactly." I nod. "And now me, too. My mother dying is my trial. I have to prove I can take it. I just need . . ." I look up at Catherine. "I suppose the plan is for you to leave soon. If you tell me you agree, I can speak to the king. Is the dowry sorted out?"

"Hal . . ." She looks distressed. "He's made inquiries about marrying me himself."

"What?"

"He's going to write to my mother."

A gull wheels over the river, squawking. I feel suddenly that I am adrift at sea, entirely alone.

"What an honor—congratulations," I say briskly. "And I'll have you as my stepmother instead of my wife. Another trial."

"Not everything's about you, you know."

Oh, but it is. She doesn't understand. It's a burden I have to bear. I am carrying everything. The enormity of it is terrifying. I lie awake at night, pinned to the bed, spinning in the blackness, dizzy with it.

She says, "I'm . . . frightened."

I almost haven't heard her. I look at her, trying to take in the words. I think of my father being ceremonially brought to the marriage bed by his attendants, as Arthur was—and of her lying there, waiting for him, in the place my mother has vacated so recently that the imprint of her body could almost still be warm. I think of Catherine's auburn hair fanning out across the pillow, her soft smooth face . . .

"You'll cope," I say, and walk away to examine a sundial. "Don't be like that."

I turn back and face her. "'The Lord is a just and merciful God, who allows no one to be tried beyond his strength,'" I say. "Saint Paul's first letter to the Corinthians, chapter ten, verse fifteen."

I'm crying. I can feel the tears streaming down my face. Dripping—like the fountain beasts' water—off my chin.

26

As the door shuts, my father is laughing—expansive, warm, his arm around my shoulders.

The envoys left behind us in the Presence Chamber—a couple of effortfully charming Venetians—probably think the door shuts out all sound. In fact, the laughter ceases the instant the door closes. And the arm drops from my shoulders too; my father walks ahead of me through the small vestibule and into his Privy Chamber. I follow. It's a different world here—quiet, secret, with just a few servants moving unobtrusively to anticipate my father's demands.

At last my father has summoned me to live at court— now I am to be always at his side, learning how to be king from his example. I am waiting for it to be announced that he will marry Catherine. I can only think that the delay is for propriety's sake; the arrangements must be in place—she has not gone back to Spain, after all.

"Get me something to eat." He's slung off his hat and is vigorously scratching his scalp as he sits down, the oiled gray hair swinging by his cheeks. No smiles now. He glances back, rakes me with a dead look. "You need to put in some more hours with the accounts today."

The food comes; his men know what he likes: a leg of meat, a puddle of sauce to dip it in. He sits on a stool to eat, his elbows on his knees, plate in his hand, like a soldier in camp. It's a wonder he can still chew meat—his teeth are few these days, and blackish. Watching him eat, I think of Catherine.

I'm determined to say something, though my heart's hammering. I grip a chairback, pressing the metal studs so hard my fingertips turn white. "She's your daughter," I say. "In God's eyes."

"What? What's the boy talking about?" My father doesn't look at me; it's an aside to the room. He spits out a gob of gristle, flicks his eyes up to Bishop Fox, who's come, followed by his assistant, into the room behind me. "Explain to him, will you, Fox?" My father jabs a chicken leg in my direction. "I haven't the patience."

Fox steers me to stand by the window. "I'm sorry, sir," he says gently. "What is it that concerns you?"

"It doesn't matter."

"The Spanish girl," comes my father's voice from the other side of the room. "It's the bloody Spanish girl he's going on about. Tell him."

Fox's normally creased brow creases even further. He says, "Your father, sir, in his great wisdom, has seen the advantage of maintaining the alliance with Spain. It has therefore been agreed with Their Catholic Majesties the king and queen of Spain that you will marry Princess Catherine. We are arranging for the formal betrothal to take place in the bishop of Salisbury's London palace. It's on Fleet Street—between Saint Bride's and Whitefriars—do you know it? It has crenellations. No matter. You will of course be notified of the date, when it is fixed—it will be within a day or two of the signature of the formal marriage treaty—"

"Me?" I feel breathless, giddy. I scrunch my eyes shut. How can everything have changed so suddenly to fit my purposes?

I open my eyes again to find Fox studying my face in concern. I say, "But I thought the king himself was going to . . ." I tip my head in my father's direction.

The bishop looks uncomfortable, rubs his long nose. "Oh. Ah. Yes. Her mother would not agree—said the mere mention of it offended her ears. Your father will look for a wife elsewhere. Of course there is the matter of it being," he waves his hand, "between the two of you also . . ."

"Incestuous?" I suggest. I remember pointing it out to my mother. "In marrying my brother she became my sister, and I am not allowed to marry my sister?"

Fox nods, wags a finger in the air. "That's it. But we have applied to the pope for a dispensation."

Fox's assistant, a large man called Wolsey, steps forward smoothly. "Our contacts in Rome indicate there should be no problem, my lord," he says.

I blink at him.

Acts will smooth your way . . .

A picture comes into my mind: grasses in a meadow bending themselves before me, anticipating the path my feet are to tread.

What does it feel like, to be chosen? I ask myself, as if

someone else were inquiring. My God, if I were not the chosen one, I should want to know! It feels like blazing sunshine—*inside*. It feels like galloping across smooth ground. Sure, certain. Knowing that nothing can make me stumble.

27

"I require and charge you both, as ye will answer at the dreadful day of judgment when the secrets of all hearts shall be disclosed, that if either of you know any impediment, why ye may not be lawfully joined together in matrimony, ye do now confess it. For be ye well assured, that so many as are coupled together otherwise than God's word doth allow are not joined together by God; neither is their matrimony lawful."

The chapel settles into a comfortable silence, broken only by a muffled snort as one of the witnesses stifles a sneeze. There is nothing to say. Wolsey was right; there was no problem: the pope did grant a dispensation. Not in time for the betrothal—which went ahead anyway—but in plenty of time for this, our wedding.

Stealing a sidelong glance at Catherine now, I catch the outline of her profile, clear against the busy background of carvings and gildings. I've hardly seen her in recent months: Today she looks thinner and paler than I remember, and I have heard rumors that neither my father nor hers is providing enough money for her household. I wish I could remedy that, but I can't. I am thirteen, which is too young, my father calculates, to be a husband yet in anything but name. So, after this ceremony, we will go our separate ways—to live, for now, as we did before: Catherine at Durham House and me at my father's side, wherever he happens to be.

I turn to the front again. On the floor, around the edges of the archbishop of Canterbury's robes, patterns of leaf shadows and bright sunlight move on the colored tiles. Against my leg I can feel the stiff gold fabric of Catherine's hooped skirt. My hand is supporting hers; her fingers feel soft and dry, the frill of her cuff lying against my thumb. I wonder if she is thinking of that other wedding day, when she married my brother. She must be.

A ring appears on a velvet cushion. I take it and look down at Catherine's hand. The nails are very short—she's bitten them right to the quick.

I pass the ring onto her thumb, saying, "In the name of the Father"—then onto her index finger—"and of the Son"—then her middle finger—"and of the Holy Ghost"—at which the blue eyes flick up to me and she smiles: a small, secret smile. And finally the ring reaches its home, sliding over the knuckle of her fourth finger. "Amen."

28

"What about the nights?"

"Oh yes, they're working nights," Harry Guildford says. "Don't worry. It'll get done in time. But the bill for candles will be enormous."

We're in the largest of my private rooms at Richmond, planning the tournament that will mark my fourteenth birthday—my coming of age. Guildford, who has developed a passion for the mechanics of these displays, is bringing me up to date with the progress made both by his father and brother, who run the Royal Armory, and by the Office of Revels, which is in charge of making the costumes and pageant-cars.

I say, "Show me the vehicle that'll hold the animals."

My feet have been propped up on the end of a nearby bench. I swing them down and lean forward as Guildford hands me the design. It's a large plan, meticulous and detailed, complete with measurements and labels to indicate building materials.

The contraption for the animals is an enclosed pageant-car, set on pivoting wheels, to be drawn by two horses dressed to resemble lions, in shaggy cloths and headpieces. The outside of the car, according to the plan, will be made to look like a mountain, topped with trees and bushes and craggy rocks.

"We'll have a girl sitting on here, a real one." Guildford

points to a boulder. "But these deer will be artificial. Papier-mâché on wire frames, painted and dressed in fabric."

"And the live animals in here?" I point to the middle of the mountain.

"Yes, two compartments inside, one for the buck and the other—here—for the two greyhounds."

Charles Brandon peers over my shoulder. "The dogs'll go mad—they'll be able to smell the buck in the next compartment."

"All the better," says Guildford. "When we open the trap they'll come out at a roaring pace."

"Make sure the division inside is strong, though," says the muffled voice of Francis Bryan, who is lounging on a daybed on the other side of the room with his hat over his face. "Otherwise you'll open the door and find two dogs having an early meal."

I hand the plan back to Guildford. "Once they've chased it round the hall and made the kill, I want the buck's head cut off and presented to my father." I think he'll like that.

Guildford makes a note in his pocket book as I cross to the table and pull a pile of papers toward me—sketches for the suits of armor. I leaf through them. Then again, more carefully. Green-and-white checkered, red striped with gold, all green, all red . . .

"Where's mine? The black one—black all over—where is it?"

Guildford, still scribbling, says, "But, sir, you are not allowed to take part."

I turn to him. *"What?"*

"Express orders of the king. I thought"—he looks up, and swallows—"you knew."

There's a silence; everyone's looking at me. Even Bryan's emerged from under his hat. I fling down the papers and stride out.

29

My father's face is stony.

I am holding myself in check, my hands clenching and unclenching by my sides. I say, "Please, sir. I have faithfully performed every task you have set me: hours with the account books, endless meetings, endless lessons. This is the one thing I *want* to do. And I have the skill, I have worked hard . . ."

"No."

I take a breath—try another tack. "To sit on the sidelines will be a humiliation. All the boys I train with are taking part. And what is jousting, if not preparation for war? One day I shall be their king. One day I shall lead them into battle—"

"Pray you won't have to."

"God may call me to lead them into battle," I say steadily, "just as you fought, sir, in your youth—and have fought many times since."

My father sighs impatiently and puts down his quill. "But I had no choice. When I was young, I was on the run, fighting for my life. Since then I have fought for my crown and the peace of my realm. This, for you, is a *game*."

We're in a small chamber, where the window is shaded by a red hanging, lending the whole space an infernal glow. It's warm, but still my father, sitting at his desk, has a fur-lined robe wrapped tight about him. Behind him on the floor stand rows of chests, strapped and locked. Before him on the table sit bunches of keys, alongside neat sheaves of papers, ledger books in meticulously squared-off stacks, and small chests with neatly ordered drawers of whetstones and penknives, quills, and small silver pots of ink.

I am standing stiffly before the desk, like a soldier reporting to his commanding officer. I say, "Not just a game, sir. My ambition, when I am king, is to reclaim the French crown. The conquests of Henry the Fifth—"

"Came to nothing!" interrupts my father, banging the desk with his hand. "Worse than nothing—disaster! Henry the Fifth's military ambitions killed him—when his son and heir was still a baby. The result? France was lost. England descended into civil war." He leans forward, looking at me intently. "Secure the succession or, no matter what your achievements, your legacy will be a *catastrophe*. This is why, incidentally, I don't want you skewered on the sports field. Do you see?" He tilts his head and speaks slowly, as if explaining to an idiot. "I—am—securing—the—succession."

There's a silence. A breeze stirs the red curtain. Tentatively, I say, "I feel sure there will be no disaster for me, sir. I am convinced . . ." I hesitate; I am loath to share this secret with my father.

"Convinced of what?" he snaps, alert and motionless like a bird, his beady eyes fixed on me.

I take a deep breath. "That I am destined to restore England's glory, sir. And I believe this means winning back the French crown. I must be trained for battle—"

A shout of laughter echoes round the room. "My God!" my father exclaims. "You don't change, do you? My son: the thoughtless oaf with the terrifying sense of entitlement. Showy, too. You've always fancied yourself a hero, but you have no idea what it means."

"And you *do*?" I snap. "Your heroics are ancient history. Look at you now! Permanently bent over your desk like a clerk! Obsessed with nothing but money!"

There is a silence. I am panting, trembling. My father regards me coldly.

He says, "I could have you flogged for what you've just said. I would like to—you deserve it. But . . . I will treat this little outburst as an opportunity for you to *learn*." He rests back in his chair and opens his hands. "Why this scorn for administrative work? Is it not *manly* enough for you? Do you think that if you ride around on a horse, brandishing your sword, the country will somehow magically run itself? And that the money to pay for your conquering armies can be plucked from the trees like fruit?

"What about taxation, trade, justice? What about the administration of estates, the security of our borders, feuds between families that have money and men enough to start a war on their own? You have spent all this time, as you say, *faithfully performing every task I set*. Were you asleep while you did it? Did you not notice that being a 'clerk' is how I exercise *power*?" He opens his eyes wide, in mock innocence. "If you think you know a better way, please share it with me."

I feel sick, but something in me knows I can't turn back.

I say, my voice quavering, "I believe England needs a lion-hearted leader. Someone to dazzle the people—someone for them to look up to. Your tasks have taught me a great deal, but some of what I have seen I . . . I cannot think is for the best." I daren't look at my father: I'm shaking, and I have to focus my eyes on the wall above his head as I press on. "The noble families of England must be allowed their pride and honor, sir. They must exercise their rightful power as your loyal servants, not be bent constantly under the weight of debts, loaded with trumped-up fines they have done nothing to deserve. When . . . when I am king, I will uphold true justice. I will reward courage and valor. I will pursue virtue, glory, and immortality." I come to a stop, feeling drained, and wait for the explosion.

The explosion doesn't come. When my father speaks, it is with scorn, but his voice is quiet. "It sounds so pretty, doesn't it?" Slowly he stands up and limps around the desk toward me. He says, "Do you honestly think your mightiest subjects will serve you out of *love*? Think of the last four kings before me. Three of them died violently, and the fourth spent years fighting for his crown." One thin hand reaches out and squeezes my arm. "Henry. As king you will be surrounded by people in thrall to their own ambition and greed. Trust none of them. Every day is a trial of strength. Not of your stupid sword-arm, idiot; your strength here." He jabs my forehead. "And here." He prods my chest.

For a moment he looks at me searchingly, then turns away. Near the fireplace there's a small table on which stand a lidded jug and cups; he crosses to it and pours himself a drink.

"You want to be admired?" he says. "I have found that it is far better to be feared. So how do you suppose I achieve that? I cannot keep a knife to the throat of every ambitious duke or earl. Yet I need them to work loyally for me when they are hundreds of miles away, defending our northern border, keeping the peace in Wales . . ."

He knocks the drink back, wipes his mouth. "Debt to the crown keeps them on a nice short lead, like a dog. Step one foot out of line and"—putting the cup down, he makes a sharp gesture, as if he is yanking a chain—"the debt is called in and they are ruined. Without money they cannot pay for their guards and their troops and their castles. And so, they cannot challenge me. In fear of this, I find they serve me well."

I watch as my father walks back to his desk; his fingers drift lovingly over his papers. He says, "The battle for control of England is fought as much *here* as on the battlefield. So—I suggest that you leave off dreaming quite so much of jousting and spend more time instead with the account books." Sitting in his chair again, he picks up his quill. "I will make a note to increase the time you spend on administrative matters."

"And if I agree to that," I say, "will you let me take part in this one tournament? Please? It is all arranged. My performance will do you honor—you'll see. It is, after all, my coming of age."

My father raises his eyes to the ceiling, pretending to consider. "Um . . ." Then his usual contemptuous expression returns. "No. And that is my final answer. You can enjoy the tournament as a spectator. You can sit next to me."

Exhausted and angry, I don't know what to do except bow and make for the door.

My father says, "Oh, one more thing."

I stop—turn.

He's back to checking the ledger. His eyesight has weakened recently; he bends low over the book—so low his nose almost scrapes it, along with his pen. With only the briefest of glances up at me he says, "You will reject your marriage to Princess Catherine. It can be undone perfectly straightforwardly if you make a formal declaration before you come of age."

I stare at him. "No."

The pen pauses; my father lifts his head. "I beg your pardon?"

"I don't want to."

"What you want or don't want has no relevance. Marriages are a matter of diplomatic strategy. The alliance with Spain is not as useful as it was. Still . . ." He frowns absently at the window, considering. "I think we won't declare the rejection publicly for now. Just have the document signed and witnessed, and then we can keep it in reserve and see which way the tide runs." He dips his pen in ink again and bends over the book.

I think of Catherine; I think of my mother, saying, *Do*

you like her? I think of the person I want to be—the person I feel God has called me to be: golden, upstanding, chivalrous, devout. I say, "It would be dishonorable."

"Dishonorable?" My father slaps his hand on the desk. "This is the difference between you and Arthur: You have no understanding of reality. . . . Oh, to live in a simple world! A world of fairy-tale ideals!" He jabs his quill at me. "You're *dreaming*. Open your eyes. Foreign rulers twist and turn every day of their lives—they promise to be your undying friend, and at the same time they make deals behind your back with your enemies. You cannot cling to some childish view of honor; you will be taken for a fool."

"I like Catherine," I say doggedly. "I need her."

My father flings down his pen, digs his hands into his gray hair, and growls in frustration. "For the love of Christ, have you been listening to *a single word* I've said? You are revealing nothing, boy, but the depths of your own inade-quacy, which, God knows, I have been made bitterly aware of already. You *need* her? Then that is an added reason for her to be sent away. You must learn to need no one. You must be prepared to strike off your right hand if it is for the good of England."

"I see you doing nothing that goes against *your* own incli-nations. Sir."

"You imagine no decision I take is hard?" He stares at me, then scrapes back his chair and bolts out of it. "I take hard decisions every day."

I manage not to flinch as he approaches. I say, "To fine a

duke you don't like and clink the coins into those chests over there?"

He is looking at me intently. He whispers, "I had to execute a man she believed might be her brother."

"She?" But I know who he means. My mother. And that man, the Pretender . . .

My father's eyes are unfocused, as if memories are replaying themselves in his mind. He says, "The Spanish demanded it. They refused to consider letting Catherine leave Spain unless, they said, not a drop of doubtful royal blood remained in England. This man had been in prison for years—I'd taken care that the queen never saw him. But she had been hoping all along it was her brother. . . . I knew that. And still I had him killed. To make an alliance England needed."

He rubs his face. "It half killed *her*, too. It weakened her health. Perhaps if I had not done it, she might be . . ." His voice tails off. He looks at me—and his expression hardens. "Do you think I don't live with this every day? I am strong—" Raising a white-knuckled fist, he thumps himself on the chest. Then he leers at me, savage and close. "Could you do it? Are you *heroic* enough?"

He is close enough that I can see the texture of his skin, the individual dots of stubble, the grayish tinge to his pallor, the hairs protruding from his nostrils. His lips are dry, flecked with white spittle at the corners; his breath is sour. Sinews at his neck stand out like ropes. The gnarled, scarred hands are ink stained. Here is the sanctified flesh of a king: ideals lost, soiled by struggle, decayed into a manipulative, frail sinner.

I have never before felt so clean and shining. Righteousness fills me to the skin. And righteous anger, too: Why have I been blaming myself for my mother's death? Here is the sorry creature who made calculations with my mother's happiness—weighed it in the scales, counted up the cost on his grubby abacus. *Thou art weighed in the balances, Father,* I say to myself, *and art found wanting.* Disgust rises in my throat like bile.

Confident and powerful, my voice no longer wavers: "It is God's will that Catherine should be my wife."

"Is it?" My father limps back to his desk. His tone is sardonic. "Well . . . it is *my* will that she should not." He leans on his hands as he lowers himself to sit. "You will reject the marriage. I command it. Or your life will become extremely unpleasant. Don't push me to devise ways to make you suffer. But be assured—I will devise them if necessary." He pulls papers toward him, dips his pen. "Now get out."

I slam the door behind me, startling the servants and guards standing outside. As I walk through the chamber beyond, I think: *I only have to wait, Father. You are an old man.*

30

As far as the world is concerned, I am good. When I am with my father—as he receives his councillors or the ambassadors from foreign courts—I hold my tongue. I contrive to look intelligent. They flick their eyes to me; they look for something—anything—to interpret. But I say not a word. My face is framed for obedience. They cannot know my thoughts.

And, on the eve of my fourteenth birthday, before Bishop Fox and a handful of other councillors in a stuffy chamber at Richmond Palace, I make a formal declaration that I protest vehemently against my marriage to Catherine and am utterly opposed to it. I state that the marriage was not binding because it was made when I was a minor. In coming to this decision, I say, I have been in no way forced. It is not true, of course—but while my father is king I have no option. I must simply bide my time.

It's only with the boys and men who joust that I can relax. There is something clean and honest about physical combat. With them, I am good tempered. It comes easily. Nothing has touched me; I know what I am for. This time—this waiting—is like the ascent up a steep hill: When my father is dead and I am at the summit, I will see it—that golden land stretching before me, bathed in sunlight. The dark years are always brought to a close by a savior. I am blessed.

31

Three years later

"She has land," says Brandon, trailing one hand in the fountain as we pass it. "My father always told me to find a rich widow."

Harry Guildford wipes the spray off his jacket. "But you are contracted to marry her niece."

"A technicality."

"I thought the niece was pregnant?"

"A slightly more, um, inconvenient technicality." Brandon smoothes his hair back with his wet hand. "I did things in the wrong order."

"It sounds to me like you did them in exactly the right order," says Compton, and gets Brandon's racket handle shoved in his gut. "Ouch."

"Sorry, it slipped," says Brandon sunnily. He shrugs. "I don't think, if I'm honest, that the aunt will live long. Then, you see, I can make things right with the niece."

Beside me, Bryan says under his breath, "Oh, *that's* fine, then."

I slap the back of my hand into his stomach. There's a party coming the other way.

Crossing the sunny courtyard toward us: a strange bouquet of Spanish maidens—one tall and thin, one plump and ruddy, the duenna sour-faced and suspicious—as well she might be, I suppose . . . and, in the center of them all, the small, upright figure of Catherine herself, her eyes angled down to the flagstones as she walks.

She sees, therefore, our feet first: a straggling row of fine leather tennis shoes. The sight makes her stop. She looks up.

I haven't seen her in ages. And though it's three years, now, since I signed a formal document in front of witnesses rejecting our marriage, my father still hasn't let her go home. Has he even told her? He's probably still trying to squeeze money out of her father.

"My lady princess," I begin, "you look . . ." She looks pale, and threadbare; in places, the velvet of her overskirt is worn smooth with brushing. "Well."

Wrong, wrong, wrong. She looks strained and ill cared for. And exquisitely beautiful.

She smiles. "It is good to see you, my lord."

When I think about it, I'm surprised that I don't bump into her more often. She lives at court now, since that's cheaper for my father than letting her have her own household. Perhaps she has instructions to show her face as little as possible.

I say, "We're off to play tennis."

"I can see that." Catherine nods at Brandon as he flourishes his racket, trying to catch the duenna's eye. "I trust you will enjoy it."

"Thank you."

Catherine moves to leave, but as she draws level with me she hesitates. Quickly, quietly, out of the side of her mouth, and in French, she says, "Your father keeps me, now, without enough money even for clothes. It is . . . humiliating. Whatever he intends, I am from the royal house of Spain. Can you speak to him for me?"

"He does not take advice."

"I understand." She drops her eyes; she's disappointed. By the time I realize what a worm I feel, she and her ladies are walking away.

It's the plump and ruddy one that answers the door. She won't admit me, but after some discussion inside, with the door pushed to, it opens again and Catherine emerges.

"You're not supposed to be here," she says.

"I know." I've been leaning against the doorframe—I straighten up. "I just wanted to tell you . . . I'm sorry, would you walk with me? Don't worry, there are servants by the entrance to the stairs. We are chaperoned, you see, but not overheard."

Catherine hesitates, glances along the passageway, then steps toward me, pulling the door to her chamber softly shut behind her.

We head away from the servants, walking slowly side by side. Hangings line the walls, in dark and heavy colors; the passageway is gloomy, even on a sunny afternoon.

"You wanted to tell me . . . ?"

"Yes—sorry. I wanted to say that it's not just you. The money. I mean, my father not giving you enough. He's obsessed. It's . . ." This is harder to explain than I thought. I

187

start again. "He fears . . . everyone. He fears that everything he has achieved will unravel. To him, money means control, you see."

"He does not need to keep me poor to control me."

"No. But the great landowners, the powerful nobles . . . He makes them swear to do what he wants—if they don't comply they are fined, so heavily that they are ruined. It works. And it has become a habit. Now he does it with everyone. Keeping himself rich, keeping others in debt to him. I've seen the coffers in his private chambers—they're stuffed full of coins."

We've come to a row of arched openings in the passageway wall, not on the side that looks out across the courtyard, but on the other side, the internal side. They give a view down into the cavernous space of the great hall.

We stop beside the arches, and I lean on one of the sills. Below me the hall is empty—a great, still space, with bright sunbeams slanting down from the high windows and, between them, a world of thin gray shadows.

At intervals along the walls stand the dark shapes of statues: kings and heroes frozen in action—trampling a dragon, holding aloft a sword, standing triumphant over an enemy bound in chains.

Directly beneath us it's the great Greek warrior Achilles; opposite—in the center of the far wall—there's a figure in full armor, brandishing a two-handed sword. It is supposed to be my father.

I nod to it. "He doesn't look like *that* anymore."

Catherine follows my gaze. "I haven't seen him in months."

"He's gray. And coughing. He's lost weight. He's . . ." I hesitate. Last week, a man in the City had his ears sliced off for suggesting my father was dying.

Catherine presses her fingertips to the velvet-covered sill, neatly, side by side, as if playing a chord on a keyboard. I notice that her nails are still bitten. She whispers, "Change is coming."

"Yes."

I turn and lean back against the edge.

Out of the corner of my eye I can see her regarding me for a long moment. Then she looks out at the hall again. "You can't blame him for not matching up to you," she says. "You will eclipse him. The prophecy—I haven't forgotten."

I turn to face the same way as Catherine, leaning my elbows on the sill. "I ask myself every day: What does it mean, what do I have to do, what do I have to be, to be this *perfect* king?"

"And what do you answer?"

"See that one, there?" I point to a statue diagonally to our right: a man in a suit of mail, with a crown on his helmet. "It's Henry the Fifth. Came to the throne in his twenties, already battle-scarred—he'd taken a crossbow bolt full in the face at sixteen and was disfigured, but you'll notice the sculptor hasn't included that part."

"I can't see from here."

"Take it from me. He hasn't." I glance at her, then look back at the statue. "He conquered France—made an

Anglo-French empire. He's my hero. *But*—he died leaving one newborn son, whom he hadn't even seen. What followed? Civil war and chaos—and France slipped through our fingers. The son grew up to be king, but he was a disaster. He was murdered in the end."

I point across to the left, where there's a statue of a young man fighting a lion. "And there, look: Alexander the Great—created one of the largest empires in ancient times . . ."

"But died leaving only one baby son not yet even born," continues Catherine. "Result: civil war and chaos, and the son was murdered at the age of thirteen."

"Exactly." I grin, impressed she knows so much. "So. I know how to do better. To be a great king, I have to achieve two things." I hold up my hand to count them off. "One: build an empire. That means taking back France—the crown is rightfully ours. And two: have sons to carry on my legacy. Strong sons, grown to manhood before I die." I meet her eyes; she's looking at me levelly. There's no scorn, no skepticism in her face. It's as if she believes in me.

For a moment we're just looking at each other. Then I say, "Did they even bother to tell you?"

"What?"

"That my father made me reject our marriage?"

"No. But I heard—eventually." Catherine looks down at her hands. Then she turns to me, her face full of determination. "Don't pity me. Please—that's the one thing I couldn't bear. All I need is money for my passage home."

32

The following winter an anonymous note is nailed up on a church door in the City of London. It's a translated quotation from the Bible, from St. Paul's letter to the Romans, chapter thirteen:

The night is past and the day is come nigh.
Let us therefore cast away the deeds of darkness,
and let us put on the armor of light.

Beside it is a drawing of a tall, powerfully built youth seated on a warhorse, with a crown on his head.

I am tall and powerfully built; I am seventeen years old.

From my closet on the chapel balcony, I watch as my father kneels with difficulty, helped down by his men. He casts off his hat and crawls along the aisle toward the altar, his gray hair hanging over his face. I can hear in his rasping breath the effort it costs him. His gnarled hands press into the carpet; if a king is to abase himself and crawl to receive communion, he will crawl on the finest carpet he has.

My lip curls; I turn away. The sight disgusts me, but it is no surprise. I have already heard that now that he sees death coming, my father is performing penance for his sins. I have heard that he weeps and sobs for three-quarters of an hour together. I have heard he tells his servants repeatedly that if God will send him longer life they will see him a changed man. So much for his strength. So much for being able to live with his hard decisions.

The spring is wet and squally. Birds nest and cats lie in wait in the long grass for their fluffy-feathered young. The world carries on with no regard for a thin old man who dreams of hellfire every night.

It is an April morning when Compton comes to me in my chamber at Richmond and says he has heard that my father, today, cannot rise from his bed.

I make my way to the king's bedchamber. It is busy with doctors and councillors, with basins and cloths and hushed conversations, but when they see me, they stop their conversations, and the nearest men fall back to clear a path for me to approach the bed.

There, beneath a crimson satin canopy, I find my father lying on his back, his arms laid out on top of the covers. His nose seems bigger, sharper: a hook of bone and old skin.

It's a moment before he becomes aware of my presence; then the eyes roll slowly toward me. "Henry." He frowns. "It's too soon." Silence; he's breathing shallowly. "You don't *know* enough. Don't try to"—it is an effort to swallow—"rule alone. My councillors . . . keep them close. Listen to them."

His eyes slowly close. I hover, wondering whether he will open them again and say more. But he doesn't—he seems to be sleeping.

Hours pass; I am still in the chamber, and I find myself

keeping something of a vigil, as my father slips in and out of sleep, and the doctors whisper in corners, holding flasks of scant and foul-colored urine up to the light.

Late in the afternoon he sees me, though I am at some distance across the room. He opens his mouth to speak, and I hurry to the bedside, as his attendants move deferentially away. I slip my fingers under his hand where it lies on the bedclothes, limp and clammy. As I watch, his mouth twitches and strains, but the attempt to speak comes out only as a breath, a wheeze, a terrible column of stinking air from inside a body that seems half-rotten already.

Then the limp hand clutches mine, and he manages at last to say, painfully slowly, "How . . . will . . . I . . . be . . . remembered? Am I . . . loved?"

I lean in to his ear. I am a fiery angel, delivering God's judgment. For a moment I could almost think there are wings on my back. I say softly, "You are hated by your people. You will be remembered only as my father."

As I straighten, his eyes lock onto mine—fierce, afraid—but he cannot respond. I smile down at him. The councillors and servants around me smile too. They think I have given my father loving words of comfort.

Later still I am at the window. I have parted the curtains to look out into the night. Occasional lights show on the river, as here and there a lone boat heads toward the City. Below me, the walled Privy Garden is an arrangement of neat, dark shapes—hedges and paths and carved decorations. Spilled torchlight from the guards stationed at the doorways picks up glints from the eyes and talons of gilded beasts, crouching on poles and holding painted shields. In the wing of the building opposite a small light winks along the windows of the gallery; someone is walking there. I think I catch a glimpse of a fair-haired young man. He stops at one of the gallery windows and looks out—directly, it seems, at me.

At that same moment, a voice behind me says, "Your Grace—"

I turn to the room. On the table by the bed, a twist of smoke drifts from a burned-out candle. Everyone has turned to face me; everyone is kneeling. On the bed, my father lies motionless, in shadow. His mouth is ajar and, from a faint glistening, I can see that his sightless eyes are fixed on the canopy above. The king is dead.

Long live the king.

PART THREE

Lift Up Your Heads

33

The embroidery on the cushion presses dints into my fore-head. My breath, with nowhere to go, blows hot against my cheeks. I am lying on my face. My arms are spread wide, in the shape of a cross. The singing of the choir echoes up to the stone vaulting. And the Holy Ghost is descending from heaven and infusing me with divine grace. Right now.

Above me the space is huge—an expanse of empty air, where drifts of incense float through beams of colored light. The windows are bright as candied fruit, the great stone columns of the nave solid as the trunks of giant trees. The whole cathedral seems to me a golden cavernous glade.

It is Midsummer's Day. Catherine, my wife of two weeks—my *proper* wife, this time—is kneeling behind me, shining in white damask cloth of gold. We are here at Westminster Abbey for our anointing and coronation. Here, in the very same place where Henry V was crowned.

At last the singing stops. Silence. There is shuffling to my right. Coughing. Somewhere distant, a low murmuring rumble. I get up, light-headed, and walk forward a short way, to face the archbishop of Canterbury, William Warham. A team of bishops steps up to unlace my shirt. I can feel the nervousness rising off them like steam. Then they fall back, job done, and I kneel.

Warham takes the eagle-shaped golden flask and anoints me with holy oil—on my hands, on my chest, on my back and head. The liquid is cold. I feel a streak of it running down between my shoulder blades. The abbot of Westminster, moving awkwardly in his stiff robes, dabs me dry—the cloth he uses, blotched now with patches of God's grace, will be burned later; a stray trace of holy oil at large in the world is a dangerous thing.

It can transform a man into a divine creature.

Later, no longer merely a seventeen-year-old youth myself, but a holy creature, an anointed king, a god-on-earth, I sit on my throne on the specially built stage before the altar. They have dressed me now in layer after layer of robes, the outer ones reaching to my feet, heavy with jewels and gold. They have brought me spurs blessed on the altar and the ceremonial sword with which I am charged to defend the Church. On my head they have placed the ancient crown of St. Edward, its jewels representing the graces God has today bestowed upon me, by which I am to rule: wisdom, understanding, counsel, strength, cunning, pity, and fear.

Remade now as king, I lead Catherine back down the nave, through a crush of my gorgeously dressed subjects: the dukes and duchesses, the earls and countesses, the barons and lords, and the merely rich. In my heavy robes and heavier crown it is a slow walk, steady and swinging, like in a dream.

Nearing the end of the nave we can hear the cathedral bells booming far above us. Then the great west doors open like the side of a mountain, and we step out into summer sunlight and a wall of sound.

The air reverberates with the pealing of the bells, echoing weirdly so that the sound seems to come from the houses opposite. Caps hurtle, spinning, into the air above a sea of faces that fills the cathedral yard. The people are clapping and yelling, chanting my name. I raise one hand to them, grinning; the cheer becomes deafening.

Then I turn to my wife, this beautiful vision in white and gold, her shining auburn hair hanging loose, her crown—with its delicate spikes of fleurs-de-lis—choked with sapphires and rubies and clusters of pearls. Her dress is embroidered with our emblems: my Tudor rose and her own pomegranate, a symbol of fertility. She is smiling. Her fingers lie softly on my outstretched, gloved right hand; I lift them to my lips. Her nails, I notice, are no longer bitten.

My grandmother, attending the coronation in robes almost as sumptuous as ours, mutters darkly that some adversity will follow. It does—for her. The celebration banquet leaves her with agonizing stomach gripes; five days later she is dead.

34

"The abbot of Fécamp, Your Grace," announces Compton. "Envoy of His Most Christian Majesty, King Louis of France."

I have been examining a miniature siege engine carved out of wood—a scale model made from my own design—holding it up between thumb and forefinger; I spy the ambassador through it: a portly figure in a black cassock, waiting beyond the open doors of the Presence Chamber.

Handing the model to Harry Guildford, I turn and bound up the steps to my canopied dais and relax back into my gold-fringed chair.

It is sunny outside; the windows are thrown open, and dust motes are swirling in the golden sunbeams. Out beyond the gardens, distant calls can be heard from the river as the ferrymen ply their trade to Lambeth and back. Around me, my friends—in expensive new clothes—are mingling with my councillors, some of whom (though not all) are my father's men, Bishop Fox and Archbishop Warham among them.

The abbot of Fécamp, envoy of the king of France, approaches. He is a fat man; he waddles up and halts some distance from the bottom step of the dais, his eyes sliding from the canopy to somewhere in the region of my shoes.

His attempts to bend at the waist in an elaborate bow are effortful. A sphere finds it hard to know the spot at which to fold itself.

I watch him, my hands dangling, weighted with rings, over the velvet arms of my chair. I chose a large diamond today, and three rubies.

Dabbing at his face with a lace handkerchief, the abbot spends some time congratulating me on my accession to the throne. It is a pretty enough speech, to which, at a nod from me, Bishop Fox replies in elegant French.

"Your Grace," says the abbot, then, "I have come to confirm the peace between England and France, in response to Your Grace's letter to my master. He was delighted by your request for a renewal of the peace treaty between our countries. This treaty was, I know, cherished by your illustrious father."

I stare at him, unblinking. Alarmed, he makes a little moue. Then, less certainly, he begins to speak again.

I interrupt him. "No, no, no. Wait. I thought—" I shake my head and waggle a finger energetically in my ear. "I thought I heard you say *my* request to renew the peace."

"I did." The abbot clears his throat. "I did say that, Your Grace."

"But I didn't make that request." I look round at my councillors. "Did I?"

"My master the king of France received your letter, sir—" says the abbot.

I am still looking at my councillors. "But why on earth

should *I* ask the king of France for peace? He daren't look me in the face, let alone make war on me!"

There's an awkward pause. Fox steps up to me and says quietly, "A letter was written. By the Council—on your behalf." He bends close to me and adds in an undertone, "Continuation of the peace is very desirable, Your Grace. While you consolidate your position and, um, decide on the direction you wish policy to take."

"Show me."

"Sir?"

"Show me this letter *my* Council wrote to France *on my behalf.*"

Fox turns to his assistant, Wolsey. "Bring a copy of the letter."

Wolsey produces a rolled-up paper from his voluminous sleeve and hands it to Fox—who hands it to me. I read it and rise from my chair.

"My lord abbot," I say to the envoy. "I hope you will pardon my councillors. There has been some misunderstanding. It will be put right immediately."

I tear the paper, over and over and over. Then I release two fistfuls of pieces out the window.

35

The birdcage is hung in the window embrasure, attached by a hook to the wall; inside it a nightingale sits on its perch, regarding me beadily. I flick my finger against the bars, and it flutters around the cage.

"I'm not a child!" I say, walking to the table. "My councillors think if they provide me with enough toys and idle amusements I'll not notice while they run the country."

I pick up a box and open it. Inside are three silver balls; I stir them round with my finger—they chime.

Catherine looks up from her sewing. "How was the tiltyard, by the way?"

"Oh, Thomas Boleyn broke three lances. And Brandon fell off." I pick up another box, open it, and angle it toward her, with a questioning look.

"Adders' tongues set in gold and silver," she says. "From my sister. Listen, Hal, you are the king. You have the power to order things as you want them."

"Do I? It feels like I can't bloody well do anything without ratification in triplicate—sending documents off to Fox for this seal, to Warham for that seal; they delay it if they don't like it—they send a grant back and tell me I am being too generous to my friends. . . . They wouldn't have dared do that to my father."

I take a shuttlecock, bounce it off the wall, and catch it again. Several masks, with and without beards, lie on a bench. Discarded caps, their feathers askew, are on a table beside them. I say, "What chance do I have of getting them to agree to an invasion of France if they won't even let me give the presents I want? *You* know what France means to me."

It's my path to glory and immortality: the creation of an Anglo-French empire. I will rule from London and Paris. I will be the father of a great dynasty of emperors.

Catherine nods. "Empire and sons. The sons being my part of the job."

"At which you seem to be doing very well." I walk to her, grinning, and she lays down her sewing. We join hands, lacing fingers, and I lean down to kiss her.

"It's early days," she says with a small frown of reprimand. "I'm not certain. So, anyway—tell Fox and Warham that you plan to invade France."

I straighten. "I've tried. *Too risky! Too expensive!* Mother of God, they're old men, that's what it is. They're looking forward to dying in bed."

"Well, at least you can be sure of Spain's support. I should have said—I've had another letter from my father."

I pull up a stool and sit beside Catherine as she produces a letter from her purse and unfolds it. "Christ," I say. "I never imagined I'd have to plan a war behind the backs of half my Council. . . . What's he say?"

Catherine traces her finger along her father's handwriting, translating as she reads. "Let your councillors renew the peace treaty with France in your name. For now. It will provide you with good cover while preparations for an invasion are made."

I groan. "It feels grubby, humiliating . . ."

Catherine looks up from the letter. "But think: You need to order artillery from Flanders. And ships must be built. It all takes time. Your destiny will come—but sometimes patience is called for." She puts a hand on her stomach. "I am impatient too."

I smile at her. Our heads are close together, and one of my arms encircles her waist; with my other hand I point to a line of writing.

"What's this part?"

"Um . . . he says it's as well to be secret, and that when you and he are writing to each other about France, it should be in cipher. Above all, the French must not suspect that the kings of England and Spain are planning to invade."

She puts the letter down in her lap and looks at me. "He is your family now, Hal. He will be a good father to you, I know it."

There's a clatter from the doorway. Francis Bryan is standing on the threshold beside Thomas Boleyn. They are oddly close together.

Catherine's already risen to go. I put out my hand. "Stay."

"Your Grace . . ." Bryan makes a face at me, silently signaling.

"There's nothing that can't be said in front of the queen." *What trouble now?* I think.

"It's just—" Bryan and Boleyn step apart, revealing the soles of a pair of shoes, which—as they come into the room—I see are attached to sturdy legs, a drooping gown, a horizontal bulky body three feet off the ground and, at the head end, a grinning Charles Brandon and a sweating and puffing Harry Guildford.

I get up to investigate. "My God!" I laugh, and turn to Catherine. "It's Fox's man." I call, "What on earth are they doing to you, sir?"

Boleyn, affecting outrage, says, "This priest won twenty pounds off Bryan at primero last night—"

"Not a crime. Congratulate him."

Guildford obliges, looking down. "Congratulations."

"But now we've just found him in the Watching Chamber cheating the page boys out of their pennies," says Bryan.

"Not *cheating*," comes a good-natured voice from beyond the large stomach. "I would say . . . beguiling."

"We thought we'd take him in hand," says Brandon. "Bring him to you, you know, hanging like a trussed boar. As punishment."

"Very well then, let me talk to this beast." I signal that they should set their captive upright.

The round face of Thomas Wolsey, the priest who is Fox's assistant, emerges as they do so, flushed but unperturbed. He straightens his robes. "Forgive me, Your Grace, but I was only whiling away the time. Hours spent in the outer chamber waiting for an audience can be . . . well, tedious." He grimaces apologetically. "And the page boys implore me to show them my sleight of hand."

I raise my eyebrows, inviting a demonstration. Wolsey steps toward Brandon, hitching back his sleeve, and raises his hand, apparently reaching behind Brandon's ear. "It seems to them like magic," Wolsey says. "They are so *very* eager." He draws his hand back—revealing in his fingers a shiny half-crown coin. He sighs. "And dim."

For a moment there's silence, and a look of concern crosses Wolsey's face. Then I let out a bark of laughter. "I *like* this man!" I motion to him to come and sit with me. "Do you drink spiced wine?"

Wolsey nods and smiles, folding the coin into Brandon's hand and patting it absently. "I'm afraid so, sir."

"They tell me I must spend more time at my desk," I say.

"On the contrary, I recommend less time."

I'm doing target practice with darts; the board, circular and edged in green velvet embroidered with gold, is mounted on a frame several feet away. Wolsey is watching, sipping his wine. My friends are playing, variously, chess and a yellow and blue instrument that produces a tune if you turn a handle.

I tap the darts on my fingers. "You mock me."

"Sir—how would I dare? I mean it. You simply need an able *instrument* to carry out your instructions; to do the desk work for you."

"And you are proposing yourself." I throw now, lining up and releasing the tiny arrows in quick succession—*thud, thud, thud.* Then I walk forward and collect them from the board.

As I come back, Wolsey inclines his head. "I would maintain a constant flow of information to Your Grace, and every decision would be yours—of course. . . . Why should your time be taken up with the mundane details of the execution of your plans? I know how quick your mind is. Simply tell me what you want achieved . . ." He drains his glass. "And I will achieve it. Try me."

I throw again. "But the seals—the sending every instruction back and forth, to Fox, to Warham—"

"Is not necessary. You can do things by direct decree. Just state that your instruction will take immediate effect, by royal command."

I look at him. "They didn't tell me I could do that."

His gaze is steady and serious. "No, I know."

The end of a bawdy song drifts to us from the far side of the room—Bryan has worked Wolsey's name into the lyrics.

"The cheek!" he exclaims, spinning round. "And me a man of the Church, too!" He sets down his cup and launches himself across the room and into a verse of his own, working Bryan, Brandon, and Boleyn's names into the rhyme and beating time on their heads with the ends of his stole.

By the time he's done, I'm spluttering with laughter and clapping. I say, "For a large man a little past the first bloom of youth, you have wondrous energy."

"For an old fat man, you mean, sir!" He laughs—a wonderful belly laugh—and walks back to me. "You will not see me flag in your service. Ever." He is suddenly earnest, intensely so. "Let me show you what *you* can do."

As my friends carry on with their music—a little more dignified now—I beckon Wolsey to the large bay window.

Within its alcove we can talk more privately. Outside the sky is a cloudless blue; clear bright sunlight streams in, creating dazzling reflections on the surfaces of a curious object that stands in the middle of the space.

It is a box, on long metal feet, the sides of which are made of glass, for the better viewing of the treasures inside. The lid, also glass, is made in two halves like doors, their frames garnished with pearls and gold thread. It's a wedding present—I forget from whom.

Idly I fiddle with the lid's catch and say, "Then give me your advice on this: I want to invade France. A number of my most senior councillors oppose me." I fold back the leaves of the lid. Inside is an agate dragon standing on a black crystal rock beside a white crystal mountain; I peer at the beast and trace a finger along its smooth back. "They tell me war is too expensive, too dangerous as I have no heir—"

"That last will soon be remedied, God willing," Wolsey says. He considers for a moment. "If one can avoid seeming to make an unprovoked attack on France—"

"Unprovoked? When the French king withholds land that is rightfully mine?"

"Indeed, I agree, Your Grace, but not all foreign rulers would see it that way. It would be better to have some additional reason for invading. So that those who are keen to stir up trouble for England cannot use it as a pretext for their own attack." He dips his head to peer through the glass at the dragon. "But there are ways . . . France, as you know, has been at war with the Republic of Venice, urged on by the pope."

I nod. "The republic is on its knees." Inside the box, the white crystal mountain has a flat top, into which a square shape has been cut—presumably it is some sort of door that opens.

"May I make a prediction?" says Wolsey. "The French king and His Holiness, once they achieve their victory, will fall out over the division of the Venetian spoils. Then Pope Julius will turn his ire upon France. *That* is your opportunity. When he calls for a holy league of nations to wage war on France, you can say: Oh, I am loath to go to war . . . but since Mother Church calls me, I am duty-bound to obey. . . ." He pulls an exaggeratedly solemn face—then his eyes flash gleefully. "You can march into France under the banner of the pope. It will be a *crusade.*"

I am flicking my nail against the edge of the mountaintop door, but it won't budge.

"Forgive me, sir, but I believe this opens on a spring." Wolsey dips his large hand into the box and pulls out a tiny pin from the mountainside. The door on the top, instead of opening, spins, and a St. George in silver armor pops up, standing on an enameled green hillock and brandishing a sword.

Wolsey grins at me. "Clever, isn't it?"

36

The child—my son—is brought to me within an hour of his birth.

It is the darkest part of the night: the first hours of the new year. I have been sitting up with Compton, playing chess by firelight, wrapped in my sable cloak.

I get up when the women enter. They curtsy low and pass him to me: I don't know how to hold him. He is swaddled tightly; he lies on my palms like a prize fish.

Two puffy eyes open, and he looks at me with a slow dark look. He blinks; he tries to turn his head. I have the women unwrap him in the warmth of the fire. He lies on the fur mantle they spread for him—uncrying, his tiny hands curled shut, his legs like a frog's. His cheek is downy to the touch and the size of a doll's.

"Look, Compton," I say. "Proof of God's favor—right there, lying on a rug."

"Such a fine child, sir. The hope of the whole nation."

It feels like standing on a ridge and looking down across a bright plain: my great future, laid out before me. Away to the right, a battlefield, where I will win great victories; to the left, a venerable cathedral, where I will be crowned king of France. And directly ahead, a youth in armor: this boy.

Empire and sons.

37

The narrow slit is all I have to see through: a thin horizontal slice of color in the black interior of my helmet.

My head can't turn; the helmet is riveted to my cuirass, to save my neck from taking the impact of a blow.

I transfer the reins into my left hand and hold out my right, blindly, for the lance, as the horse steps and shifts beneath me. Out of my vision, two grooms bring the lance to me, upright, and place the great, weighty hilt of it in my hand. I feel for the balance of the thing and rest the end on my thigh.

My blood is pumping at double speed. The barrier is in my sight. I catch a glimpse of the armored horse and rider at the other end. I am on a good alignment to run. My horse stirs eagerly. The trumpet signals the start.

Now.

It is February: bitingly cold. The tiltyard is packed. Hearts are in mouths to see whether the king can give blows and receive them without harm.

I use the hardest technique: riding in with the lance upright; dropping it at the last moment to its target.

It strikes. There's a jolt, unbearable pressure against my grip, then all at once release, and a great crack as the wood of the lance shatters. Splinters fly and the crowd yells its delight. My horse slows as it reaches the end of the tiltyard, and I bring it into a turn. I drop my broken lance; signal for another.

I run and run, until the horse is exhausted. I am hit, repeatedly, but never unseated. I break seven lances. The people see that, by the aid of God, I am in no danger.

At one end of the tilt is my pavilion: blue and gold and topped with a white hart holding a standard. While the others run their courses, Compton helps me out of my armor and into a close-fitting coat of cloth of gold.

I emerge again on a gray horse now; the cloth covering its flanks is blue velvet, decorated with beaten gold hearts and initials—mine and Catherine's.

She is watching from a viewing gallery. I halt the horse directly before her, unsheathe my dagger and, reaching down, slice a gold heart from the cloth.

Dismounting, I hand the reins to a groom. Then I climb the face of the gallery, finding footholds on carved rows of portcullises and painted roses. I swing my leg to sit astride the sill as Catherine gives me her hand, laughing. "There are steps, you know, at the back."

"It's more interesting this way. I've brought you a present." I give her the golden heart. And kiss her, which sets the crowd yelling and whooping again.

The next moment, I've jumped down to the sandy floor and am back on my horse. I spur it into a thundering circuit of the tilt, and make it leap and prance for the crowd and lift its hooves to drum on the wooden barrier with a noise like a volley of gunshots.

I laugh, exhilarated. No other knight can approach even

half my skill. I am first among warriors, first among men. I only wish I were in France right now, on the battlefield. But it will come. I can do anything. I am bigger than this tiltyard, bigger than this city and all the creatures in it. I hold them in my palm. I am England.

In the pavilion afterward, I'm dazed. Ordinary things seem strange—ludicrous. I'm thirsty, but how can I need to do something so mundane as take a cup in my hand and drink? How can I need to eat and shit and sleep like ordinary men? My heart is hammering so hard I feel it might burst. I need another challenge. I'm sweating.

"Fetch some more beer."

Compton goes to do it; the tent flap closes behind him.

I can't sit; I have to pace. As I turn to put down my cup, my eye is drawn to the shadows beyond the table. There is a figure on the floor, huddled against the fabric wall. Its back is to me. Its straw-colored hair curls over its collar.

Instantly I am drenched in cold. It is *him*. The ghost or vision or whatever devilish thing it is that I have seen before. He has not appeared to me for some time—not since my father's death. But now he is back.

This time he looks taller, older—no longer a boy, but a young man like me. Still, in my mind I cannot call him anything else but *the boy*. As I stare, he turns to face me, rolling his head against the cloth wall as if it were solid brick and he were leaning on it. He looks fit, healthy; his clothes—a doublet and hose such as a gentleman's servant might wear—are plain but clean. His face, though, is horrible. Mouth gaping, dribbling, he is crying from his deeply shadowed eyes. I can see the glisten of wet eyeballs and of fat, rolling tears. He makes no attempt to hide his shame or to wipe the snot and spittle from his face.

Rage seizes me. I throw my cup. Solid though he looks, it passes straight through him, hits the fabric wall, and drops, leaving the cloth rippling.

He is still crying. I throw the jug, too, though I know it's useless, and the balled-up tablecloth; I pull off my surcoat and throw that. I am in a frenzy. I think: *Why has he come to me now?* This tournament is the celebration of the birth of my son and heir: Why must he poison my moment of triumph? Is he jealous? Is he the ghost of my murdered uncle, one of those boys killed in the Tower, tortured by the sight of me leading the life he should have had? Is he weeping in rage?

If he is, I have no sympathy. I wish him in hell, where he belongs. I tell him so—can he hear me? God only knows— then I rip aside the tent flap and stumble out into the cold of the yard.

38

Seeing the boy leaves me with a feeling of inexplicable dread. A few days later, looking back, that dread seems like a premonition. I have been visited by calamity. My infant son is dead.

I sit, staring out of the window. I don't recall when I last moved. It is raining. I am watching the rain.

"After all," says Wolsey quietly, standing somewhere behind me. "Your incomparable mother lost three."

Outside, black branches drip, and, as a bird takes flight, a remnant of gray slush slides and splatters to the ground. The wind whirls, blowing raindrops hard against the glass.

"And you are young. There will be—"

"Others. I know."

But fifty-two days, as I have discovered, is enough to become attached to a child.

He died very quietly, they said. Not much fussing and fretting. I would have liked to hold him, but I do not admit this. I comfort Catherine and talk robustly of our future. Then I come and sit, and watch the rain. I feel hollow, as if I have been carrying my son inside me—as if he filled every inch of me—and now he is gone. In the space he has left there is a dark feeling, dark as the black branches.

I say to Wolsey, "I have a task for you."

"Sir?"

"You will get my Council to consent to a campaign in France."

"Ah. Yes."

"As you predicted, the French king and the pope are no longer allies. Rome will support us."

"Indeed, Pope Julius will be delighted." Wolsey pauses. "Your Council less so. But I can bring them round."

"The Spanish king is ready to invade in the south. We will open a second front in the northeast," I say. "And I will lead our troops myself."

"Now, *that* the Council will certainly oppose. Without . . ." He hesitates. "Sir, without an heir, they will argue that the danger to the nation is too great."

The raindrops on the windowpanes collect, shimmering, and run. "Tell me what you want achieved, you said." My voice is quiet, and absolutely stony. "So I am telling you."

39

The whole ship vibrates as the cannon fire; I can feel it in the rail I'm gripping—I can feel it through the soles of my boots.

Gun smoke drifts sideways in the evening sunlight. To the starboard side, the fortress town of Calais is sliding into view, the outline of its cathedral showing above the high walls, proud against the skyline. The cannon on board our ship— and those on the rest of the fleet—fire booming salvo after booming salvo, answered by the guns on the walls of the town.

We're pounding nothing but our ears: It's a celebratory display as I arrive with my fleet at this English city on the northernmost tip of France, the last remnant of what used to be our vast territories on this continent. Eighty years ago, Henry V's son was crowned king of France, but since then the crown and the land have been lost in war, and only Calais and the surrounding area remain in English hands. Now I am here to rectify that injustice: I am here to win back France.

The guns are so loud, I can't help laughing. "It sounds like the end of the world!"

Beside me, Wolsey smiles. He is still a little green and has only just emerged from his cabin. "Compton's offering odds that they can hear it at Dover," he says.

To Bishop Fox, who stands beyond him, I say, "This man has the constitution of an ox. But no sea legs." I clasp Wolsey round the shoulders. "Remind me not to make you an admiral."

Brandon appears at my other side to survey the flotilla of small boats, decorated with flags and overladen with waving people, which are weaving their way out of the harbor to meet us. Slanting sunlight shines off Brandon's breastplate and gauntlets and picks out the ridiculously large rubies on his sword hilt. "Ever get the feeling the Almighty's smiling on you?" he says. "Someone should tell the king of Spain he jumped the wrong way."

"He'll realize soon enough."

Three months ago I lost Catherine's father as my ally: He double-crossed me and made peace with France. So much for being a good father to me. But I don't need him; Wolsey has proved as adept at finding replacement allies as he is at producing coins from Brandon's ears. He has delivered me, instead, the mighty Emperor Maximilian as my fighting partner. Maximilian rules a sizable chunk of middle Europe; he is a powerful ally.

Fox's thoughts have turned to Maximilian too. "The emperor is said to be the most unreliable man in Christendom, sir. We must watch him at every turn."

I smile at Fox. "I rely on you to foresee all difficulties."

Nothing can dent my mood. I have been lost in the planning of this campaign for so many happy days at Greenwich— kneeling over huge charts spread out on the floor of my chamber: marching formations and plans of camp, designs of pavilions and of new types of siege engines.

Now at last we are here. Yesterday, they say, there was terrible rain in the Channel; today we have had a perfect passage in glorious sunshine. I have stood on deck throughout, the salt wind in my face, flags fluttering above me: the papal banner alongside the lions of England.

I'm even *wearing* a miracle, for goodness' sake: a suit of armor that's easy to walk in. It has a thousand joints that move as I do, every which way. Over it there's a tabard of white cloth of gold with the red cross of St. George the Dragon Slayer on my chest.

And best of all, back in England, Catherine has a new child in her belly. God smiles indeed. This time, it will be a boy who lives.

40

On my first night in the field there is a downpour. As darkness falls and the trumpets sound for the watch sentries to take up their positions, teams of pavilioners are still struggling to stem leaks in the officers' tents.

One of my largest pavilions—the walls six feet high and double layered—is up and secure, but still I can't relax. I call for a horse to be saddled up, and, wrapping myself in a hooded cloak, I set out for a tour of the camp. Just like Henry V: On the rain-soaked night before the Battle of Agincourt, he toured his camp to raise the morale of his troops. I have brought my *History of Henry V*—the translation I made myself—packed in one of my trunks. I intend to keep it to hand.

The rain has extinguished campfires; the dark is inky, the tents looming hulks with the occasional glow of a light within. In front of me the lantern-bearers squelch through the mud and step low, suddenly, as a foot goes into a water-filled rut. Rain drips off the front of my hood; my legs are soaked already, and the damp is seeping through the thick lining of my gloves.

The camp is pitched to a design I perfected myself: a square plan, with two main "streets" dividing it, each thirty paces wide, intersecting in the middle in a cross. It is a little city, and the largest tents have signs outside like taverns; they swing and creak in the wind and provide running points for water. The Chalice is home to the chaplains, the Gauntlet to the master of the armory. The Beds is where the surgeons are bedding down, and one of Wolsey's collection of pavilions goes by the name of the Inflamed House—which is a stretch for any place in this weather.

Farther toward the camp's perimeter, ordinary men are huddled in the rain, getting rest as best they can. Some are sitting wrapped in small sheets of canvas, like old women in shawls. Others have collected branches and made rudimentary huts. Pale faces appear as I pass.

"I am in the same condition as you, tonight, comrades!" I call to them.

A moment's hesitation—realization—then they scramble out and stand to attention.

I stop in front of a man who has emerged from a well-constructed shelter. "Your officers would do well to take advice from you, my friend—you are expert, I see, at shifting for yourself in any weather."

"It's all in knowing how to make your hut, sir," he says. "I'm snug as a small pig in there, sir."

"Good man. And you?"

His neighbor is squeezing a woolen cap nervously in his hands, sending a fair trickle of water, unnoticed, onto his feet. "An Englishman is not afraid of the damp, sir."

I ride on, my horse stepping carefully through the mud. At the outer edge of the camp wagons are stationed in a protective circle, interspersed with artillery. The soldier guarding the nearest wagon kneels as I approach. I jump down from my horse and squelch over to him.

"Get up, man. You're wet enough as it is. What's in these wagons?"

"These, Your Grace? Bows and bowstrings, sheaves of arrows, demilances, and whole spears. Oh, and stakes to drive into the ground in front of the archers."

"For the French cavalry to skewer themselves on."

The man grins. "That's it, sir."

I make my way to the nearest gun carriage. "This is called an organ, isn't it?"

The man guarding it opens his mouth; then, finding that no words come out, nods.

It is a many-barreled piece for firing grapeshot through a breach in a city wall or at a body of troops.

"And this?"

"The bombard, Your Grace, sir," says another man. He holds up several layers of canvas for me to see.

I run my hand over the smooth metal of the cannon. The bore is enormous; looking down it by lantern light is like peering into a cave. "How much gunpowder for this monster?"

"Eighty pounds to charge it, sir."

"Your skill," I say, looking round at them, "is worth more than the whole Jewel House to me."

The same Jewel House that, incidentally, I have brought with me: a fortune in jewels and ornaments housed in a well-guarded tent called the Flagon, several hundred yards away. I will need it when I play host to Emperor Maximilian—I am determined to make an impression.

When I return to the center of the camp, they have finished putting up my timber house, which has traveled from England in sections that pack flat into carts. The place has two rooms, lantern-horn windows, and fireplaces and chimneys. Its outside is painted like brickwork, and the inside is hung with golden tapestry. My bed is full size, carved and gilded, and hung round with cloth-of-gold curtains.

Compton helps me out of my wet clothes and into a nightgown that has been warming by the fire. I climb into bed, and he pulls the hangings closed. Even in the dark, the gold threads glow.

Strangely, the bed starts to trundle. It seems to be on wheels.

I dream that I am in a fountain made of russet satin, curiously decorated with snakes, modeled in paper and painted; around me eight gargoyles are spewing cloth-of-silver water from their mouths. I am trying not to laugh. Not that anyone could see it, beneath my helmet—but sitting in my armor like this, with the lower edge of my cuirass pressing into my thighs, laughter is painful.

Brandon is in a litter somewhere behind me, and is, I know, wishing he had drunk slightly less wine. As we are drawn round the tiltyard, the crowd cheers, and there's a thunder of stamping on the wooden boards of the grandstand.

With a great noise of trumpets, my fountain stops in front of one of the many triumphs of Harry Guildford's carpentry team. It's a huge fortress: entirely black, with THE DOLOROUS CASTLE written above it in silver, on a painted wooden board cut to look like a waving pennant. Standing high on the battlements there's a knight in coal-black armor, with black ostrich plumes sprouting from his helmet. Though the visor is down, concealing his face, I have a nagging feeling I should know who he is. I just can't for the life of me remember.

41

"Enemy troops are assembling some distance to the south, sir, near Enguingate. It looks to me like an attempt to resupply the city." Sir John Neville's hair is standing up in spikes. He has his helmet, just now pulled off, under one arm; with the other he holds the reins of his horse, which is stamping and shifting beneath him.

"Then for God's sake let's stop them," I say. "The city will hold out indefinitely if supplies continue to get through."

It is dawn. After ten days' march, we have reached the city of Thérouanne, to which the foreward and rearward of my army have spent the past month laying siege. A well-fortified French stronghold, it sits on the north bank of the river Lys six miles upstream from Aire. Emperor Maximilian has made a strong case to me for its capture.

Now my bodyguard of mounted archers parts to let Francis Bryan ride in; I give him permission to speak. "A messenger's just arrived, Your Grace, from the Earl of Essex and Sir John Peachy. They took a prisoner three miles south of here—he says the French will come in from the north and south simultaneously."

"They'll distract our troops on the north side—and make a quick dash in with the food on the south. That makes sense," says Brandon beside me, his horse's harness jingling as it tosses its head. "They will think the south wall is still unguarded."

I nod, looking down from the hill we stand on to where long columns of men, horses, and wagons are snaking slowly across the river. "Then we have the advantage of surprise."

Until our arrival with the last section of the army, my troops have not been able to encircle Thérouanne completely—and so the French have continued to resupply the city. Now my section—the middle ward—must move to the south of the city to complete the stranglehold; this means taking sixteen thousand men and all our wagons, tents, artillery, and ordnance across the river, which skirts the southern wall of the city.

With timber brought from England the carpenters have spent the night constructing five bridges; now, in the hazy light of dawn, the army is making its crossing.

I turn to Bryan. "Instruct the troops on the north side to prepare themselves for battle. Rhys ap Thomas can take a detachment of cavalry forward to engage the French first. He may be able to hold them off entirely."

As Bryan leaves, my bodyguard closes round me, and we ride down to cross the river.

Once across the water, the wagons and provisions establish themselves in defensive order out of range of the guns on the city walls; the fighting men move south to face the plain where the French will have to make their approach. It is bordered by a forest on one side and a ridge of hills on the other.

I instruct the gunner commanders. "Use the ridge there.

I want a row of the lighter guns to give cover as I send scouts forward."

"Sir."

I place a bank of archers where they can cover the plain too. Shielded behind a hedge, they take up position, planting their arrows point-down in the ground in front of them. I ride up to Compton and say, "You and I can take the cavalry forward first, infantry following."

Compton hesitates, then says, "Sir, please stay back. The Council won't countenance you riding out in the first wave."

"The Council be damned. I am here to lead my men."

Brandon, who has heard, turns his horse to approach closer, and says in a low voice, "Hal, the French are only trying to bring supplies in. If you go down in the first push, for the sake of a side of bacon . . ."

I stare at him. "Christ, have you been listening to Fox?"

He makes a movement that, if it weren't for his armor, might be a shrug. "This isn't Agincourt. But something else might be. Stick around for it."

In the distance I can see splashes of blue and gold now against the brown-green fields. It is the French cavalry, riding toward our lines.

I look back at Brandon and, beyond him, to where the arms of England billow in the breeze, held high by Harry Guildford, to whom I've given the job of standard-bearer. "If I'm sitting out, then so are you," I say. Then I turn my horse and ride away.

From the safety of high ground, with Brandon beside me,

I survey the mass of waiting troops: the mounted knights at the front; behind them infantrymen hidden beneath a forest of pikes and bills, the vicious spikes glinting silver. A dull thick heat is gathering; inside my helmet, sweat trickles down my temples.

On the ridge to my left a flag drops and the guns fire across the plain. The French cavalry, weighed down by large saddlebags—no doubt the food for the city—have stopped some distance from our lines; it's clear they haven't been expecting to meet such a large body of troops in their path.

Hesitating, they are now sitting ducks; a cloud of arrows streaks up from behind the hedge. A hundred feet up, the chisel-tipped points turn and plunge toward the French. Arrows whistle and sing; horses scream and whinny as the missiles find their targets.

The French riders turn and begin to retreat, but they run straight into the next line of their countrymen coming on from behind. And, at that moment, my cavalrymen spur their horses into a headlong charge.

The ground, churned by hooves, is muddy; in the melee men and animals slip and are trampled. There is shouting, metallic clanking, and the strange piercing shrieks of horses overcome with pain and fear. It is thrilling; it is like a vast, vicious tiltyard.

Brandon points with a metal paw. "My God, the French are throwing down their weapons! Look! They can't retreat fast enough!"

I can see in his eyes exactly what I feel: it's unbearable to watch.

"Coming, then?" I say, and I see him grin.

We slap our visors down, and I signal to the captain of my guard. Then I draw my sword and spur my horse to gallop full pelt down the ridge. I yell to Brandon, though he'll never hear—with my visor down, it's like yelling in a bucket:

"Who says, eh? Who says this isn't Agincourt?"

We pelt down the passageway, hand in hand. Catherine is half running, skittering in soft pink slippers, her free hand supporting the curve of her belly. I'm striding, dressed all in silver cloth today, my sword wagging at my hip.

Forest animals on tapestries bob and ripple as we pass; the dark wooden paneling is carved into trees and fruit; the light sconces jut like branches from the walls, golden flame-leaves flickering.

We reach the double doors of the Council Chamber; I punch them open. Faces turn: a row down each side of the long table. Bony hands lie on the board, flat and dry, some stained with ink, none with blisters from handling swords or lances. There's a shuffle and a scraping of chairs. Gingerly the noblemen and bishops lower themselves and kneel; they look like wizened children, barely able to see over the tabletop.

"Well? Didn't I tell you it would be a triumph?" I say to my Council. "Get up off your knees, all of you, for God's sake. Sit. I have called you together so that you can offer me your congratulations."

I draw up a chair for Catherine and stand behind her, my hands on her shoulders.

One councillor has creaked to his feet. "We offer our heartfelt congratulations, Your Grace. And to you, dear

Queen, on your most blessed impending event—you carry the hope of the nation within you." Catherine nods, placing her hands contentedly on her stomach. "But most of all, sir, we give fervent thanks to Almighty God that you are returned to us safely."

"I would like less opposition next time," I say as he sits down. "I would like less skepticism. Consider, gentlemen: You advised against this glorious expedition."

"And would do so again," says another voice.

It's Archbishop Warham. I stare at him. "An *obstinate* skeptic! Do you put no value on what we have achieved?"

He's remained sitting; he looks down at his hands, which twitch a little as they lie on the table. "If you will forgive my plain speaking, Your Grace," he says, "in my view the expedition has not been a great success."

"I would be interested to hear you define your terms." I swipe a lavender sprig from a vase and sit, twirling it in my fingers. "I have entirely destroyed one of the best-fortified towns in France; I have captured and occupied another. I have won a glorious victory—to rival Agincourt. And I have brought back as my prisoners some of the leading noblemen of the French court. What more, Warham, do you want?"

"Indeed, Your Grace, but in doing all this you have spent enough to fill a well of gold." His doleful gaze lifts to me. "To what purpose? One French dog-hole is destroyed, another has become an outpost that will eat up money and men. What use to England is a single landlocked city surrounded by French territory?" He shakes his head slowly. "It will cost a fortune to maintain; it will cost a fortune to defend. It gives us nothing: nothing strategically, nothing commercially. The only person it benefits is the emperor."

A murmur goes round the table. I wonder if someone will stop him, argue the point—but he goes on uninterrupted, "Did you never wonder why Emperor Maximilian advised you to destroy Thérouanne and capture Tournai? They are strategically important in relation to *his* territories, not yours; it is mightily convenient to him that they are out of French hands. You paid for the enterprise; you even paid him to fight for you. I am sorry to say it, sir, but he has won this round of the game hands down."

I am sitting entirely unmoving now, staring at the archbishop. There is a burning in my stomach. I say quietly, "I am on the brink of conquest."

He does not reply. I crumple the lavender in my fingers and rise. "Do you think because I have brought the army home that I have finished? The job is only half done. The troops are back because summer is over—the campaigning season is over. But we will return next year." My fists are on the table; I am leaning toward him.

Behind me, Catherine says to Warham mildly, "My father, King Ferdinand, has realized how foolish he was in not taking part in the invasion. He has already indicated he wants to join with England next year."

I have not taken my eyes from the old man's face. "So. Next summer I will return to France with a larger force and in alliance with both Emperor Maximilian *and* King Ferdinand of Spain. There is no way France will be able to withstand the onslaught. I shall be crowned at Paris before the year is out." I smile, but not amiably. "I wonder, sir, if you will live to see it? Let us hope so. You can apologize to me then.

"In the meantime, gentlemen, those among you of a less pessimistic disposition have much work to do. We must prepare to rule France."

43

"And perhaps my sister's son could stand as godfather?" Catherine shifts to face me, her hair fanning out across the pillow; here, with the bed curtains shut, it's like a little private world of our own.

The only light comes from a candle burning just above us in its niche on the carved headboard. In the golden glow it casts, Catherine's cheeks look creamy, her eyes darker than usual and shining. I put my hand under the covers and lay it on her belly; I like to feel the child moving. She says, "Where do you think we should have him brought up?"

"Half here, half in France. The people must know him in all his territories—not feel he is a foreigner."

"I meant which house! Perhaps, Eltham or Richmond . . . Oh, don't send him away too young, will you?"

I smile and prop myself up on my elbow. "I see how it's going to be. He'll have you twisted round his little finger."

"Absolutely," says Catherine. "In Spain they say the English hate their children, beat them too much, and pack them off to live in other men's houses."

"Do they? Funny, that. In England we say that the Spaniards are thieves, the Germans are tipplers, the French unchaste, the Scots perfidious, the Danes bloodthirsty . . ."

A fine linen pillow hits me full in the face. I grab it from her. "What? Isn't that right? Maybe the *Spaniards* are tipplers, the *Germans* unchaste—"

We're both laughing now—well, she's growling and laughing, and trying to tug the pillow back out of my grasp. Suddenly she stops with a small gasp, and rolls away from me.

"What?" I say. She doesn't move. I can only see a jumble of nightdress and bedclothes and hair. "Don't sulk."

"No, it's not that." She's curled up; her voice is muffled.

"What, then?"

"Hal." She turns and looks at me bleakly. "I'm bleeding."

44

"Benedixit, deditque discipulis suis, dicens: Accipite, et bibite ex eo omnes, hic est enim calix Sanguinis mei . . ."

He blessed it, and gave it to his disciples, saying: Take and drink ye all of this, for this is the chalice of my blood . . .

Beyond the small grille-window of the partition, the priest's voice rises and falls in its familiar pattern, intoning the words of the morning mass. I'm in my private closet, the one adjoining my Privy Chamber. Beside me, Wolsey sits making rapid notes in the margin of a dispatch. There's a pile of discarded papers at my feet.

Wolsey says, "How is the queen?"

"Fine."

Stupid answer. She's not fine at all. She lost the child—a boy. They said the half-grown thing was formed enough that you could see its face. But her body is healing. And I have next season's invasion of France to think about.

"Remind me of the original proposal."

"Sir?"

"The treaty with Spain. Come on, I want to go hunting as soon as Mass is over."

Wolsey nods. "It is proposed that King Ferdinand will invade Guyenne or Aquitaine—"

"Before next June."

"Yes. With fifteen thousand foot soldiers, one and a half

thousand heavy-armed cavalry, one and a half thousand light-armed cavalry, and twenty-five pieces of artillery. Of which twelve will be large and thirteen small."

He's reeling this off without reference to notes. His memory, I reflect—not for the first time—is prodigious. I say, "And all land he takes will be handed over to us."

"Exactly."

"Money?"

"You contribute twenty thousand gold crowns a month, from the point when he starts fighting."

"Meanwhile, we invade Picardy or Normandy—also before June—and each of us puts a fleet to sea before the end of April."

"Yes."

"My God, he ought to be happy with that. It's more than generous. What's his problem?"

Wolsey raises his eyebrows, inhaling deeply. "He wants to enlist six thousand German mercenaries and asks that you bear the cost of their transport *and*, before the beginning of June, send a year's pay for them, at twenty thousand crowns per month."

"As a lump sum? That's outrageous." I think for a moment. "Could we do it?"

"We'd need to raise a tax. Sir—" Wolsey gestures toward my kneeling desk, which stands in front of the grille-window.

I kneel in silence while the priest takes communion. Then I cross myself and stand up. "What else?"

Wolsey draws a paper out of the stack beside him. "Just one more thing. Our agents in Rome report that, now that the pope wants everyone's hands free for a crusade against the Turk, His Holiness plans to ask you to renounce your claim to France."

"When I'm just about to conquer it? The answer is no."

"And, in return for this, he will," he reads from the document, "'let the king of England have the rule of Scotland, which belongs to his one-year-old nephew.'"

"Interesting . . ."

"Indeed." His eyes flick up to me. "But there is something further you should know. It has been reported that your sister, the queen of Scots, will agree to this, because she expects her son to inherit England in due course."

I stare at Wolsey. He is talking about my sister Meg; she married the king of Scotland soon after our mother died. I say, "She expects *what*?"

"I quote: 'Since the king of England has no children, his nephew will be next in line to succeed.'"

"*Yet.* I have no children *yet*, Meg. Give me that."

I read the dispatch. It reports that the general view is that this latest miscarriage proves that Catherine is unable to carry a healthy child who will live, so there is no prospect of an heir.

The room is still as I scan the paper a second time; next door the priest's voice drones on.

I take a breath—shake my head. I feel winded. "This is ridiculous. There is time."

"Of course there is."

The paper crumples in my hand; I throw it to the floor. "There *is* time."

45

Of course there's time. A new year has begun: It is spring, again, and Catherine is pregnant—again. This is the year I will conquer France; this is the year I will have a son.

Surely.

A fresh-scented morning: Everything outside is unfurling, new green and dewy. I'm just back from hunting; I stink of horse sweat and my sweat; I'm smeared with animal blood and comprehensively mud splashed. I am also happy. My thoughts are still with the chase: the hard riding, the perilous jumps, the horn blasts, the howling and barking, and the wonderful sight of the bucks going down—lurching, torn, glassy eyed.

As the grooms of the wardrobe deliver the clothes I want to the door of my bedchamber (only a select group of people, of course, are allowed to touch my sanctified flesh), a letter arrives. It is from Wolsey, who is deep in business—papers and ink, seals and figures—in his rooms at Westminster.

Reading, I swat away the men who are trying to unlace my sleeves, take a step back, and lean against the wall. My heart has done a flip; my hands are shaking; my pulse seems to be thumping in my stomach. I read the letter twice, get blood on it from my gloves, and then leave the room at speed, pounding along the gallery in my riding boots and muddying the new rush-matting.

Guards twitch aside their halberds as I reach the entrance to a chamber; I slam open the door.

"Did you know he was going to do this?"

I've caught a glimpse of a tableau: ladies sitting in well-bred poses in a sunlit bay window, gable headdresses bent over their sewing—a scene of industry and quiet conversation. Now all heads turn to me. Seeing my expression, the faces suddenly blank; each lady gets up from her stool and sinks immediately into a deep curtsy. Some of the sewing—some of it my own shirts, halfway through being embroidered—has slipped down the sides of skirts to the floor.

The ladies remain in their curtsies; the figure in the center rises again—very upright—and says, "My lord?" Catherine is studiedly formal; she is signaling as strongly as if she were waving her arms: *Wait. We are in public.*

I don't give a damn where we are. I shout, "Did. You. Know?"

A small movement of her hand to her ladies: *Go.* The ladies straighten and file out, almost stumbling in their eagerness to get away. The last shuts the door carefully behind her.

Once they've gone, Catherine moves forward, her hands reaching out to take mine. "Hal, what's happened? What's the matter?"

I sidestep to keep my distance. "He's pulled out of the agreement."

"Who?"

"Your father!" I throw the letter at her. She makes a swipe to catch it, but it zigzags through the air. She stands looking at me. I shout, "Your bastard, pox-ridden father! Not only that, he's persuaded the emperor out of it too. They've made sodding terms with the French. There will be no invasion." I walk up the room and back again, take a glass dish from a table and smash it into the hearth.

For several moments Catherine hasn't moved. Now she stoops, with difficulty in her boned dress, to pick up the letter from the floor—I don't help.

She scans the paper, looks up at me. "Hal, he's done this before. Can't you still—"

"Yes, he's done this before," I say in a singsong speaking-to-an-idiot tone. "But *this* time I don't have the money to mount a campaign on my own. I. Am. Destroyed." I dig my hands into my hair. "*This* was the year. Christ! *This* was the year I was going to be crowned in Paris."

"Any agreement made with the French won't last."

I stride over to her, take her shoulders. "Were you in on it? That's all I need you to tell me. Because I know you have this, this"—I grimace in disgust—"*private* correspondence with your father, and I'm sure he advises you on how you should string me along like a dog, and I want to know just how much the two of you have been making a fool out of me."

"He can write what he likes; my loyalty is to you."

"Then it's so strange—isn't it?—that you don't deliver."

Silence. We hold each other's gaze. I say, quietly and

distinctly, "This is what you are for. Do you think I married you for love? I married you to give me an alliance with Spain. And sons." I look down at her belly. "Will this one live, do you think? For a change?"

My God, her control is magnificent. Not a single muscle in her face twitches. But her eyes . . . She looks as if she is drowning.

Six months later, on a clear and crisp autumn day that I spend flying hawks, another small coffin is placed in the crypt of the friars' chapel at Greenwich.

46

Four more winters pass. How do I stand it? I cannot even bear waiting while they dress me in the mornings.

The old king of France dies in his bed, leaving no sons to succeed him. The king of Spain—Catherine's father—dies too, before I can take revenge on him for his shitty betrayal of my glorious plan.

I find that I am no longer the youngest ruler in Christendom. A horse-faced young duke named Francis is the new king of France; he is as keen on empire-building as I am and has his sights set on Italy. In Spain the new king is Catherine's eighteen-year-old nephew Charles, who has been brought up Dutch, and whose mother, they say, is mad.

How curious the world is.

And now the campaigning season has come round again. I am not in an incense-clouded Paris cathedral or even a gun smoke–filled battlefield. I am not in France in any capacity. I am at Hampton Court, Wolsey's redbrick palace on the Thames. In a garden. Waiting, still, for my empire. Waiting, still, for my sons.

There is a child, though: a girl. Mary. Two years old now, she is standing next to me on the gravel path, staring at a clump of marigolds and pointing one small finger toward a bee.

"Stripy," she says gravely. She watches it for a long

moment, then she looks at me. "The bee is buzzy." She frowns and corrects herself. *"Busy."* Then she smiles delightedly. "The bee is buzzy, too!"

I swing her up into my arms. Her face is level with mine. Carved beasts on green-and-white wooden poles stand sentry at intervals along the clipped borders: lion, dragon, greyhound, antelope, dun cow, unicorn. The unicorn is odd, short snouted and fierce looking, its white-painted body lit by bright sunlight against a background of dark, gathering rain clouds.

Seeing it, Mary squeaks and hides her face in the crook of my neck, one hand gripping the gold chain that lies across my shoulders.

In her stiffened bodice and thick skirts she is a solid little bundle, though she is small for her age. If I shut my eyes and open them again, can I will myself to be holding a boy?

"Look at it," I instruct her. "You are not afraid of anything."

She lifts her head. She is a pretty child, her eyes the same blue as the sapphires edging her hood. Her gown is violet tinseled satin, the cuffs fur-edged, the sleeves lined with green silk. She is studying the jewels on my collar now, tapping them to see if they will pop, like bubbles.

"Look at it."

She looks. Then she brings her hands up in front of her, fingers curled like claws, and makes a little growling noise.

"Stop laughing, Papa," she tells me. "I am fiercing the monster."

As I set the girl down, Catherine says, "Her women tell me she never cries."

"Of course she doesn't. She's my daughter."

The small girl in violet satin runs off, stops, comes back, does a wobbly curtsy to me, and runs off again. Catherine turns and walks after her. I watch my wife's retreating back for a moment—the long thick skirts, the black veil. From the back you cannot tell that she is carrying a new child. It has been a long wait, this time: the first pregnancy in two years. But she has begun to have children who live. First the girl—and now I am certain that she is carrying the boy.

"The betrothal can take place this autumn, sir," says Wolsey, suddenly at my shoulder, "but I am stipulating that they must not be married until the dauphin is fifteen. That gives you plenty of time to change your mind. And, of course, time may change it for you: The dauphin may not live to be fifteen."

He is talking of Mary's marriage; we are engaged in a dance of negotiations with the new French king. Francis has lately been blessed with a son—this dauphin. So, if Mary marries the boy, my son (the baby Catherine is now carrying) will rule England, and my grandson—Mary's son—will one day rule France. Except, of course, that I will conquer France long before that. There is time, as Wolsey said, to change my mind. For now it is just another finger in the pie.

"And they've agreed, have they? To the delay?"

Wolsey waves a hand dismissively. "They will."

I look at him, expectant.

"Oh," he says, "there've been lots of ridiculous queries

and quibbles. You know the French; they're incapable of a straightforward yes."

I start off down the gravel path toward the house; Wolsey follows. I say, "Queries? About what?"

"Well . . . most recently, the validity of your marriage."

My pace slows. For a moment I'm silent, then I laugh uproariously. "God, don't they love to take the piss? Ridiculous. Do they need to see the bloody dispensation?"

We pass through a door and climb the private stairs that lead to my lodgings. Wolsey says, "Sir, I would like to set a date for Princess Mary's betrothal ceremony. Would you prefer it to be before the queen's confinement—or afterward, so we know the outcome?"

Outcome. He means: Whether or not the child is a boy. Whether or not it lives. Whether or not, if Mary were my only heir, I would want to send her to France.

"There is no doubt of the outcome." We reach the head of the stairs and turn left; as I approach the door to a chamber, it is opened for me; the view inside is of a handful of men talking and laughing and lounging on benches. One of the youngest looks pink with annoyance, as if he's being teased. "We'll have the ceremony at Greenwich, as soon as it can be arranged. Spare no expense. I want the French dazzled. All right?" I pat Wolsey on his well-padded shoulder and say to the room, "Tennis?"

"Yup." Brandon's already on his feet, reaching for the case of rackets.

"You're too slow for me these days; I'll play with Norris." I take the case and sling it to Henry Norris, one of my new younger gentlemen of the Privy Chamber, an easy and dependable youth. Brandon is standing astonished, opening and closing his mouth like a fish.

"I don't blame you, Brandon, but you do sometimes forget that you're older than me. You're, what, nearly thirty-five now? You've done well to keep up with me as long as you have."

At this there's general laughter and a sardonic comment from Bryan's direction featuring the word "grandpa."

"And you," I say. Several men start forward eagerly. I click my fingers. "Damn it, I've forgotten your name. Boleyn's son."

A dark-haired youth, the victim of the teasing, steps forward, flushing pink again—but this time with delight. "George, sir."

"George, come and run the book." I grin at Wolsey. "Forgive me, father. You know I'm just *not* interested unless there's money on it."

47

"Chances?"

"Ten to one. Against."

It's November—less than a month since Mary and the French prince were betrothed amid breathtakingly expensive celebrations at Greenwich. The dauphin, who is not yet even a year old, did not attend in person—instead the Admiral of France, as his stand-in, passed the large diamond ring onto Mary's finger. Mary herself behaved well, although she became fidgety during the sermon and had to be picked up.

Since then we've stayed on at Greenwich, and tonight Catherine is in labor.

At one end of the Great Hall Norris has set up an archery target on a wooden frame. In front of it, on a stack of boxes, stands a candle in its holder. We're laying bets on whether I can put the flame out with a shot.

Some say you don't need a direct hit to do it; the arrow's tail feathers make enough wind as they pass. They don't—I know from experience.

I'm not just aiming to hit the candle; I'm aiming to hit the wick.

"Come on, it's impossible." George Boleyn shakes his head. "Even if you were sober. Let's make it interesting. Fifty to one."

"One shot only."

"Right."

We've been shooting all night. We've been drinking all night too. Chairs, with cloaks slung over them, are ranged haphazardly around the great fireplace; on a long table nearby the cloth is bunched and rumpled, littered with remnants of food and with cups, some upright, some not.

Now, as I pass the shaft of my arrow under the bowstring and rest its head in position against my knuckle, I am watched by the eager faces of Boleyn, Norris, my cousin the Marquis of Exeter, and Thomas Wyatt, the handsome young son of one of my councillors. Compton is there too, but he never looks eager, just amused and watchful.

I nock and draw.

I think: *become* the arrow. See it hit the target before you've even released it. If you can do that, everything else drops away. It's a beautiful feeling. There's only the arrow and the target—and they're not even two separate things any more. Arrow-target. Joined. All one.

Reflections of firelight and candlelight play in the dark panes of the hall windows. Beyond, under a black, empty sky, the world is crisp, clear, and bitterly cold.

The arrow flies. It hits the wick; the flame goes out.

"I'm too damned good. Aren't I?" I beam at George. "Cough up."

"Um. I'll write you a note."

"This'll do." I take a spare arrow and hook it under the gold chain around his neck, lifting it clear and dropping it into Compton's outstretched hands. Everyone laughs.

We send for more drink, and I expound—somewhat woozily—on the relative merits of my son being called Henry, after me, or Edward, after my mother's father.

Meanwhile, Wyatt and Boleyn have formed a plan to mark the moment the glad tidings arrive: They've ordered up a cask of good wine from the cellars and are even now rolling it, with curses and mishaps, up two ladders.

Wyatt, a tall youth of usually impressive strength, is now laughing so hard he has to stop and cling to the ladder weakly, leaning his forehead on a rung.

When he's recovered himself, he and George hoist the cask up to balance on one of the crossbeams of the hall roof, at the end nearest the main doorway, where they tie it to the corner truss with a messy net of ropes. The cask's end overhangs the beam, with its stopper clearly visible. They've adjusted the stopper carefully so that it's slightly loosened, but not leaking.

"So, sir," George explains to me, "the man comes in, gives the news, you shoot off the stopper, and we hold him under the waterfall—"

"*Wine*fall," corrects Wyatt.

"Mouth open . . ."

"He'll be the first to drink the prince's health," says Exeter, looking suddenly solemn. "An honorable dousing."

"Don't worry," says George. "We'll give you next turn." Exeter grins.

By the time the man arrives, more wine has been downed, and the room is very slightly pitching when I walk.

I'm wondering what the odds are now of me hitting the cask at all, let alone the stopper.

"Well, sir, is my son born?" I've aimed, drawn the bow-string back. My eyes are on the stopper. Out of the corner of my vision, I can tell by the way they're standing that Norris and Boleyn have taken the startled man by the elbows and maneuvered him to stand under the cask—which of course he hasn't seen. Momentarily I wonder about the whole cask coming loose from its ropes and landing on the poor sod's head; the thought makes me laugh and is not helping my aim.

My arms begin to ache. I realize, abruptly, that the man hasn't answered. That there is, in fact, a weird silence in the room.

"Is my son born?" I repeat, my eyes still on the stopper.

"Your Grace . . . ," begins the man. And hesitates.

Keeping the bow still full-drawn, I swing my arms down; the arrow is now trained directly on the man's face. "Is my son born *alive*?"

In the silence I have sobered up in an instant.

"Does the child live?"

The man's eyes are swimming. Despite his terror, he cannot hold my gaze. "Saving Your Grace, it . . . it is a girl. That is to say . . . *was* a girl. She lived for a few minutes. Long enough to be held, they said."

I change my aim fractionally and shoot. Not at the messenger—the man's legs buckle in relief. Instead a pane of glass in the window shatters. Shards of painted glass—pomegranate seeds and rose petals, Catherine's emblem and mine—rain into the black garden.

48

The sunshine on the water dazzles; reflections dance on the inner wall of the fountain, back and forth, back and forth—rippling, repetitive, like my thoughts.

"There is a message from the queen, sir."

"Later."

My hands are on the saddle. I swing myself up, turn the horse toward the gateway, and canter out of the courtyard. My company of young men follows.

We head toward the hunting park. Despite the early hour the day is already bright and hot; the air quivers in the distance above dry fields. The colors are garish: burning blue, lush green, and gold.

Another winter has passed, and a spring. There is something pressing on me. An emptiness that expands to fill everything until I cannot breathe.

At night I hardly sleep, by day the thoughts in my head run at double speed, while everything *out there* in the world seems slow and stupid, and strangely distant. When people speak to me, it feels as if I am underwater.

"The beaters have been out since early, sir," says Norris, as if from far away. "We will have good sport."

"How many horses stationed for me?"

"Ten, sir."

It is the same today as every day: We leave early; we stay

out until dark. The horses tire before I do—I need eight or ten a day. Wyatt complains I turn hunting into a martyrdom. It is simply that he cannot keep up with me.

When we reach the forest, the relief is intense. The rustling glades refresh me like water. The horses tread through sweet woodruff and violets, sorrel and cranesbill. Creepers swarm up trunks; ferns hold out their many-fingered hands. Dappled light flickers as the wind moves the tops of the trees. On the bark of one tree I see the deep grooves of heavy scratch marks, made by great talons or claws.

Time seems to pass in an instant. Now there is sweat running into my eyes. My breathing is loud and harsh. I am suddenly aware of the horse's exhaustion—yet it seems only moments since we started the chase.

Occasionally, at times like this, I will see something strange: a waking dream. Sometimes it is a dark-haired girl riding ahead. The sun glints off her—white and gold—as if she is wearing armor. Sometimes it is the serpent that I saw once, years ago, in a dream.

Today it is a white hart. Automatically I draw an arrow from my quiver, loose the reins to nock it, and shoot from horseback. One fluid movement—smooth and quick.

For a moment as the arrow flies, the hart seems to be a fair-haired youth, running. I blink, and the creature is the hart again, the arrow dodged, his back legs kicking up as he jumps a fallen tree.

They are nothing, these visions. It is just that I cannot sleep.

49

When I get back, Wolsey is waiting for me. It is very late.

He is in my chamber, sitting by the fire, hefty and solid as a piece of furniture. The curtains are drawn against the dark sky. His shadow lengthens toweringly upon them as he gets up: a fat man with a thin shadow.

I slump into a chair, call for wine. "What are you doing here? I thought you were busy banging heads together in pursuit of your peace treaty. Sit down, for God's sake."

"Something has occurred to me. An idea."

"Don't tell me—an alliance with the Turks because it is cheaper than a crusade? Heaven save us from your *ideas*. Talking of which, at what point are we going to break off my daughter's betrothal? We can't have that French brat in line to be king of England."

There is a short silence; Wolsey is looking at me placidly. I see my knee shaking and still it.

Wolsey says, "Do you sleep?"

"Like a log." I drain my glass and hold it out to the shadows, where the servants lurk. "Another."

I drain that, too.

"Stop," says Wolsey gently. *"Stop."* He waves his hand; the servants melt away. The door clicks shut softly behind them.

I fix him with a look that would fry a lesser man. He simply blinks at me.

A spasm in my chest: Something cold is coiled around my heart, squeezing. I get up and take a turn about the room. My whole body aches, but I can't relax. "It seems unfathomable how I have got to this point. How *you* have got me to this point. Empire and sons? What a joke. The eleventh year of my glorious reign and what do I have? A treaty with France and a daughter."

"Perhaps God gives you what you want, but not in the way you expect."

"Christ, don't give me a *priest's* answer! I am looking over the brink into . . ."

"Into what?"

"A void. Absolute nothingness."

"Your Grace. May I tell you my idea?"

"If it's quick."

"The emperor is in trouble. He needs help—quite desperately, I believe—to crush the rebellions in Spain. He has no money left."

The man carrying the title of "emperor" these days is no longer Maximilian, the most unreliable man in Christendom, as Fox once called him. *He* sleeps—reliably dead—in his grave, while the young kings of France and Spain have fought a crippling financial war to win his imperial crown. It came down, in the end, to threats and bribes. And, at the cost of one million gold florins, King Charles of Spain won.

So, Charles now has to his name Spain, Burgundy, the

Netherlands, Germany, Austria, some Italian states, parts of the New World . . . and no money. *Perhaps God gives you what you want, but not in the way you expect.*

Wolsey says, "It occurs to me there is a prize to be won here. Greater than we could ever have anticipated."

"Don't pause for dramatic effect. I'm not a congregation. Get on with it."

"You give Charles the ships and money he needs for Spain. In return, you demand a joint invasion of France, and his hand in marriage for your daughter."

I stop. I am at the far end of the room. Absently I reach out and touch the tapestry-covered wall in front of me: David's crown, rendered in gold thread, glinting in the candlelight.

Behind me, Wolsey rises from his chair. "See: You conquer France. Princess Mary, as Charles's wife, becomes an empress. She will have a son, your grandson—shall we say he is called Henry? This grandson will rule not only all the lands Charles rules now—numerous as they are—but France and England too. His empire will be on a scale unknown since Caesar's time."

I lean my forehead on the wall.

"It makes *sense* of what has happened," says Wolsey. "If you had a son, the empire could never be so vast. This way, your grandson will establish a new world order. There will be no one to challenge him."

My eyes are shut; I take a deep breath. Some terrible creature releases its coils from my heart and slinks away.

"Who knows?" says Wolsey, at my shoulder now. "Charles may die young. Then you will rule this new empire as regent until your grandson comes of age."

The greatest empire in the world.

Yes. This makes sense of it all. Doesn't it?

50

The most powerful young man in Christendom has not waited in his chambers—he bounds down the grand stairs to greet us, passing lines of guards in their best new liveries, passing trumpeters at the great doorway, who are now confused about whether or when to play. He is a vision in gold damask and red satin—with spindly limbs, all knees and elbows, and such an outsized jaw it could do service as a spade.

I cross the courtyard, arms extended. My bear hug closes on air—Emperor Charles V has dropped onto one knee on the flagstones and snatched off his bonnet.

"Honored Father," he says in French, and I look down at his dark head, as his neatly cut hair swings forward, momentarily concealing the colossal jaw.

Through Catherine I am his uncle, but I'm not old enough to be his father—still, this is like a pack dog deferring to its leader. All at once, I am in a marvelous mood. I raise the youth by the shoulders, embrace him, and pound him on the back. Winded, he smiles at me awkwardly. But he is not long on his large, narrow feet. He and Catherine kneel to one another at the same moment—and laugh, and embrace where they are. "I can see my sister in your eyes," she says. As she clasps his hands, an embroidered loop on her sleeve catches on a cluster of his doublet's pearls; laughing again, they disentangle themselves. He helps her up. Tears are coursing down her face; she is smiling and smiling.

The trumpeters take a decision: A blast echoes round the courtyard as I lead him inside. Through the padding at his shoulder, I feel him start.

We are at Dover Castle, my gray stone fortress overlooking the Channel. Out in the deep water Charles's ships are lying at anchor, with flags, banners, and streamers fluttering from every line of rigging and, flying highest, his imperial standard, the black two-headed eagle, splayed like a butchered pheasant on rich cloth of gold.

Our talk takes place across an intimate lunch—larks and quails set out on gold platters, on a table of marble inlay—and, as the small bones crack, so, just as easily, are the agreements reached. I will supply cash and ships to crush the Spanish rebellion. Charles will supply himself—as husband for my daughter Mary, whom we will withdraw from the French marriage—plus forty thousand troops for our joint invasion of France. Both of us will swear before God not to recall our army or fleet until each recovers what belongs to him.

So. There will be no end to the war until I am king of France.

Charles's manner is earnest and diffident, his speech slow, broken by long pauses for thought. But eating is his greatest struggle. Due to his deformed jaw, chewing is difficult; he has to mop up spittle with his napkin. It is not pretty—and yet, the more awkward he seems, the more I find I warm to him.

Dabbing with a cloth at my own mouth I say, "The king of France, as you know only too well, cherishes his ambitions in Italy. It seems to me you can encourage him to overreach himself there . . ."

Charles's dark eyes slide up to mine as, with both hands, he lifts his cup. He takes a sip, then says, "Providing the perfect opportunity for our invasion, in his absence?"

"Exactly."

He wipes his mouth again. The napkin, removed, reveals a slow smile. "What a wonderful idea."

Look at him. This boy who rules vast territories. So simple. So pliable. I see with delight what God has put into my hand.

51

The sword gleams in the torchlight. When I grasp the hilt and lift it, the balance is perfect. The blade is tapered to an elegant point, bringing its center of gravity close enough to the hilt to allow me to slice the air with just a turn of the wrist. And so fast that it makes an eerie little singing sound. I run my thumb along the edge—it is properly blunted, as a tournament sword must be.

Still gripping it, I jump up on an arrow chest. In front of me in this, the largest of the arming pavilions in the Greenwich tiltyard, a crowd of knights are talking, drinking and laughing, swapping boasts and private challenges. They're bareheaded—some balding, some bearded, some so young they're barely out of boyhood. Edges of breastplates gleam beneath the zinging colors of their tabards; at their hips hang scabbards covered in velvet and jewels—casings for swords as insanely expensive as mine.

I touch Compton's shoulder with my blade and he calls for quiet. There's shuffling and clanking, and faces turn to me.

"God knows, my lords, it has been a long wait. But this New Year we are on the brink of glorious victory."

Emperor Charles has taken my advice, as I knew he would. He has lured the king of France to cross the Alps.

I say, "We have all heard reports of the French king's foolhardy campaign in Italy. Who but a madman would make his soldiers spend the winter in the open field? They are weakened and disease ridden. And France is weakened by the absence of its king and its finest troops.

"In short, the French are terrified we will attack."

There are muttered comments. A bearded figure at the front—who is still, after all these years, built like a tree trunk—says, "Is this your best New Year's present?"

"I did like your gold plates, Brandon, but I think this inches ahead." Those within earshot laugh.

I raise my voice again. "So, gentlemen—I am watching closely. This is not simply a tournament. This is preparation for France. The Emperor Charles only awaits my word, and together we will launch our invasion. I have not yet decided who will fill the key command positions. Show me today how you deserve them." I shoot my sword into its scabbard. "Let's go."

Outside the pavilion lies the vast, wind-whipped tiltyard. We mount our horses, put on helmets, with visors raised, and set off in procession around the arena.

It is one of those winter days that never seems to get properly light; the sky has a dim leaden glow, and around the tiltyard's perimeter, torches are burning, even though it is the middle of the day. Beyond them, ruddy with cold, float the faces of the spectators, who are packed together on the benches of the grandstands, wrapped in furs or woolen cloaks, keeping warm with stamping and chanting, and burning their fingers and mouths on roasted chestnuts sold in twists of paper.

At one end of the tiltyard stands a huge mock castle— *The Castle of Loyalty*—its turrets rising fifty feet from the sandy floor. The battlements are lined with boys from the chapel choir, posing as ladies in gowns and long wigs. As my horse approaches, I can see that chestnut shells are being lobbed at them from the stands; they duck below the parapet to retrieve them and chuck them back. Above them, real ladies—Catherine's maids of honor—stand on each turret top. Most are waving in response to shouts from the crowd, or struggling with veils flapping in their faces. One, however, is looking at me.

I return her stare with interest. It's not that she is beautiful; Catherine has other maids of honor who are prettier. But she seems somehow compelling, significant: It's as if I have been told something about her, though I can't remember what, or as if I have seen her in a dream.

Her dress is white and gold, like the others'—but on her, it puts me in mind of armor. Her hair—what little of it shows beneath her hood—is dark. She stands very erect, seemingly untouched by the wind. And her eyes . . . Even across this space I can see there is something commanding in that black gaze.

But the moment passes: I turn my horse, ready to head back up the other side of the tilt. I put those dark eyes out of my mind.

First event: an assault on the castle. Francis Bryan and Tom Wyatt have volunteered to defend the west face of the

fortress against my team of four, which is n
besides myself—George Boleyn, Henry Norris,
letic young courtier named Edward Seymour.

The north and south sides of the castle are b
a deep ditch—but not the west side. Here there i
rampart: nine feet of packed earth, its surface smoo
out handhold or foothold. At the top, behind a fen
of wooden stakes, Bryan and Wyatt are waiting.

We are armed—ready. The trumpets blow and we
into the attack, yelling, swiping, and stabbing at the two
with our long-handled pikes.

It is fiendishly difficult to fight men above you. You m
direct the power of your blows upward; you will find yo
arms, neck, and lungs are quickly in distress.

Nevertheless, we go at it hard. I can see that Seymour,
beside me, is eager to impress. We are both tall, with a good
reach; there is lashing, striking, and clanking as we engage the
pikes that jab and slash at us from above.

Up there on the bank, Bryan's lean figure is busy and
flashy as a theatrical, while Wyatt is a confident heavyweight.
He changes weapons: His sword's edge may be blunted, but
still, one horizontal swipe is enough to splinter the shaft of
Norris's pike.

Norris calls for a replacement weapon and we fight on.
I swap pike for sword and manage to scramble some way up
the bank, but Wyatt beats me back with a few smart blows.
Seymour, following in my scraped and smeary footprints,
returns just as quickly.

Drenched in sweat already, my chest heaving for breath,

back up and run at the mud bank again. Planting my feet wide apart as I run to combat the steep incline, I get close enough to the top this time to fight hand to hand, but can't get my balance. My free hand flails for the fence; I can't reach it. I'm forced back.

I call my team to regroup a little way from the bank. Quick conference; hard to speak between gasping breaths. I give instructions: fresh assault, new tactic.

Boleyn doesn't have Seymour's height, but he's belligerent, like a tough little dog. He and Seymour now attack from the ground with their pikes so vigorously that Bryan and Wyatt can scarcely look over the fence.

Meanwhile, Henry Norris and I, under cover of this assault, use our swords to dig holes in the bank to make footholds for climbing.

It works. I climb, and manage to grab hold of one of the palings of the fence before I can be beaten down. Holding on, I fight hand to hand with Wyatt, all the time being supported from below by the blows of my comrades' pikes. One of my best strikes leaves Wyatt's shoulder armor half hanging off.

By now Norris has made it up his scooped footholds too. The fight is fierce; Bryan and Wyatt must combat two of us at the fence, and two others making their way up. At last Seymour and Boleyn get close enough behind to help Norris and me climb over the palings, and, with a trumpet blast and deafening cheers from the crowd, the herald declares the battle ended.

We walk unsteadily back to the pavilions, panting and exhausted, bruised and muddied, leaving the earth rampart pitted with digging and smeared with scrambling footmarks. As he unbuckles his helmet and wrenches it off, I see Wyatt looking back and up—up to the castle turrets.

That reminds me.

"Compton, who's that girl?"

He's holding open the flap of my private tent, hand out ready to take my helmet. He looks the way I'm pointing. "Mary Talbot, sir."

"No, next to her. The one on the right."

He pays more attention. "That's Thomas Boleyn's daughter. The younger one. Lady Anne."

Oh, yes. So I have seen her before. Thomas Boleyn's children have all been at court for some time. She's just one more among the many offspring of my friends. I watch her: She's no longer turned my way, but the strange feeling lingers. A sense of recognition. Why haven't I felt it until now?

Trumpets blast. The first men are coming out for the tourney. I take a final glance around the arena. Away to the side, Catherine sits in her canopied viewing gallery. After so many pregnancies, she is a rounder figure now than she once was—solid as a pudding, her expression benign.

I pass into my tent.

52

The door shuts. I don't even bother to look up.

"If you're feeling better it's because you've stopped taking all those bloody medicines," I say, reaching for my gilt compasses and taking a measurement on the drawing in front of me. "I knew you had too many."

I can feel Wolsey smiling. "And good morning to you, Your Grace. I am perfectly recovered, thank you. It was just a little fever. It didn't stop me working." To prove it—as I see when I do look up—he's carrying a hefty sheaf of papers.

I am in my private library at Greenwich, in the tower closest to the river. Cold, lemony sunlight shines flat across my desk, where large plans are spread out—for siege engines, and guns, and armor. My own designs.

"I want to speak to someone from the armory."

"I'll arrange it." Wolsey sorts through his papers, and brings one to me. "May I? There really aren't too many this morning." He slides it in front of me. "This is the money for the repairs at Tunbridge and Penshurst."

I sign, and go back to my drawing. A mortar and a large-bore cannon, which I want cast in bronze. I say, "George Boleyn's sister—the younger one. Wasn't she supposed to be married into Ireland?" I'm sketching details for the decorative engraving, now—roses, lions, dragons. "I half remember giving consent to a match."

"With the Earl of Ormonde's son." Wolsey brings another document; waits—then lays it down. "The wardship of the Cluny boy."

I sign. "And it hasn't happened because . . . ?"

"Sir?"

"The marriage."

"Oh, the usual—the families can't agree on terms." Wolsey returns to his papers, which lie on a nearby table; I sit back and watch him. He is huge, and impressive in red. The hem of his robe lifts an inch as he leans over the table— I see the backs of his wide velvet shoes and his ankles, puffy in white silk. A wrestler in velvet shoes and silk hose. He says, "Harry Percy has been showing interest in her too—and he's a much better catch. She no doubt fancies being Countess of Northumberland."

"That's ridiculous. She's not the right rank for Percy." I reach for a knife and cut a few shavings from my red-ocher pencil. Then I test the line it draws. "And there's a wife already picked out for him, in any case."

"Yes, the Talbot girl. He doesn't like her."

"Since when did that count for anything?"

Wolsey laughs.

A gilded leather box on my desk holds drawers filled with silver boxes of ink, pairs of scissors, penknives and small whetstones to sharpen them, a tiny mirror, hawks' hoods, odd keys, and the occasional jewel. I sort through looking for the narrowest-nibbed pen, find it, dip it in ink, and bend over the drawing again.

As I draw, I say, "Whatever there is between Percy and Boleyn's sister, make sure it's broken off, will you?"

"With pleasure, sir."

There's a tap at the door. Wolsey moves to answer it, has a brief, murmured conversation with someone outside, and comes back into the room, holding a letter. I lean back in my chair and stretch, turn my head, move my shoulders, look up at the ceiling—at the antique mermaids fashioned in painted leather mâché, their cheeks rouged as brightly as an actor's.

"My God, half an hour doing anything at a desk and I've had enough. How on earth do you manage more?"

"I am constantly inspired by devotion to my master." Wolsey's grinning. He holds out the letter.

"What's this, then?"

"Sir, I believe it's news from Italy."

Catherine's at prayer when I burst in: a stout bundle of ornate clothes, kneeling at the altar in the far corner of her bedchamber. She starts, crosses herself hastily, and stands up.

I'm across the carpet in two strides—I see her flinch minutely as I reach for her. What is she expecting? Whatever it is, what she *gets* is a picking up and a whirling round. She shrieks and loses a slipper, which goes spinning into a corner.

"By Saint Mary! Hal! What is it?"

I set her down, her bell-skirt swinging. I put my hands on her shoulders. It takes an effort to speak steadily. "There's been a battle in Italy—at Pavia. Your nephew . . . *our* nephew,

Charles . . . God has given him such a victory over the French, Catherine! Thousands of them dead and King Francis captured. In imperial hands. Right now."

There is silence—a delicious silence. She's not even breathing. Then her hands reach for the soft green hangings at the bedpost beside her; she hides her face in them and weeps.

"Read it to her!" I tell Wolsey, who's come in behind me, brandishing the letter. "Read the bit about Francis stuck under a horse!" I laugh and clutch his arm, then bound back to Catherine and turn her gently in to my shoulder. "Listen to this."

She leans against me as Wolsey reads: "'The French were attacked where they camped in the great hunting park outside the city walls. As the battle raged, the thick forest hampered the movements of their cavalry. By eight o'clock the emperor's pikemen and arquebusiers were closing in from all sides. The French king fought on, but his horse was killed beneath him, and fell upon him, injuring him and pinning him to the ground. As he lay, Spanish troops plucked the plumes from his very helmet. He was taken prisoner and carried from the field—'"

"Might he die from his injuries?" I say to Wolsey. "Huh? Do you think?"

"God willing!"

"We'll pray for it! Won't we? But he might as well be dead for all the use he'll be to his country when we invade. Charles from the south; us from the north." I can't stand still; I detach myself from Catherine and pace about. "Christ, this is it! This is perfect! At last, at *last*!"

I open the windows—all of them—unlatching and pushing on casement after casement. It has rained, and the wind that blows in from the river is strong and fresh, whipping the last droplets from the creepers on the walls outside. Past the river I see a clear expanse of country and, beyond it, sunshine breaking on the hills.

I can breathe again.

I turn back to the room. Compared to the brightness outside, the light is soft and green, as if we're under a canopy of trees. Wolsey stands like a red-robed Merlin, his hands tucked into his sleeves. Catherine's tears have stopped; her face is shining as she looks at me.

I go to her and take her hand. It is soft and pudgy, these days, like a child's. I rub the back of it gently as I say to Wolsey, "We must mount the invasion as soon as possible. All ships in our ports, of whatever nationality—have them detained for use as transport. And dismiss the French ambassador. We need to send to Flanders to buy horses, too. But most of all we need money—fast."

"My last calculation was eight hundred thousand pounds, sir. Parliament will hate it."

"Then to hell with Parliament! Find another way."

"Of course. Nothing can possibly prevent the invasion now."

"Go on, then. Go and start work on it."

"Your Grace." Wolsey bows and leaves the room.

Catherine is still looking at me—and it's a look to bask in. *This* is why I married her: She has brought me Emperor Charles. She has brought me this moment.

I kiss her. I have not kissed her on the mouth for years.

53

It is wet and red and weeping fluid. It is on the side of my left leg—a three-inch gash where I fell from my horse in the hunting park here at Windsor yesterday and ripped my flesh open on a piece of splintered wood. The leg is bound now and propped up on a stool; but I have been watching a spreading stain seep through the bandages while the ambassador talks.

Now I interrupt him, "Commander, with all *due* respect"—which, if he looks into my eyes, he will see is very little—"what the hell are you talking about?"

Commander Peñalosa clears his throat and starts again. "His Imperial Majesty requests that you send the Princess Mary to Spain without delay, along with her dowry."

"You've said that already. What I'm asking for is an explanation." Peñalosa blinks at me. I am clicking the underside of my rings on the chair arm. "Look. We have an agreement. A treaty. Remember? Which states that I am to send my daughter to Spain in three years' time at the very earliest. Not *now*. She is only nine, for Christ's sake. The emperor cannot take her to his bed. . . ."

"He would not think of such a thing, of course, Your Grace."

"I'm glad to hear that, at least. So. I send her in three years, with her dowry, yes, but *minus* the loans I have already given to your master. Not the full amount. Let alone the full amount *plus* another six hundred thousand ducats. It is . . . well, many different words spring to mind but, shall we say, *astonishing* that the emperor should demand this. And I am under no obligation to pay."

Peñalosa, an experienced military man, keeps twitching his fingers to the place where his sword hilt should be. I get the feeling he would rather be on a battlefield at this moment, engaged in the straightforward business of killing—or being killed. He says, "Your Grace, the money is not demanded as an obligation, but as the kind of help a father gives to a son."

"I have given your master a great deal of fatherly help already. Without it, he would not still have control of Spain."

"His Imperial Majesty is constantly aware of all you have done for him and is full of gratitude. He sees this request now as a very moderate sum"—at this Wolsey, who is leaning on the fireplace, yelps, but the Spaniard plows on, raising his voice a little—"considering that every penny of it will be spent on a war which will benefit England . . . and, moreover, that when Your Grace has claimed the crown of France, your wealth will be greatly increased."

"Yes, it will. *When* I am king of France. But now, I am *not* king of France. Now, I cannot pay. It is hard enough to raise money to put my own troops in the field." I take a deep breath; I attempt pleasantness. "Commander. I understand—the emperor would like to try and squeeze me for more money. Perhaps he thinks I am a soft touch. Please tell him, it was a nice try."

"That is not his view——"

"Whatever. The answer is no. Let us move on." I smile, and Peñalosa winces. I say, "The emperor and I have a solemn, binding agreement to invade France together. An agreement sworn in the chapel here at this very castle. This man"—I point to Wolsey—"saw us do it. At the altar. It would not only be against God to break that agreement. It would be—frankly—madness, considering that your master now holds the king of France prisoner." I regard Peñalosa narrowly. "Unless, of course, there is something you are not telling me."

"I am being entirely open with you, sir. But the request for money cannot, I'm afraid, be put to one side."

"So you are saying that if I do not pay, the emperor will not invade France? Is that it?"

"The war in Italy has been ruinously expensive, sir. He simply lacks the funds. If you refuse to help, sir, his only course of action would be to make another marriage immediately, with another princess who would bring him a large dowry."

Oh God.

"I cannot believe your master would . . ."

I stop, remembering the huge jaw, the slow look. Did I misjudge him? Did that simple mask conceal—Christ!—*cunning*? All at once I feel exhausted. I rub my eyes. "Is he thinking of anyone in particular?"

"The princess of Portugal, sir, would bring with her a good sum of money. And she is of childbearing age."

"And if he marries her, we invade France straightaway, do we?"

"Well, sir, in point of fact . . ." Color mounts to Peñalosa's face; he rearranges himself, tugging his cuffs, shifting his stance, and then launches in, talking fast. "In point of fact, the emperor, my master, in order to satisfy his own conscience and the wish of his subjects, has sent certain worthy personages to the French king to inquire whether he is willing to return—of his own free will, and without compulsion—those lands which he holds unjustly and by usurpation from my master and from . . . from you, sir. Until he has an answer on this point, my master cannot say how and where the war is to commence—that being the reason why he has not yet written to Your Grace announcing his intentions. However, I have no doubt that, a definite answer being obtained, the emperor will not fail to acquaint both Your Grace and the cardinal with his plans."

The man finishes triumphantly, and looks sick.

There is a moment of silence.

I say, "How kind of him."

The room is full of shadows. My leg wound is throbbing. "Leave us now."

"Sir, what shall I report as your answer?"

I look at him. "Leave. Us."

Commander Peñalosa cannot retreat fast enough. The door shuts behind him; Wolsey and I are alone.

Outside, it is a dismal summer day, gray and squally. A tendril of creeper scratches the window with each gust of wind—a high-pitched, grating sound.

Still leaning on the fireplace, Wolsey says, "The emperor knows, of course, that his demands are preposterous. They are designed to be refused. This is his way of pulling out of the treaty."

"There will be no invasion, then."

He doesn't need to answer.

"And no marriage."

I am sitting perfectly still, but something moves. It feels as if I am inhabited by things that shift and crawl inside me. I say, "I don't understand."

Wolsey stares into the fire. "The emperor finds himself in a position of strength," he says. "He has routed the French. He has their king as his prisoner. He calculates that he no longer needs us. Why should he, now, help you become king of France? Or wait to take a wife until Princess Mary comes of age? As the man said, his parliament is urging him to marry *now* and produce an heir—"

"No. I don't understand," I say, "how you could have got it so wrong."

He turns to look at me. "Your Grace—"

"You told me: This makes sense of what has happened. You told me: God gives me what I want. Not in the way I expect, perhaps, but he gives it to me nonetheless. So. What is God giving me now? Another ally who has betrayed me. And a minister who has failed me. Not *another* minister— the same one. Who, it seems, fails me again . . . and again . . . and again." I get up, with some difficulty, and walk away from Wolsey, to the window. The courtyard below looks grim and unlovely, the water-spewing creatures on the fountain grotesque. I lean my forehead against the cold glass.

"Your Grace," says Wolsey again, but I don't turn. "Sir, to deal with foreign rulers is to deal with lies and deceits. All the time. A French king, a Spanish emperor—any one of them—will swear he is your friend, while in truth he has his own agenda that he is pursuing, mercilessly, behind your back. It is"—he sighs deeply—"the way the world works. The key is to recognize that, accept it, and keep moving. Keep stepping lightly as the squares on the checkerboard shift beneath your feet."

He's at the window now, looking down at the courtyard too. I roll my forehead on the glass, so I can look at him. "What is *your* agenda?"

"Sir?"

I straighten up. "Well, as you say, a man will swear he is your friend, while in truth . . ." I slap the sill, with some violence. "It's the way the world works."

"I was talking of foreign rulers."

"Really? You see, I am asking myself why you were so keen to sell this alliance to me. Were you working with the emperor? What was it *for*? So that he would deliver you the papacy and you would deliver him your king, on a platter—"

"No, sir—as you see, I am not pope—"

"—to be humiliated, to be laughed at, to be used, when the need arose, and then cast off, like so much baggage."

Wolsey is very still, looking at me. He says, "Your success is my success. Everything I have, I have from you."

Silence.

"Your Grace, we need only a new strategy. Listen. We can make a league with the French. Not with the king, I mean with the government left behind in Paris. If Princess Mary marries the dauphin, I'm certain they will have the boy crowned king. King Francis isn't popular—they won't give a shilling for his ransom. Then you can rule as regent until the boy comes of age."

I step toward him; we are toe to toe. I say, "I have had enough of your ideas. They are nothing. They are"—I blow in his face—"hot air."

I turn away. "I find that I cannot rely on anyone but myself."

"You can rely on me, Your Grace. Just give me a little time to arrange things. I will find a way. . . ."

I am at the door. I don't look back.

54

Today I dine in the Presence Chamber, sitting in state, alone at the table, though the room is packed. It is an honor to watch the king eat.

The scene before me jumps and crackles with color: the gilded blue of the ceiling, the polished gold of the plates, the crimson silks and purple velvets of the courtiers who stand around me, the yellows and greens of slashed satin and draped cloaks, the jarring glitter of jewels and spangles, the frantic colors of a million threads in the tapestries lining the walls.

The food appears. Steam rises from the pies as they are slit open like stomachs—curling tendrils of steam that wind their fingers into the air, melting the colors of the scene behind.

I watch the colors begin to run, to drip, to collect in dark puddles on the floor. And as the colors melt, the people around me seem to exude a rank smell, mingled with sickly gusts of perfume. As they bow, I notice the grease of their hair; as their hands move objects on the table, I see flakes of skin fall; I see the yellow rind of their nails, their rheumy eyes, their pox scars. A man leans in to set down a plate, and I catch sight of a boil on his neck, only half concealed by the collar of his shirt.

My gaze is drawn to the doorway at the far end of the chamber—the doorway to the next public room. The space is packed with people, but for an instant, in that sea of ugly faces, one stands out.

It is a young man with straw-colored hair. He is deep in the throng, his body hidden by the bodies in front, but what I can see of him is peculiarly vivid, as if he is somehow closer to me than all the rest: the yellow hair, the darkly shadowed eyes; I can see the texture of his skin—coarse and sallow. He looks ill fed; his face is angular, more gaunt than I remember. But what is most arresting is the calm, unswerving certainty of his gaze. No crying today. He seems to fix me with a terrifying scrutiny.

Lurching to my feet, I turn away. I head for the other door, the door to my private apartments. Insects crunch beneath my feet. Something scutters across the floor in front of me and disappears beneath the hangings.

Away from the crowds, I walk along the gallery, past windows that make a rhythm of shadows on the floor: light, dark, light, dark.

Outside, the rain is a gray curtain; we are closed in by water. Beyond, unseen, I feel the forest on the march, eating up the open grassland, strangling the clipped gardens.

Reaching my secret study, I dismiss the servants and sit alone.

No candles are lit. The paneling is dark, the corners dingy—the shadows reach out, consuming the light, swallowing it whole, like an egg.

Time passes. Perhaps minutes, or hours.

I struggle to think. I have no empire, no sons. And now my last hope—that I will be king of France, and that my *grandson* will be a great emperor after me—is snatched away.

Yet how can it have come to this? My glorious destiny was foretold in the prophecy: It is *God's will.*

Surely there can be only one explanation: God is telling me that something is wrong—that something displeases him. That, until I correct it, my destiny will not be fulfilled.

What can it be that is wrong?

I am God's chosen. That is the basic fact—irreducible—from which all thinking must begin.

So, it follows that the thing that displeases God cannot be me.

Now, coming from the darkest corner of the room, I hear a faint scraping and scratching, as if a creature with talons or claws is crouching there. I sense rather than see movement in the pitch-black; I detect a shift in the current of air.

Frightened, I grip the arms of my chair, widening my eyes to stare into the shadows. But I can see nothing there.

Slowly, in creeping steps of logic, I reason it out: If the thing that displeases God *cannot* be me, then it must be a thing—or person—other than myself.

Oh merciful God, speak to me. Show me who it is that displeases you.

Nothing answers. I feel as if the darkness could engulf me. Somewhere in the impenetrable shadows, where the unseen creature crouches, I imagine the black mouth of a bottomless pit.

Then, at last, there is a sound from the far end of the room: the door, opening—and closing again.

Someone has slipped in. At first I can make out only a vague shape: an arched block of color, like a church window. It is a woman.

It is Catherine.

PART FOUR

Which Way I Fly

55

Surfacing, I push my wet hair out of my eyes. The clean white linen of my bathing shirt clings to my skin, heavy and dripping, as I wade to the side of the pool.

"I asked God to speak to me. He *has* been speaking to me—for years. With each dead child." Rolling into the water again, I lean back and stretch my arms along the stone edging. "Catherine is the problem. I need a new wife."

Wolsey, sweating in his heavy robes, is sitting on a bench by the wall. He is blotting his face methodically with a large handkerchief, which he folds and refolds, searching for a dry surface. "You know, sir," he says from behind it, "there's a man of mine—by the name of Thomas Cromwell—says his mother gave birth to him at fifty."

"I am not floating ideas. Neither am I asking for your advice—or your opinion. I am issuing instructions."

The handkerchief stops. He lowers it, examines it on his lap, smoothing its fringed edging of Venice gold and red silk. At last he says, "Are you sure about this?"

"I've never been so sure of anything in my life."

I watch my legs floating in front of me, the loose fabric undulating in the water. In the corner of the room the stove gurgles; it is green glazed and bulbous, like a huge, water-heating toad. Wolsey passes a hand over his face, gets up, paces. "For the pope to annul the marriage would not be unprecedented, of course. Louis the Twelfth of France put aside his first wife . . . and Louis the Sixth before him . . ." He stops. "A slight problem might be posed by the dispensation . . ."

"Oh, I'm sure you can find a way."

He meets my gaze. "Yes," he says steadily. "I'm sure I can." He walks again, trailing one hand on the tiled wall. "And the queen, sir. Have you . . . ?"

"There's no need to tell her yet. I want everything arranged first, so that when it happens, it happens fast."

Wolsey has stopped. A square of light shines down from a window, high up on the wall behind him. Beyond it, he is in shadow. I realize that his hand is not touching the wall idly; it is there to support him.

"Are you in pain?"

For a moment he doesn't move. Then he shakes his head. "No, sir, it's nothing. Just stomach gripes. They pass." Another pause. He pushes himself off the wall, stepping into the light. "There. Better now." His face is pale and waxy; he smiles. "Well. A new marriage presents a wonderful political opportunity. Do you have anyone in mind? Say, a French princess?"

"I'm not having one of the emperor's pox-ridden sisters, if that's the alternative." I hold my nose and prepare to go under. "You can draw up a list."

56

The names are chalked on the slate at the top end of the bowling alley:

Edward Seymour
Henry Norris
George Boleyn
Thomas Wyatt
The King

"Compton? Not you?"

"I'll do the usual, sir."

"So self-effacing," mutters George Boleyn. "Does he have no competitive instinct?"

"On the contrary, George, I think he's so competitive he daren't risk losing." I sling Compton my bag of coins. "He'd never survive it."

We're all to play together. I elect to be the last to bowl, since my favorite tactic is to knock the other woods out of the way.

Both sides of the bowling alley are lined with unglazed windows, open to the gardens beyond. At the top end, where we wait to play, there are seats and wooden windowsills to lean on. Compton throws the jack, and Seymour is the first to bowl; I gaze out at the orchard, where the trees are laden with blossom.

"Oh, nice. If it just hadn't curved away at the end . . ." Boleyn grins, ignoring Seymour's glare. "Norris? Are you going next?"

I turn to the gardens again. Something outside is irritating me. Bees drone, stop, and drone again, as they crawl into flowers and swing away; birds chirrup repetitively, all on one note.

Among the fruit trees, several of Catherine's maids of honor are walking with some gentlemen of the Privy Chamber. I watch the teasing social dance: The men bend in, solicitous; the women step away, and laugh.

Seeing the ebb and flow of a group as it moves— conversations beginning or ending, people breaking away, fresh gambits made, accepted, or refused—you can tell who holds the most power.

Here it is an unlikely figure: a slight girl with a face too odd and pointed to be beautiful. It is the same girl I saw on the turret top that day at the tournament: George's younger sister, Anne.

I see men, intrigued, trying to make her laugh—trying to say something clever enough to win her approval. I see women, in spare moments from their own conversations, glance at her with mistrust or plain dislike. It is a puzzle: She hasn't the rank, the money, or the looks to be so assured.

"Good shot!"

Wyatt turns away, dusting off his hands and grinning. It's me up next.

At the far end of the alley, the woods—each the shape of a squashed sphere, like a whole cheese—cluster around the small white jack. Some of the woods have been overshot; others, too tentatively thrown, have fallen short.

I swing my arm back and launch my wood. It arcs up the curved bank of the clay wall, overtaking Seymour's and Norris's, and descends at speed, knocking out Boleyn's, which rolls on, into a corner.

There's applause all round as I walk back up the alley. I'm limping, still—my left leg, though the skin has healed, is uncomfortable and swollen. But I don't sit; I lean on the sill again and stare out at the orchard.

In recent months I have caught myself thinking more and more about this young woman—God knows why; it makes no sense to me. What is she? An insignificant girl with nothing to recommend her but a quick wit and those strange dark eyes—eyes that can flash with merciless hilarity, then look blank as a frozen pond.

I have even gone so far as to make my interest plain. But her response has been confusing, drawing me in one minute, pushing me away the next. Which is downright impudent.

She is no great lady, after all; she is a girl about court, who should be worth no more than a brief bit of fun—some easy entertainment—and then forgotten.

But it is getting worse. The feeling, the interest—whatever

it is—has become an annoyance, like my leg wound, which itches and aches, and festers.

Seymour's just thrown. "Best shot yet," Compton calls from the far end. He holds up a finger and thumb. "Inch off the jack."

Norris throws, then Boleyn. Wyatt's wood cannons Seymour's out of the way.

"A lucky kiss," says Wyatt, holding up his hands.

As he walks back up the alley, Wyatt keeps turning to the windows; he has been watching George's sister too. There is something pained in his expression that I recognize all too well.

"Sir?"

I turn.

"Your wood, sir." Norris hands it to me.

The last throw. I step forward to take it. It is another good shot: The wood swings in from the wall as before and comes to rest only just beyond the jack.

Compton hops about, looking at the balls from different angles. "Close-run thing. It's between you, sir, and Wyatt."

So Wyatt and I approach to examine the state of play.

On the little finger of my right hand there is a small ring—a woman's ring. A topaz only—nothing costly. I slip it onto my index finger—it cannot even pass the first joint—and point to the jack.

"Wyatt, I tell you it is mine." I'm grinning.

Wyatt catches sight of the ring, and his eyes flick up to my face. He knows where the ring comes from: It is Anne's.

He hesitates—then, grinning too, he digs inside his doublet and produces a small pearl on a length of ribbon.

"But if you'll just let me measure the distance, Your Grace, I hope I'll find it's actually mine."

The pearl, the ribbon: I recognize them. Anne's too.

Wyatt kneels and stretches the ribbon between the two woods and the jack, comparing distances—looks up at me, and, seeing my expression, instantly blanches. The ribbon goes slack; he slowly rises to his feet.

Before he can think what to say, I am gone, striding as fast as my sore leg allows, back up the bowling alley and out through the door into the orchard.

Everyone hears the door bang; groups split and fall back before I reach them, clearing a path to let me through.

At the end of one line stands Anne. I stop in front of her, breathing heavily. She curtsies low and then straightens, perfectly composed.

"May I speak with you a moment?" I say, and take her upper arm without waiting for a reply. I steer her toward a half-built arbor a short way off. I know my grip is uncomfortably tight, but she doesn't complain, just walks quickly to keep up with me, steadying her skirts with her free hand.

The arbor is a stone bay window, glassless and roofless. As we step in, I let go and she turns to face me.

"Have you . . ." My voice sounds strangled. I clear my throat. "Have you given yourself to Wyatt?"

For a moment her eyes register something disconcertingly like curiosity. Then she says, "Your Grace. If this is about the pearl, I didn't give it to him; he stole it from me three days ago and has been taunting me with it ever since." She folds her hands against her dress. "As for myself, sir, I give myself to no one."

"Anne, forgive me." I feel suddenly desperate. "You are plaguing me."

She raises her eyebrows.

"In my head, I mean. I . . ." Exasperated, I snatch off my cap and rub my hair roughly. "Look—did you read my letter?"

"Which one?"

I stare at her, then press on. "My offer still stands. You could be my acknowledged mistress. No one has been offered that before."

She blinks, catlike, saying nothing.

"You will have status."

Still no response.

"And I will not even so much as glance at another woman."

"Except your wife."

"Of course, but—"

"Then, sir, I thank you for your favor, but I must ask you to look for your *amusement* elsewhere." She gestures toward the garden. "There are plenty of eager, pretty little things out there who would consider it an honor to please you, surely?"

I look at her. She doesn't flinch.

"Anne. I'm not enjoying this. It's irritating. It's . . ." *Torture,* I could say. I take a breath, effortfully. "I will not ask like this again. I don't know where this stupid feeling has come from—or why. But I can train myself out of it. I *will*."

It is a threat, and I like my threats to be met with alarm and apology. Instead I sense amusement—something side-long, quick, and mischievous in her eyes—as if, wherever my thoughts are heading, she's gotten there before me and is waiting farther up the track, hidden by the trees—watching me, laughing.

She says, "I would have hesitated to use the word if you had not used it first, sir, but I agree that it is *stupid* to urge me to give up my honor. My future husband and the children God will grant us would not thank me for throwing it away."

There is a silence. I find that I am shaking.

"Then you may consider this—whatever it is—at an end. My lady."

I walk away—not back to the orchard, but on, toward the palace. I want to go inside without looking back, but I don't make it. Almost at the door to my private stairs, I turn. In the distance the girl is gliding away across the grass, heading back to the orchard, trailing picked stems of poppies against her skirts. Untroubled.

I watch her go. I know full well that nothing is remotely at an end. On the contrary, it occurs to me that she has issued a challenge.

57

"Marry *her?*"

Wolsey has turned the color of porridge.

"And when . . . when did this idea occur to you?"

I don't reply. Under my gaze, Wolsey sinks to his knees. "Sir, I am begging you. Not to."

Silence. We are in a small chamber at Westminster; Wolsey is kneeling in a patch of sunshine, squinting against the light.

He opens his mouth, closes it, starts again. "Sir, kings do not marry for love. Surely you agree? That is what mistresses are for. Royal marriages are political alliances—made with foreign princesses. Not with the daughter of one of your own courtiers. This way, we . . . you, sir, would lose every single scrap of advantage that a new match could bring. . . . And it would make the annulment a—a thousand times more difficult to achieve."

I walk slowly into the shadows behind him. "I know why Lady Anne has refused me. Because she is sent by God."

Wolsey turns and stares at me. "To be your *wife?*"

Bending to his ear, I whisper, "You are very quick."

Then, briskly, I say, "And the annulment will not be so difficult to achieve as you pretend. Anne has already consulted her chaplains—" I see Wolsey's expression. "*Secretly.* They advise that it is a sin for me to keep Catherine as my wife a moment longer."

There is a chair to one side of Wolsey. An embroidered chair, fringed with gold and decorated with his own coat of arms. I sit in it, hook my toe under a page's stool to drag it toward me, and prop my leg on it. I say, "The case is watertight. The Bible clearly states that a man may not marry his brother's widow. The dispensation originally given was in error—what is written in the Bible is divine law, and the Pope cannot dispense with divine law."

I spread my hands—*see?* I say, "We can open a private court—you can pronounce judgment within a fortnight. What are you papal legate for, after all?"

Wolsey is looking at my hands, unfocused.

"I *am* able to think for myself," I say—and smile. "You should be proud. Your pupil has come of age at last."

58

The key is new and ornate; I have had all the locks changed. I slip it back into the purse at my belt and push the door open.

"Go on." I nod to Anne.

She passes me and enters the small room, stopping in the middle of the floor to turn slowly and look about her.

It's one of my most private spaces: a tower room built long ago for my mother. The small lattice windows are painted with her coat of arms. Outside it's sunny, and the colored glass shines like jewels, but the room is shady and cavelike. Most of the wall space is taken up with cupboards and shelves stuffed with boxes and bags, books and documents.

In the dim room I see the gleam of Anne's eyes and her small white teeth as she smiles.

"Feel free," I say. "Explore. No secrets."

She approaches a wall, trails a finger over a cupboard latch, along a shelf edge. She's not sure what to open first. Her hand reaches a box, covered in painted decoration. She lifts it down.

"What's this?" she says, staring at the contents.

"A dragon. Dried."

"Really?" She studies it with renewed interest, then puts it back.

She investigates shelves cluttered with astronomical instruments, leather- and velvet-covered boxes, and several ornate clocks; cupboards out of which flop drifts of papers, others crowded with chessmen and jeweled hourglasses.

She loosens the strings of a green sarcenet bag and peers in. "A pair of spurs. Gilt. Old?"

"Henry the Fifth wore them at Agincourt."

I'm lounging on a chair, enjoying watching her. I see her open a small box. "Scissors . . ." she says. And another. "Perfumes?"

"Probably." Some of the boxes are so old I've forgotten what's in them.

Next her fingers light on a flat case, covered in black velvet. She opens it. "Oh. And you."

Inside, if I remember, is a carved wooden cameo. Anne considers it, her head on one side. "I think it's quite like you."

She grins at me quickly, then slides it back onto the shelf.

I say, "You'll find jewels in there." Her hand is on another cupboard door.

She glances at me again then dives in, fishing out boxes lined with small drawers—and in the drawers ropes of pearls, bracelets and brooches, necklaces, loose jewels, trimming for hoods and sleeves.

"You can have any of them you want."

"They're pretty," she says at length, putting them back. "But I want Catherine's jewels." She shuts the cupboard. "When I'm queen."

I watch as she picks up a dog collar. Sometimes she leaves

me winded. Before I've recovered she says, "So. What's the news from Wolsey?"

I push myself up and pretend to look for something on a shelf. "Oh, there's a—uh, a small delay."

"Why?"

"He says he needs to take advice. It's all in hand."

"Is it?"

She reaches out and tugs me toward her, by the sleeve; she pulls me very close. In the shadows there seems to be something fierce about her, something otherworldly in the silky skin, the long neck, the pointed, elfin face.

"Are you sure?" she says.

"About what?" I stroke her cheek. "I'm sure about you."

"Sure that it's all in hand . . ." She closes her fingers round my wrist. "It's a failing of mine; I don't trust others much. I like to know exactly what's going on. . . ."

I study her. "But I think you do know . . . everything. It's eerie. I think you can read my mind."

"Can I?" She smiles. "Yes, maybe . . ."

We're both laughing now, and I'm kissing her.

As I begin to kiss her neck, she tilts her head to one side. She says dreamily, "Tell me about Wolsey."

I stop. We look at one another. Her gaze is entirely serious—not dreamy at all.

I disengage and lean my elbow on a shelf. "All right, he's adjourned the case. He says it's too difficult and he needs to take legal advice. But he's given me guarantees—"

"Too difficult? Because?" Her eyes have narrowed.

302

I let out a breath. "The Bible clearly states in the book of Leviticus that a man may not marry his brother's widow. But elsewhere in the Old Testament there's a text contradicting that—"

"In Deuteronomy, I know." Anne moves into the light. She looks cool and elegant and human again. "But it deals with ceremonial law. It applies only to Jews, not Christians."

"Ye-es. But not all theologians agree on that, do they? Wolsey thinks it's unavoidable . . ." I hesitate.

"What is?"

"That the pope must be involved."

Anne has picked up and opened a box; now she snaps the lid shut. "But imperial troops have overrun Rome; the pope is the emperor's prisoner." She paces about. "If the trial is held there, do you imagine for *one moment* that the pope will be allowed to make a judgment against Catherine, the emperor's own aunt?"

"The trial won't be held in Rome. It won't come to that. Wolsey has plans."

Anne makes a noise in her throat, something like a laugh.

"He's asking the pope to send a document specifically granting him authority to decide this case."

Anne has stopped by a table; she's fiddling with the stopper of a bottle. She says, "Do you ever doubt his loyalty?"

"Wolsey's?" I glance out the window. "I've known him a long time. Longer than you've . . ."

"Been alive?"

I smile. "Not far off it."

She lifts the bottle, examining its surface. "Still. Catherine's known him just as long. He may be working for her. What has she said?"

There's an awkward silence. Anne looks at me sharply.

"You haven't told her."

I don't move. I say, "I will."

Silence again; we're looking at each other. Suddenly I notice that the bottle she's holding is engraved with an entwined *H* and *C*—I go to her and slip it out of her hands. I say, "I just need to find the right moment."

"Do you remember what my chaplain said? That it would be a high crime against God if you didn't repudiate her straightaway?"

"Progress is being made. Wolsey—"

"And what about *my* right moment, anyway?" she says. "I've turned down offers for this. I could be married and pregnant by now. I need to be sure." Her thin fingers are on my arm again; their grip is surprisingly strong.

"Sure?"

She nods. "That I'm not wasting my time."

59

"I didn't want to trouble you when you've been so busy with these . . . these negotiations. I mean with the French. So I ordered them anyway. One is purple velvet edged with ermine, three are cloth of gold, and then"—she counts on her fingers—"there's one purple tinsel, one cloth of silver, and one tawny cloth of gold—"

"Catherine—"

"Oh, and a couple of hoods. Black velvet lined with satin. The gable style suits Mary best, don't you think?"

"Catherine."

"Yes?"

We're alone in her chamber. It faces south, across the Greenwich parkland, and today the sunshine is streaming in—bright light, almost unbearable. Having edged into the room, I'm standing in the shadows, just inside the door, sweating beneath my clothes.

God is all around: Icons look down at me from every wall—Christ wearing the crown of thorns; Christ as the Man of Sorrows, bleeding and attended by angels; the Virgin Mary with diadem and scepter, balancing the Christ child on her knee. On an altar by the window a gold monstrance blazes in the sun. At its heart, encased in crystal, lies a dull black splinter: a piece of the true cross.

Catherine is standing in the middle of the room, solid as

a velvet-upholstered man-of-war, her prayer beads looped at her waist. A gold cross, heavy with gemstones, presses into the doughy flesh below her throat. Above it her face bears an expression of such innocence—such openness. I am about to shatter her world.

I take a breath, then start, quickly. "Several wise and learned men have come to me with terrible news. They say that we are living in sin and always have been. They say our marriage is against the law of God."

In my hands is a volume of the Old Testament, its embroidered cover imprinted on my fingers where I've been gripping it too tightly. I fumble for the page marked by a ribbon, then turn the book round and hold it out.

"Leviticus, chapter twenty, verse twenty-one. Read it."

She doesn't register the book—she's still looking at me. I shove it at her; she doesn't take it.

"Hal—"

"All right, then." I turn the book back and read, translating the Latin: "'If a man shall take his brother's wife, it is an unclean thing . . . they shall be childless.' It means without sons."

I glance up at her, then stare. "You're not surprised?"

Her eyes are full, but her gaze is steady—tender. She says, "Something's happened to you."

"My conscience is disturbed."

"I don't mean that. What is it?"

I look at her, at a loss. Then I say, "Nothing. It's nothing."

A fly has come in through an open window; it lands on Catherine's sleeve. I watch as it moves across the fabric, stops, moves again.

I look down at the Bible text; it swims slightly. I say, "There was a day . . . a while ago . . . I sat down to eat . . ." The colors of the illuminations are sliding and merging; I blink hard. "I don't know. Nothing looked the same."

I haven't heard her move, but suddenly here she is easing the book out of my hands, drawing me toward the window seat. I let her lead me. As we sit she says gently, "Go on."

"Everything was so ugly." The scene rises before my eyes again: the Presence Chamber; the crush of people, come to watch me eat; the greasy sheen of their hair; the pockmarked skin; their rank odor. And the colors of the tapestries, melting and running as I watched . . .

Our knees are almost touching; Catherine is holding my hands. She says, "And . . . how does everything look now?"

Like a child, I bury my face in her shoulder. The smell of her skin is so familiar; it feels like home.

After a while, without moving, I say, "Catherine, our marriage is cursed."

"We married in good faith."

"We were wrong."

There's a pause. She is breathing steadily. She says, "This isn't the way to go."

Abruptly, I sit up. Then stand. Move backward, facing her. I say, "You have nothing to fear. You will be treated with great honor. You will lose no comforts: clothes, horses, land, jewels . . ."

She is standing too. "You are not yourself. You need me."

"I need to be *free* of you," I say, and leave the room.

60

Behind me the packed courtroom watches me go: the law-yers, clerks, bishops. And the judges: two cardinals in their red robes. One of them is Wolsey, the other an ailing Italian named Campeggio, present at the pope's insistence. At the lower end of the chamber the common people gawk as I pass, making no noise except for shuffles and whispers. Merchants and their wives, shopkeepers, laborers—all have shoved and jostled for a viewing spot, and many who did not make it are squashed into the anteroom beyond or on the stairs.

I am wearing my public face: sober, dignified, gracious—fitting for a man struggling with his conscience, fitting for a man coming away from the opening day of the trial that will determine the validity (or otherwise) of his twenty-year marriage.

I don't descend the packed staircase; instead I walk on, into an adjoining first-floor gallery heading north, and then strike northwest as another gallery takes me diagonally across the friary's gardens and orchards. This leads straight into a new-built covered bridge that crosses the River Fleet and links Blackfriars, inside the City wall, with my palace of Bridewell just outside it.

It is a gray day, but hot and airless. The Fleet is an open sewer, its banks a public highway. The crowds here are as thick as the stench, their dusty, muddy clothes as brown as the water. As I pass the bridge's windows I raise my hand to them in acknowledgment, suppressing the urge to grimace at the smell. A lone child shouts and waves—the rest gaze up at me dumbly.

Once over the bridge, in Bridewell Palace, I walk faster. Guards stand to attention as I approach, courtiers bow and curtsy. I don't acknowledge them—I have dropped my public mask.

One of Wolsey's men is waiting outside the door to my chamber: Thomas Cromwell. He's a bruiser of a man in black velvet. I stop in front of him, dig my finger into his chest. "You can tell the guards: *Never* let the common people into my court again."

"Yes, Your Grace. Your Grace—"

He's got something to ask or tell me, but before he can say it I pass into the room and kick the door shut; it slams in his face.

Slumping into a chair, I press the heels of my hands into my eyes.

"Drink, sir?"

It's a goblet, held out by one of my men. I take it and smash it into the hearth.

"They shout for her. Why not for me? Eh?"

"Who do?"

"The common people. The bloody rabble." I fling my arms wide and yell at the ceiling: "'Care for nothing, Queen Catherine! Heaven favors you!' Damn them!" My fists strike the chair arms. "Can't they see it's an act? It's calculated. She's been *coached*, for Christ's sake."

I find that I do need a drink—urgently. I go to the sideboard and pour it myself; some of it slops over the side of the glass. "She went on her knees. Do you know that? Groveled at my feet in front of the whole courtroom, asking for pity, saying that she's a foreigner and at my mercy, that she's humble and obedient. And they treat her like she's the bloody Second Coming."

I gulp the drink, wipe my mouth. "And then when *I* stand up and say I have been in agonies of conscience . . . say I would be glad to find the marriage good if only someone could *prove* it to me, what do they do? They snigger behind their—their shit-covered hands."

"Because they think you're lying."

I turn. My gentlemen attendants have melted away—perhaps at a nod from Anne. She is standing, unmoving, in the corner.

"Oh I *see*," I say with sarcasm. "And do *you* think I'm lying, Anne?"

She looks back at me evenly. "No."

It is nearly midsummer. The windows are open, but the muggy heat is unforgiving. Anne—impervious, it seems, to the weather—is dressed in black, with only her face standing out pale in the shadows.

She says, "I think you *would* be glad to have it proved. But the only possible proof would be your son, standing here beside you now, aged sixteen."

"Seventeen," I say quietly. That child who lived for fifty-two days. "He would have been seventeen, this last New Year."

She looks at me, impassive. "Do you dream of him, ever?" she says. "He is your height, perhaps. Your coloring. Strong. A great horseman. Skilled enough with a longbow to rival the best captain in your army. A leader of men in the making. Who loves and fears his father as a god."

"You know, sometime I really must ask your brother about your favorite childhood hobby. I believe he will tell me it was tearing the wings off birds. Or drowning puppies."

"I'm not being cruel. I'm reminding you why I am here."

"You are showing me the prize, Anne—a son, an heir—without giving me the means to achieve it."

Her eyebrows rise a fraction. "I have given you the means already."

She has shown me books and pamphlets setting out arguments about the role of the Church. Saying that ancient histories and chronicles declare this realm of England to be an empire. That, as such, it is free from the authority of any foreign ruler. And that I, as king of England, have no superior except God.

Where, these writings ask, does it say in the Bible that a pope should have authority over a king?

Anne walks forward. In the center of the room there's a table strewn with papers relating to the trial. She stops beside it. "Have the case decided here," she says. "Not like this." She waves a dismissive hand over the papers. "Not under the pope's jurisdiction, under *yours*. Change your judges. Get rid of Wolsey. He has made so little progress he must be either incompetent or working against you: a nice choice. Get rid of this decrepit Italian cardinal, Campeggio. The pope, I guarantee you, has given him a secret mission to delay and delay until I am beyond childbearing age or we all topple into our graves from the tedium of it, whichever is the sooner. Instead have the archbishop of Canterbury try the case."

I snort. "Old Warham? We'd get nowhere. He refuses to act against Rome."

"But what is he now—seventy-nine? Eighty? He can't live much longer. Then you can appoint a new archbishop who sees the truth."

I pour myself another drink, knock it back, look at her. "And if the case is decided without agreement from the pope," I say, "what then? Do you think he sends me a letter of congratulation and wishes me every happiness? Hm? *I* think he excommunicates me and invites all the kings of Christendom to come and deprive me of my throne."

Anne walks up to me. She stands very close. She says, "Since when did England fear? Since when did *you* fear . . . anyone? France will support you against the emperor. We Boleyns alone will give you ten thousand troops. Free of charge for a whole campaign season."

I smile. "If you can raise that many, I've given you too much land."

"I will lead them myself if necessary."

"Christ." I slip my hands around her waist. "I believe you would, too."

"This is not about me," Anne whispers, her face close to mine. "Or Catherine, or the pope. It is about you—only you. God has spoken to you. So. Do you want to provide this empire of England with an heir—or don't you?"

61

With a window-shattering boom the great guns of the Tower fire, greeting the arrival of the water procession. The Thames is a riot of noise and color as far downstream as the eye can see.

A huge model dragon, terrifying as a pagan god, rears up from one barge, surging along in shuddering bursts as the oarsmen pull their blades through the water. Its head swings from side to side, its mammoth jaw drops open, spews out flames and sparks, and then snaps shut again.

In another barge monsters with bulbous eyes, grotesque limbs, and lolling tongues spit more fireworks, while hideous wild men in suits of straggling fur roar and snarl beside them.

A third barge carries a floating craggy mountain, topped by a golden tree stump. On this, a great white falcon has landed. The bird—molting a scattering of real feathers as a stray streamer slaps it on the wing—wears a crown on its head, and where its claws grip the gilded wood, flowers are sprouting: red and white roses, in fertile abundance.

In among these monstrosities the wherries nip and weave, the silk- and tapestry-clad barges of the City guilds plow in formation (their on-board musicians laboring valiantly against the din), while the lords and bishops, in their own barges, vie for attention by the ostentation of their display.

And all about, flags and bell-tipped pennants snap and jingle, and the sunshine flashes where it can on the odd inch of free water.

I, meanwhile, am waiting.

From this chaos Anne emerges at last, climbing up the wharf steps from her own barge, like the sun creeping over the horizon. She is a golden creature emerging from the filth of the Thames—a phoenix of renewed hope, rising from my blighted past.

The wharf is packed with people. Down a corridor of spectators I see her; she comes toward me, stepping carefully on her dainty, golden-slippered feet.

Her cloth-of-gold mantle trails behind her, wiping away the old ashy lies and untruths, the blasphemies and superstitions. Her strange, elfin face is a shining vision of triumph and certainty.

I have met her challenge.

I have broken free of the pope, broken with a thousand years of mistaken tradition, and asserted God's truth: that I am the supreme head of the Church in my kingdom, and that no one has power over me but God himself.

Old Warham has died; by my permission my new archbishop of Canterbury has judged the case and declared that Catherine and I were never truly married in the eyes of God. And so at last, I have a wife: I have married Anne.

She was right (as she so often is): Wolsey was no help. And now he is dead too. Taken by illness, he breathed his last on the way to the Traitors' Gate of this very fortress, whispering to his friends that Anne was a night crow who haunted me like an evil spirit.

But the evil was in his own heart only, and here's the proof: look at her now.

Her slight frame is swollen by the child in her belly: my son.

I am standing on the drawbridge that links the wharf to the Tower. This is Anne's formal reception into the Tower as my queen—in three days' time she will be crowned in Westminster Abbey. Before me stands a greeting party: my lord chamberlain, my lieutenant and constable of the Tower, and those noblemen and bishops not already on the river.

Behind me stands the monstrous edifice of the Tower itself, the fortress I once saw as a swallowing beast, a gate to hell, a place of horrors. Today, Anne will shine a light in its darkness that will burn away the evil: That light is my son, in her belly.

I think of the child I once saw in a dream, the little boy walking down beams of light toward me from a bright black sun. Now I feel as if it is my son coming down the beams of light toward me, as I stand here in the darkness—the darkness of the Tower, the darkness of my years of struggle. He will stretch out his small hand to me. And I will take it and step into the light. He is my bloodline, my future, the beginning of my glorious dynasty that will live on forever.

Anne walks past the bowing lords and bishops. She reaches me, and her black eyes shine brighter than her golden robes.

In a ringing voice that all can hear I say, "Welcome, my adored wife and true queen." I take her shoulders and kiss her; more quietly I add, "Welcome, Anne."

And, turning, I take her hand and lead her under the shadowy gateway, and on, into the dark Tower itself.

The required feats have been performed; I have won the hand of the golden maiden. Now my destiny stretches before me, as the prophecy made in this very place, all those long years ago, foretold:

Oh blessed ruler . . . you are the one so welcome that many acts will smooth your way. You will extend your wings in every place; your glory will live down the ages.

Now, at last, the waiting is ended.

Empire and sons.

62

It is three months since Anne's coronation; it is September and it is squally. The wind whines around the gardens and courtyards here at Greenwich, seeming unsure of the way out, buffeting the heraldic beasts on their poles and stirring the waters of the fountains. Inside my thick robes I shiver.

September, for months, has been my goal. By now I was to have been deliriously happy. Because by now the child would have been born.

And it *is* born. Anne has been delivered safely. She and the child are both alive. It is a fine-looking infant. Healthy, robust.

But it is a girl.

When the news was brought to me I took in a sharp breath. Now, five days later, I feel as if I have not yet breathed out again.

This I never expected.

Not this, not this, not this.

It is unthinkable.

The river today looks cold and gray in the flat north light. I am standing in a bay window, staring out; someone behind me speaks. It is a bishop, one of my councillors. In his hand he holds a dispatch: Begging Your Grace's pardon, but there is an urgent question regarding the matter of the ships from Lübeck. . . .

I snatch the paper: I can read it for myself. The bishop makes a nervous little prance toward me and back, urging me to let him summarize—in scanning the paper I soon see why. Not just news of ships and mercantile quarrels: There is news from our man in Flanders of rumors, too. Rumors circulating that Anne has been delivered of a monster—or else a child that is dead, and that if I do not take back Catherine as my wife the pope will summon all Christian princes to make war on England by Easter next. Oh yes and, to cap it all, these Flemings liken the king of England to Count Baldwin of Flanders, who was plagued by diabolic illusions. . . .

I crush the paper—tight, tight into a ball—and take it to the fireplace and throw it in the flames. As it catches light it begins to unfurl; the edges flare brightly as they burn.

Behind me the bishop's voice patters on anxiously, bland and soothing: What ordure it is, sir, but it is as well to know what is said on the streets, what is said anywhere in fact; it's astonishing of course how evil the slander can be. Nevertheless we can circulate counter-rumors, even as far afield as Flanders; and now perhaps we can come on to the matter of those ships from Lübeck?

I don't turn; I stare into the flames as they curl around the blackened remnants of the paper. These last few nights I have dreamed of monstrous births myself. Such events have genuinely happened in certain German and Italian cities—I have seen woodcuts of the things born. One woman produced a creature with bird's wings and a single leg ending in a clawed foot. Another had a child with bat's wings and two legs, one bearing a devil's hoof, the other an eye at the knee. I have dreamed of Anne bringing forth a serpent, with a scaly hide and great tearing claws.

Each time, I have woken to find Anne lying beside me in the dark: this astonishing being sent me by God, as ready for battle as if she wore armor. And I have wondered how I can dream such things. She has given me a healthy girl. Next it will be a fine warrior son.

So Anne tells me—and she is right. She is as defiant and determined as in those dark years of struggle over the annulment of my marriage to Catherine, and she is delighted with our daughter, too—whom I have named Elizabeth, after my mother. She is delighted with Elizabeth's strong limbs and her vigorous cry, her dark Boleyn eyes and her tuft of red-gold Tudor hair.

When I look at the child, I am also proud. But as soon as she is taken away, the feeling fades. I think: The boy Anne was carrying when she climbed the wharf steps at the Tower, the boy who shone his brilliant light in that place of dark horrors—where has he gone? He existed; I knew him. I put my hand on her belly, and I felt him move and kick.

Behind me, the bishop has paused now; he is waiting for a response, though I have no idea of the question. I tell him I will deal with the matter later and I leave him, walking through my Privy Chamber and my Presence Chamber and a short gallery to my private closet on the first-floor balcony of the Chapel Royal.

Norris has followed me. At the chapel door I tell him to remain outside. As I enter, I see the dean and one of the chaplains below me, standing near the dark-wood choir stalls; I dismiss them. I want to be alone. When they have gone, I descend the spiral stair that leads into the main body of the chapel, approach the altar, and kneel.

What is it I want to say to my God? That waiting a single moment longer for my son is an agony, that I have done too much waiting these last twenty years, that I am pulled taut, as if I am lashed to a wheel, or on the rack. I waited so long to marry Anne. Marrying her meant the *end* of waiting—I thought.

I know God has a plan for me, but I do not understand why it should require this. Perhaps, then, I am praying for strength. Perhaps I am asking God to reveal to me his reasons. . . .

The chapel is a cold and empty chamber. Candles are lit at the altar and beneath the stern-faced statues; from time to time a wick sizzles. Gradually I become aware of the stillness of the space behind me. It seems eerily like a presence, like something waiting.

I look over my shoulder. The balcony is dark and seems unoccupied; beneath it there is no movement in the shadows.

I turn back and bow my head. But now I can hear something, an indistinct brushing or scraping. I think of nesting birds. I think of rats. I try to block it out—to focus on my prayer. I hope the sound will stop. I don't want to see what makes it.

But the sound doesn't stop. And I feel compelled to find its source.

In front of anyone else I would never move like this, would never *edge* toward a sound, which I now sense comes from behind the pulpit to my right. I don't want to see, but I must see; I am already clammy inside my clothes.

Peering slowly, inch by inch, round the edge of the pulpit, I spot a sliver of something dark, down near the floor. The sliver shifts in sudden jerks—it is part of something active; I am not alone.

I cringe against the pulpit's wooden paneling—then force myself to look. The sliver I saw was the edge of a doublet: dark fabric. Its wearer is kneeling on the floor; the soft scraping sound I heard is made by his fingernails as he drags them in great tearing sweeps along his skin. The scratching is violent and brutal. Unlaced at the wrists, his sleeves are pushed back—red tracks are raised on the surface of his forearms, intermittently speckled with blood.

As I watch, he bends his head, puts his hands—like bony rakes—beneath the straw-colored hair at the nape of his neck and drags them downward around the curve of his throat, leaving fork-tracks of red. The effort pulls from him a guttural grunt—the effort and perhaps the pain.

The sight is contemptible, disgusting; I lean against the side of the pulpit, then stumble up its short staircase and lunge for the Bible as for a talisman that will ward him off.

The great book is lying open on the lectern. It takes me a moment to focus on the words. To drown out the sound of him—the thing, *the boy*—I read loudly the first sentence my eye falls on: "'Be sober and watch, for your adversary the

Devil as a roaring lion walketh about, seeking whom he may devour . . .'"

I can still hear him; still louder I read, declaiming the words as if to a congregation: "'The God of all grace, which called you unto his eternal glory by Christ Jesus, shall his own self, after ye have suffered a little affliction, make you perfect; shall settle, strengthen, and establish you. To him be glory and dominion forever, and while the world endureth. Amen.'"

"Sir?" At the back of the chapel Norris has put his head around the door; his mild brown eyes are puzzled and concerned. He could hear me outside, no doubt, and must have wondered at me shouting in an empty space.

I have stopped shouting now. The scraping sound has stopped too; I know, without looking, that the boy has gone.

My hands are on the open book; I am breathing hard, as if I have just fought a bout. Why do I suffer this? Is it part of God's purpose? Does he show me this hideous apparition—this ghost or whatever it may be—to remind me that there is evil in the world that I must fight too?

I don't need to look far for it. Plenty of my own subjects wish me ill. There have been predictions—some would call them prophecies, but I do not grace them with that name. A monk declared last year that if I married Anne the dogs would lick my blood as they licked Ahab's. And a nun who claimed to see visions foretold that I should not remain king one month after the marriage.

When I hear such things, I am ready to lick the blood of the traitors that circulate this filth. But look: The months have passed and none of it has come true. It is more than half a year since Anne and I were married, and I am still king.

As I move among my smiling courtiers these days, though, I wonder: How many in their secret hearts believe I deserve death—for breaking with the pope, for heresy; how many of them hope my grave is gaping for me even now?

"Norris," I say, coming down from the pulpit, "call in all keys—the master keys and the by-keys. And send for my locksmith. I want a new set of locks made. Larger and more complex. More secure. Perhaps I will design them myself."

"New locks for the royal apartments, sir?"

"For all the rooms in the palace, Norris," I say, passing him. I head toward the spiral staircase that leads back to my apartments. "In *every* palace."

63

The piece Anne's playing is very difficult. Her fingers move swiftly over the keyboard; her brow is furrowed in concentration.

I lean across and play a flourish on the low notes. She slaps me away.

"You are very irritating," she says, but her tone is teasing.

My chair is right beside hers. I put my face close to her ear. "I-love-you-I-love-you-I-love-you."

She swats me away like a fly. Grinning, I return my attention to the astrolabe I'm holding. "My wife is *so* heartless."

The astrolabe is a thing of beauty: a gilt brass disk and dial, engraved with sea monsters and signs of the zodiac. It can be used for navigating on board ship, for telling the time day or night, for casting horoscopes, and for surveying land. When the new child in Anne's belly is born, I'll be able to calculate his natal chart with this thing—for I was right: God has brought the next child, the boy, to us swiftly; the infant Elizabeth is only a few months old and Anne is pregnant again.

I move the astrolabe's dial, examining the gradations marked on the rim. I say, "Have you felt him move yet?"

"It's too early."

We both return to our preoccupations. Outside the winter

sun is watery and cold, weeping a trickle of light through a dank fog. Here in my private gallery, torches in sconces on the walls throw patches of flickering orange onto the ceiling. A great fire blazes in the grate, but drafts still swirl at floor level; my bad leg is propped up to escape them.

Anne sings a phrase or two as she plays, then breaks off. "If you love me so much . . . What . . . then"—she plays a note for each word—"would . . . you . . . give up for me?"

I laugh, still fiddling with the astrolabe. "What have I *not* given up for you?"

She turns and looks at me severely; I raise my eyebrows—*what?* Then I relent and play the game; I put down the astrolabe. "All right. My hunting. I would give up the chase."

She pretends to consider the offer for a moment—then turns back to playing. "Not enough."

"What? That's huge! All right then . . . I would give up gambling. Of any kind. No money will be staked by the king on anything ever again."

She plays a little more, breaks off, shakes her head. "Uh-uh."

Reaching over, I take hold of her chin and turn her face to me. I say, "I would beg alms from door to door for the rest of my days."

"To keep me in finery, I hope."

"Of course. And I would lie at your feet in my stinking rags like a dog, and you could feed me scraps from your plate." I kiss her. "Is that enough?"

I kiss her again. She wrinkles her nose and says, "Maybe."

I kiss her repeatedly—kiss, kiss, kiss. I say, "Maybe, hm? Maybe."

Suddenly I feel Anne tense, though she doesn't move away. I realize that someone has come in. A bulky figure is standing in the shadows beyond the window. I let go of Anne, stretch, get up—say, "Cromwell, my diligent man, what have you brought in your ink-stained hands for me now? Come on. How many things on your list?"

The hands holding today's documents are thick as a blacksmith's. Cromwell is a fighting dog, born in a back alley—a start in life so unheralded that he doesn't even know his own age. I like his savage teeth; I like his charm. He is quick to see my purposes. God's purposes. He gets things done.

Right now he is scanning his list. I say, "Oh, don't depress me. Just start." I turn to Anne. "Business is troublesome. Yours should be all happy thoughts. Take yourself to your ladies. For the child's sake."

She's standing beside the virginals, queenly and authoritative. She says, "I'm fine."

"For the child."

She shoots me a withering look—and a concession. "I'll sit down."

Cromwell's first subject is Catherine, whose title now is not queen, of course, but—as my brother's widow—princess dowager. He says, "Your Majesty. The latest report from Buckden says that the princess dowager hasn't been out of her room for an entire month. Except to hear Mass in a gallery." Anne gives a snort of exasperation, gets up again.

Cromwell refers to his notes. "She won't eat or drink what her new servants provide. The little she does eat is prepared by her chamberwomen. And her room is used as her kitchen—"

"So—what?" I slap the sideboard next to me. "What should I be doing about it? Did I order any of this? This squalid situation is"—I beat my hand on the wood for emphasis—"*entirely* of her *own making.* What does she think? That we intend to poison her?"

"Of course," Anne says. She follows me with her eyes as I cross to one of the windows. The fog seems to press against the glass. Below, dim silhouettes appear and disappear in the near distance—the builders are doing what they can despite the weather. This palace of Hampton Court is to have entirely new queen's lodgings; we are impatient for them to be finished.

Cromwell says, "The princess dowager complains that the house at Buckden is too near the river, sir, and that the damp is destroying her health."

"Nothing will destroy her health so well as keeping to her chamber, taking no air or exercise, and thinking nothing but obstinate and vengeful thoughts." I turn to face him. "But if she is determined to hasten to her grave, I will not stop her."

"And she asks, again, to see the Lady Mary."

The Lady Mary, our daughter—our illegitimate daughter, since she was born during an invalid marriage. Now no longer princess, and now almost eighteen years old.

Anne answers quietly: "Mary can see her mother when

she tames the obstinacy of her Spanish blood and recognizes that she herself is a bastard."

Cromwell's eyes flick to me: checking.

I say, "Exactly. I expect Lady Shelton has told you—Mary is playing the same trick as her mother and keeping to her chamber, so she won't have to encounter our daughter Elizabeth."

"And *curtsy* to her," Anne puts in.

"Catherine must be encouraging her. No doubt the emperor's ambassador has been in touch with her too. Are you intercepting correspondence?"

"Of course," says Cromwell.

The emperor's current ambassador, Chapuys, is a mincing little twig of a man, and an inveterate gossip. "He can go to hell," I say. "I loathe him."

Cromwell rubs his sausagey fingers over his chin. He's clean-shaven, but his hair is so dark that the skin there is permanently gray. He says, "But I'd suggest, sir, that you shouldn't say anything—yet—about the advice Chapuys is giving her. It would reveal our surveillance—and bring it to an end. We're waiting to land a bigger fish: We want to know whether the princess dowager is sending messages to the emperor, asking him to invade."

"Yes . . . Christ. I know."

"There is a different matter though, sir, on which you might decide to act," Cromwell goes on. "I have spies in Chapuys's household. They tell me he has been heard saying something . . . *interesting* . . . lately. Saying that when Parliament is bullied into passing a law, that law is worth nothing. And that men can, with a clear conscience, disobey it as soon as a signal comes from the pope or the emperor to do so."

For a moment, no one speaks. The fire spits and hisses.

My focus is all on Cromwell. I seem to see him down a tunnel. I say, "So. Let me get this straight. An act—say, the Act of Succession you're preparing, the act that will confirm this boy-child as my heir . . ." I point, without looking, in the direction of Anne's belly. "This act can be passed by Parliament, signed, and sealed, and then, as soon as the emperor lands an invasion force, *my own subjects* are absolved from any duty to obey it? They can fight beside the emperor's troops to put some usurper on the throne instead of me or my true heir? Is that what he means?"

"I believe so, sir."

Evil surrounds me. *Be sober and watch,* the Bible says, *for your adversary the Devil as a roaring lion walketh about, seeking whom he may devour . . .*

My hand goes to my belt as I walk forward. "Bring Chapuys to me. Bring the nasty little shit to me. To hell with ambassadorial protection." I have drawn my dagger; I hold the blade up, glinting, in front of Cromwell's nose. "I will gut him myself. I will *flay* him." Turning, I throw the knife at the wall. It embeds itself, shuddering, in the wood paneling. I press my palms against my forehead—pushing back hard, stretching the skin. My head feels fit to explode.

I hear a cool, dogged voice: "If he is saying it, others will too."

I whip round to face Anne. "So I will have them all killed. No one will stand in the way of my son succeeding. I will slaughter them like beasts; I will hang them from every gibbet. Let every town stink of rotting meat."

Cromwell says, "I have a solution to propose."

"Christ." I cross to the windows, then back again. My leg is hurting. "Tell me. Tell me what it is. Quickly." I keep walking; I can't stop.

"Have an oath prepared," says Cromwell steadily. "Make each citizen swear to maintain this act. Swear"—he counts the points off on his fingers—"to obey Your Majesties, to uphold the right of your children to inherit the crown, to accept the validity of your marriage, to deny the power of the pope . . . Then it will be on each person's conscience, before God, to obey—or risk the damnation of their soul."

I am still walking; I mutter, "Yes. Yes."

Anne says, "How can you possibly swear everyone?"

Out of the corner of my eye I see Cromwell grin. "Anything can be done, Your Grace."

I don't need to look—I know that she doesn't smile in return; she is waiting for more. Quickly Cromwell adds, "Appoint commissioners. Use every landowner, every justice of the peace, every bishop, abbot, and friar—give each one responsibility for the swearing of every person under their charge. I will organize it."

I stop walking in front of another window, put my arms up, and lean on the mullions, glaring out at the blank, gray view.

Behind me Anne says, "And what if people refuse?"

"Simple," says Cromwell. "Then the treason laws will take their course."

Which means the death penalty. So the choice is this: Swear complete allegiance to me or die.

64

"It's not complicated, Norris. Well, not *that* complicated." I'm coming down the stairs, slapping my riding crop on the side of my boot.

Behind me, Norris says, "I just can't quite imagine it, sir."

At the turn of the staircase, I stop and pull out my hunting knife. "Look, the barrel runs along the back of the blade—the blade's single-edged and deep like this one. And the barrel's very narrow." I hold the knife level and show with my thumb and forefinger where the pistol's barrel lies. "I'll show you when we get back to London. You can have a go at firing it."

George Boleyn, waiting farther up the staircase for us to move on, says, "Give me notice, sir—he's a terrible shot. I'd want to take cover."

"I seem to remember he beat you at the butts a few months back," says Edward Seymour beside him.

I'm at the More, one of Wolsey's old houses in Hertfordshire. There's always good hunting here, and it's a glorious day outside; we're ready in our boots and green hunting coats, and Boleyn—who, among his other titles, is my master of the buckhounds—has assured me that the dogs and their handlers are ready.

Reaching the bottom of the stairs, I say, "That branch of

the moat that lies farthest west—should I have it filled in?"

"Sir?" Norris looks confused. He's still troubled by the idea of a combined knife and pistol.

"The moat here." Facing Norris, I'm walking backward. "The branch of it nearest the river. You know? It would make a better run for the hunting if it was filled in, don't you thi—"

I cannon straight into someone behind me. I turn to see the top of a gable headdress; it's one of Anne's maids of honor, curtsying now, with her head bowed.

"I—I'm so sorry, Your Majesty," comes a small voice from under the headdress. In her hands she's holding a pile of clean linen.

I regard her for a moment—a moment she evidently finds uncomfortable. Then I say, "You are forgiven. Go on your way." She scurries off.

"Seymour, isn't that one of your sisters?"

"Yes, sir."

I watch her hurried progress down the passageway. "Which one?"

"Jane, sir."

"Does she always shake like that?"

Seymour begins to apologize; I slap his stomach with the back of my hand. "Don't worry, man. I like it. It makes a change from what I get from—"

I stop. In the shadows under the stairs there is a bundle of clothes. Except it is not a bundle of clothes. It is *him*—again. Crouching, his bony knees drawn up. The boy.

What's shocking this time is how much worse he looks—ravaged, emaciated, sinewy. His clothes are frayed and worn and hang limply from his thin frame. He is eating like an animal—in front of him on the floor are strewn pieces of a small spare carcass. He is picking at the bones with his fingers, shoveling morsels quickly to his mouth.

As I watch, he lifts his head to me. I see the wet gleam of his eyes in the gloom. He drops his food and extends his arms, his greasy clawlike fingers reaching out, scratching the air. A voice sounds in my head, insistent and demanding:

Comfort me.

The boy's lips have not moved, but I know the voice is his.

"Sir?" says Norris beside me. "Are you all right, sir?"

My heart is hammering; I am sweating. I hardly dare acknowledge it, but with an unsteady hand I point. "Norris, do you see anything?"

"Where, sir?"

"There—under the stairs."

He goes over—peers into the shadows.

The boy ignores Norris, stares past him straight at me. Looking half-starved as he does, he should be weak, but I have the feeling that his power is growing, that in his physical deterioration this creature is showing more and more of his devilish nature.

Comfort me!

That voice again.

Norris shakes his head. "What kind of thing am I looking for, sir?"

"Huh? Nothing. Trick of the light," I say, holding the boy's gaze.

It is an effort to turn away, but I do it. Turn and walk to the door that gives out onto the courtyard. As I am about to reach it—about to escape into the sunshine outside—a clatter of footsteps brings a page boy, running down the corridor, scrambling to a halt.

"Your Majesty, I have a message from the queen."

I turn back. From here I cannot see the space under the stairs. Instead I see the page boy, straightening from his bow. He looks pale, shocked. Behind him I see women coming and going from the direction of Anne's apartments. Holding linen, like the Seymour girl. Hurrying. Heads bowed. I realize that some of them are crying.

Around me, my men are waiting—tense for my reaction.

Disconcerted by the silence, the messenger looks to Norris for instruction—should he go on?

Norris says gently, "Will you hear it, sir?"

There's a pane of glass between me and the world—the page boy, my men, the whole scene is distant. Here, where I am, there is only me. And the voice:

Comfort me!

I say, "What?"

"The message, sir," says Norris. "Will you hear it?"

But I don't need to hear it. I have seen the crying women, the fresh linen, the shocked messenger. It is too soon for Anne to be delivered of a live child.

I feel a rising panic: I will not hear the message. I will not hear the words. I cannot. I say to Norris, "No."

And I turn again toward the open door. For a moment I have to steady myself against the doorframe. The sunshine outside is dazzling: a bright black light.

65

In a dark little room, stuffed with books bound in deep shades of red and brown, the man's clean, white, disk-shaped collar stands out, as if his head is sitting, like John the Baptist's, on a plate. He says, "According to the law as it stands, refusal to swear the oath upholding the validity of Your Majesty's marriage to Queen Anne and the succession of Your Majesties' heirs carries the maximum sentence of life imprisonment. It cannot carry the death penalty."

I sit back in my chair and regard him: Audley, my current lord chancellor, is an able if unappealing man, with a salt-and-pepper beard and an irritating attachment to legal niceties. Still, his care for detail, alongside Cromwell's own, is what, day by day, makes possible this extraordinary task of swearing the entire nation.

Whole villages at a time are being assembled to take the oath. All males above the age of fourteen are called. And those with most responsibility have it driven home to them—by Cromwell himself—how closely they are watched. Bishops, you are responsible for the obedience of your clergy; abbots and friars, for the brethren in your institutions; landowners, for your tenants. Most are stumbling over themselves in their hurry to submit. Most fear the consequences of refusal. Those consequences, then, cannot be anything less than terrifying. If I make a few grisly examples, it will be enough to steady any wavering minds that remain.

Through clenched teeth I say, "According to the law as it stands? Then change the law."

Audley glances down at his hands. He seems to be hesitating. Then he says, "Begging Your Majesty's pardon, might I put before your remembrance some of those who have refused to swear the oath? The bishop of Rochester, Sir Thomas More—"

"Your point?"

He blinks at me. "Sir, the bishop is an old man. Held, internationally, in high esteem. He was your grandmother's confessor . . ."

I say under my breath, "My grandmother—what, that old witch?"

"He preached at your illustrious father's funeral . . ."

"Oh, I *see*. He can be excused treason for, what, *sentimental* reasons? And I suppose Master More, too—because I have called him my friend and have walked of an evening with my arm around his shoulders, discussing I-don't-know-what— then he may lead a rebellion to depose me or do as he pleases? Is that what you think?"

"He has no intention—"

"Really? But his refusal to swear is as good as a declaration of intent. To support the pope, to declare me a heretic, to deny the right of my son to rule."

My son that is not yet born. Not yet even conceived.

I say, "That is acceptable, is it?"

Audley's gaze drops to his hands again. "No, indeed not," he says.

"Indeed not."

I get up from behind my desk and walk to the window. It is dark outside; I see my silhouette reflected in the window-panes. The candles behind me seem to flare out of the top of my head. What did they do with the dead fetus Anne was delivered of, that day I saw the boy under the stairs? It occurs to me suddenly that I never even asked. Did he—for it was a male child, I did ask that—did he end up on the fire, along with the blood-stained linen?

I take hold of the nearest curtain and pull it round me, so that I can see into the darkness outside. I say, "God makes trials of his chosen ones—my life is proof of that. The Devil looks about for hearts to enter, to test me, to smite me. Who will he choose? Those *closest* to me. My friends. Don't you think?"

Audley doesn't answer. Below, a short distance away, I can just make out a wherry plow its way across the black water of the Thames. On the far bank torches blaze at the land-ing stairs by Lambeth Palace. The flames, the inky water—I might as well be looking at the gateway to the underworld.

I say, "Evil stalks the land. If you don't believe it, you are a fool." I turn back to Audley, tugging the curtain shut behind me. "So—what do you suppose evil looks like? It wears a mask. It looks like anyone—you." I grin at him.

"Or you." I approach a young man hovering by the door—a lutenist who was playing for me before Audley arrived. I have forgotten to dismiss him; he is looking now as if he would like to melt into the wall hangings.

I say, "And it smiles." The young man smiles automatically, nervously; an instant later his smile vanishes when he realizes what I've just said.

"And then it murders you in cold blood the first chance it gets," I say, turning back to Audley.

A few minutes later we are walking along a gallery, beneath a ceiling fretted like a gilded cobweb. On the wall, frozen painted figures—Orpheus and the beasts, Death visiting a banquet—glow in the candlelight. The sound of laughter and the scent of spiced fruits drift to us from the rooms ahead. I have an appointment for supper, dancing, and a few hands of primero in Anne's apartments tonight.

I am saying to Audley, "So, it must be made high treason, punishable by death, not only to wish bodily harm to come to us, but also to deny us any of our titles, or to say or write that we are heretics or tyrants."

Audley pulls at his lower lip, thinking as he walks. He says, "This will require a new Act of Treasons."

"So speak to—"

Suddenly: Anne. Standing in the bulge of a bay window, she's been out of sight as we've approached. Now all at once we are upon her; she is talking with her brother George and with Norris—laughing with them. She turns. Her mouth is open; I am too close. She is laughing in my face.

"—Cromwell," I finish.

In the gap between two words—a measure of time no

longer than a heartbeat—I have been hit by a stray thought.

The Devil looks about for hearts to enter, to test me, to smite me. Who will he choose? Those closest to me. . . . Don't you think?

I groan.

"Sir?"

For a moment I am dazed. I turn to Audley, struggling to remember what I've just said. "Um . . . Speak to Cromwell about it, would you?"

"Yes, sir."

Audley leaves and I greet my wife. I watch her speaking; I do not hear what she says. Have I not noticed before how hard, how complaining her mouth is? The long neck seems grotesque; the pale, delicate-jointed fingers adjusting her cuffs are like white spiders' legs. She is wearing dark fur and black velvet and damask. What did Wolsey call her? A night crow.

Just a moment ago, the world seemed entirely different. Absently my hand moves to the crucifix pinned to the front of my doublet.

66

The quintain is in the shape of a cross, one arm ending in a shield, the other in a hanging weight. The aim is to strike the shield with your lance—as you would your opponent in the tilt—and set the quintain spinning. The trick then is to avoid being struck by the weight as it swings round.

Today—a December morning—the tiltyard is a vast barren plain of frost-hardened sand. I am here with a dozen others, practicing for the New Year tournaments. For me the quintain is a useful warm-up, but no test of my skills. For some of my younger companions, however, it is more of a challenge: A few hard knocks have already been taken, and a few falls endured, by the time I spot a stocky figure walking toward me from the outer courtyard gate. I pull up my horse to wait for him.

He is dressed in black, his cloak drawn close about him, his sable-lined bonnet pulled down over his ears.

"Well?" I say when he comes within range.

Cromwell doesn't reply until, having bowed, he is standing right by my horse's nose. He says, "Your Majesty, the doctors fear for the princess dowager's life."

I've jettisoned my lance already. Now I dismount—without too much difficulty today—and pass the reins to a groom. I say, "How long? Months, weeks, days—what?"

"Days—weeks at most."

"Yes!" I fling my head back. The shout floats heavenward on a cloud of warm breath.

Cromwell doesn't react, but others in the tiltyard look my way. I yell to them: "The princess dowager is dying! We'll be free from the danger of war! There'll be no reason for the emperor to attack us when she's gone!"

Energized, I put my arm around Cromwell's neck—lead him away from the grooms and other riders. "So much for Catherine. Let the Almighty gather her to his bosom as soon as he likes. I want to talk to you on another subject." I lower my voice: "I believe I may have had a sign from God, Thomas. About Queen Anne."

We reach an empty corner of the yard. I turn to face Cromwell, keeping a grip on his shoulders. I say, "I may have been tricked into this marriage."

"Tricked?"

I nod. "By witchcraft. Seduced. She is . . ." I shake my head; start again. "I have seen her true nature. I believe I might take another wife." I touch my gloved finger to Cromwell's mouth. "Shh. Our secret."

He regards me thoughtfully. For a big man, he has small eyes—and they are as sharp as a rat's. I suppose he is making quick calculations. He says, "Sir. One thing. In such a circumstance . . . would the queen, do you think, retire quietly? To—" He pushes out his lower lip, a facial shrug. "To a life of honorable seclusion?"

I look at him. In the distance I hear a double impact as a rider takes a blow and falls heavily to the floor.

It is very cold, standing like this. Cromwell's nose is red. I don't answer his question. Instead I say, "There will be a further sign. She has told me she is pregnant again. This new child she is carrying will prove it. Surely? God will speak through this pregnancy." And, patting Cromwell's shoulder as I pass, I walk back to my horses.

67

Today, every step is painful. But movement is a distraction; it is worse to sit and rest. Using my stick, I try to put as little weight on my left leg as possible as I walk.

Still, nothing prepares me for the pain that rips through me as I reach the middle of the room. I cringe against the nearest table, my weight on my elbows. I am panting, wondering if I will vomit, as saliva drips onto my hands. My attendants rush forward to help.

"Get away from me!"

They hover, uncertain. My stick has fallen; one of them makes a dash forward to pick it up. He slides it onto the table then backs off, fast.

I turn, still leaning on one elbow, my legs still buckled, and swipe the stick round at the lot of them, but they are standing just out of reach. "Don't treat me like a bloody invalid!" I snarl. "Leave me alone! Go and cower behind doors and spy on me through keyholes as I know you do!"

They blink at me stupidly.

"*Go on!*"

Hesitantly at first, and then all in a rush, they beat a retreat.

I am alone in the Privy Gallery, where I have come to try to walk off the pain. The old wound on my left leg is ulcerated and badly swollen. It needs to burst and discharge its evil humors. Until then it will not heal. Until then I am—intermittently—in agony.

The gallery is a long space—my private walkway—where decorations twist and creep up every available surface. On an evening like this it is lit with wax candles on the fireplace and in the windows, and torches in sconces on the walls. Behind the windows' shimmering reflections, the night is black and bitterly cold.

For now the pain has subsided; I walk again, haltingly, to the end of the room, and stop, gathering the energy to turn.

Which is when I hear it. The sound of a slow, shuffling tread on the stairs. And something like . . .

A tapping. No, no—more like a scratching. Listen—there it comes again.

Who said that once? My mother? I have no time to think. Fear makes my heart race; my head is pounding.

The staircase lies at this end of the room—a small spiral of stone steps leading up directly from my private garden. The door at the top stands ajar. The one at the bottom is—or should be—locked, and checked regularly by the guards of the night watch.

No one could possibly be climbing those stairs.

I listen, not breathing. There is a moment of silence, as if whoever is on the stairs is listening too. And then the footsteps resume.

I cannot move—and must move. I retreat crabwise, my eyes on the door.

Slowly the footsteps come nearer. It seems to take an eternity. Then I see thin fingers grasp the edge of the wood.

As the figure slips through the gap, it turns to look first in the wrong direction, at the empty end of the gallery.

I have a split second to see without being seen—and turn away.

Leaning on my stick, my back to the door, it takes me a moment to regain control. Then I say, "The quivering rabbit. Are you still quivering?" I turn to face her. "Yes, you are. Why did the guards let you through?"

The Seymour girl, Jane, has dropped into a deep curtsy. "I—I don't know, Your Majesty," she says. "My brother told me they would."

"How interesting."

Her brother, it seems, has convinced the guards I have authorized her admittance. What presumption. I find I am both amused and annoyed.

Thinking this, I am watching her. She squirms under the scrutiny, looks at her hands, the floor, the windows—then begins to fumble with the fastenings of her cloak.

I say, "I saw you the day the child died—remember?"

Her fingers freeze on the cloak's lacings. "Yes."

"I remember seeing you."

Another silence. Jane resumes her task and succeeds in untying the bows. She takes the cloak off, in the smallest, most self-effacing movement possible, and hangs it over one forearm, like a lady's maid carrying the garments of her mistress.

I say, "Are you here to seduce me, Jane?"

"No!" The shock jolts her, makes her look at me directly, if only for an instant. "No. Lord, no . . ." I watch as a deep blush spreads over her entire face and throat, and her hands clutch each other, fingers twisting painfully.

I think: *Whatever her brother's up to, he has kept her in the dark. Is she really so simple?*

I say, "Then why *are* you here?"

She bites her lip. "I would like to . . . My brother says I should ask . . . if you would like me to play some songs on the virginals for you. He thinks it might help you rest. . . ."

Christ. And she thinks this is what her brother genuinely means. Poor, artless cow.

I say, "Does he? And what do you think . . . Jane? Do you think it will help me rest?"

Her eyes flick up to me, return to the floor. She says, "I think perhaps you might find a little comfort in the quiet company of a simple girl who has no . . . no opinions or demands . . . who wants only to serve her sovereign in whatever way she can."

Ah. Maybe not so artless after all.

For a moment I remain, watching her. Then I turn and walk to the far end of the gallery—to the door to my apartments.

I open the door without glancing back. I could shut it behind me—I almost do.

Almost, but not quite. For a moment I hesitate. Then I stand aside, holding the door open—leaving room for her to pass.

68

I stride down the passageway, fast. Guards fall back as I slam into the room.

"Up. Up. Get up."

Faces turn; women servants, startled in the middle of their domestic tasks, drop what they are doing and curtsy hastily.

I drag open the bed curtains. Anne's face—angry, alarmed, puffy eyed from crying—stares at me from a mountain of pillows.

"I want to see the body that killed my son. *Again.*"

This new pregnancy has indeed produced a sign: another male fetus—dead.

Anne's hands are gripping the coverlet. I grab one thin wrist and pull. She has a job to get to her feet in time before I drag her bodily from the bed.

The servants have disappeared. She stands on the rug, her feet bare, her white nightshift falling straight to her ankles; but she stands as erect as if she were wearing the crown jewels.

I walk round her, twitching up the cloth of her nightshift, which she snatches from me and holds in fistfuls. I say, "Tell me. What is so rotten in this body that it cannot hold a child?"

"It can."

"A *boy* child. Girls count for less than nothing. As you know."

She looks at me, feral, glaring, her long hair disordered, strands of it across her face. She says, "It was the shock of your accident."

I stop. There is a table beside me. I lean back against it, my hands on the edge, and regard her with interest. I say, "Ah, I see. It is my fault, then?"

My left leg has healed, but at last week's tournament, forgetting how weakened it has become, I misjudged a maneuver in the joust and took a bad fall from my horse. They tell me I lost consciousness for two hours.

Anne's eyes flash with something like fear and something like contempt. She says, "No, I didn't say that. But I was so alarmed by the news that you were lying senseless . . ." She stops, compresses her lips, begins again: "In other pregnancies you have been concerned for my . . . my peace of mind. Now you should comfort me. But instead you taunt me."

Comfort me. I think of the ravaged figure I saw under the stairs the day she was delivered of the last dead boy. I say, "Taunt you? With what?"

"The attentions you are paying to"—she lowers her voice to a whisper—"that whey-faced bitch."

"I'm sorry, to whom?"

"To another lady. Don't think I haven't heard. I know what has been going on."

I raise my eyebrows. "Well. I am glad to hear that your spies are giving you such good service. Sometime I must remember to find out who they are and punish them. In the meantime, I would advise you to close your eyes, madam, as your betters have done before you. Remember, I have elevated you—and I can humble you again in an instant."

I turn to go—and get as far as the door before fists pummel my back.

"Why are you cruel to me? You love me!"

I turn, and in one quick movement catch her wrists and jerk them up, together, in front of her face. "Sweetheart, I really cannot imagine"—she has lowered her head; I dip mine to meet her eyes—"what I ever saw in you." She struggles; I tighten my grip and she stares at me, shocked and defiant, refusing to cry out in pain.

She struggles again. I transfer her wrists to one hand and, with the other, take hold of her hair and drag her head back. The throat is exposed, the ridges of the windpipe stand out beneath the pale smooth flesh. It reminds me of a hunted beast at the kill; this is what the dogs would want to bite.

Pulling her about behind me, I walk across the room. There are noises from her, but not many. She stumbles and struggles—not to get away, but simply to keep her feet and take the weight, dragging, off her hair.

It is when I turn toward the door again that I see, in the corner by the fireplace, the boy. He is crouching on a stool, his knees wide, his hands between, gripping the stool's front edge. His cheeks are hollow, his eyes glittering in the deep shadows beneath his brows; he is watching with avid interest.

My grip loosens, and I am vaguely aware of a thudding sound as Anne's head hits the floor.

I reach my bedchamber; I don't even remember leaving Anne's room.

Servants hover—bowing, frightened, writhing like maggots in fancy dress.

"Clear the room. *Go!*"

I lean over a chair—my hands on its arms. Beyond the sound of my own breathing, I hear footsteps coming up the stairs.

There are no stairs.

But, then . . . this time it is not Jane who is coming for me.

I draw my sword and set about methodically, energetically checking the room—batting at tapestries, slashing down bed curtains. I see figures in every fold of the hangings. Surely that one covers a face? Surely there a hand is gripping?

I find nothing. But still there is a sense of menace, of something behind me that swings round behind me again each time I move, something that can see me and is studying me intently—but I can't see it. I turn and turn like a baited animal.

At last I stand in the center of the room, holding my sword before me.

I think: *Come—I am ready. Let me confront you properly now.*

My empty left hand is extended, palm down, fingers spread. And that is where I see it first: a mist running from my fingers' ends. I drop my sword and hold out both hands. Like sand running in the wind over the surface of a beach it comes: something vaporous from my fingers, something that pours out of me to fill an unseen form, like liquid that reveals a bottle's shape by filling it.

The shape in front of me is quickly filled. It is him. As if I am standing with my fingertips touching a mirror, his shape mirrors mine: His fingertips seem to touch mine, though I cannot feel them. And just as quickly as the vapors fill his shape, so I am filled with horror. I called him, and he has come. I have conjured him, as they say a witch can conjure the Devil.

He is rattlingly thin, his clothes ragged; he looks squalid, contemptible. His eyes have the cold gleam of a wild beast; his fingers are sharp like claws. Aged and ageless at once, his face bears deep lines now, but they seem more like the lines of a malnourished child than the wrinkles of an old man.

I stare at him, aghast. I say, "Who are you? *What* are you?"

The boy drops his hands; our link is severed. Then a voice speaks, close in my head.

You tell me.

I think: Y*ou look like a creature of hell.* I say, "Are you a ghost?"

Slowly, he shakes his head.

"Then I believe you are Lucifer."

A soft, horrible smile curls the edges of his mouth.

Oh, come. Don't be dramatic.

He blinks at me. He is still waiting.

So I say, "One of Lucifer's servants, then? Some lower class of fallen angel?"

This causes him genuine merriment; he throws back his head, his mouth gaping, a black hole of mirth. And as he laughs, rage shoots through me. I think: *This* thing, *this hellish vision, plagues me only because I am an archangel, a warrior of light, battling the dark forces. It is my virtue that draws him.*

With a roar I swing at him, putting all my weight behind a punch—but it passes right through his jaw. I stagger. I have swung round to face the opposite direction—yet here he is, in front of me again.

He tips his head to one side and stretches out his arms, a look of mock pleading on his face.

Comfort me?

He *is* a devil: He must be. He is a herald of evil. And look what he is showing me now . . . *Comfort me.* That is what she said—Anne. He is showing me that Anne is his creature. He must have fashioned her precisely to trick me . . . he made her look like the golden maiden who would provide me with sons. But she was the exact opposite: the Devil's serpent sent to entrap me.

Just as Jesus Christ was tempted by the Devil in the wilderness, so have I been tempted by Anne Boleyn.

And here is my choice: to relinquish my God-given destiny, the glory for which I have fought so hard, sacrificed so much . . . or to take courage and destroy this devil in all its forms.

A surge of joy runs through me. I feel ecstatic, sure of my blessed vocation and my virtue. I rejoice in it. And I rejoice that God tests me: that he enables me to see the Devil clearly, as others cannot.

The night is past and the day is come nigh.
Let us therefore cast away the deeds of darkness,
and let us put on the armor of light.

I hear something behind me. I turn away from the boy. On the opposite side of the room the sill of the window has become a horizon, beyond which something is rising. I hear a slow tread on invisible stone stairs. A swaying, monstrous head emerges; scaly claws and short, muscular legs plant themselves above the cliff edge. I know this serpent: I dreamed of it. I crouch quickly to pick up my sword from the floor.

When I straighten, the serpent has become Anne, climbing the wharf steps, her dainty feet stepping in golden slippers. The train of her mantle leaves behind a bloody trail of stinking, rotting flesh.

The next moment it is a serpent again; its neck weaves back and forth. The ridges of the windpipe stand out against white flesh. Against scaly flesh, green and gray.

The serpent's jaws swing toward me, gaping, stinking, and dreadful. I step forward, ducking to reach the neck. I slash and slash and slash.

My sword cannot make contact. The creature advances. I begin to back away. Quicker now. My legs collide with something and I turn.

I yelp. I have backed into the bed, and now I see the boy, lying there under the covers. He is like a wife, waiting for me. Like a hideous parody of a wife—his hair greasy and shorn, where hers would flow over the soft white linen of the pillow.

I drop my sword and draw my dagger. I stab and stab and stab—his face, his eyes, his neck. He lies there—he does not struggle; it is like stabbing a corpse. But his eyes are open; he is looking at me. There are hands restraining me now. My servants have returned.

"Fools!" I swing round, slashing one of them across the cheek.

Someone calls for a doctor.

I look back to the bed, panting. I have stabbed the bolster, nothing more. There is no blood, no mark to say he lay there. I am sweating and I am cold.

69

The fire is blazing. Beyond its glow, the room is dark. I am sitting wrapped in torn bed hangings, my dagger planted point-down in the table in front of me. I am watching the movement of the flames' reflection in the sheen of the blade.

In my peripheral vision, I am aware of the pale mass of Cromwell's face, floating like a dumpling in dark soup. We have been sitting for some time in silence.

At last I say, "Anne must die. And it must be handled quickly. I'm not interested in the mechanics. You will find a way."

"Poison?"

I shake my head. "Nothing underhand. I would be suspected instantly. It must be clear to everyone *what* she is."

I look at Cromwell. I can see that he understands me completely.

70

The sunshine is eye watering, glinting off trumpets and gilded armor, off swords and shields and cloth-of-gold sur-coats. Drifts of blossom from the orchard at the tiltyard's western boundary flutter on the warm spring breeze and land: a stray petal here on a herald's crimson cap, there on a horse's braided mane, a sprinkling of pink and white against the wooden fencing of the arena's perimeter. The sky is a daz-zling blue, the only clouds high thin streaks of translucent white.

We are celebrating May Day, but I am not competing; instead I have arrived on my white charger as king not knight, have taken a turn about the tiltyard to the cheers of the crowd and a trumpet fanfare, and have retired into the building known as the Tiltyard Towers to enjoy my role as spectator.

Emerging now from the spiral staircase into the viewing gallery, I come round a corner and take a sharp breath: She is there, Anne, perfectly dressed in cloth of gold and bright green satin, jewels winking in the sunlight at every available edging of cloth, at her ears, fingers, and at her throat; but none of them as bright as her sharp dark eyes upon me.

I smile. I touch my lips to her hand and watch as an expression of relief and gratification floods her face. She sees only my perfect shell; she thinks her charm has soothed me.

The viewing gallery is a loggia—open to the air on the tiltyard side. We sit in full view of the crowd. Anne's brother George, armed and mounted for the joust, stops his horse below us and, in the language of chivalry, asks her humbly for a favor. I watch as she leans forward and drops a gold-trimmed handkerchief onto the ground. George sends a page to retrieve it and twists it round the fabric band on his helmet.

The tournament begins. The sand is churned by hooves, by falling men, by lances cast aside, and pages running. It is raked and churned again. Norris's horse refuses to run; I lend him mine, and the crowd roars its approval.

As two new riders line up and gesture for their lances, a letter is passed to me. I break the seal—stamped with Cromwell's crest—and read.

Down in the yard, there is a crescendo of yelling as the horses thunder in and a booming crack as a lance makes contact and splinters. The hit rider, bouncing like a rag doll in the saddle, slumps down toward his stirrups as his grooms run forward.

I refold the letter and rise. I do not look at Anne. I speak to no one as I leave.

71

"She has had lovers. Many. Norris among them. And . . . and her own . . ."

I look down at my hands—at the brooch I'm turning compulsively in my fingers. I can't speak the words.

Jane is sitting to my right, halfway across the room. Meek on a low stool, plain as a mouse, even in the new clothes I've given her. Softly, she says, "Yes?"

I take a shuddering breath. *"Brother.* Her own brother."

"George?"

"George, yes, George. She's only got one. Christ!" I lean my elbows on the chair arms, press my forehead to my fists. "She plotted with them to murder me. If Cromwell hadn't found out in time I would be in my grave by now."

Jane whispers, "No."

My eyes snap open. She adds hastily, "Forgive me, sir, if I can scarcely believe it."

I raise my head and look at her. I can find nothing snide, nothing calculating in her face. I say, "Evil is shocking to the godly, Jane. Your innocent mind could never conceive of the depravities these people have committed."

Looking down again, I open my hand; the brooch has dug red grooves into my palm. It is decorated with five diamonds and five rubies; above the rubies gold letters spell out

TRISTIS VICTIMA—"sad victim." I ordered it some weeks ago for a masque: I was playing the part of someone struck with the dart of love—now it seems all too appropriate in a different way. I sling it onto the table beside me; it sits spinning on the polished wood.

Jane says, "What will happen to them, sir?"

I push myself out of the chair. "They are in the Tower."

"The queen, too?"

"Of course." Near the window, on another table, there is a pair of virginals. I lift the lid and play a few notes. "It is out of my hands."

For a long while after this I stand motionless, looking toward the window. We are at Chelsea, at Thomas More's old house on the river. It is a convenient place for Jane to lodge in—for now. The garden is well tended, and, as the late afternoon shadows creep and lengthen over its herb beds, scents drift through the open window. Somewhere in the distance a dog barks. I hear a soft rustle of skirts. Gentle, tentative fingers touch my sleeve. "Sir?"

I take the fingers and kiss them. Quietly I say, "You can't imagine, Jane, what it is to come so close to evil. To have the Devil so near that he almost . . ." I shut my eyes—shake my head.

Wherrymen are shouting on the river. Somewhere down in the servants' quarters a door bangs. In the aviary below the window a nightingale begins to sing.

"I thank God for my narrow escape, Jane," I say. "I thank God for granting me life." I smile at her: at the grave little concerned face. "Life to share with you."

72

My dearest Jane—

They tell me that the execution has been set for tomorrow. In the afternoon, about three o'clock, I should be able to send you a messenger with the good news that it has been done. Then I will come to you myself by river, and we shall be betrothed the next morning. It will be the happiest day of my life.

73

Seventeen months later

I am holding a boy-child again. And his strange, serious eyes are looking into mine. He is swaddled. Just a tuft of hair peeks out at the center of his forehead. The hair is my color. He is my son. Edward.

The cloth he is wrapped in is gold; my clothes are gold; the altar-cloth before me here in the chapel is gold. Gilded angels look down on me from the gold-starred ceiling; icons covered in gold leaf shimmer in the light of a forest of wax tapers.

It is evening. The chapel is quiet and still. I have come here for a private moment of thanksgiving—with only my gentlemen for company.

The baby purses his tiny lips and makes a gurgling sound in his throat. His brow furrows—wrinkled as a walnut—and blurs as I begin to weep, great blotting droplets that darken the brilliant colors of his wrappings.

Almighty Father, humbly I thank you for giving me strength to endure my sufferings. Through them, like Christ, I have brought salvation to my people.

Here is that salvation: here is peace and prosperity, lying in my arms. Here is the glorious future of my bloodline. My triumph.

To be on my knees like this is an agony; my leg is bad again. I indicate that I wish to rise—my gentlemen hurry forward on either side, steadying my elbows, their hands on my back, enabling me to straighten, slowly, while still carrying the child.

The men stay with me, supporting me, as I turn and walk from the altar.

Outside the chapel door, one of my favorite young Privy Chamber attendants is waiting.

"Yes, Tom?" I say, pausing by him.

Tom Culpeper straightens from his bow. He is a pretty youth, with a hard edge of ambition in his eyes that the ladies do not spot. I, however, see it and like it; he is from no great family—he relies solely on his king to get what he wants. Which is as it should be. He says, "I have news from the queen's physicians, Your Majesty."

From Jane's apartments, just a courtyard away.

"Well?"

Culpeper steps close and says in a low voice, "Sir, they report that Her Majesty's condition is worsening. Her fever is high and getting higher. Her confessor is in attendance."

I nod, and move off along the passageway, in the direction of my own apartments. Culpeper breaks into a trot to catch up. "Your Majesty?"

I stop.

"Forgive me, sir, but I am instructed to ask what your plans might be for going hunting at Esher. Will you delay here another day, sir?"

"If the queen is better tomorrow morning, I shall leave for Esher immediately."

"And . . ." The young man hesitates. "If she is no better, sir?"

The birthing chamber turned sick room . . . the thought of such a place fills me with an ancient dread. I cannot be waiting for news. I cannot be waiting for Compton to come . . .

I glance at Culpeper. He is not Compton. Compton has been dead these half dozen years or more, carried off by the sweating sickness one summer. I miss him and yet . . . With new men like Culpeper, I am free of the past.

Culpeper is waiting for my response. I say, "Let them tell the queen I am still here. If she asks for me, let them say that I am coming—that I am delayed in some meeting; they can make up a reason. But I cannot wait. Whatever happens, I leave for Esher tomorrow."

In the event, she does not ask for me, and no one has to lie. Near midnight that night, before I have had the chance to leave Hampton Court, Jane takes leave of it herself. At the other side of the palace, I am woken to receive the news.

PART FIVE

Weighed in the Balances

74

"There has been a wax doll found—a baby. It was half-buried in a churchyard, here in London. With two pins stuck through it."

The face of Sir William Sidney, chamberlain of my son's household, pales behind his beard. "God preserve the prince!"

I incline my head in agreement. I'm standing next to a table covered in a mess of papers, remnants of drinks, and candle ends. It has been a bad night. I am still in my dressing robe.

I say, "So . . . you see the seriousness of your task. Though Edward—though *my son* is a gift from God for my consolation, and for the comfort of the whole realm, though he is the guarantee of peace and of the continuation of my blessed dynasty"—I take a steadying breath—"and though he is a defenseless infant barely a year old, yet *still* there are people out there—astonishingly—who wish him dead."

Outside, under a gray sky, the rain is driving sideways across the courtyard. It is as light as it will ever be this morning; the candles are still lit.

"You already check his food." I begin to paw my way through the pile of papers on the table, letting them slip to the floor as I discard them. "Double-check it. Triple-check it. Not a single substance must pass his lips that has not been tested in large quantities."

"Yes, sir."

"Where did I put the list?"

From the shadows behind me, Cromwell starts forward. "Sir?"

"The *list*. I made a list, damn it . . . in the night." I step back and flap a hand toward the pile. "Find it."

Cromwell leafs through the papers quickly, pulls one out, hands it to me.

As I take it, I feel something move in my mind. I am experiencing it more and more these days. It is as if there is something else that looks out through my eyes—some other being. I think that perhaps it is God. I scan my scrawled writing and glance up at Sidney. "All right: No page or servant boy must be allowed to set foot in the household. Not one. They can't be sufficiently trusted. And they carry infection."

Sidney nods.

I look at the list again. "No person below the rank of knight is to enter Edward's presence."

"A formal document will be issued, containing all these points," Cromwell puts in.

I pace, haltingly, on the carpet before the window, holding the list in front of me. "Next: No one—*no one*—is to touch Edward, no one is to so much as kiss his hand, unless they have had my express permission to do so. And—even if I *have* given permission—either you or Lady Bryan must be in attendance when the contact occurs."

Turning, I stop to consider Sidney. Gray-bearded but still strong, he is an experienced military commander. But is he enough to protect Edward? How can anyone be enough?

I limp over to him. "You answer for the safety of my son. With your life."

Sidney meets my look, standing to attention. "Yes, sir."

At that instant pain strikes up through my leg. Beside me there's a chair; I grip its back.

I manage to say, "Cromwell will give you the list of other measures."

"I will fulfill every one with the utmost diligence."

"Yes . . . you will."

Sidney bows and exits; unseen behind me, Cromwell must have indicated that he should go.

Cromwell says, "Shall I call the doctor, sir?"

I shake my head, breathing heavily. "Passing now."

The wave of pain subsides; I stay leaning on the chair for a moment, enjoying the relief. Then I move over to the long table, where a new map of the south coast's defenses is laid out. Looking at it, I say, "It was wrapped in a winding cloth, this—this wax thing?"

"Yes. Apparently. Would you like it fetched for you to view?"

I shudder. "No."

The map shows all the places an enemy fleet might land; every sandy bay is drawn, every inlet, every fort and town and cliff-top beacon. I have been annotating it myself—showing where I want new, better fortifications. The threat of attack is now greater than ever: The pope has declared that I am no longer the rightful king of England. Even now his envoys are exhorting the emperor and the king of France to deprive me of my throne.

"Look, I can build all this," I say, indicating the map. "I can design the best gun towers this country has ever seen. I can buy the heaviest guns. I can smash every nation the pope urges to invade us, but . . ." I turn to Cromwell. "But what I *fear*—what makes me wake in a sweat at two in the morning—is some godforsaken carpenter sticking pins into a wax doll in Smithfield."

Cromwell looks back at me, pasty-faced, his eyes baggy and red rimmed; he looks as if he's at his desk every night until two in the morning. Which he probably is. But there's something else in his eyes: a glint that is not the glint of a pen pusher.

He says, "That carpenter is not sticking pins into anything now, I can assure you, sir. His hands are"—he flexes his own fingers thoughtfully—"not as useful to him as they were. I supervised his interrogation myself."

"Give me the list of staff for Edward's household."

Cromwell sorts quickly through his papers and hands one to me.

I look down the names. "How can I tell that one of this lot isn't doing the same? These women who are his rockers—I know, they all . . . they all have spotless reputations, they've all been thoroughly checked—but how can I *know* . . . These men"—I jab my finger at the list—"these gentlemen of the bedchamber. How can I be certain of their loyalty? How can I know their secret intentions?"

"Each person has been selected with the utmost care."

I sling the list aside and take hold of Cromwell's face.

He smells of clean linen and tooth-soap. Not the blood and fear of the interrogation room. I say, "The Devil's disguises are the best. I want to see—I want to see in here." I touch his forehead. "And in here." I prod his chest.

I let go of Cromwell and turn away. "Some old hag's got a doll of me with a pin through its leg, that's for sure."

"It's all superstition, sir," says Cromwell evenly. "It is unpleasant to think of, but a doll can have no effect—other than to point us the right way to find a traitor."

I take the list and drop it on top of Cromwell's pile of papers. "Check them out again. All of them."

"Yes, sir." He shuffles the papers deftly. "If I could just ask Your Majesty about a couple of other things? The munitions ordered from Antwerp—"

"The thing that astonishes me," I interrupt, pacing again, "is that *however* much God does to show that *I* am the vicar of Christ for my people, that *I* am the channel for divine grace in this country, a number of my miserable subjects will work against me. What was that report from . . . was it Kent? The idiot who said, 'If the king knew every man's thought, it would make his heart quake'—was that it?"

"The man was in Cranbrook, in Kent," says Cromwell. "His name is Skarborow. He is in custody. Regretting his words."

"God has blessed me with a son and shown that what I am doing pleases him. They have only to obey. Is that really so hard? God speaks to *me*. Not to them. To *me*."

The room is still. The wind sounds down the chimney, a low eerie note. I realize that I have been shouting.

After a moment Cromwell says, "Alongside measures for the prince's security, it would be wise to speed negotiations for a new marriage, sir. All loyal subjects long for the birth of a Duke of York."

I let out a breath. Then I flop into a chair and prop my bad leg on a nearby chest. "What have the French said? Will they bring the princesses to Calais for me to view?"

"They say they are not willing to parade them like horses at market."

"Sod them." I pick up a candle-end and lob it into the fire. "Always an insult. The sodding French arrogance."

Cromwell perches his bulk on a stool close by me, his elbows on his knees. "I have, though, received the report from Dr. Peter about the Duke of Cleves's sister."

"All right," I say. "Tell me."

75

I can ride again. The roads are murder: The mud is frost hardened and rutted worse than a plowed field. But I can ride again. The wind on my face, the movement of the horse— even the cold drizzle needling my eyes—is pleasurable for a man who has been lame half the winter.

We number six, my party: six gentlemen in matching multicolored cloaks, traveling incognito into Kent. Despite the roads, despite the weather, we make good progress from Greenwich, down the great Roman thoroughfare of Watling Street, toward Rochester.

Cromwell has arranged a marriage for me. I am riding to meet my bride. She is the Duke of Cleves's sister—the Lady Anna—and she is resting in Rochester after her Channel crossing. She expects to meet me at Blackheath in a few days' time, from where I will lead her into London, to receive the City's welcome.

It is just that I cannot wait that long.

"What was it Fitzwilliam said?" I ask Anthony Browne, my master of the horse, as our horses pick their way side by side over a particularly muddy stretch of road. "About her looks?"

Browne pushes his hood back; the drizzle has stopped. It is New Year's morning, and, though his face is more than usually pale after last night's court celebrations, under his cloak he is dressed as meticulously as ever. He is a man who takes notice of appearances. I wonder if he will have to give up any of his jeweled buttons or gold lace-ends; a good deal of money was lost at the gaming tables last night.

"He certainly praised the lady's beauty, sir," Browne says now, flicking a wet leaf off his sleeve. "Though, I regret, I don't remember the exact words. He had more to say, I think, about the card games he taught her while they were waiting for a fair wind at Calais."

"Someone said that, in beauty, she outshines the Duchess of Milan 'as the golden sun outshines the silver moon.' Was that Ambassador Mont?"

"The Duchess of *Milan* . . ." Tom Culpeper whistles. He is riding at my other side with a hopeful sprig of mistletoe attached to the hood of his cloak.

I laugh and reach out to dig him in the ribs with my riding crop. The Duchess of Milan, a very young widow, was another marriageable candidate on the list Cromwell compiled for me. I had her portrait taken—and I have kept it, just for its decorative value. Which is high: The duchess is sixteen, dimpled, and breathtaking. Anyone outshining *that* must be practically an angel.

Approaching Rochester, we find the city looking far from celestial. The city walls and rooftops huddle gray under a gray sky, while the damp finger of the cathedral spire stirs the low-hanging clouds above.

We dip through the shadows of the city's northeast gate

and emerge into the cobbled streets beyond. Doorways are hung with holly and yew, small boys run past with pies for the cook shop, and shabby loiterers call out New Year greetings, as they might to any group of well-heeled gentlemen from whom they have hope of a penny. I pull my hood low over my face and leave it to my companions to dish out coins.

Our destination is the bishop's palace, not far from the cathedral. Browne rides ahead to warn the bishop's staff that a party of the king's men approaches. My presence is not announced; I want to surprise my bride.

Back at Greenwich now, had I stayed, I would be leaning against the cupboard in my Presence Chamber as my courtiers queued up to present me with their New Year gifts: jewels and gold plate, clocks and curiosities. As it is, I am making my own way to the best gift of all.

"Ready, sir?"

Our horses have halted, stamping and snorting, just inside the palace's main gate, and Browne comes forward to tell me he has forewarned the staff. The lady remains in delicious ignorance.

"Keep your cloaks on, gentlemen. No clues," I say, and dismount, with Browne's help. "Where is she, then?"

"In an upper chamber at the back, sir," he says, pointing across the courtyard. "She's watching a bull-baiting in the yard beyond."

"Ah, hence the racket." Barks and shouts are carrying clearly through the cold air. I turn to Browne. "Right. Go to her. Say her New Year's gift from the king has arrived. I'll follow."

Browne strides ahead to the entrance to the main staircase: an imposing arched doorway in one corner of the courtyard. Energized, despite the long ride, I follow him quickly. I even manage to take the stairs two at a time.

At the top of the staircase I head past a rank of startled servants, through the great hall and on—following the billowing shape of Browne's parti-colored cloak—to the palace's best suite of private rooms. My heart is pounding and I feel flushed; my pulse seems to beat in my face.

Reaching the lady's chamber door, I meet Browne coming out. "She will receive the gift," he says, and grins.

"How is she?" I ask, gripping his sleeve. "Is she stunning?"

A ghost of pain seems to cross Browne's face—no doubt because I am crushing some very fine gold-thread embroidery. I release his sleeve. "No, don't tell me. I'll see for myself."

We enter as a pack, my men and I, our matching cloaks giving no clue to our—to *my*—true identity. The chamber air hits us: a warm fug of cinnamon and cloves. It is a comfortable if old-fashioned room, with antique tapestries on the walls and the bishop's coat of arms carved monumentally large above the fireplace.

Straight ahead, there's a figure at the window.

Good God, the German fashions are strange. The lady's wearing a high-necked dress and a peculiar wide bonnet that makes her head look like a coal bucket. I can tell from her bearing she's alarmed to see so many men burst into her chamber. A lifetime ago I used to play this trick on Catherine, dressed as Robin Hood or a Turkish sultan. Her astonishment, I thought at the time, was very pretty.

"Greetings, Lady Anna," I say, removing my cap with a flourish and walking forward. "The king has sent you this token." I work a ring off my little finger and hold it out to her.

Lady Anna of Cleves is not dimpled; she is not breathtaking. Hers is a long-nosed face—though not, I think, without potential. My enthusiasm is running, after all, at full gallop; I cannot pull up now.

"Good day, my lord," she says in a thick accent, laying out each word carefully. "I . . . thank . . . His Majesty."

As she reaches to take the ring, I catch hold of her hand and raise it to my lips; then, with a quick tug, pull her in for a kiss on the cheek.

Ladies of the English court greet such games with giggles and teasing looks, with delight and pretty blushes. Lady Anna gasps and jerks her head away. Below the long nose, her mouth is twisted with disgust.

For a moment, we are frozen. It is an ugly pose. My neck is still stretched forward, my head still inclined for the kiss, meeting nothing but empty air.

Then I release her hand, and she moves away swiftly, brushing her palms down her skirts and saying something in her own grating language to a lady-servant standing in the corner, who shrugs at her mistress and shoots me a scandalized look.

My bride then resumes her stance at the window.

Resolutely staring out, willing me to leave. In the yard below, the tormented bull bellows, and I hear the scrape of its chain against the ground. The bulldogs are barking; I wonder, distractedly, whether one of them has already sunk its teeth into the bull's snout.

Thinking this, I am still watching her. My heart is still beating as fast as when I climbed the stairs, as fast as when I grabbed Browne's sleeve outside the door. But all the hope and excitement I had then has shriveled.

I turn. My men, still in their damp-stained cloaks and muddy boots, avert their gaze, each one finding sudden interest in his gloves, the floor, or the weave of the wall hangings.

I push past them out of the room.

76

"I like her not." Absently I line up the purses on the trestle table: orange velvet, pink satin, white leather, cloth of gold. I don't see them; I see only that long-nosed face. I say, "She is ugly. She looks like a horse. I can tell you now, I will not be able to get sons on that . . . that *woman*." I turn to Cromwell and smile—but not pleasantly. "So, Thomas. What remedy?"

Cromwell is standing by the cupboard displaying the gilt cups and plates. We're in the Presence Chamber at Greenwich, where my New Year's gifts are on display. Against all those burnished surfaces he's looking clammy and pale. And edgy. He says, "I know none, sir. But I am very sorry for it."

"Really? That's odd. You've never told me before that there is no remedy." I pick up a pair of spurs, test the spikes, put them down. "In fact, I seem to remember you saying once—I don't remember the occasion but I remember the words quite clearly—'Anything can be done.' *Anything*. So. I want you to get me out of this marriage."

"But . . . ," Cromwell begins, and checks himself, runs a hand through his hair, starts again. "Sir, as you know, this is not simply a marriage; this is an alliance. With Cleves. To strengthen us against our enemies, who are every day threatening to invade." He spreads his meaty hands. "And . . . look, sir, the lady is *here*. She has completed a long and arduous journey from her homeland. To reject her now would be a very public humiliation, both for the lady and for her brother, the duke. And if the duke is pushed into the arms of the emperor—"

"He will join the long list of rulers working to deprive me of my throne. And no doubt my life."

Cromwell rubs his fingers over his mouth and chin. His shoulders give the ghost of a shrug: He can't bring himself to nod, but it's clear I've hit the nail on the head.

"Well, what a marvelous situation you have brought me to. Let me see. I am forced into a marriage with a hateful woman. I have rulers queuing up to depose me. Tell me. You're not working for one of them by any chance, are you?"

Cromwell says, "The Duke of Norfolk would like you to think so."

The comment is accompanied by a rueful grin: He has enemies at court, and he's making a joke of it. But I asked if he is betraying me; who dares brush away that question? In two strides I'm across the room with a fistful of Cromwell's fur-trimmed black gown in my hand. His grin has vanished.

"I am prey to no man's influence," I say, my spittle flecking his pasty face. "Not Norfolk's, not yours. Do not imagine that you know what is in my mind. If I thought my cap knew my counsel I would throw it on the fire. It would delight me to watch it burn."

77

A slash of color appears across my vision, like a horizontal door opening. I am in darkness; out there, blurred figures move. They loom and swing away. I seem to be lying down. Have I fallen from my horse?

Someone bends near. Who is it? The face is lit from one side only; the other side melts into shadow. It looks sinister. The mouth is moving, but I can't hear the words. Only the blood rushing in my ears. It sounds like the sea. Am I on a ship?

All is dark again. The pain is bad. My leg is on fire.

I have to move. Have to turn onto my side.

Gingerly, I shift my position a fraction. It's agony. I stop. I daren't breathe.

"The sore must be kept running." The words swim to me from somewhere. I can't see who's speaking.

"Cut it open, then."

No. No one is to cut anything. I open my eyes—try to speak. No one responds. Patches of candlelight show black-robed figures moving at the end of the bed. I am seized with fear.

How long have I been here? Hours—days? Weeks?

What's the last thing I remember?

I try to think . . . and then the light is different. Paler, washing in from high up on my right. Time has passed. Did I sleep? I am clutching a hand. Someone is gibbering and whimpering. It's a disgusting sound: pitiful moaning.

Pain. *Pain pain pain pain.*

Figures tower over me—a line of them along each side, like coffin bearers. But they are not lifting me, they are pressing on me. I am being held down.

I try to mash the hand I'm holding—crush it. The knuckles roll against each other as I squeeze. A face is near: Culpeper's, wincing. I have never been so grateful to see him in my life.

That sound comes again, the whimpering. It's me.

At the height of the pain nothing else exists. I need every ounce of energy just to get from one moment to the next.

Then, when there's a lull, I rest, panting. I feel the pleasure of just lying. The lightness of no longer being held down. The softness of the pillows. I attempt to speak. I manage: "They . . . poison . . . me. Fetch Cromwell." I swallow drily, and try again. Culpeper is leaning in to catch the words. I say, "Don't tell. Fetch him. Quickly."

Culpeper's hand slides out of mine as he stands up. He moves away; I see him talking to a figure. Not in a black robe—a red figure. I want to shout: *I told you not to tell them—*

Terror, now. Like a wave crashing over me; I'm gasping for breath. Is Culpeper in on it? Is this slow murder? Where is my son Edward? Do they have Edward, too?

The red figure expands; it wears a courtier's doublet; it has a face. Anthony Browne's neat fringe and dark eyes hang in a moon-white disk. The mouth says, "Cromwell is dead, sir. He has been dead these last six months."

I turn a little; curl up slightly. He cannot be gone. He was so solid. Where have they hidden him?

And yet they all leave me, eventually.

My pillow is wet. I whisper, "What was it—plague? The sweat?"

It's a moment before Browne answers. "You commanded his execution, sir."

78

The light is soft, tinged green by the leaves of the climbing rose that has spread across half the window. It is like being in a summer glade.

I'm sitting in a chair and my eyes are half-closed. There's a gentle hum of conversation in the room behind me, a chink of glass as drinks are poured, a few rippling notes of the virginals as someone begins to play, a snatch of singing, broken by laughter. Mesmerized, I watch the flickering pattern of light and shade on the sill before me as the wind stirs the leaves.

A rustling sounds close by. Silken arms slide around my neck and a kiss brushes my cheek.

"Sweetheart." I draw her onto my lap. She is only nineteen: the Duke of Norfolk's niece and a dainty little thing, with velvet eyes and the softest skin. Her name is Kate Howard.

She says, "Join us. Tom proposes a game."

"Does he?"

"And you know how I like games." She traces a finger along my jawline, looks at me: a secret look, just for the two of us.

This is my new world: Cromwell is dead, and this beautiful creature is my wife. The marriage to that German woman, the Lady Anna, happened—as it had to . . . but I made sure it was annulled as soon as possible. My lawyers studied the documents and found their reasons—did she not have a pre-contract to marry the Duke of Lorraine's son? And besides, witnesses heard me say I could not bring myself to take the woman in my arms, let alone put a son in her belly. Without physical union, there is no union in God's eyes.

Chief among those witnesses was Cromwell. I kept him alive long enough to see that the annulment was achieved. He died the same day I married Kate. There was a certain neatness in it.

Now I kiss Kate lingeringly and haul myself up to stand. "See—I can't resist you," I say, and she laughs. One of the men moves my chair to a place in a loose circle they are creating in the center of the room, made of stools and benches and cushions.

There, I sit again, with Kate beside me, her plump hand resting in mine. As the others settle themselves in the circle, I lose myself in gazing at her: at the way the light falls on her, at the way she smiles, at the way a pearl that hangs from her ear catches on the soft frill of fine linen at her neck, swings, and catches again as she turns her head. She is covered in jewels. She asks for them as a child asks for sweetmeats and toys. She looks so pretty in them, and so pleased; I can deny her nothing.

Our young companions are settled now: the men with their bright-colored legs stuck out in front of them, slashed and jeweled arms slung languidly over the backs of chairs or propped on knees, the women with their skirts arranged, the pomanders and trinkets hanging from their girdles gathered into their laps.

"Take a slip of paper and read it out," says Anthony Denny, one of my gentleman-servants, passing round a basket. It stops at Kate first. She dips her hand in and unfolds a paper, eager and excited. She says, "It's a question. 'What quality would you most like the person you love to possess? And, since everyone must have some defect, what fault would you choose they should have?'"

"Sir?" Her eyes are on me. "What would you say?"

"Beauty, sweetness of nature."

"And a fault?"

I smile. "Only that she is too innocent."

Culpeper, sitting on Kate's other side, says, "That she is already married." Oh, roguish boy; he cannot resist playing the gallant.

It makes Kate laugh. "How can that be a fault?" she says, turning to him. "It would be the fault of the other, to have fixed his affections on a lady who is beyond his reach."

I say, "Quite so, my love, but how can anyone help it?" I smile at her again, and she smiles in return, and I see that her eyes are lit with adoration.

As the discussion continues round the circle, my thoughts drift again. I think: She will give me sons, that's certain. Look at her: Her flesh seems edible—it has a sugary sheen. She's like one of those marzipan goddesses the confectory makes for banquets. The sons she gives me will be ruddy and healthy. Edward is only three years old, and too pale. Whey-faced, like his mother. Someone said that once. Who was it?

Now Tom Culpeper is reaching into the basket.

"'If you had to be openly mad,'" he reads, "'what kind of foolishness would you be thought most likely to display?'"

"Lovesickness," Kate says, and blushes deeply.

At that moment I am suddenly aware that, on the other side of the room, there is an interested spectator.

The boy—the thing, the specter—is standing against one of the curtains, staring at me. As exact and real as every other person here. He is ragged as a tramp, his skin yellow and seemingly patched with sores; he looks young and old at once, alive and dead. His hands are held, dangling, slightly away from his sides. He's wearing glossy red gloves. Intermittently, the gloves drip.

"Sir?" says a voice—Denny's. Miles away.

Those are no gloves. The boy's hands are the red of a butcher's hands, a surgeon's hands. The hands of an executioner who has delved deep into the belly of his victim. The spots of red on the floor are merging into small pools.

My heart is pounding. I struggle to rise—the boy watches the attempt.

"I thought I was rid of you," I say to him. "You showed me the evil and I destroyed it. I have my son now." At last I'm on my feet, twisted awkwardly to keep the weight off my maimed leg, one hand gripping the chairback. "Why the—" I point to his hands. "Why the blood?"

"Sir, what is it?" "Sir?" Kate and Denny's voices now, together.

The boy says nothing. His pose is tranquil, as if he has stood there for an hour and intends to remain there an hour more. But there is something horrifying in his look: His stare has such intensity—a kind of fury of interest.

"Speak, damn you!" I start forward across the circle. "You were right. She was the Devil's creature. So I destroyed her and I got my son. What evil are you here to show me now? Will there be a death? Surely not Edward, please! God would not allow it. . . . Or is it evil in someone's heart? I am constantly watchful. I continue to do God's work. But now your . . . your appearance frightens me—the blood . . ."

He does not blink; I cannot bear that he does not blink. His hair is moving a little, as if in a draft I cannot feel.

Panic constricts my throat. I croak, "What do you want from me? *Who are you?*"

I'm aware of a shifting at the edges of my vision. In the circle around me there is fear—and embarrassment. Behind me Denny says, "The king is tired. He has overexerted himself today." There's a clatter and shuffle as people rise, eager to leave.

"Stay!" I put out my hand, still staring at the boy. They sit again.

No movement but the stirring of his hair. No reaction but the continued ferocious determination of his gaze.

And then his voice speaks, as if whispering in my ear.

Whom do I resemble?

Hair the color of straw. Hollow, haunted eyes. A livid pallor on the young-old face. I say, "No one. Evil. Death."

Now there's movement in the face at last. He smiles, and his grayish teeth seem longer and sharper than before.

Try again. Whom do I resemble?

I stare at him. I am loath to admit what I am thinking. "My family. My *mother's* family. One of her brothers? I said once before I thought you were a ghost. But what does it matter? A devil can take any shape."

No. You are close. But not close enough.

I am close indeed. An arm's reach away now. He looks so real. I can see every pore of his sallow skin, every strand of hair against the blue of the curtain behind him. I cannot bear it. I stagger forward, yelling, "Who is it this time? What evil stalks me? *Tell me!*"

I reach out, grabbing for his scrawny neck. My hand closes on something too soft—fine blue taffeta. The curtain. I wrench it aside.

I find myself looking into the boy's eyes: amused, savage, triumphant.

But the eyes are in my face. It is a mirror.

My forehead crashes into the glass. With a crack the mirror splinters into a fan of jagged pieces. Sections of a queasy, jarred room. Sections of a face—my own—that do not fit together. The eyes are mine again, but one is closer than the other, grotesquely unaligned.

"Call the king's physician."

"Get off me!"

"Sir, you are bleeding."

Slowly, I lumber round to face the room. Since when did my body become a ship that is so hard to turn? I am breathing heavily. Terror has opened like a pit at my feet. I sway and stagger back to catch my balance.

A circle of faces, staring at me—afraid. Among them,

Kate's. I see that in her alarm she has clutched Culpeper's hand. Her fear is so innocent, like a child's in a thunderstorm.

There is blood trickling into my left eye. I wipe it with the back of my hand and hold the hand out to her. Almost reluctantly, she rises and comes to me.

"Don't worry, sweetheart," I murmur. "It's those damned medicines they give me. They bring strange daydreams. But, as you see, the dreams pass in a moment." She's looking at the floor now. I tilt her chin up; I manage to smile. For a brief moment I have the strange sensation that something else is looking out through my eyes, smiling at her too. I say, "There is nothing to fear."

79

But there *is* something to fear. I fear to look in the mirror, in case I see his eyes in mine. I fear an empty room, an unturned corner, the slightest sound whose source is not instantly clear.

The boy's appearance is an omen. I do not know what is coming, only that *something* is. And so I fear not just him, but everyone—men close at hand, men far away. A face in the crowd—any face. Disease.

I am diseased—dis-eased. On edge: I cannot sleep. And yet, for the hours in the day when I am with Kate, for the hours in the day when I am without pain, I think I am the happiest I have ever been. It is a strange, contradictory existence.

As summer approaches, I plan a progress: I will take Kate and my court to the third of my kingdom that I have never seen—to the north. To those benighted shires where the most brutish of my subjects still cling to the lies peddled by the bishop of Rome—the one they call pope—and where the weeds of rebellion spring up year after year and must be hacked down in cold blood. These northern men have never seen the magnificence of their king, nor his might. A thousand soldiers will accompany me—it will be a show of strength.

But as I turn to the north I must watch my back, too: in London, the Tower must be cleared of prisoners before we go, to alleviate the risk of unrest in my absence—for who knows what form the evil will take this time. I insist that the job be done thoroughly: Even the elderly Countess of Salisbury, my daughter Mary's erstwhile governess, is hustled out one windy morning to the block. Her pope-loving sons intrigue against me in their exile, abroad. I cannot be too careful.

And so, in July I set off—with my queen and court, with my soldiers, with five thousand fine horses and two hundred tents and pavilions. It is unseasonably wet, and the carts and wagons of our vast baggage train founder in the flooded and muddy roads. But at last we make it: to Lincoln and Pontefract, to Hull and York.

We wear cloth of gold, my simple-hearted, loving little Kate and I, our outfits embroidered with each other's initials. In the cathedrals we have incense swung and prayers said over us, calling on God to grant us long life and many children. My subjects kneel to me in their hundreds, cheer for me in their thousands. But I am scanning the crowds, always—scanning the faces for signs of ill intent.

As the days of the progress pass into weeks, however, my agitation begins to ease. I begin to settle more fully into my happiness. I begin to look forward to the birth of the Duke of York—for surely Kate will give me a son soon.

At the end of October we return, in easy stages, to Hampton Court. I order a thanksgiving to be held in the chapel there for the joy Kate has brought me. I attend it on All Saints' Day and hear Mass in public beneath the blazing blue and gold of the ceiling. Gilded angels hang above me, stars twinkle in the man-made firmament, and my motto declaring my divine right to rule, written in gold, stripes the sky like the tail of a comet.

The next day is the Feast of All Souls. I go to Mass again, but more privately this time: in my closet on the chapel's balcony. Entering it, I see my familiar cushions and prayer books, my spectacles resting as always on a folded silk handkerchief—plus something unusual.

There is a letter on my chair.

"This is a lie." The door to my closet bangs against the wall as I come out. I'm holding the letter. "This is an evil lie. Bring me the person who cooked up this filth."

Half a dozen of my gentlemen are standing in the passageway, rigid with alarm. No one moves.

"Christ! Jesus *Christ!*" I crumple the letter and throw it, hard, down the passageway. I grab the nearest man by the doublet. It's Denny. "I. Am. Happy. With. Her. You understand?" I shove him aside; Denny staggers.

The letter contains accusations against Kate. That her innocence is a pretense. That she had lovers before we were married—several. But more than this. Much more. That, on the progress just completed, in Lincoln and Pontefract and York, she and Tom Culpeper met by night while I slept in my apartments.

Tom Culpeper? That pretty, roguish boy? I can believe he is a fool, but he is no traitor. His accuser must be a jilted woman, or a man jealous of his looks and charm.

And Kate . . . my devoted, artless Kate. Is this what the

boy's appearance signified: not a death, but an attempt to destroy my happiness?

I yell, "What are you waiting for? Bring me the wretch who did it. Bring me the man who spewed up this stinking, putrefied *fantasy*."

Denny, having straightened his doublet, hesitantly steps toward me, with something in his hand. "Sir?"

"What?"

"You might need to take a look at this, sir."

Another piece of paper. He pushes it at me quickly then steps back, as if I will bite.

"What is it?" Holding the paper, I'm still looking at him. He sucks in his lips. He won't answer.

I look down. It's a letter, closely written.

Master Culpeper . . .

I recognize the writing—awkward, clumsy. It is hers. What trick is this?

> *I never longed so much for anything as I do*
> *to see you . . .*
> *It makes my heart die to think that I*
> *cannot be always in your company . . .*

I am confused; it *cannot* be hers. I look to the end.

Yours as long as life endures, Kate.

And a fault? she had said.

That she is already married, he had replied.

And she had laughed.

I take a step back and jolt against the wall. My legs buckle; the letter crumples as I do, sliding down. My bad leg won't bend—I fall part of the way, catch myself with my hand against a wooden chest.

I turn myself into the corner between chest and wall. My fists are shielding my face. I am sobbing.

80

Dark, dark, dark within. I am plagued by strange dreams, from which I wake smothered by sweat-soaked sheets and an undefinable feeling of dread.

And I begin to see *him* everywhere. Scan any mass of people long enough, and I will spot him. In a crowd-lined street, in the stands at a tournament, glimpsed among a huddle of courtiers: He is always there—he is always watching me.

Some days I gaze in the looking glass and see him behind me. Or I see his eyes in mine. Through an archway, I spot him, waiting. If I glance down into the garden he will be standing in the shadows, looking up at me. Sometimes he peeps at me through a half-open door.

But if I lunge for him, he is never there. I learn not to do it. I learn to endure his appearances. To turn away. I know now that he will never leave me.

And sometimes I feel movement in my mind, and sometimes none. I am no longer so sure that it is God. And I think of the Devil, and evil spirits, and I shudder . . . but I know that however viciously they attack me, I will not be defeated; I am a creature of light and blessedness.

Culpeper goes to the block in December, Kate two months later.

Evil stalks the land. If you don't believe it, you are a fool.

What is this sense I have of being in a speeding cart, racing, horseless, down some steep slope? I dream of it. . . .

The days pass so quickly—I blink and a year is gone. And somehow the hours of pain are drawn out and lengthened. The pain, and the night. While the sunlight flees from me, and the flowers bloom only for a breath.

Sometimes I wake and think *she* is beside me in the dark. Anne. Watching me, her eyes glittering with laughter.

I wake to find my fingers clawing at the bedcovers, scratching the silk.

81

"Sir?"

"Mm?" I open my eyes.

"The bandages on your leg. Are they more comfortable now?"

"A little. You are gentle. Your fingers are more skilled than those infernal doctors'." I gesture vaguely. "You may read again."

The young woman opens the book at its ribbon marker; I settle myself against the cushions piled behind me.

It is summer again. I have married again. A widow, this time: Kathryn, the sister of one of my knights of the Garter, William Parr. She is a young lady with a grave, gentle face, a dependable, thoughtful nature, and a known past. This morning she has been reading to me from a new translation of the Proverbs of Solomon. As she scans the words, she frowns a little.

"'Let mercy and faithfulness never go from thee; bind them about thy neck, and write them in the tables of thine heart.'"

"Amen to that," I say. "Put a mark in the margin."

She rests the book in her lap, takes a pen from the table beside her, and dips it in ink; I watch her draw a small pointing hand on the page.

The windows are shaded, the room a softly lit clutter of books and papers, maps and medicine boxes. The only sounds are the scratch of the pen and a repetitive tapping as the weighted hem of a curtain, lifted by the breeze, scrapes against the edge of a table. I know that if I were to go to the window, I would see *him*, somewhere outside, watching.

Kathryn puts down the pen and looks at me, considering. "Later, sir, if you are not too tired, might you like to watch Prince Edward in the tiltyard? You expressed an interest. He has been working hard. And your daughters are keen to accompany you, if you wish it."

I close my eyes. "They're both here, are they? I thought Mary was at Hunsdon."

"She was, sir. But she arrived here yesterday."

I don't reply. After a moment Kathryn adds, "You are blessed with such loving children, sir. They are all eager to have the honor of seeing you."

Beside my daybed stands a silver pan in which perfume is being heated. Gusts of rose-scent drift to me with each gentle inrush of air from the window. They cover, mostly, the smell of my ulcerated leg.

The tiltyard does not see much of me these days. I grunt and indicate the book with my hand—Kathryn resumes reading.

I go as far as the orchard in my carrying chair, my feet supported on its footstools, four gentlemen bearing the weight, one at each corner.

I don't, though, want my son to see me in it; I have the men put me down well before the tiltyard gate and I walk the rest of the way, my arm through Kathryn's, my other hand grasping my black and silver stick. The sun is warm; by the time I reach the gate I am sweating.

There is hardly a breath of wind—the flags at the top of the tiltyard towers droop against their poles. In the sandy space before the building they have put up an open-fronted pavilion to provide some shade. Two figures start forward from it to greet me: dark shapes gliding across the dusty ground.

"Your daughters, sir," Kathryn murmurs. I set off toward them.

Walking takes all my concentration. I do not see that I am upon them now; that they have halted in front of me and dropped into curtsies, their heads bowed. I stop, my breathing harsh in my own ears. I swallow. I say, "You may both rise." I hold out my hand to each in turn for them to kiss.

Mary is dressed in black today, Elizabeth in red. Elizabeth is only ten—or is it eleven? I forget. Whatever she is, she is disconcerting; watchful like her mother, and precociously self-possessed. Despite the heat of the day, her long, pale fingers feel cold as they touch me; I withdraw my hand quickly.

Mary—bony, sallow Mary; where did the pretty little scrap of a child go?—is, by contrast, disconcerting only in her continued presence. Being well into her twenties, she should have been married off long ago. But her status as the product of an invalid marriage has proved a . . . well, a cause for uncertainty, shall we say, among the royal bridegrooms of Europe.

Now, as she straightens and releases my hand, her bird-sharp eyes are checking for the smallest sign of approval or dissatisfaction. At least she is eager to please, these days. That, in itself, pleases me.

My daughters step back to either side, revealing a smaller figure some way off, just now breaking free of a cluster of gentlemen-servants: a perfect knight in miniature, hurrying toward me, the sunlight catching blindingly on the surface of his gilded armor.

Edward—already, at seven, the most significant person in Christendom, who will be, when I am gone, the greatest king to walk this earth since the days of Solomon and David—stops in front of me, biting his lip, and kneels.

I ruffle the red-gold hair, then raise him up and pinch his cheeks—pinch some color into them. "My jewel. My boy."

He smiles, pleased and a little awkward. "It is an honor to see you, sir."

I turn him to face the girls, holding him in front of me by the shoulders. I say, "Kneel to him. Both of you. One day you may have to beg him for your lives if you have displeased him. Eh, Edward?"

"Yes, Father," he says, as Mary and Elizabeth each obediently pay him homage. "I will always be merciful to my sisters."

"Promise nothing, Edward." I bend to whisper in his ear. "Trust no one."

The boy, for a moment, looks profoundly uncomfortable. I pat his shoulder, my rings clinking on the metal. "Well then, son. Show me what you can do."

I retreat to the shade of the pavilion. I think I glimpse a figure in the shadows of its farthest corner; determinedly I turn away, toward the light, and sit in the large chair provided. Edward takes the sword a servant passes to him—an elegant blade, the perfect length and weight for his size.

Not far from me a wooden stake five feet high has been set firmly into the ground. It is thick and has been gouged with a pattern: Lines and crude features make it look like a man—a docile opponent with whom to practice single combat.

In a moment I'm on my feet again.

"Step in and out quickly! Quicker than that! Vary the attack! Come on: head, sides of the body! Go for the thighs!"

I watch, growl, swipe the air with my arm. Then I hurry to Edward, haltingly; I have jettisoned my stick.

"Look. With a sword like this, a thrust is safer than a chop." I grasp his hand, the one holding the sword, and guide it, demonstrating. "It inflicts more damage and puts you in less danger. See—your body's less exposed. But once you've dealt the blow you *must* move out of range *quickly.*"

"Yes, sir."

"Show me again."

I hobble back and sit down.

Kathryn says, "He is nervous in front of you."

"So he should be." I shrug. "And you think he wouldn't be nervous in battle?"

Edward's second attempt with the sword is a little better. After that, still panting, he puts on his helmet and demonstrates, with his master of defense, the moves he has learned with the two-handed sword and the quarterstaff.

Kathryn applauds him readily and smiles as fondly as if the boy were her own son. She leans toward me. "He's skillful for his age, don't you think?"

"I want to see him ride at the ring."

"Have pity on him, sir. He is young; he has done enough."

"The horses are already here." I clap my hands to get the servants' attention. "Anyway, this is nothing. The lances I've had made for him are very light."

There is a flurry of activity among the servants. The target is set up: a wooden frame, placed beside the long wooden barrier running down the center of the tiltyard. From a high crossbeam of the frame a small ring is hung. The lance must be aimed at the ring's center; if this is done accurately, the thread the ring hangs on will break, and the rider will carry the ring away on his lance.

A white palfrey is brought, and Edward mounts smartly. He is given a lance.

"He sits well in the saddle, at least," I say.

"He is trying very hard to be perfect," Kathryn says quietly.

Edward takes his horse to the far end of the yard, steadies his aim, and gallops in. He misses the ring, and his efforts at the last minute to swing the lance toward it make him lose control. The lance dips wildly. He loses his balance in the saddle and slides. He tries to hang on, dropping the lance and clutching at the saddle. The horse, feeling a painful drag on the reins, jumps and kicks. Edward hits the ground as the horse speeds on; he rolls over in the dust.

In an instant, I'm on my feet. His attendants are running in.

I yell, "Again! Do it again! Get up!" My voice echoes across the yard. I am hurrying, limping fast. *"Get-up-get-up-get-up!"*

He is huddled—to the extent his armor allows—against the barrier, his back to me. His head is angled forward; beneath the rim of his helmet his fair hair curls over his metal collar. As I reach him, I see he is making small shuddering movements—as if he is whimpering.

I am seized by something like panic. *"Get up, you pathetic little insect!"* My hands are on the barrier now; I am bending over him, bellowing. *"Get up! Get up! Get up! Get up!"*

He scrambles out from under me and stands. Wrenching off his helmet, he stares at me, shocked, breathing hard—as I am. He looks sick.

Grooms and gentlemen, approaching from all directions, have stopped short of us in a ragged semicircle. I glance around; they look appalled. Kathryn emerges through their ranks—she has hurried to us from the pavilion.

With an arm raised as if she would put it round Edward, she makes a move toward him, then stops herself. She clasps her hands together; she says gently, "Are you hurt?"

Edward can only shake his head and bow to her—it seems he cannot trust himself to speak.

I pass a hand over my face; it is slick with sweat. I say, "You have done enough, sir." I reach forward and see my son conquer his instinct to flinch. My clammy hand slides off his shoulder. "You need more strength."

"Yes, Father."

The hurry, the bending, the yelling—I pay for it now with a spasm of pain. For a moment I cannot move—can do nothing but grip Edward's arm. Even in armor the limb feels fragile.

When the pain subsides, I release him. The horse has been subdued now—a groom is leading it back to the far end of the yard. I see Edward's eyes darting to it with something like dread. He fears I will make him run again. I am uncomfortable, aware of wanting to make amends.

"You like hunting?"

"Yes, Father."

"Good, good. I will take you hunting, when . . . when this—I have a slight . . ." I wave a hand toward my bad leg. "I will take you hunting soon. I'd like to see you kill a buck. Have you been blooded yet?" I look round at the men. "Has he been blooded?"

The men shake their heads; Edward says, "No, sir."

"I will do it myself, eh?" I say and, reaching out, I rub my thumb across his forehead and cheeks, as if smearing the animal's blood there right now. He still looks sick. I turn to search for Kathryn's arm, turn to go. "That's right," I say, patting him one last time. "That's right."

82

I often dream about a forest. I am on horseback—hunting.

There is a dark-haired girl riding ahead. She looks back—the wind has blown a strand of hair across her mouth. She pulls it aside with her fingers—pale fingers, ungloved—and laughs. She laughs because she wants to be caught, but she won't let me catch her.

The forest seems important—the relief is intense, as if I have ridden into the cool shade out of glaring sun (though the time in the sun is never in my dream).

Then I wake, and at first I don't know where or who I am. The room around me takes shape slowly—the clutter, the hangings, the drifts of documents spilling out of my desk—but still the damp, brackeny smells of the forest are in my nostrils, and I can feel the breeze on my cheek. I want to hold on, but I have learned that the dream disappears more quickly that way, so instead I try to still everything—just let the sinking-out-of-it happen as slowly as possible.

I feel more at home in the dream than here. I *belong* there. It is like a trick of the light, except it is a trick of the years. One moment I am a young man, fit and healthy, able to ride for so long that I can get through eight horses in a day—the next I am young, still (aren't I? It feels that way), but trapped in a body that no longer works. And there is a different girl beside me. Always a different girl.

I turn my head. This girl today has hair that spills across the pillow like rich brown syrup. She has a gentle, grave face—even in sleep she frowns a little. How did I come by her? For a moment I cannot remember. Has she borne any dead children yet? They all do, sooner or later.

I have been dreaming. I open my eyes. The head beside me on the pillows is alarming. My vision is blurred. But the head is gray—that is wrong. And odd shaped.

I try to turn over. Figures are moving, speaking in an indistinct murmur so that I cannot hear them. They have strapped something around my ribs to hamper my breath. I am desperate to raise my head—I could breathe better if only I could raise my head. Or sit up. God, yes—someone help me to sit up! There is a weight on my chest as if a devil is crouching there.

My eyes have shut again. Colors pop and swim against the darkness. Voices float and mingle on the air.

"I have told the king he must prepare for his final agony."

"Did he hear you?"

"I can't say."

I drift. The dark is liquid; the current pulls me under. I don't know for how long. And then, without warning, I surface—I can see light. The thing beside me on the pillows is not a head. It is a basin. Metal. Dull reflections move on its surface. They take all my attention, but they make no sense.

After a time I see something beyond the basin: a small, blurred shape. It is farther away than the basin. It is a person. It is my son—standing against the wall.

Thank God. Thank God he is here. He will watch what they are doing, the sinister figures that move and whisper about me. If they are poisoning me, he will see it.

"The archbishop has arrived—to hear His Majesty's confession."

"I fear you are too late, my lord. The doctors say he is beyond speaking."

I say—or perhaps think, I cannot tell which:

Edward.

I never did take him hunting.

Someone close by says, "Perhaps he can hear me still?"

"Perhaps."

The small figure starts forward toward me. He has heard me. The black and white robes of the archbishop, bending at my side, block him from my view for a moment.

"Your Majesty." The archbishop has put his face close to mine. "If you cannot confess your sins, it will be enough if you give me some sign, sir, either with your eyes or your hand, that you trust in the Lord. It will be enough for your salvation."

Has it come so soon?

A hand swims into focus: thin, clawlike fingers extended. My hand is lifted.

I say: *You.*

It is *him*. Not my son, the boy. That thing. He looks like a corpse now: The contours of his sharp bones are visible under a thin layer of grayish skin. His ragged clothes are stained with mold or old blood. Something tiny wriggles at the corner of his mouth; a dark tongue darts out and licks it away. He says:

Get up. Up. Up.

I can't.

You can.

His hand looks skeletal but is of preternatural strength. Holding it, I am able to rise from the bed, stepping out of that great, fetid carcass as if discarding a too-heavy coat. No one around me turns; none of the figures bending over the bed see me go.

Behind me the archbishop says, "He pressed my fingers; he did give a sign."

The boy leads me to the window and pulls aside the hangings. Outside there is bright, cold sunshine—harsh and beautiful.

Is this the end?

Oh yes.

But it can't be you that has come for me! Why are you here—some final test? Oh Lord God, hear me: I have endured all your tests; I am your chosen; I am a warrior of light. Where are your angels? Where are your handmaidens?

The boy turns from me, unconcerned. He leans on his forearm and stares through the window.

Coming from beneath me, such heat: Waves of hot air fan upward from some invisible source.

The prophecy, says the boy, without turning his head. *The "blessed ruler," the "glory down the ages."* God's chosen. His tone is scornful. *It wasn't you. It never was.*

I am reeling; I want to tug at his sleeve, to slap his face. *Yes. It is me. It is. I know—I have known all my life . . .*

It is as if an abyss has opened at my feet; limitless space yawns below me, though I am standing, too, somehow, on the floor. The wall is in front of me still, the panes of the window set into it—but I know that if I fall I will meet with no resistance. I am trembling.

The boy does turn his head now; he looks at me with such pleasure—with triumph—and as he does so, images flash into my mind with dizzying speed: a burned-out candle by my father's bed; a door opening with thin fingers gripping it; a boat crossing dark water; a dark-eyed woman turning to laugh in my face; the boy's own face crying; those dark, dark shadow-eyes; a sense of falling. Something comes to hit me like a speeding slamming lance, and it is horror. White-hot horror.

The boy grips the window mullions—hard, as if there is an earth tremor and he is steadying himself, or as if he will break them apart. He stares out at the world, drinking it in urgently, drinking it in as though he will never see it again. No, it is not the boy: It is me. It is him in me and me in him—it is us. We are gripping the stone; we are staring through the window. Outside, the winter sunshine slants into the courtyard below, slicing it diagonally in half—half brilliant, blinding light, half deep shadow.

Quickly, desperately, I blurt, *If the blessed ruler of the prophecy is not me, then it must be my son, Edward—*

No, you fool, interrupts the boy's voice, a voice in my mind. *Look there . . .*

A figure is crossing the courtyard below me, emerging at that very moment from the murky shadow. A girl—no, a young woman, slight but tall, with red-gold hair. At first I do not recognize her—then with a jolt I realize that it is my younger daughter, Elizabeth. Anne's daughter.

Her? A girl?

She stops as if she has heard and, turning, looks up. At that moment birds take off from the roof above me; I hear their hoarse croaking. She lifts her head and watches as their large black shapes wheel against the sky. Then her gaze slides down to the window. For an instant her eyes—her mother's dark eyes—look directly into mine.

A slight frown crosses the girl's face, as if she is puzzled, as if she thinks she sees something at the window. A shadow, the smudge of a pale face moving? There is the tiniest shake of her head: no, nothing. But a small smile flickers at the corners of her mouth as she turns back into the sunlight and continues on her way.

Q & A WITH H. M. CASTOR

Where did your inspiration for VIII *come from?*

I can't remember a time when I wasn't obsessed with Tudor history. It started when I was at primary school—back then it was the outfits and the executions that intrigued me most! For years I skirted round Henry himself—if you'd asked me, I would have said I was more interested in his wives, his children . . . but Henry was like the spider at the middle of the web: Once I'd looked at everyone around him, I came to be fascinated by what was going on at the center. And I began to feel that my impression of Henry was not really the same as any of the other versions out there.

How did you find your way into this well-known story?

I didn't have to find my way in: Rather, the feeling of having something I needed to say grabbed me and wouldn't let go. And this was despite a lot of resistance—in me! After all, you could line shelves and shelves with the books written about Henry VIII; there are so many—and many of them are utterly fascinating and brilliantly written. How could I possibly dare to add to them? But I became convinced I had something new to say. That was immensely exciting. The urgency of it really took me over—sometimes I couldn't sleep.

What was it that felt so new?

The more I read about Henry, the more forcefully it struck me that I hadn't ever found a satisfactory explanation of *why* he did what he did. And some of the things he did are so incredible—so apparently contradictory—that the question just nagged at me.

Though in a way the story is well known, the well-known part is, in fact, only that: a part. Yes, he was that famous image: the fleshy, powerful-looking bearded king who had six wives. But just look at him earlier on. He's an extraordinary boy: hugely talented, with astonishing warrior skills, and he's said to be a model of virtue. What went wrong? How did that boy become one of the most villainous kings in British history?

How did you find it inhabiting Henry VIII's head?

I had to try and sweep all the baggage out of the way, all the preconceived ideas I—and other people—had about Henry. One trick that helped was to use the name Hal rather than Henry—because as soon as the name Henry even sounded in my head the iconic image from the Holbein portraits came to mind. I couldn't climb inside that icon.

At first it was daunting, but in the end it became amazing—intoxicating and intense. Always difficult to get myself there, mentally, but once I *was* there . . . well, I felt as if I'd created a whole world, a place to go to in my head—and now I'm reluctant to let go of it!

Why did you choose to tell the story in the first person?

Two reasons. I absolutely didn't want there to be a distance between the reader and Henry. I didn't want anyone to open the book and think, "Oh, this is someone who lived hundreds of years ago; he's nothing like me." Because of course Henry lived in a world that was in many ways very different from ours, but he still felt fear and rage and love and frustration like we do. He still got the hiccups, you know; he still tripped. He was a human being, waking up in the morning, not knowing what was going to happen next in his life.

Secondly, I didn't want to look at Henry from the outside; I knew that being on the inside and looking *out* at the world through his eyes would change the story entirely. I wanted to get a vivid sense of the particular world Henry inhabits in his mind—the claustrophobia of it, if you like, and the extent to which his thoughts shape what he perceives to be reality.

How much research did you do before writing?

I never stopped; I didn't shut a book and think, "Okay, that's the research done; now I start writing." In a sense I've been researching *VIII* almost my whole life (I've been reading about the Tudors since childhood, and I studied the sixteenth century at A level and then again at university)—but still, as the book developed, the story showed me how much more I needed to find out. For example, when Hal and his mother ride through London in the first chapter, I had to know their exact route and what they would see as they went along, so I needed to find sixteenth-century maps of London. For the sword fighting, I read as much on the subject as I could find—there's a wonderful book called *English Martial Arts* by Terry Brown that was especially helpful. But I also wanted to know what it felt like to face up to a real opponent—so I started martial arts lessons.

I spent many hours glued to a website called British History Online (british-history.ac.uk). It has fantastic quantities of original documents: You can read letters, accounts, ambassadors' reports (some of them deliciously gossipy!), and dispatches. But even so, my book list was enormous: I read psychology books, biographies of Henry, books on his palaces, his clothes, his government, his army maneuvers in France, plus the wonderful huge inventory that survives of all his possessions at his death—it's utterly fascinating stuff. It's especially fascinating to see from the inventory that, in his palaces, there were cupboards stuffed with old, worn-out, and broken things, not just the new and the sumptuous. He still had belongings confiscated from old friends he'd had executed. He still had a robe that was his brother Arthur's. No doubt he kept some things for sentimental reasons, as most of us do. And many of the items set me thinking—the cap-badge bearing the words *Tristis Victima* that appears in part four, chapter XVII, for example, was prominent in this list of possessions at his death. It gave me a shiver; it seemed to me so apt for one aspect of his self-image.

How much of what happens in VIII *is fact and how much is fiction?*

As you might guess from my answer to the last question, I've tried to be as historically accurate as possible. My training as a historian makes this very important to me. Of course, I am telling a story, and I have had to imagine what it felt like to be Henry, what thoughts were in his head—but beyond that, I've used evidence from the time everywhere I can, down to the smallest detail. Very nearly every object you see is mentioned in an inventory somewhere, for example. I've worked reports of real conversations into the dialogue and used surviving evidence as the basis for descriptions. The details of the tournaments are almost all taken from the time, though I've sometimes changed who is taking part, as otherwise the book's cast of characters would have become too huge!

You've portrayed Henry's relationship with his father in an interesting light. What led you to it?

When I look at the adult Henry and the extraordinary things he did, the decisions he took—other kings failed to have sons, for example, without reacting so devastatingly—the question for me is: What shaped this personality? What was it, early on, that constructed his emotional circuit board, if you like, and made him react as he did? So I looked at his childhood. And his relationship with his parents is fascinating to think about, particularly because of their own traumatic past.

The years before Henry's birth were years of bloody struggle—the Wars of the Roses. Both of his parents were profoundly and very personally affected by the violence and upheaval, there's no question of that—but, as to the exact lasting emotional effects on them, that's an area for speculation. How did Henry's mother feel about her young brothers who had apparently been murdered? How was his father affected by being on the run for so many years and then winning the crown in battle? It's easy to say that last phrase, but when you think about the reality of it—the carnage, the murder of the previous king, and the possibility that the same thing could happen again, which was a very real danger—well, then the effect not only on Henry's father but on Henry himself becomes a very interesting question to ponder.

What's next?

Ah, I'm writing about an equally fascinating subject now! And in a way it's a sequel. It's a book about Henry's two daughters, who both became queens: Mary I and Elizabeth I. They're half sisters, and much of what happens to them is a shared experience: Each is born heir to the throne, a feted princess; each is then declared illegitimate and loses her title and status. Each loses her mother in heartrending circumstances caused directly by her father—and yet each comes to revere Henry and identify herself with him.

But, though so much is similar, the way Mary and Elizabeth react to these events is utterly contrasting—they have dramatically different personalities. How did they feel about one another? To have a sibling is a common thing, one many of us can relate to, but how does sibling rivalry feel when your sister has not only knocked you off your perch as an only child, but has also taken your title of princess? And how does sibling rivalry feel when your sister has the power to put you to death?